A GIRL IN THE HIMALAYAS

DAVID JESUS VIGNOLLI

Published by
ARCHAIA

COVER BY
DAVID JESUS VIGNOLLI

DESIGNER
SCOTT NEWMAN

EDITORS
CAMERON CHITTOCK & SIERRA HAHN

 ARCHAIA™

A GIRL IN THE HIMALAYAS, April 2018. Published by Archaia, a division of Boom Entertainment, Inc. A Girl in the Himalayas is ™ & © 2018 David Jesus Vignolli de Mello. All rights reserved. Archaia™ and the Archaia logo are trademarks of Boom Entertainment, Inc., registered in various countries and categories. All characters, events, and institutions depicted herein are fictional. Any similarity between any of the names, characters, persons, events, and/or institutions in this publication to actual names, characters, and persons, whether living or dead, events, and/or institutions is unintended and purely coincidental.

BOOM! Studios, 5670 Wilshire Boulevard, Suite 400, Los Angeles, CA 90036-5679. Printed in China. First Printing.

ISBN: 978-1-68415-129-5, eISBN: 978-1-61398-868-8

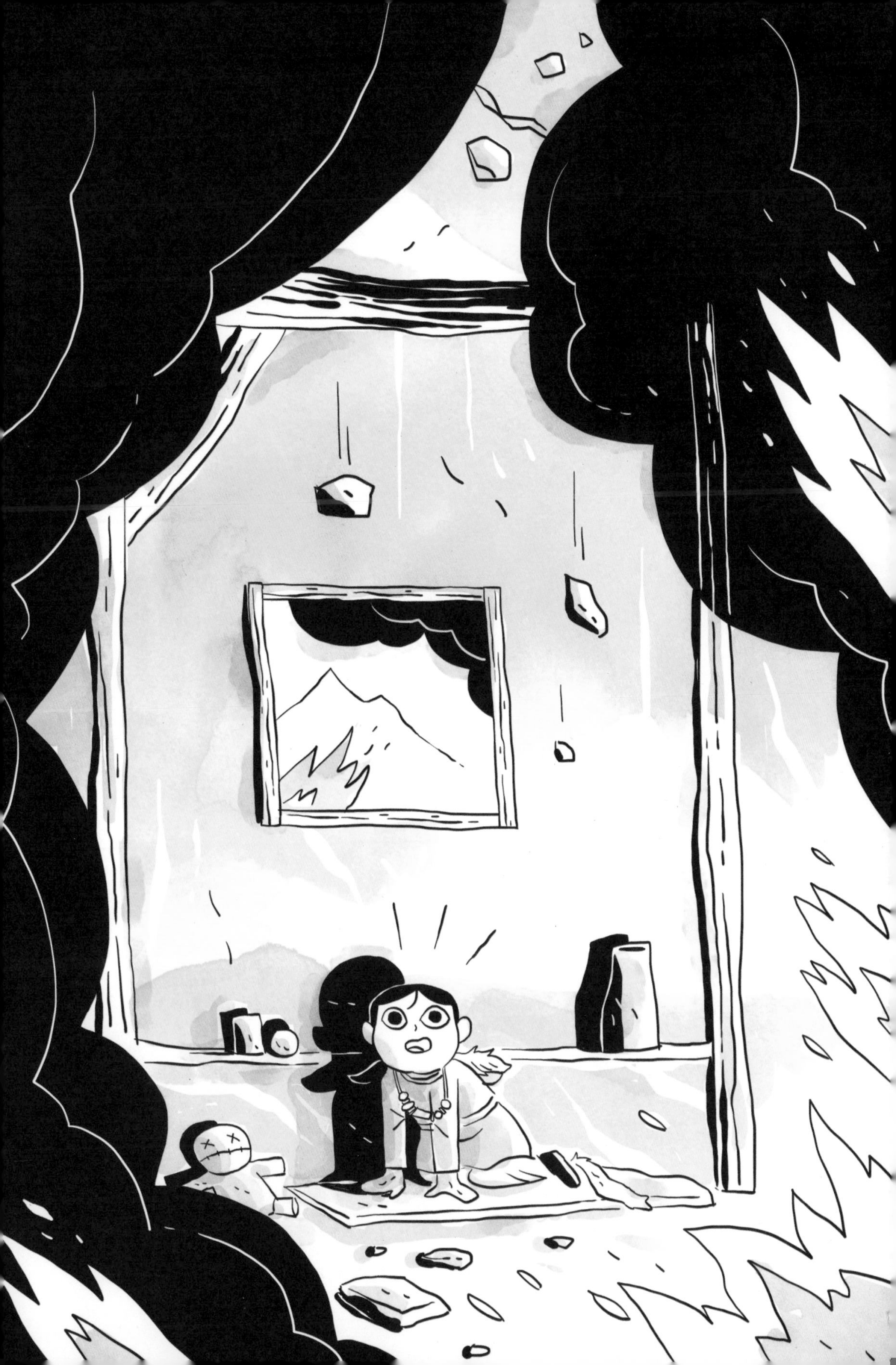

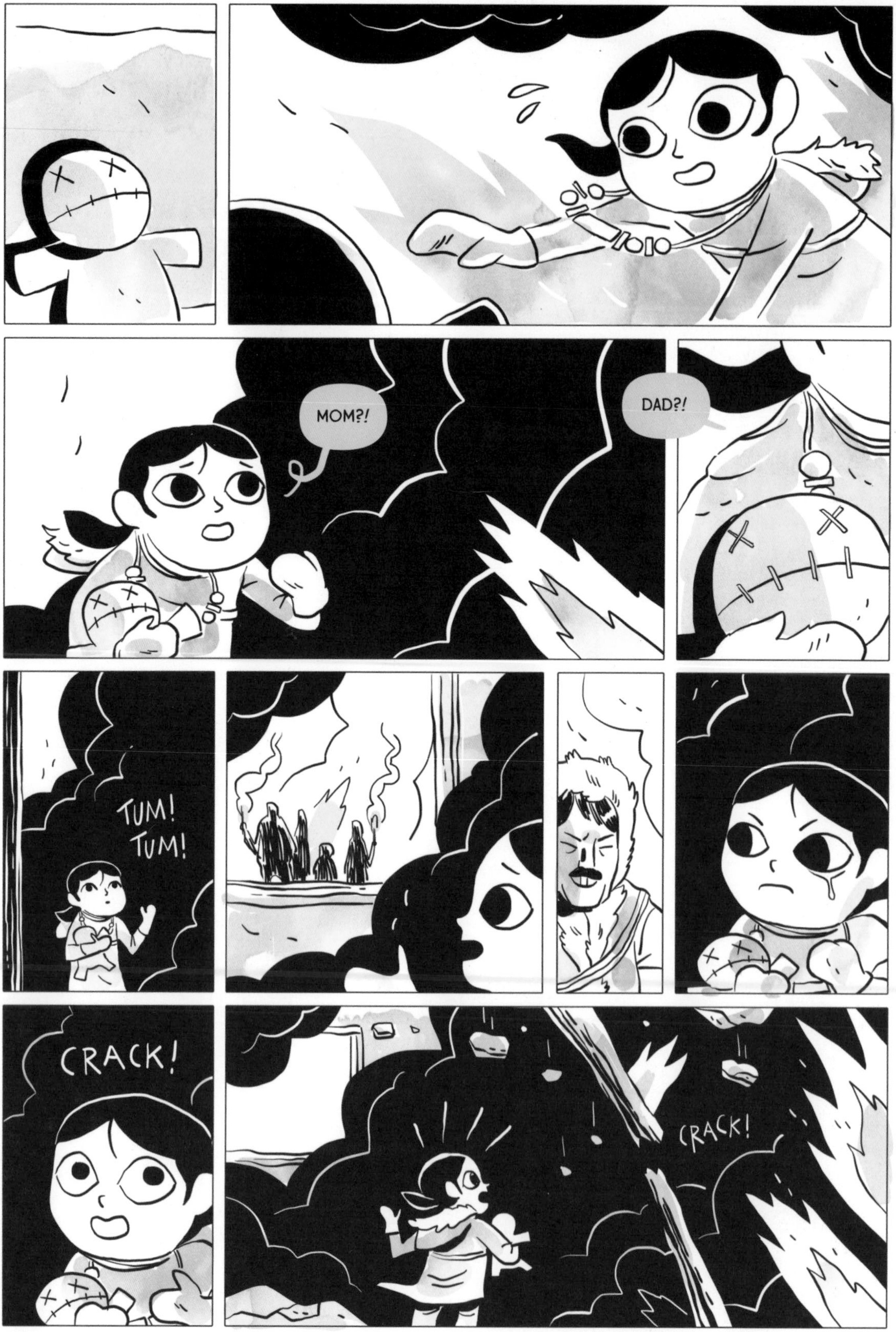
MOM?!
DAD?!
TUM! TUM!
CRACK!
CRACK!

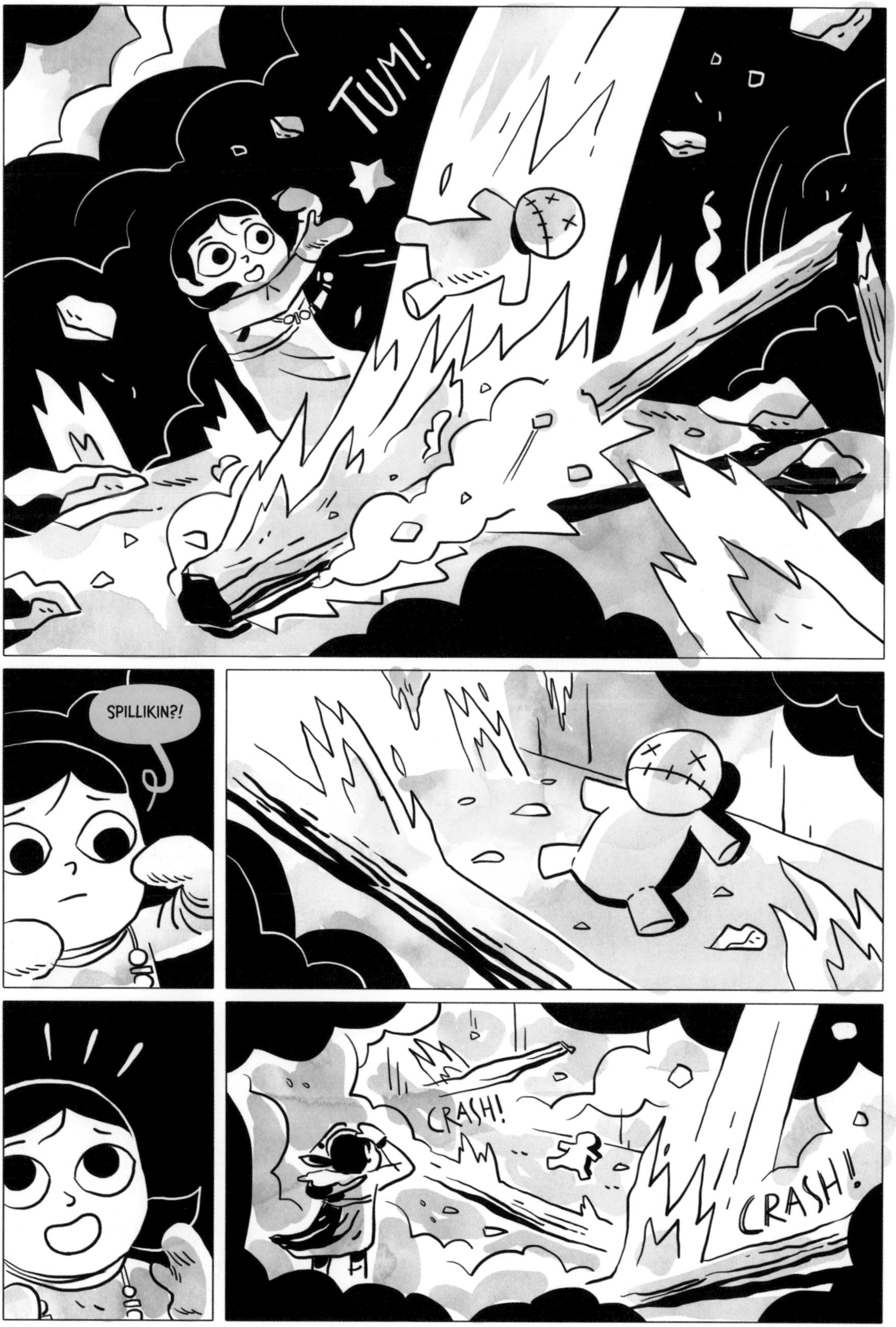
TUM!
SPILLIKIN?!
CRASH!
CRASH!

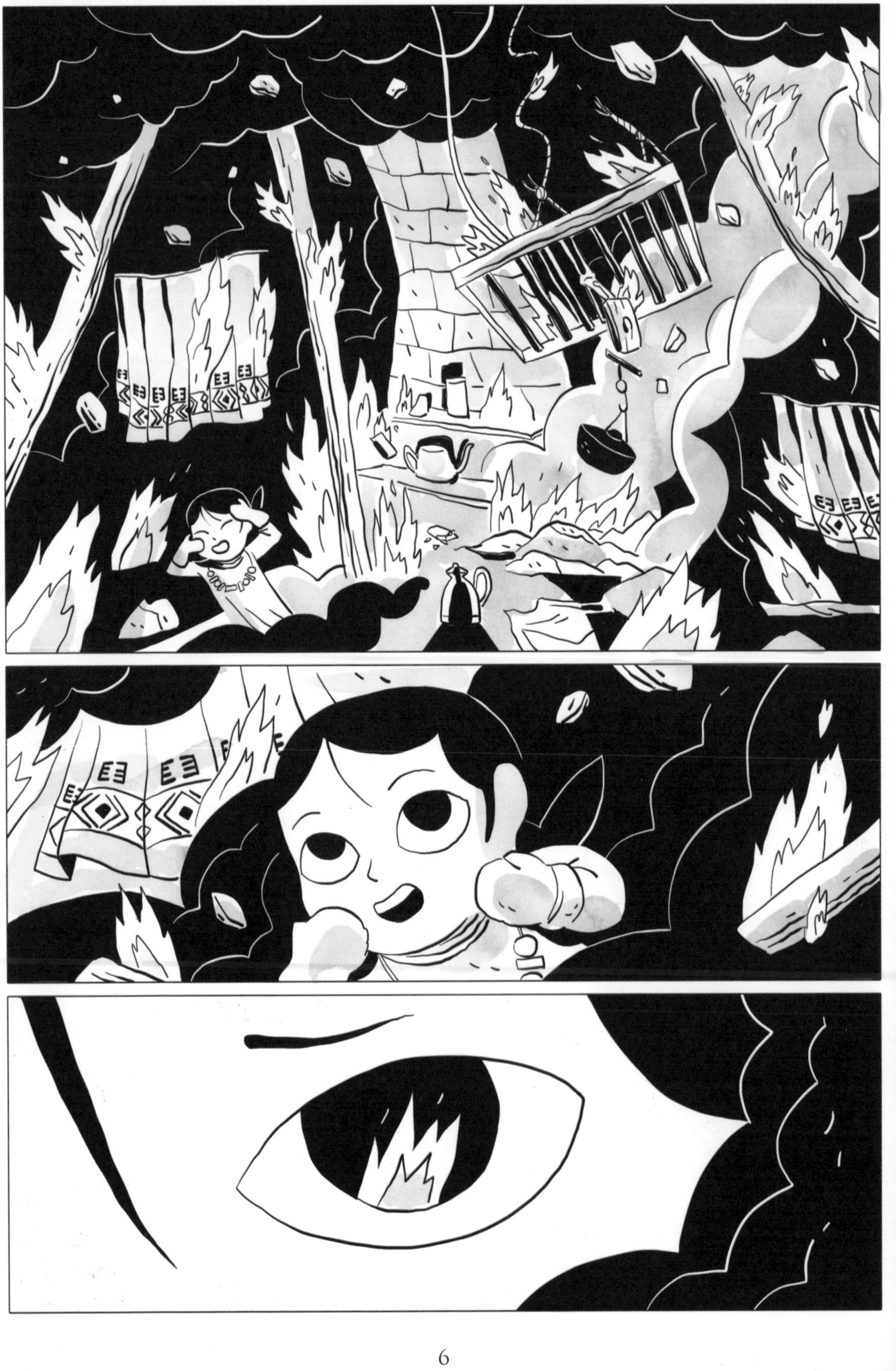

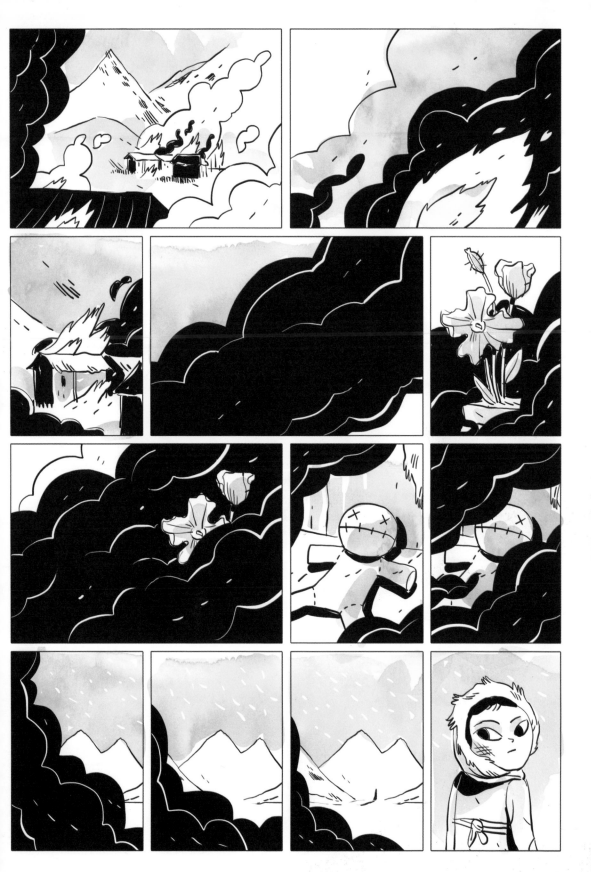

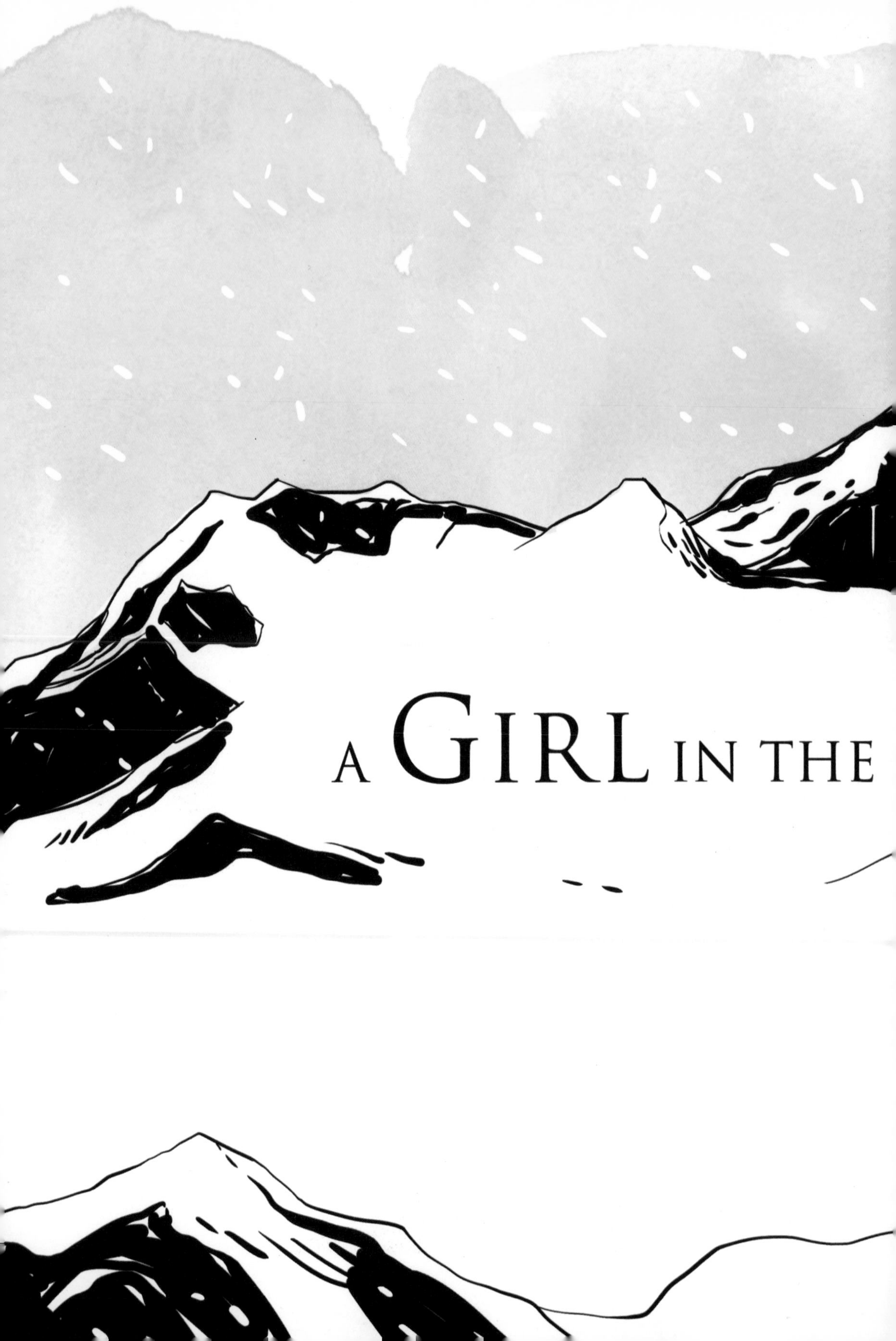
A GIRL IN THE

HIMALAYAS

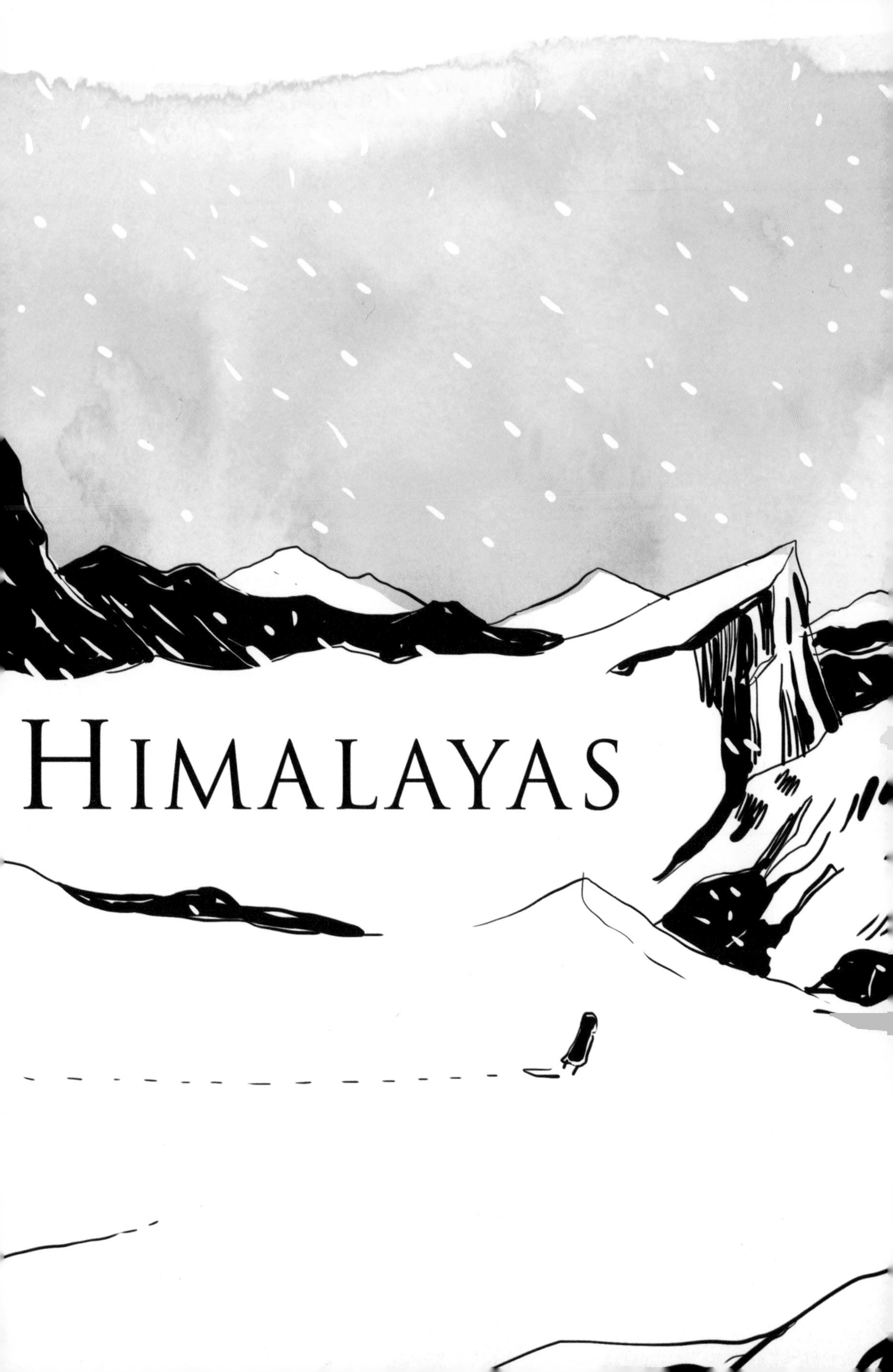

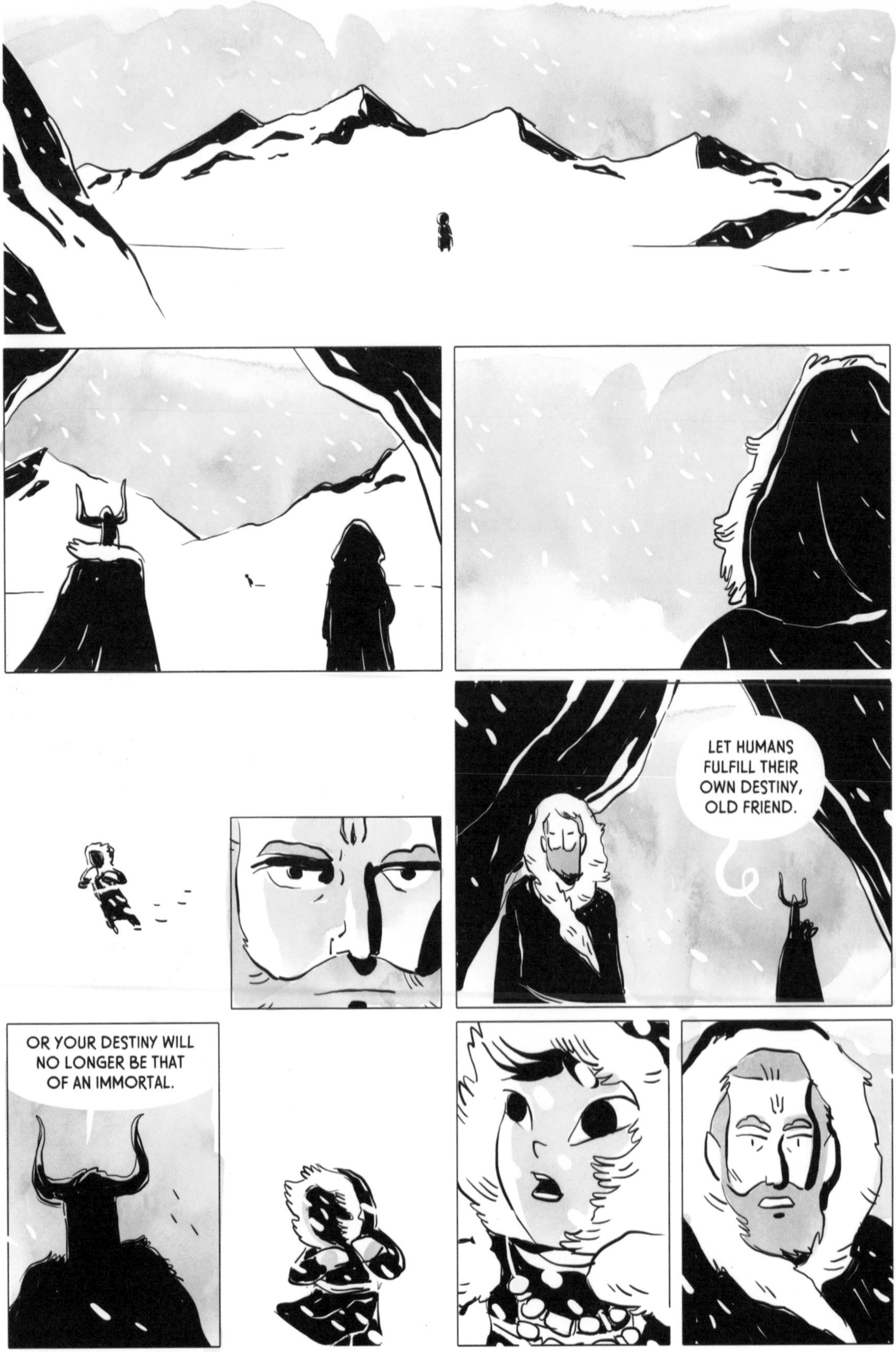
LET HUMANS FULFILL THEIR OWN DESTINY, OLD FRIEND.
OR YOUR DESTINY WILL NO LONGER BE THAT OF AN IMMORTAL.

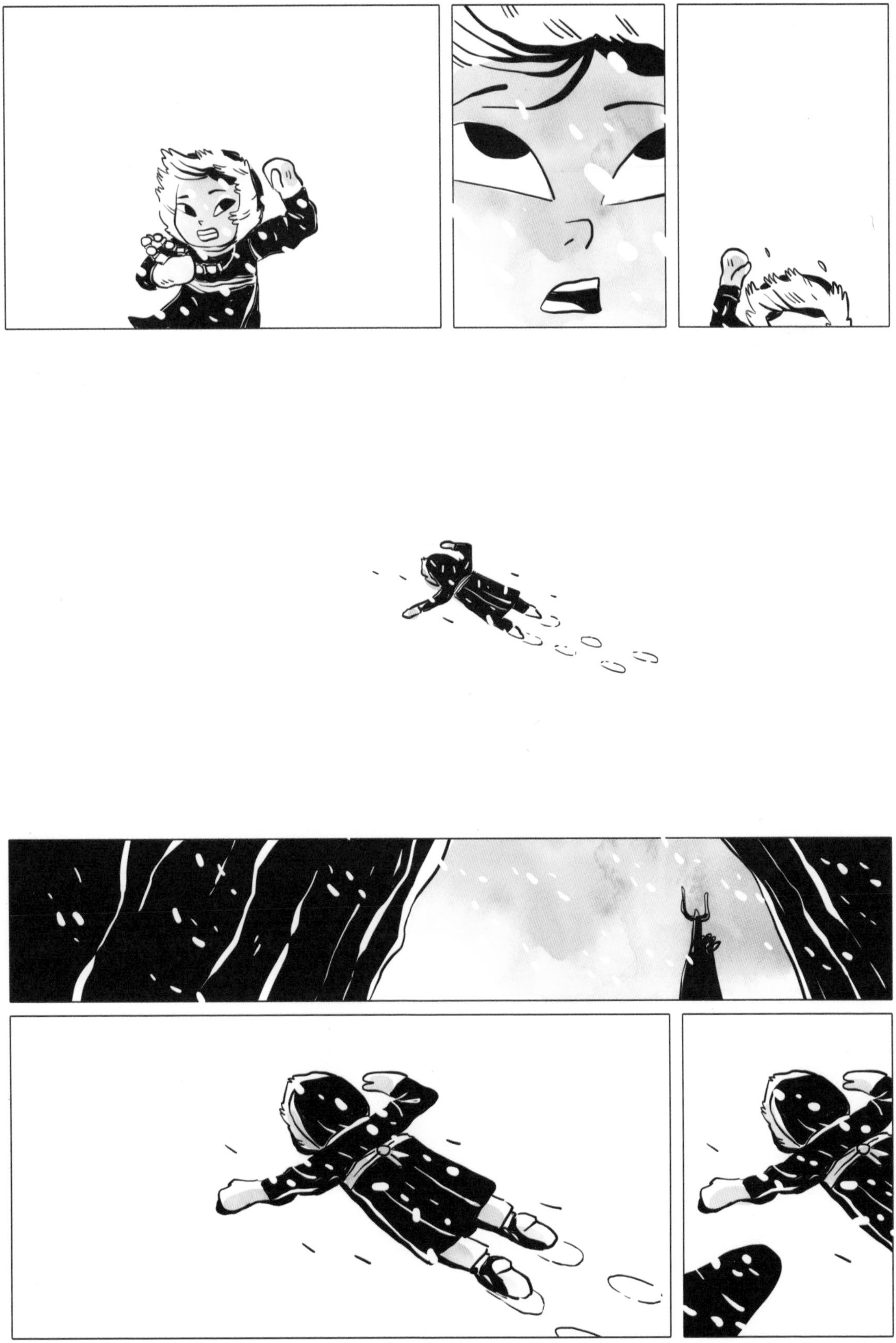

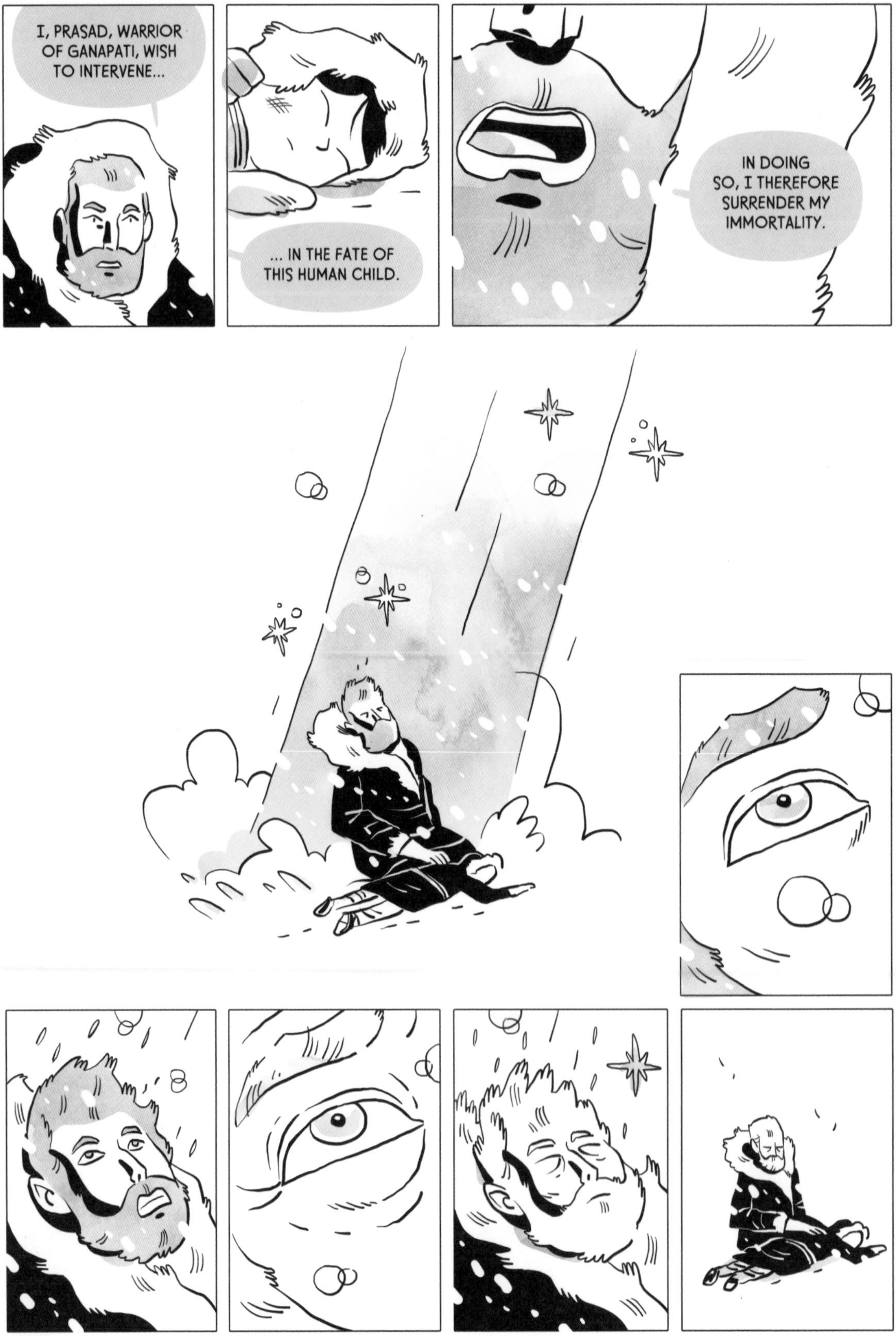
I, PRASAD, WARRIOR OF GANAPATI, WISH TO INTERVENE...
... IN THE FATE OF THIS HUMAN CHILD.
IN DOING SO, I THEREFORE SURRENDER MY IMMORTALITY.

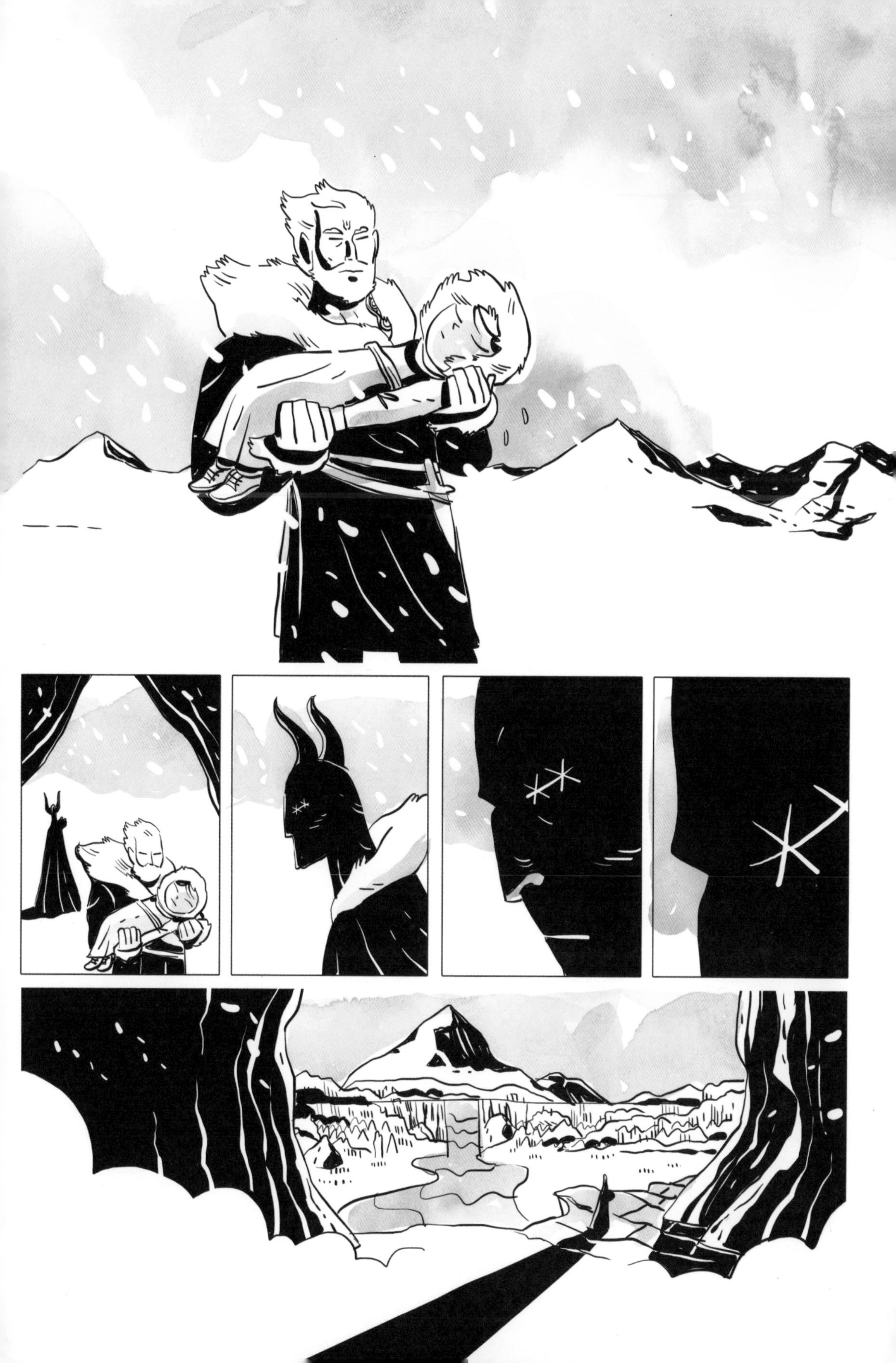

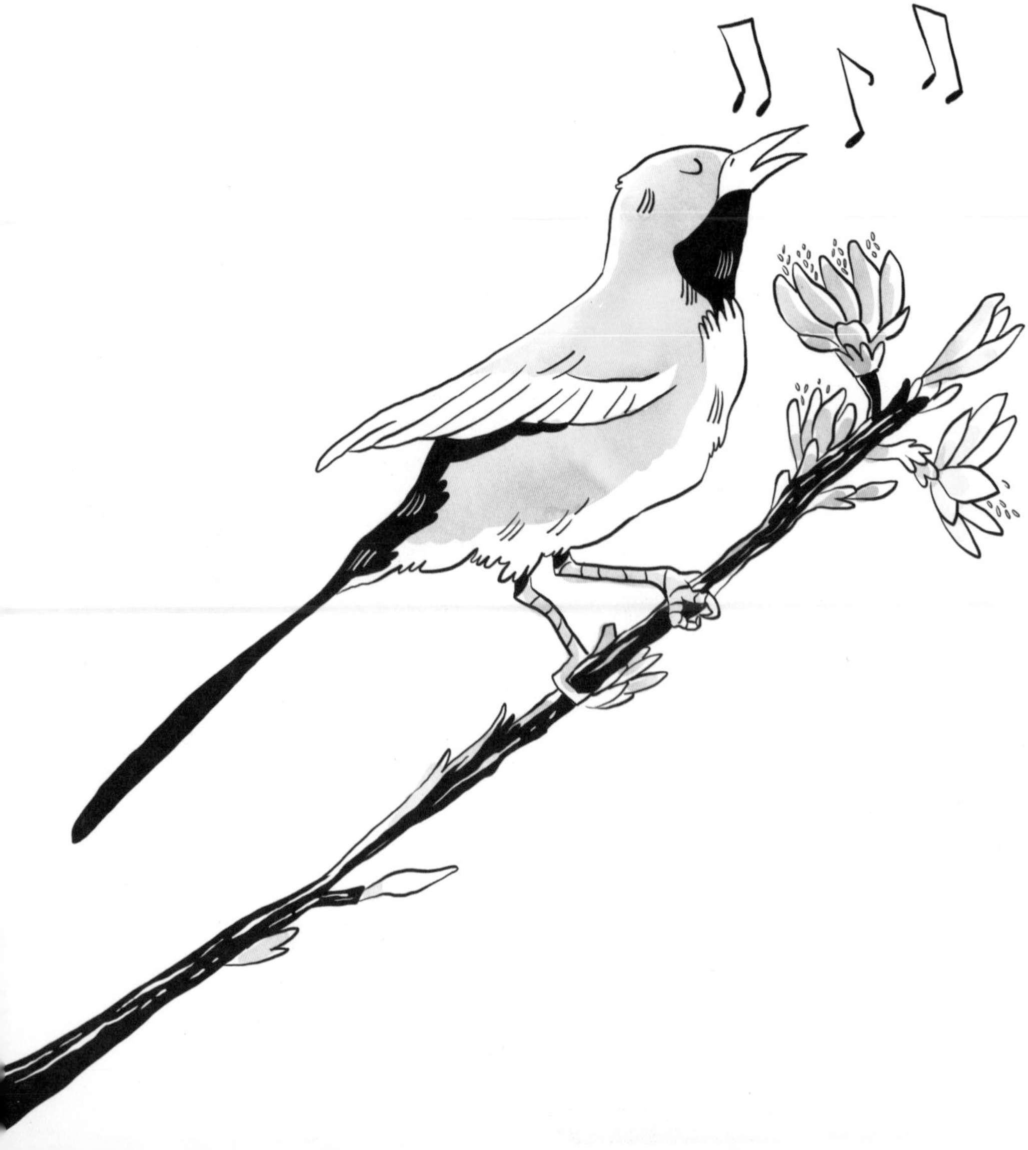

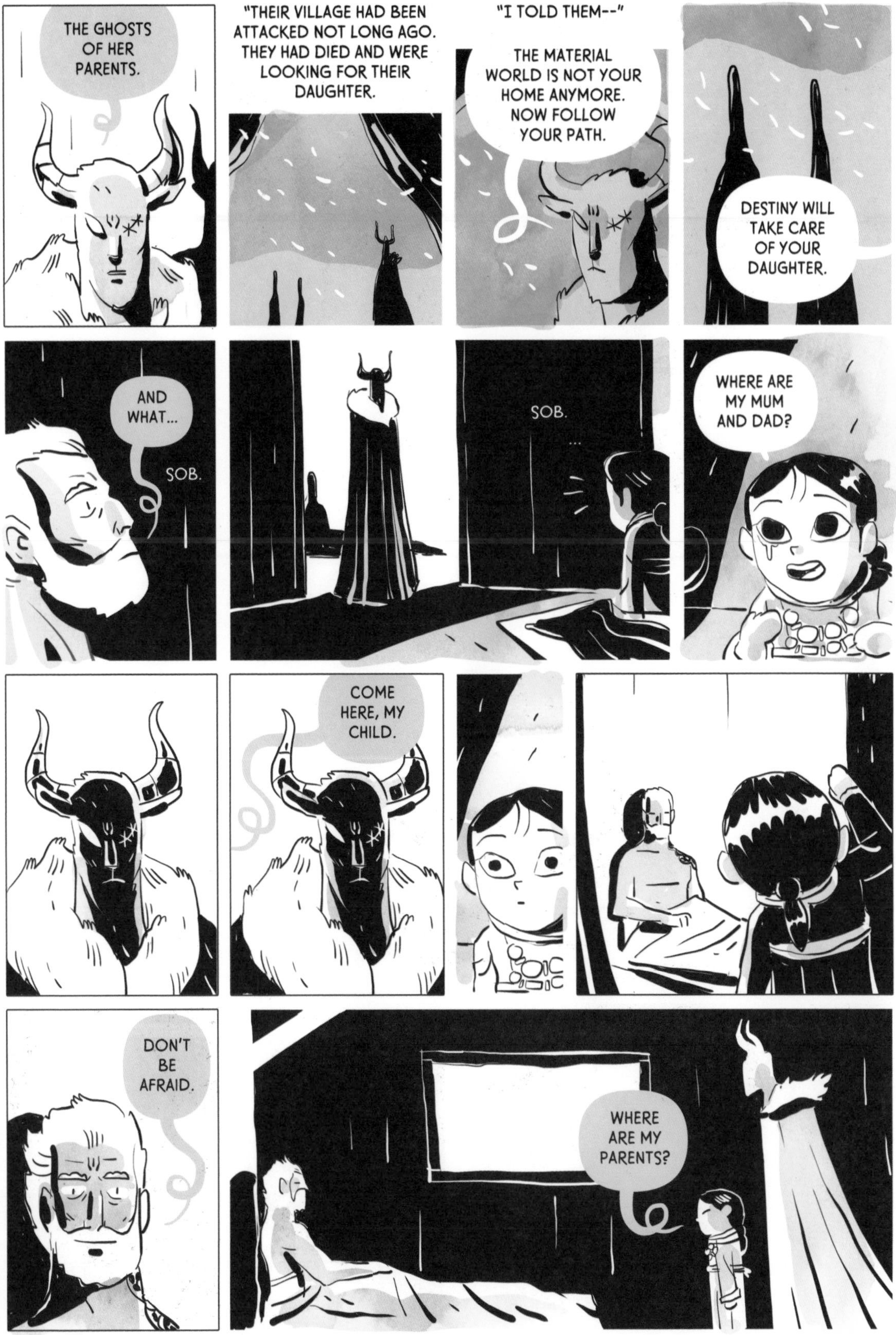
THE GHOSTS OF HER PARENTS.
"THEIR VILLAGE HAD BEEN ATTACKED NOT LONG AGO. THEY HAD DIED AND WERE LOOKING FOR THEIR DAUGHTER.
"I TOLD THEM--"
THE MATERIAL WORLD IS NOT YOUR HOME ANYMORE. NOW FOLLOW YOUR PATH.
DESTINY WILL TAKE CARE OF YOUR DAUGHTER.
AND WHAT...
SOB.
SOB.
...
WHERE ARE MY MUM AND DAD?
COME HERE, MY CHILD.
DON'T BE AFRAID.
WHERE ARE MY PARENTS?

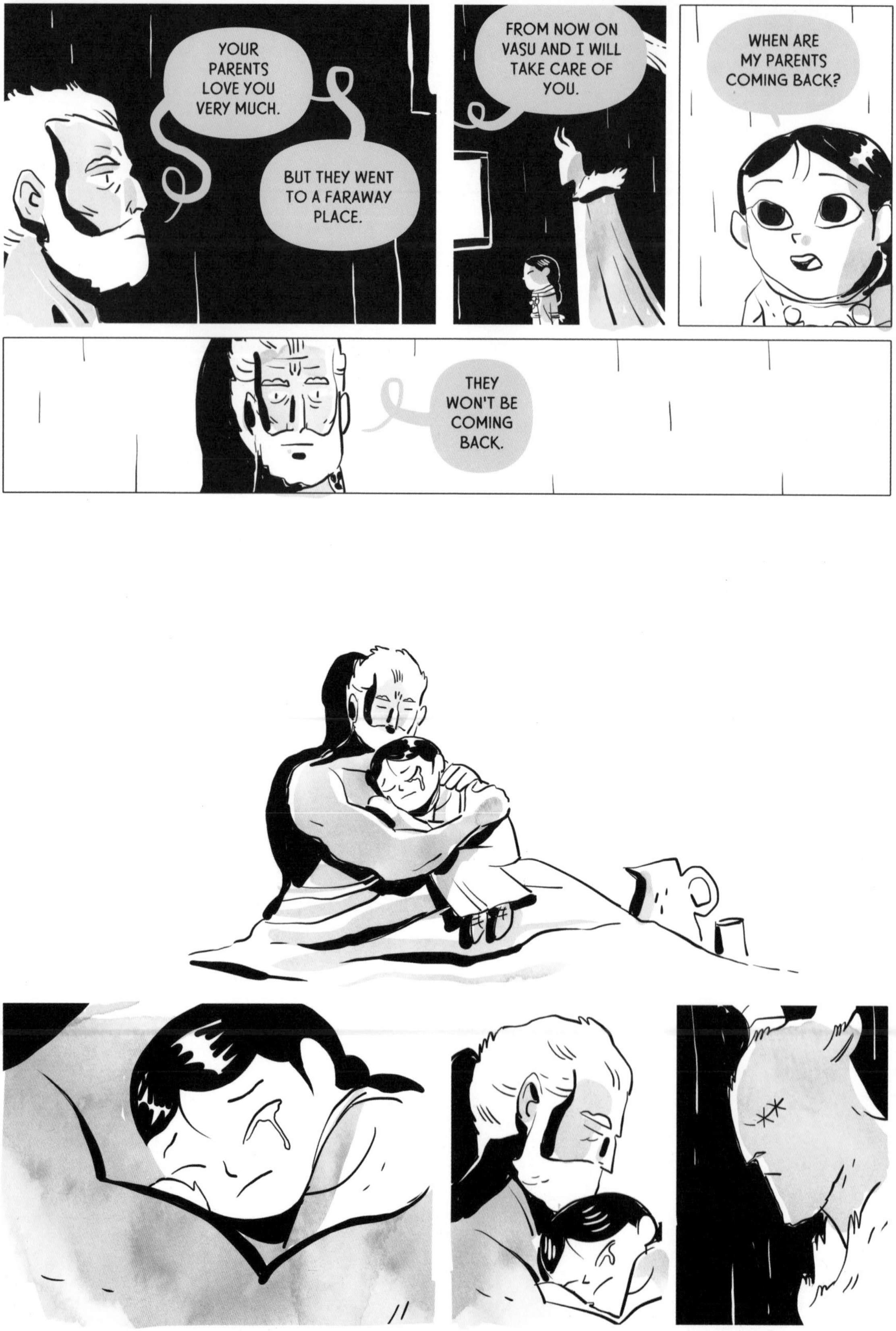
YOUR PARENTS LOVE YOU VERY MUCH.
BUT THEY WENT TO A FARAWAY PLACE.
FROM NOW ON VASU AND I WILL TAKE CARE OF YOU.
WHEN ARE MY PARENTS COMING BACK?
THEY WON'T BE COMING BACK.

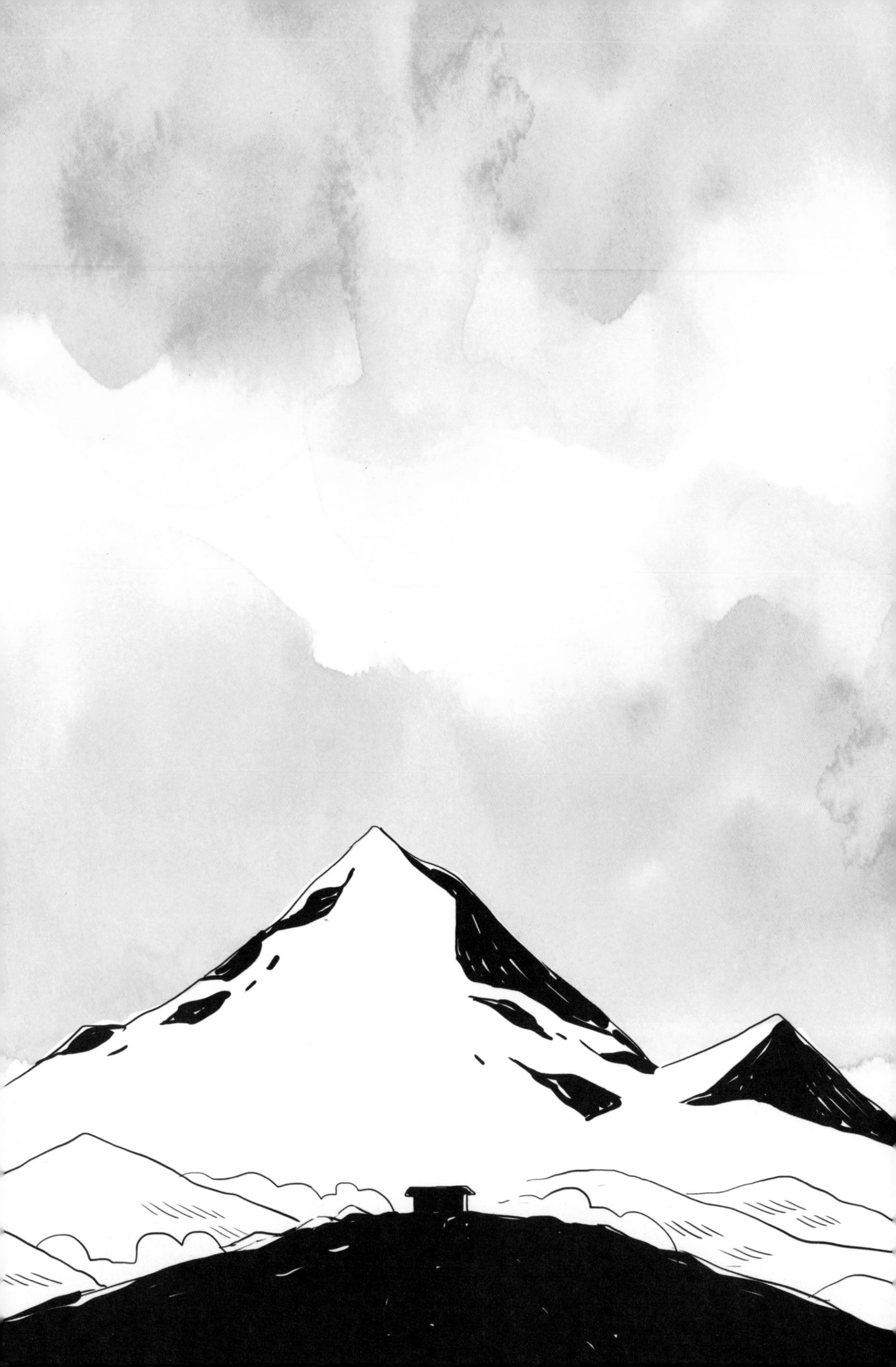

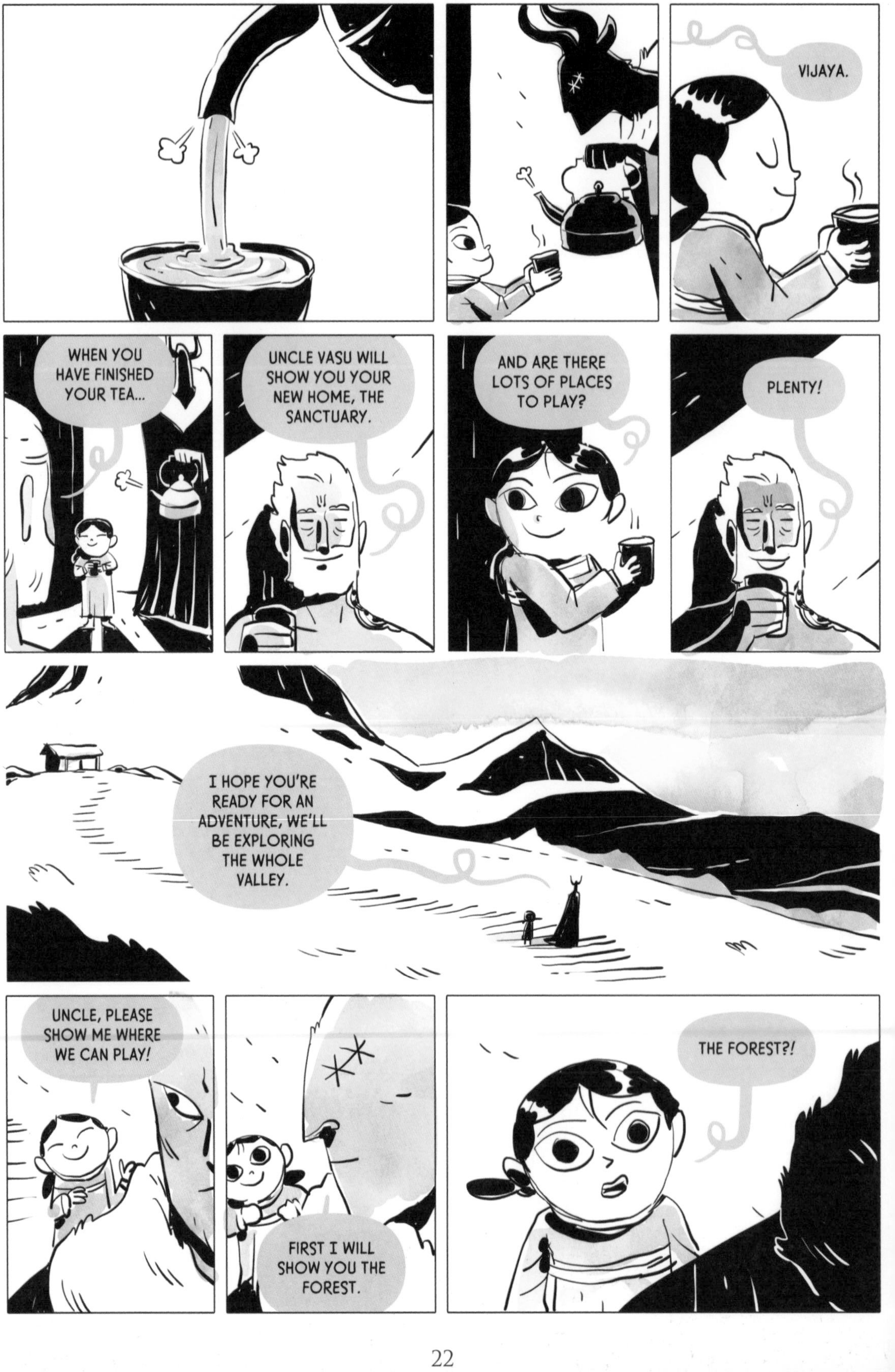
VIJAYA.
WHEN YOU HAVE FINISHED YOUR TEA...
UNCLE VASU WILL SHOW YOU YOUR NEW HOME, THE SANCTUARY.
AND ARE THERE LOTS OF PLACES TO PLAY?
PLENTY!
I HOPE YOU'RE READY FOR AN ADVENTURE, WE'LL BE EXPLORING THE WHOLE VALLEY.
UNCLE, PLEASE SHOW ME WHERE WE CAN PLAY!
FIRST I WILL SHOW YOU THE FOREST.
THE FOREST?!

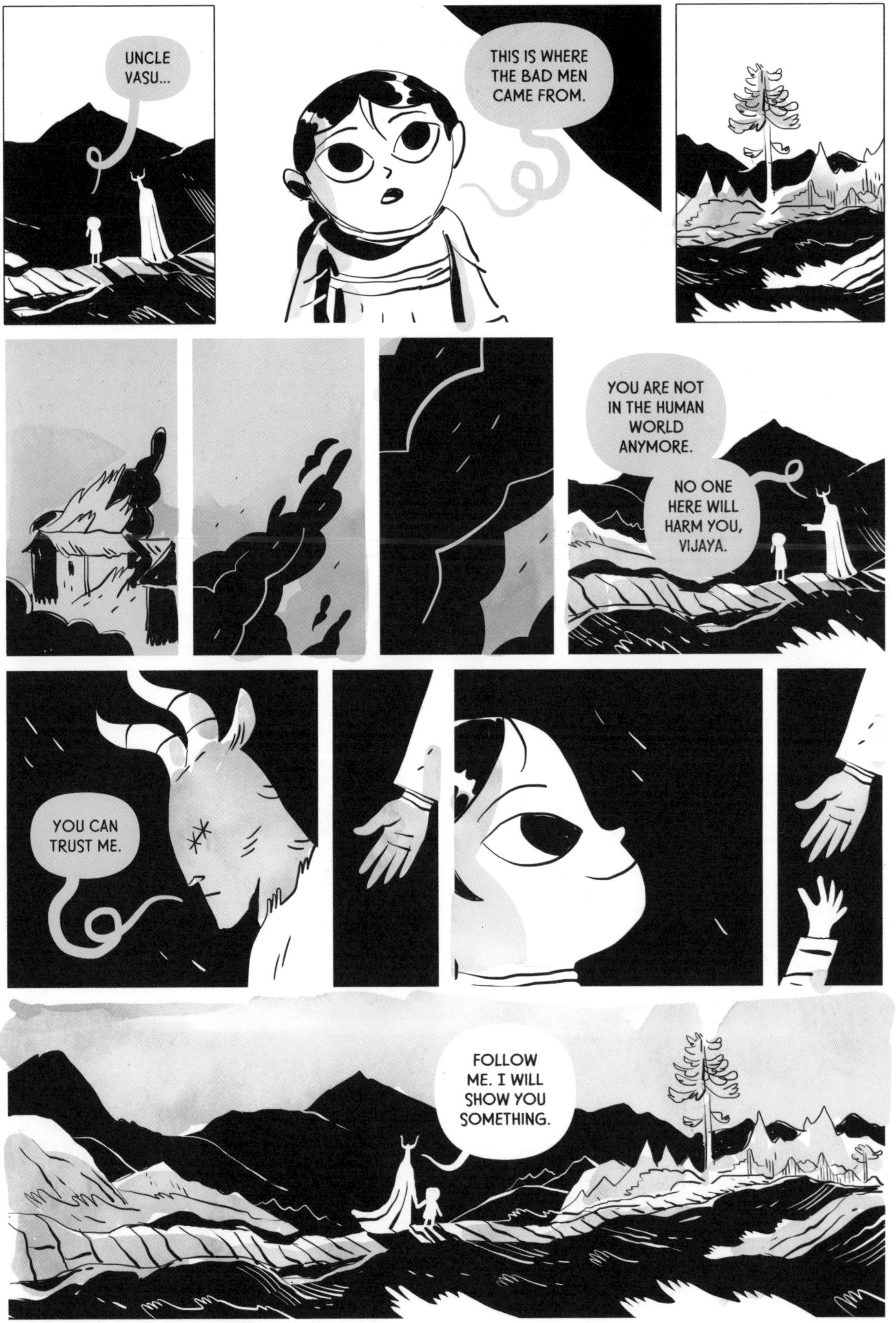
UNCLE VASU...
THIS IS WHERE THE BAD MEN CAME FROM.
YOU ARE NOT IN THE HUMAN WORLD ANYMORE.
NO ONE HERE WILL HARM YOU, VIJAYA.
YOU CAN TRUST ME.
FOLLOW ME. I WILL SHOW YOU SOMETHING.

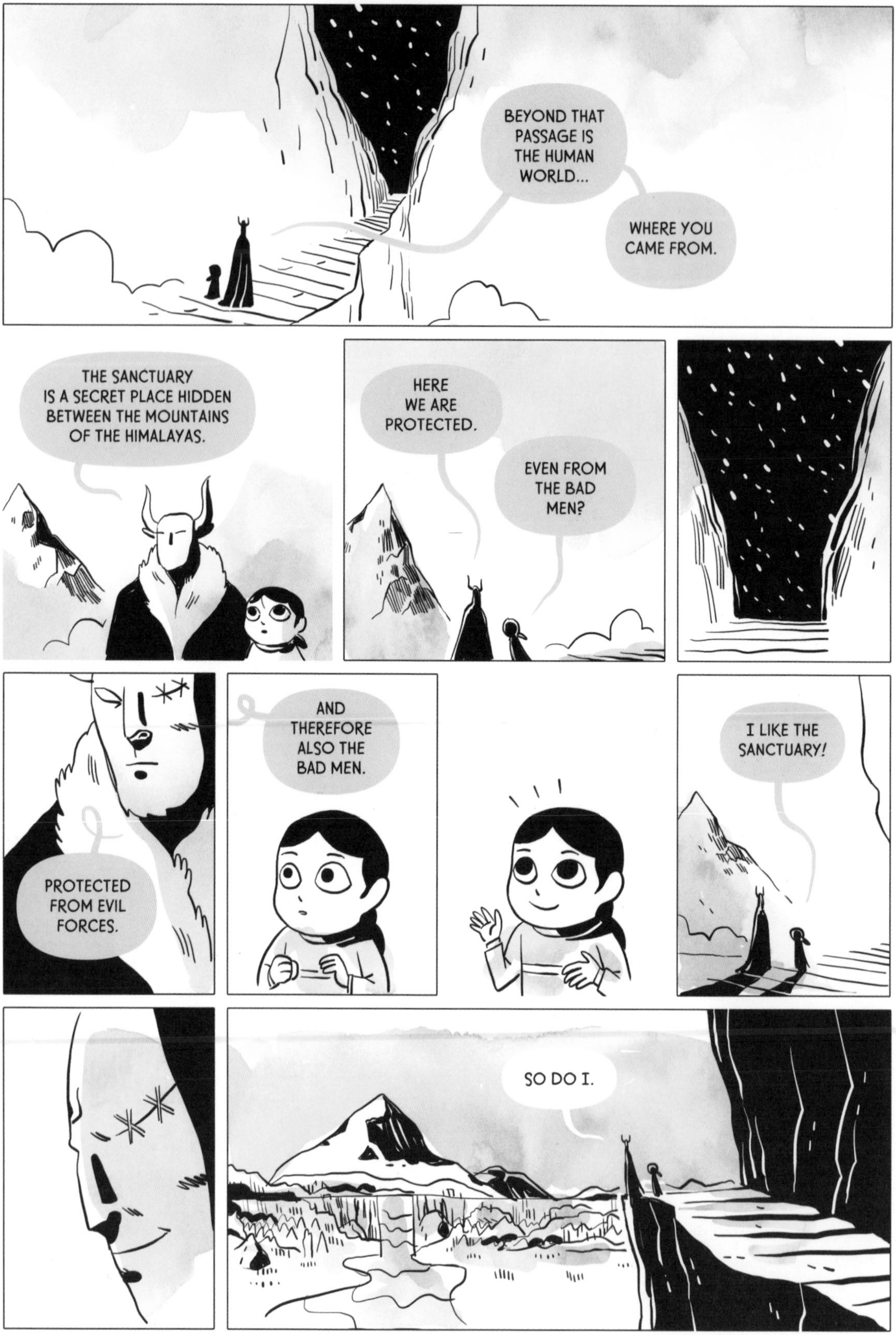
BEYOND THAT PASSAGE IS THE HUMAN WORLD...
WHERE YOU CAME FROM.
THE SANCTUARY IS A SECRET PLACE HIDDEN BETWEEN THE MOUNTAINS OF THE HIMALAYAS.
HERE WE ARE PROTECTED.
EVEN FROM THE BAD MEN?
PROTECTED FROM EVIL FORCES.
AND THEREFORE ALSO THE BAD MEN.
I LIKE THE SANCTUARY!
SO DO I.

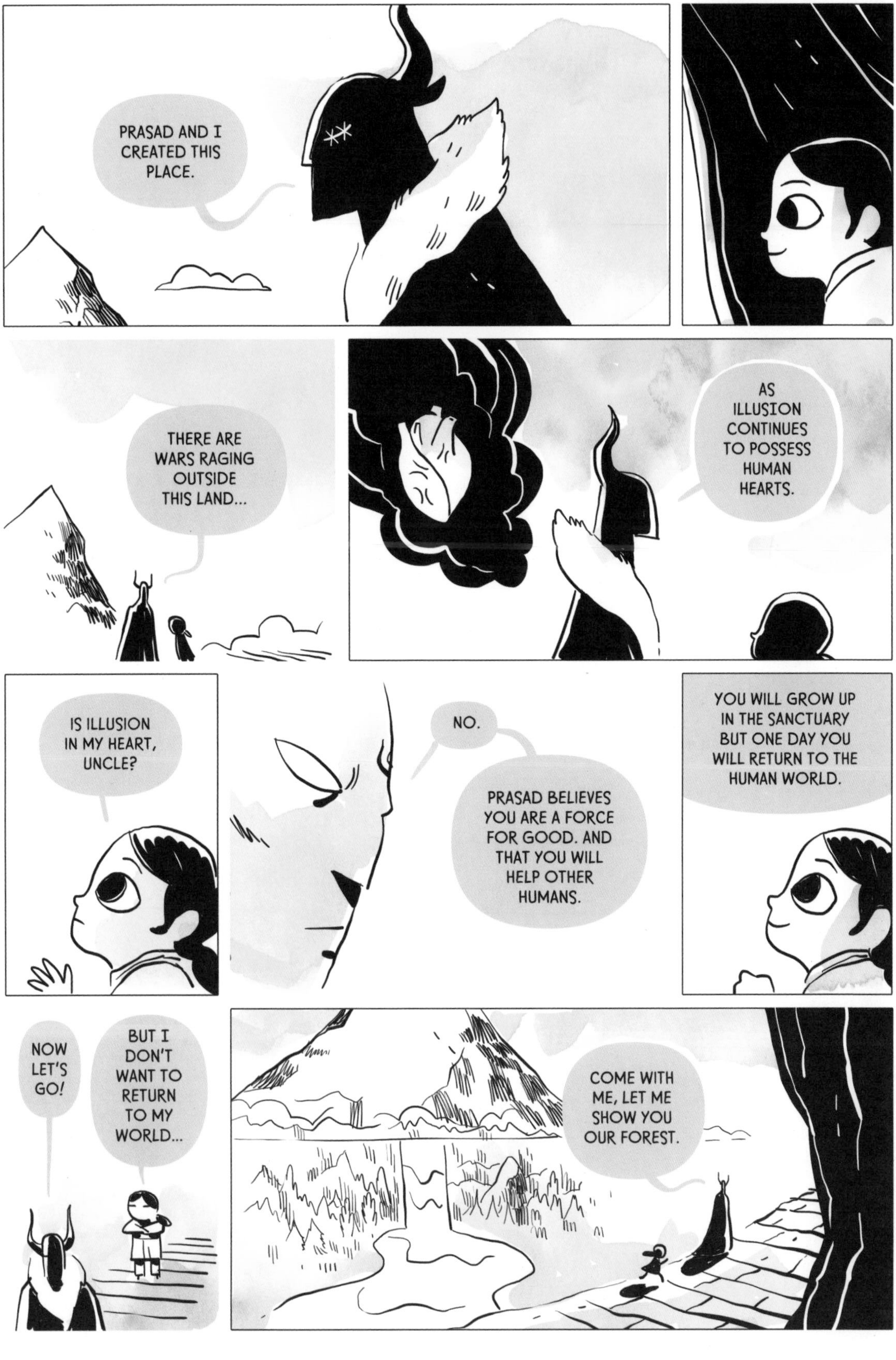
PRASAD AND I CREATED THIS PLACE.
THERE ARE WARS RAGING OUTSIDE THIS LAND...
AS ILLUSION CONTINUES TO POSSESS HUMAN HEARTS.
IS ILLUSION IN MY HEART, UNCLE?
NO.
PRASAD BELIEVES YOU ARE A FORCE FOR GOOD. AND THAT YOU WILL HELP OTHER HUMANS.
YOU WILL GROW UP IN THE SANCTUARY BUT ONE DAY YOU WILL RETURN TO THE HUMAN WORLD.
NOW LET'S GO!
BUT I DON'T WANT TO RETURN TO MY WORLD...
COME WITH ME, LET ME SHOW YOU OUR FOREST.

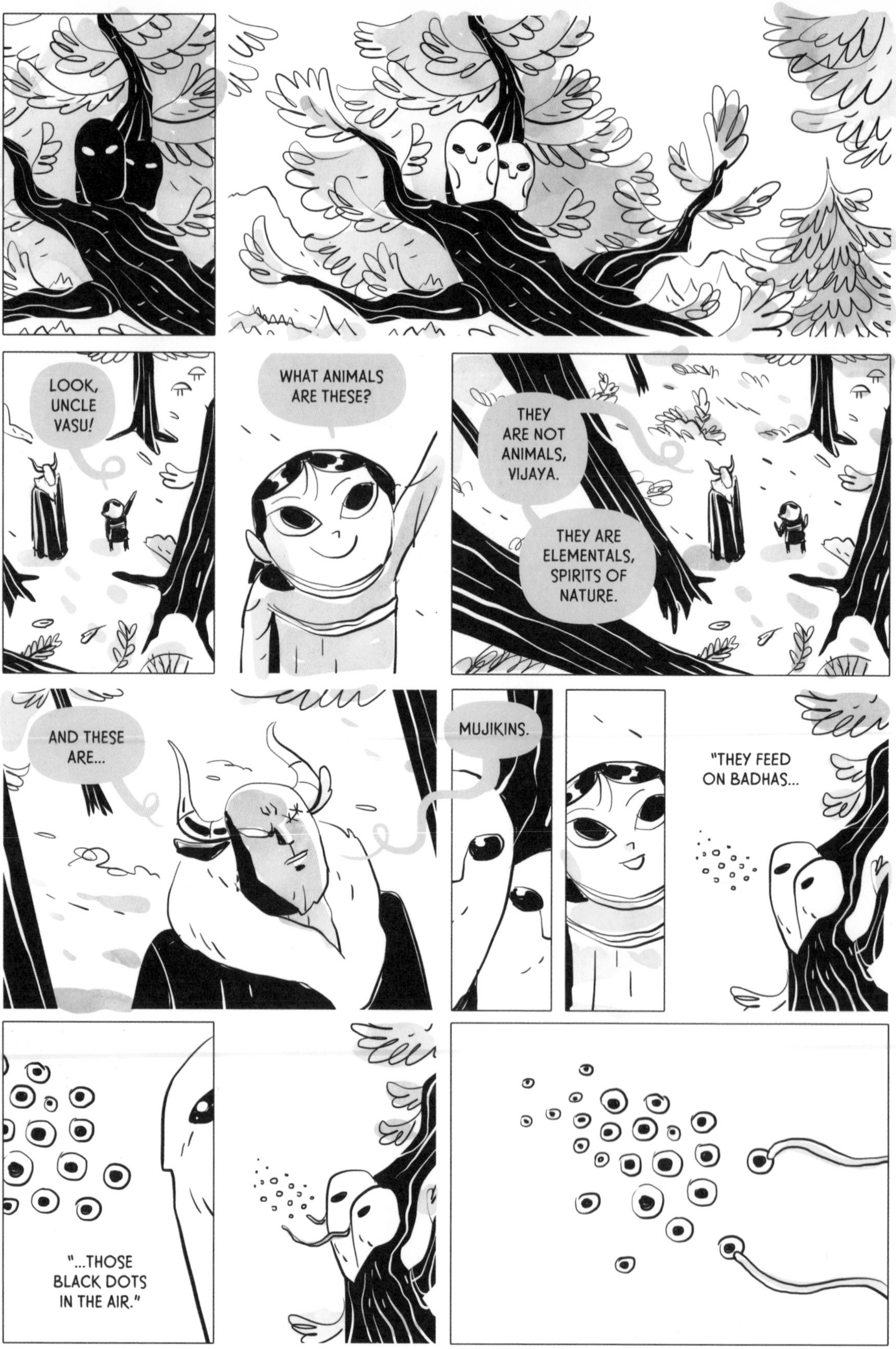

LOOK, UNCLE VASU!
WHAT ANIMALS ARE THESE?
THEY ARE NOT ANIMALS, VIJAYA.
THEY ARE ELEMENTALS, SPIRITS OF NATURE.
AND THESE ARE...
MUJIKINS.
"THEY FEED ON BADHAS...
"...THOSE BLACK DOTS IN THE AIR."

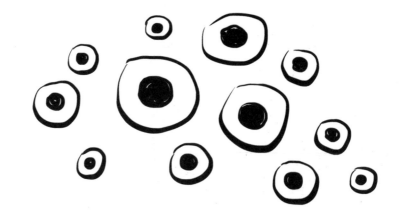

"BADHAS ARE THE SOULS OF DEAD ANIMALS AND PLANTS THAT DID NOT FOLLOW THEIR EVOLUTIONARY PATH.

"AND LOST THEIR WAY.

"AND MUJIKINS PURIFY NATURE OF THESE EVIL BEINGS."

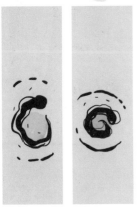

"MANY OF THESE BADHAS TURN THEMSELVES INTO VIRUSES.

WOW!

27

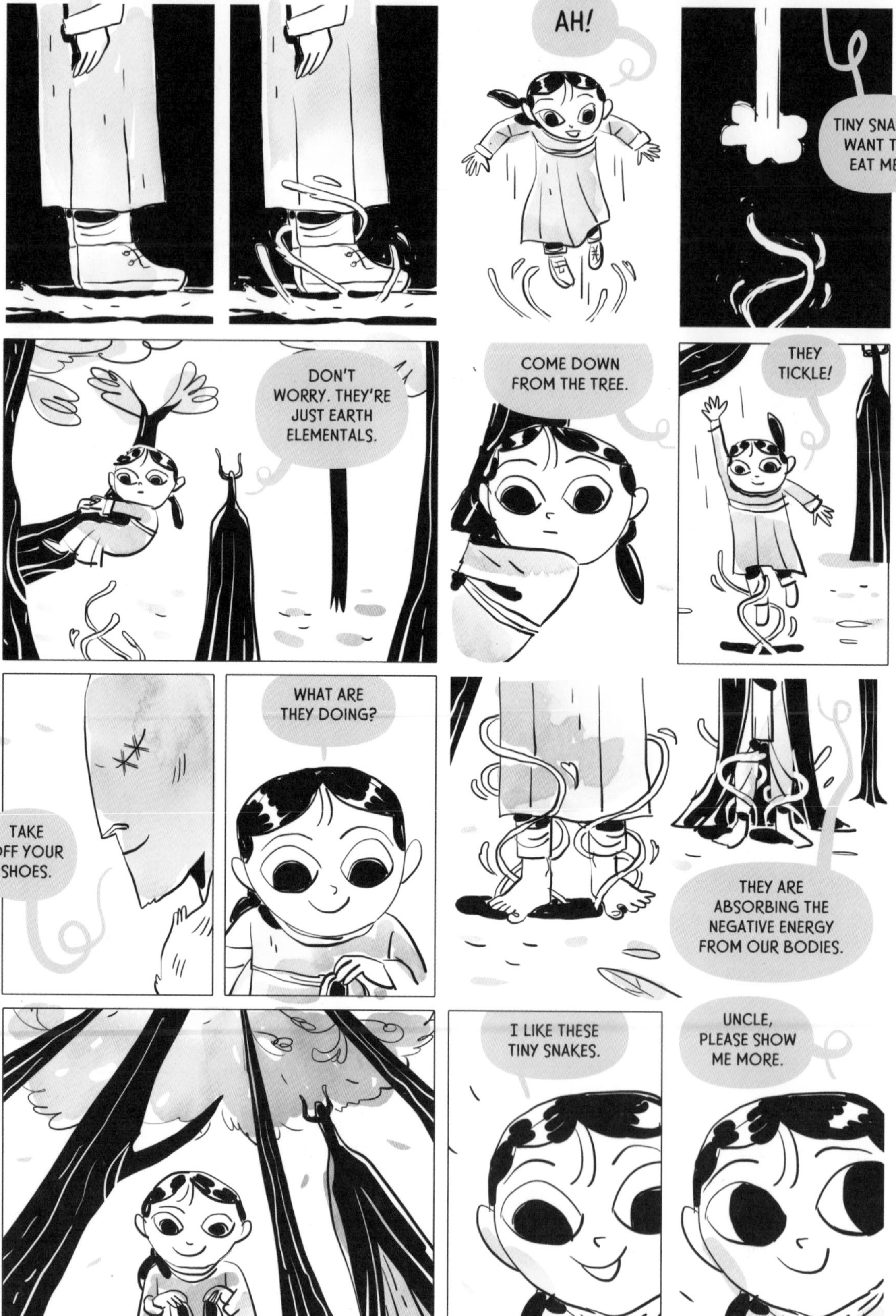
AH!
TINY SNAKE WANT TO EAT ME!
DON'T WORRY. THEY'RE JUST EARTH ELEMENTALS.
COME DOWN FROM THE TREE.
THEY TICKLE!
TAKE OFF YOUR SHOES.
WHAT ARE THEY DOING?
THEY ARE ABSORBING THE NEGATIVE ENERGY FROM OUR BODIES.
I LIKE THESE TINY SNAKES.
UNCLE, PLEASE SHOW ME MORE.

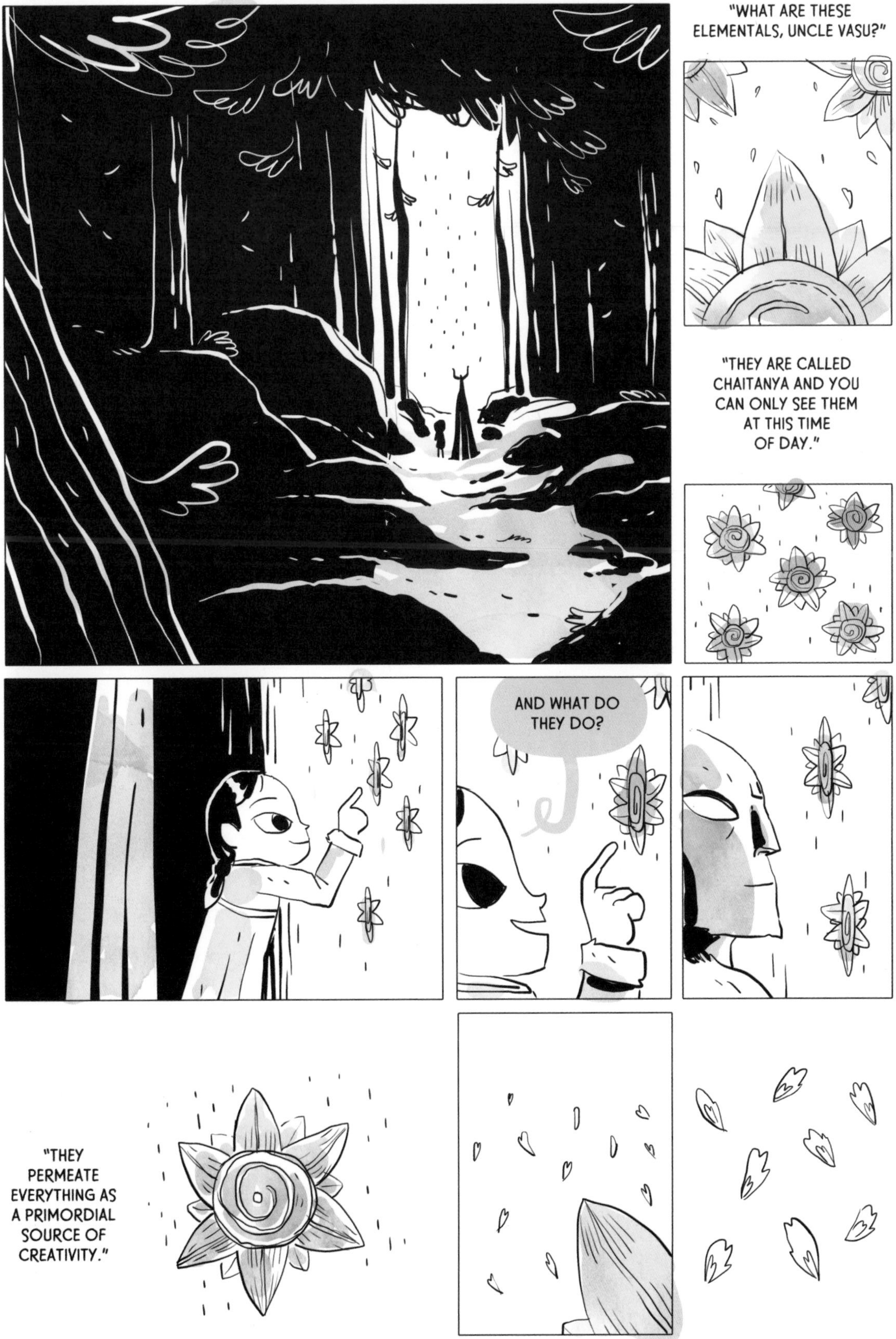

"WHAT ARE THESE ELEMENTALS, UNCLE VASU?"
"THEY ARE CALLED CHAITANYA AND YOU CAN ONLY SEE THEM AT THIS TIME OF DAY."
AND WHAT DO THEY DO?
"THEY PERMEATE EVERYTHING AS A PRIMORDIAL SOURCE OF CREATIVITY."

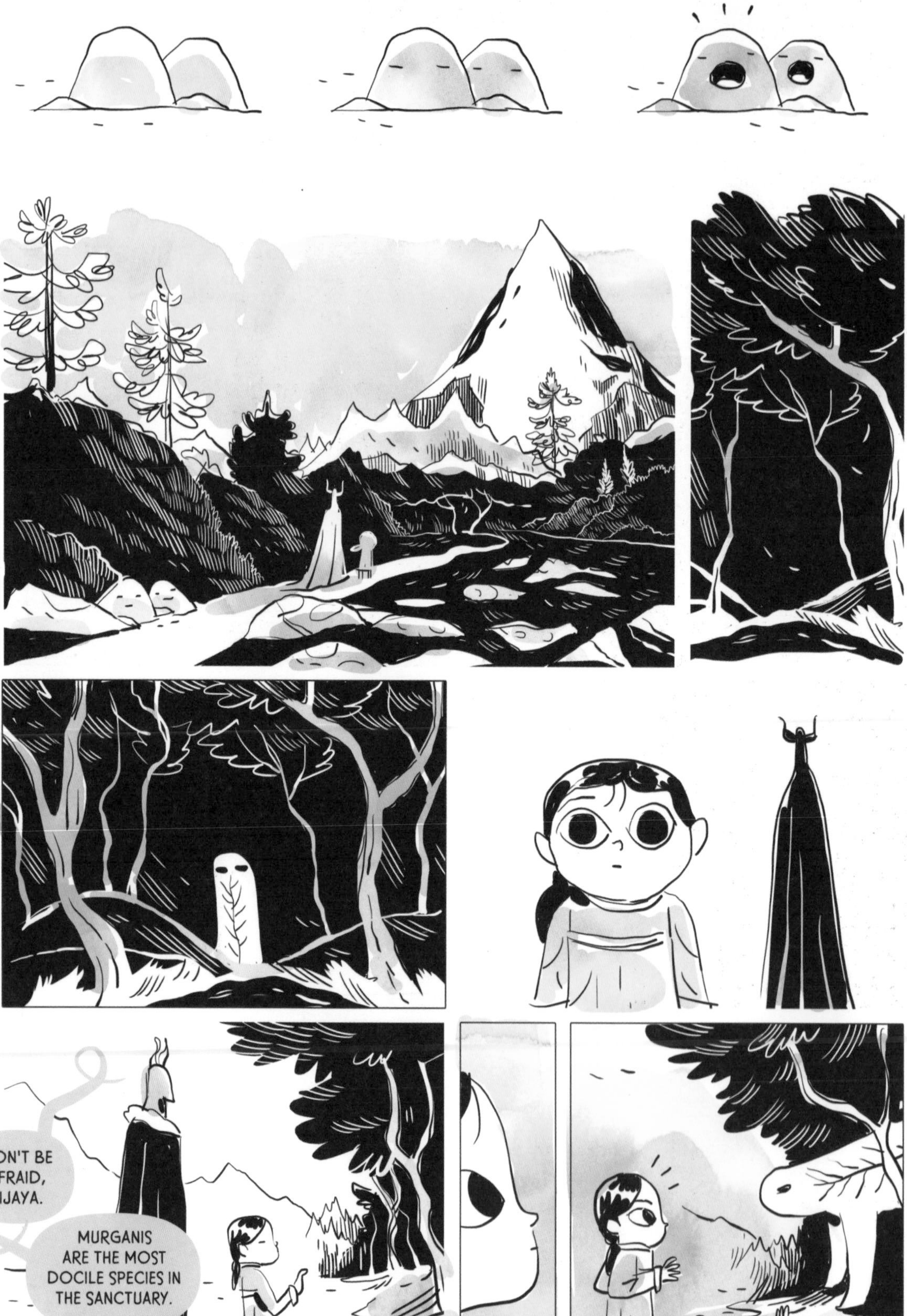
DON'T BE AFRAID, VIJAYA.
MURGANIS ARE THE MOST DOCILE SPECIES IN THE SANCTUARY.

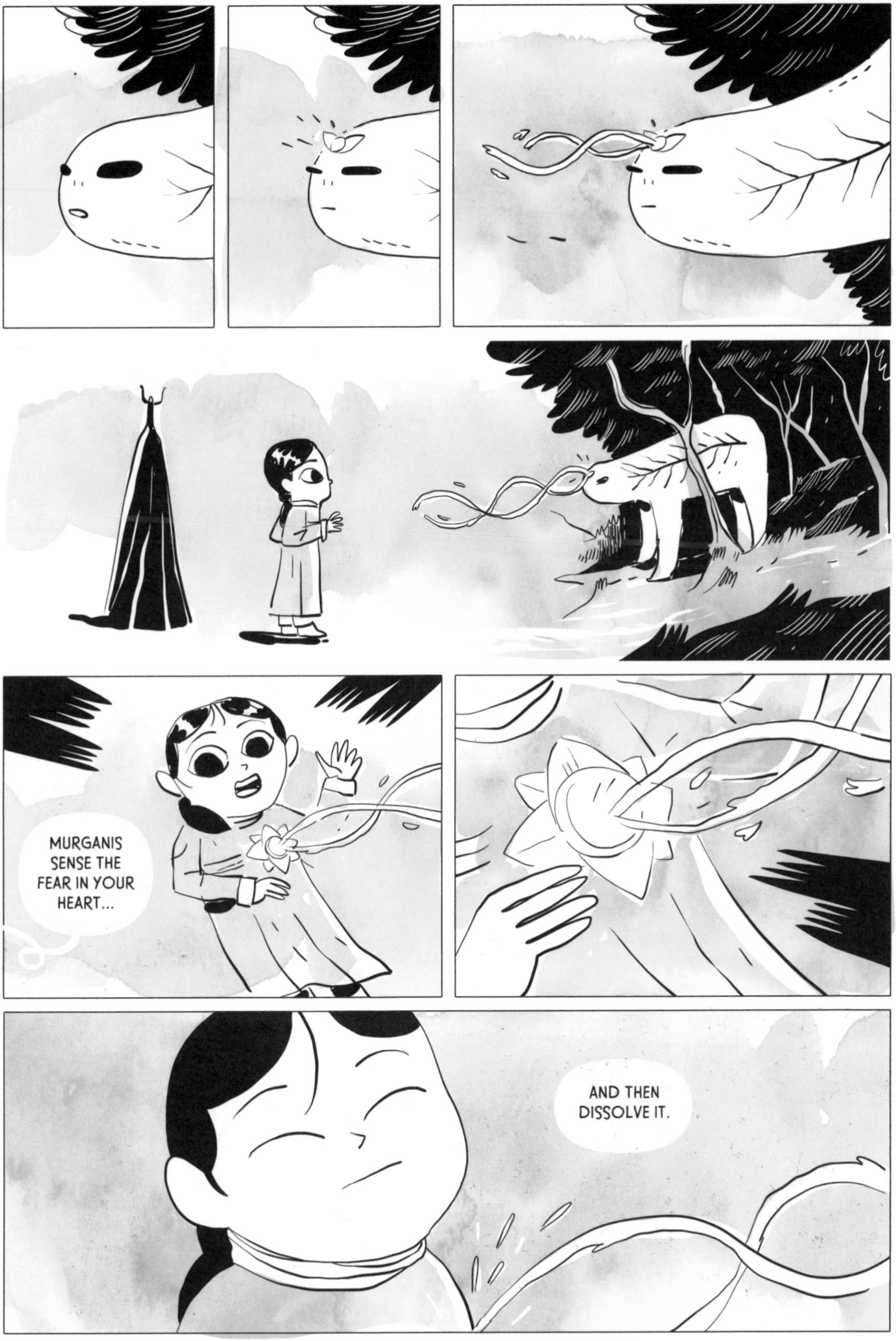
MURGANIS SENSE THE FEAR IN YOUR HEART...
AND THEN DISSOLVE IT.

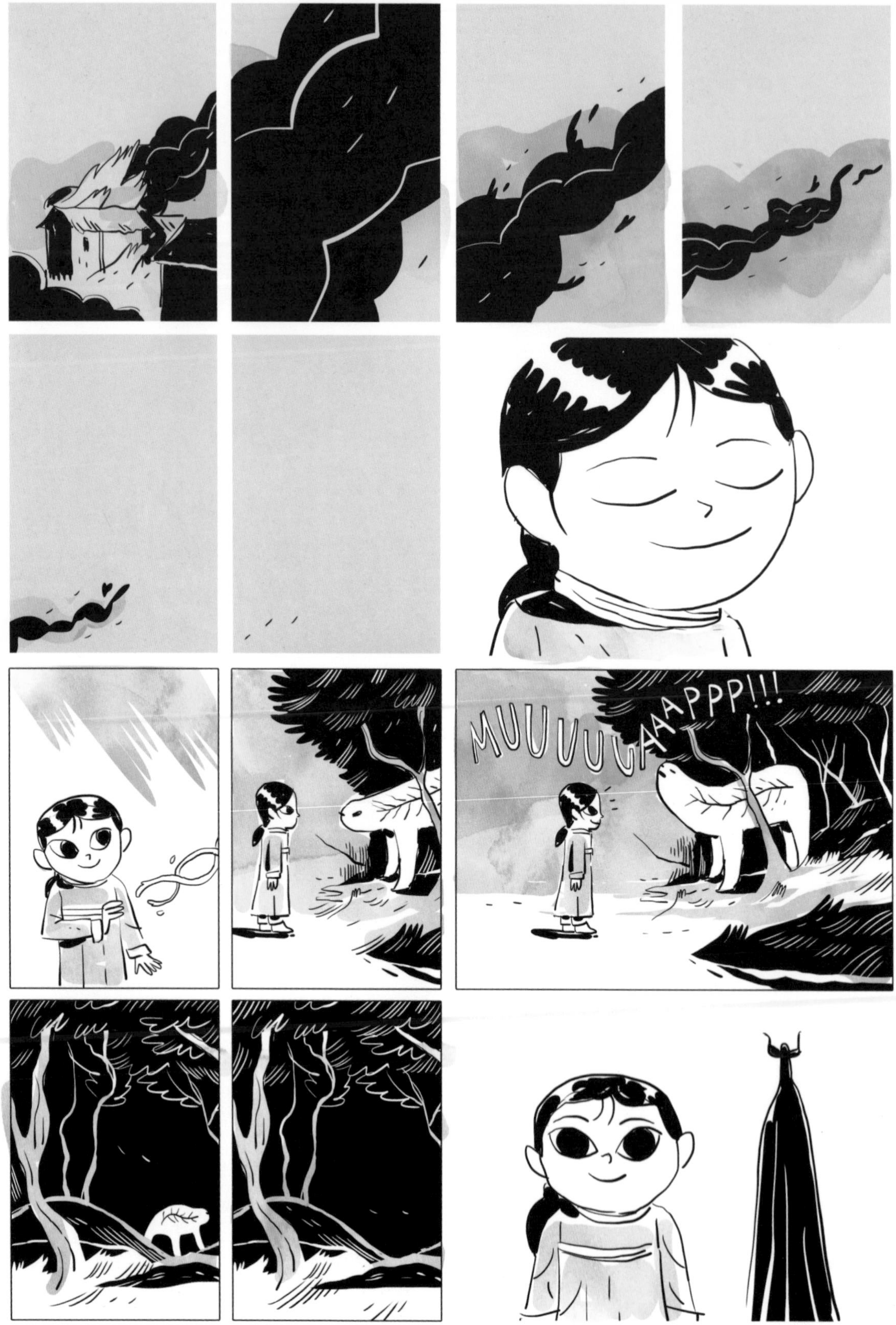
MUUUUUAAPPP!!!

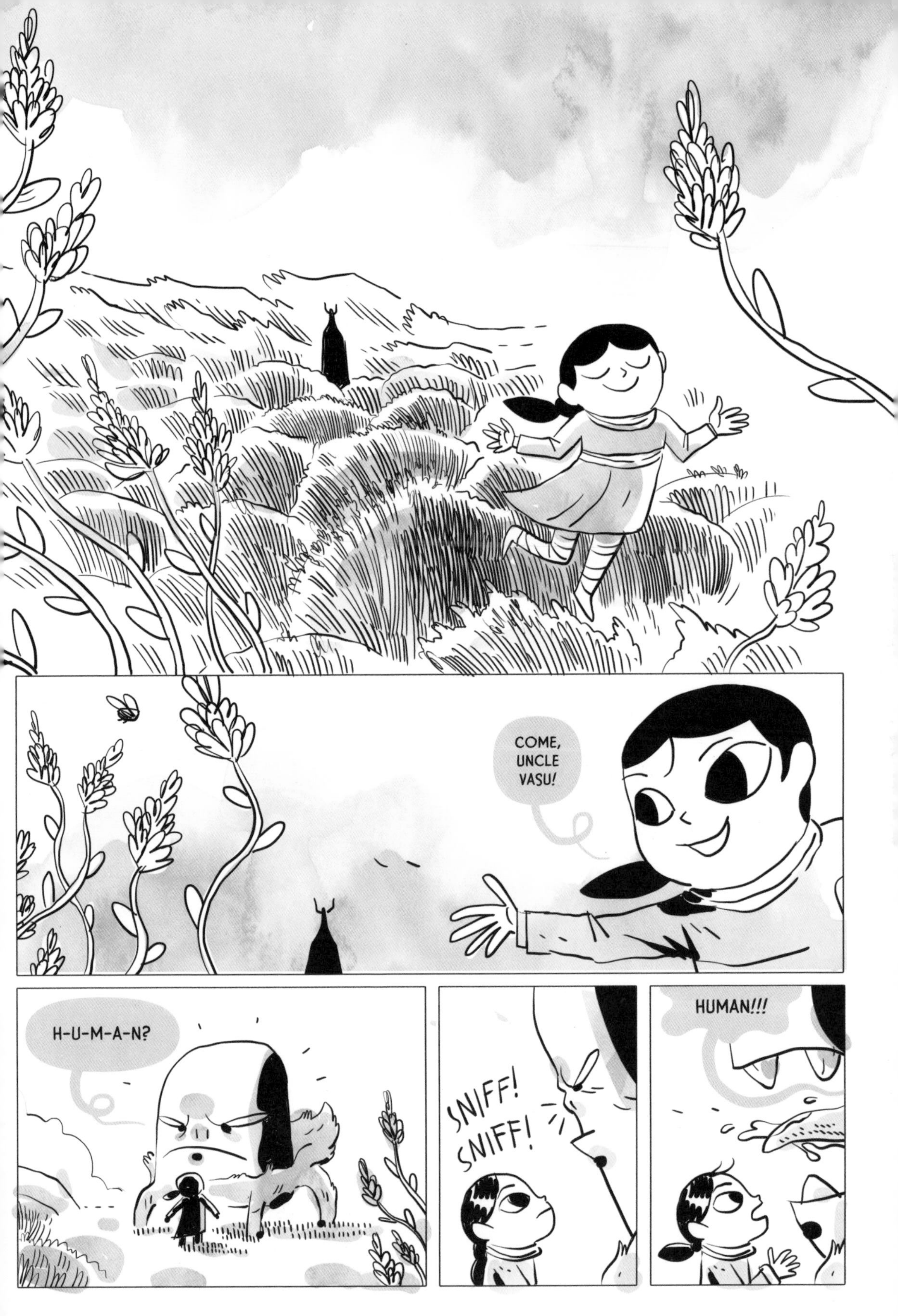
COME, UNCLE VASU!
H-U-M-A-N?
SNIFF! SNIFF!
HUMAN!!!

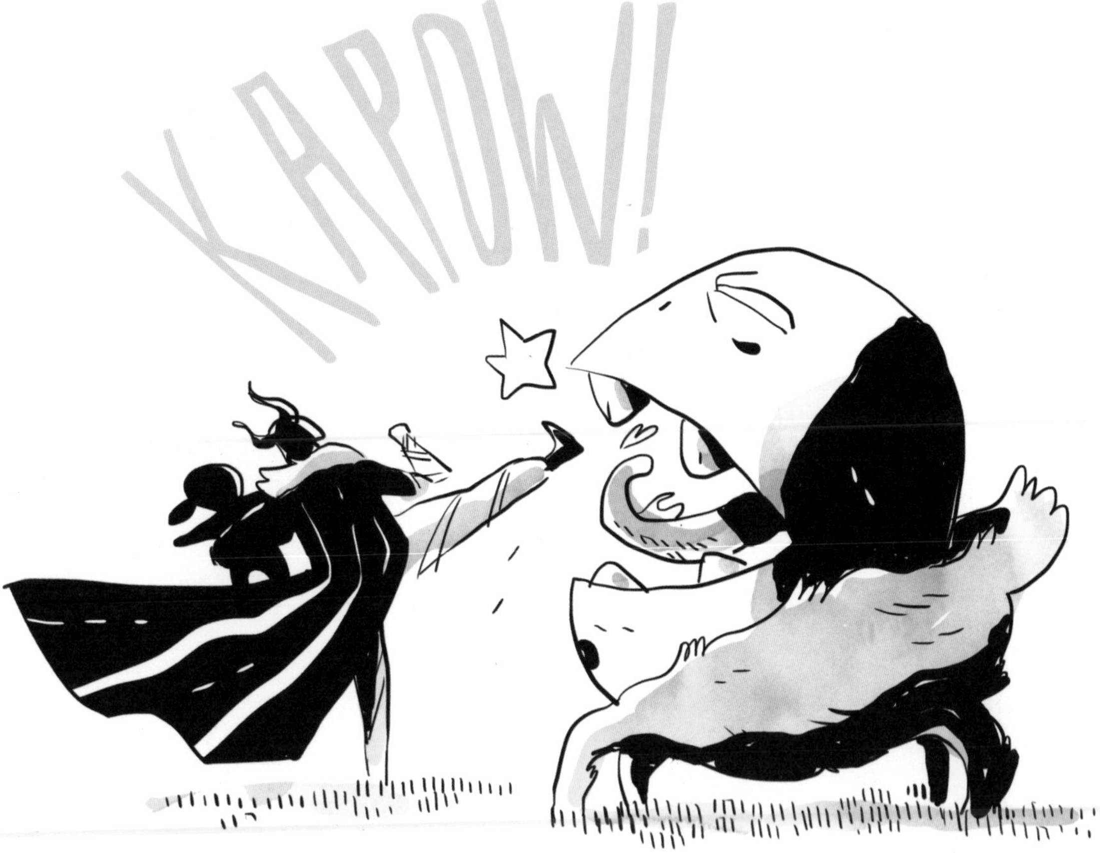
KAPOW!

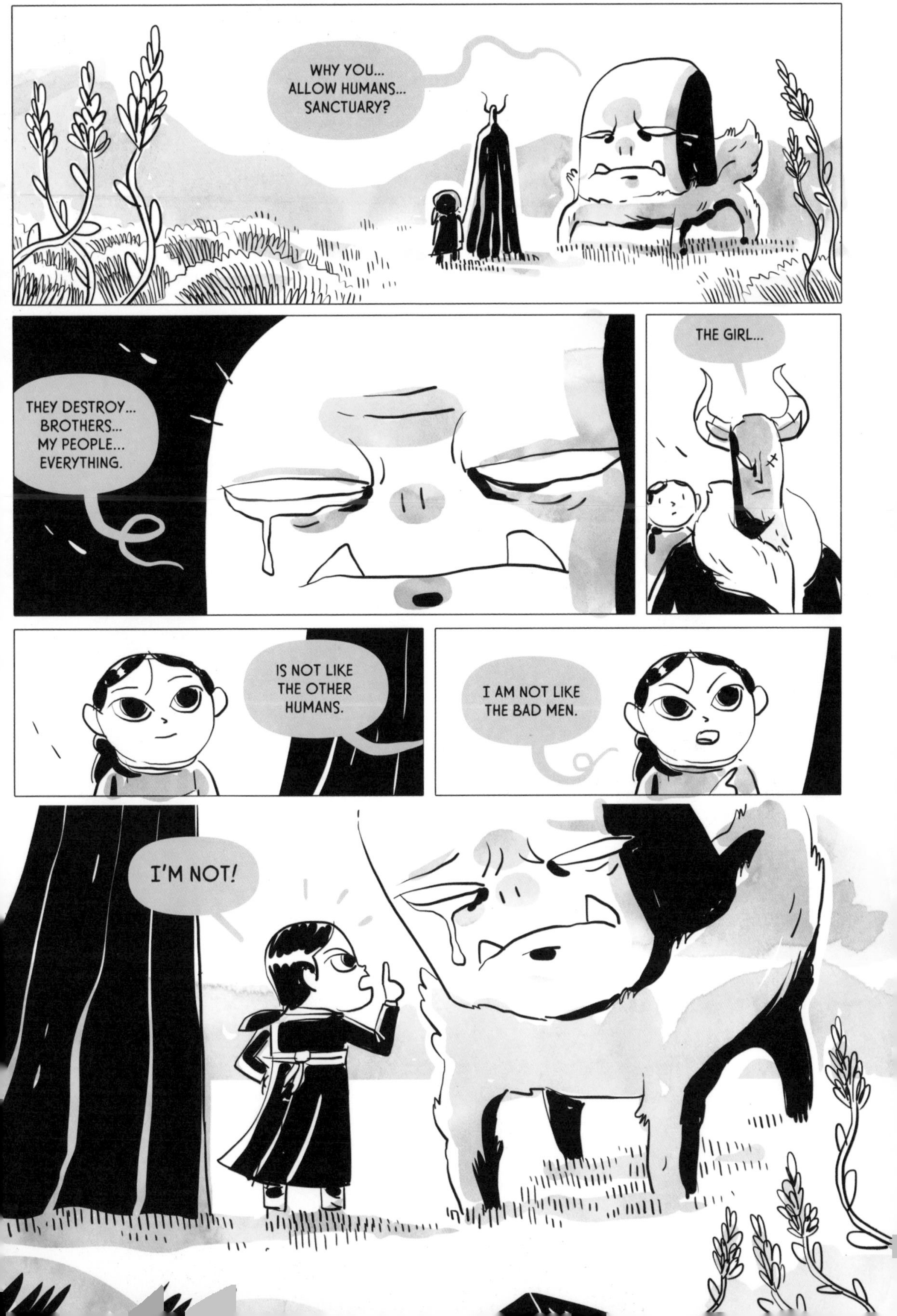
WHY YOU... ALLOW HUMANS... SANCTUARY?
THEY DESTROY... BROTHERS... MY PEOPLE... EVERYTHING.
THE GIRL...
IS NOT LIKE THE OTHER HUMANS.
I AM NOT LIKE THE BAD MEN.
I'M NOT!

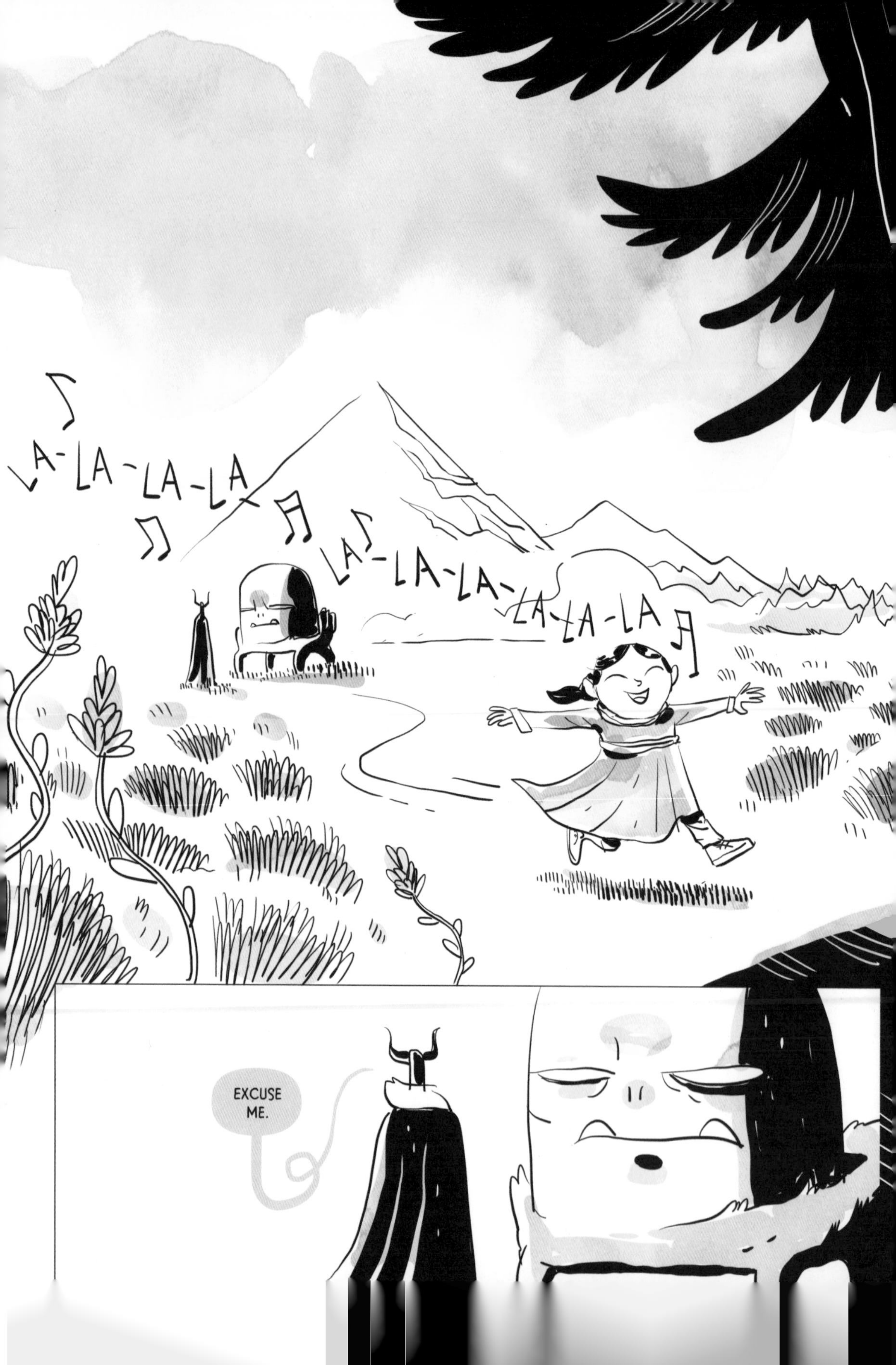
LA-LA-LA-LA
LA-LA-LA-LA-LA-LA
EXCUSE ME.

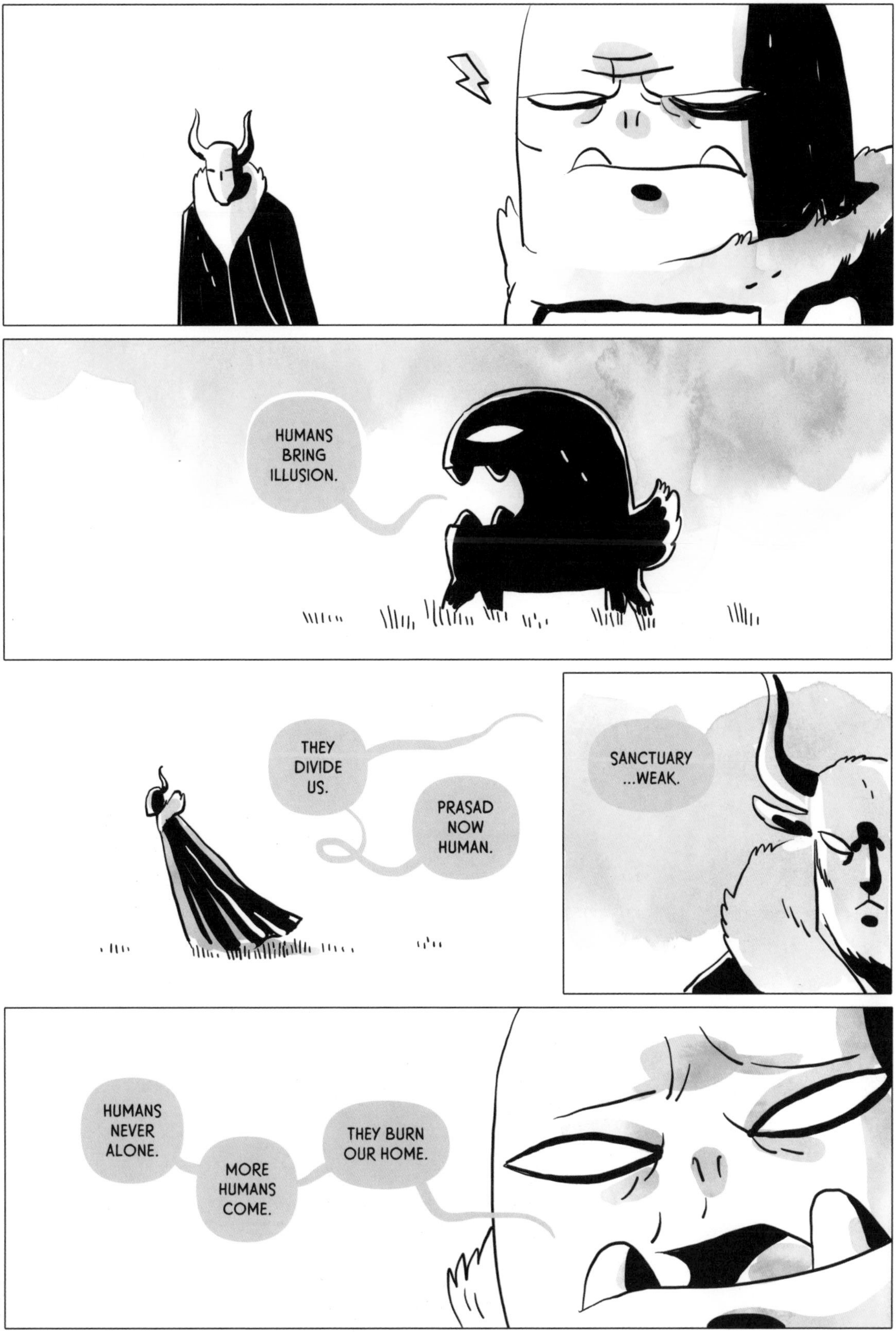
HUMANS BRING ILLUSION.
THEY DIVIDE US.
PRASAD NOW HUMAN.
SANCTUARY ...WEAK.
HUMANS NEVER ALONE.
MORE HUMANS COME.
THEY BURN OUR HOME.

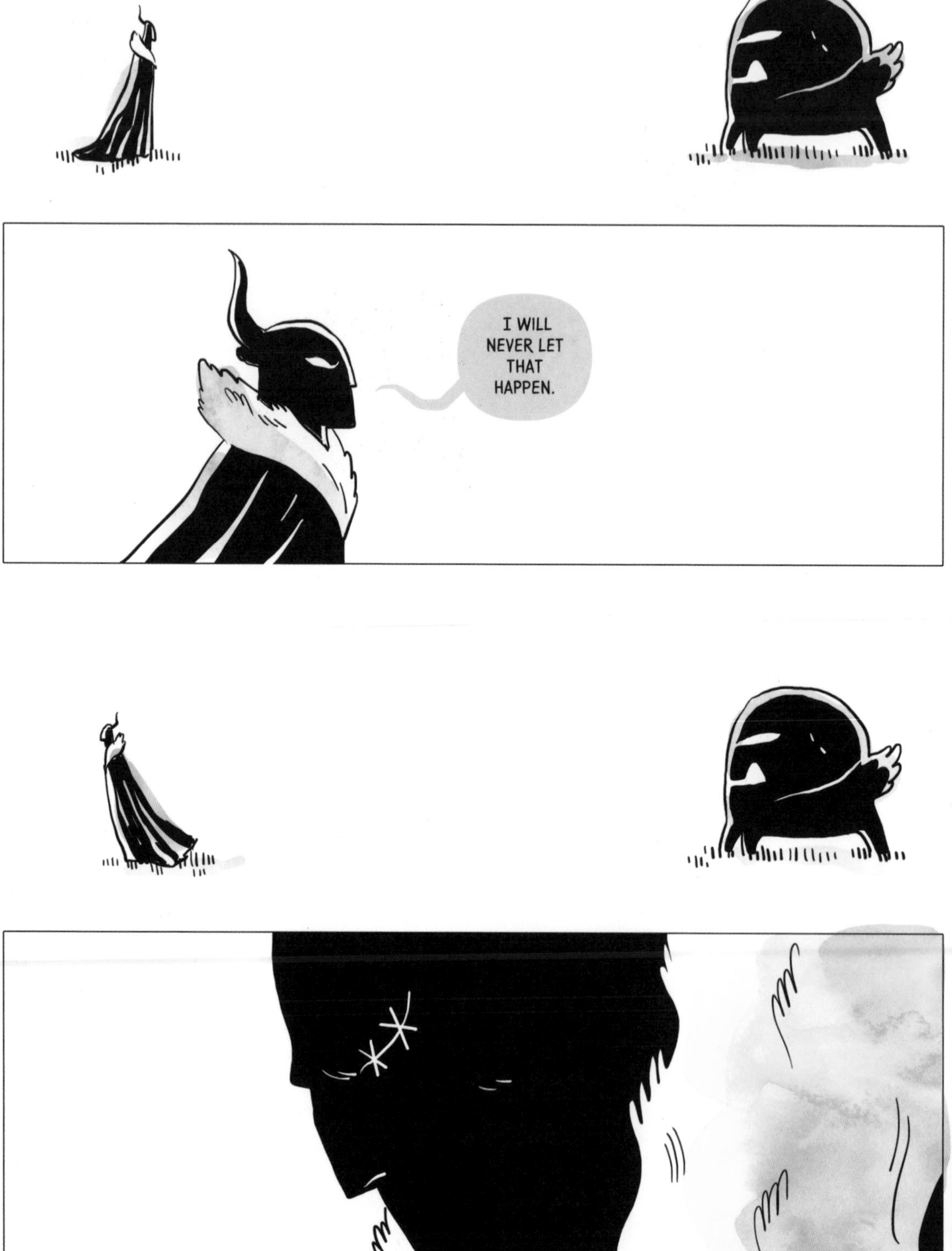
I WILL NEVER LET THAT HAPPEN.

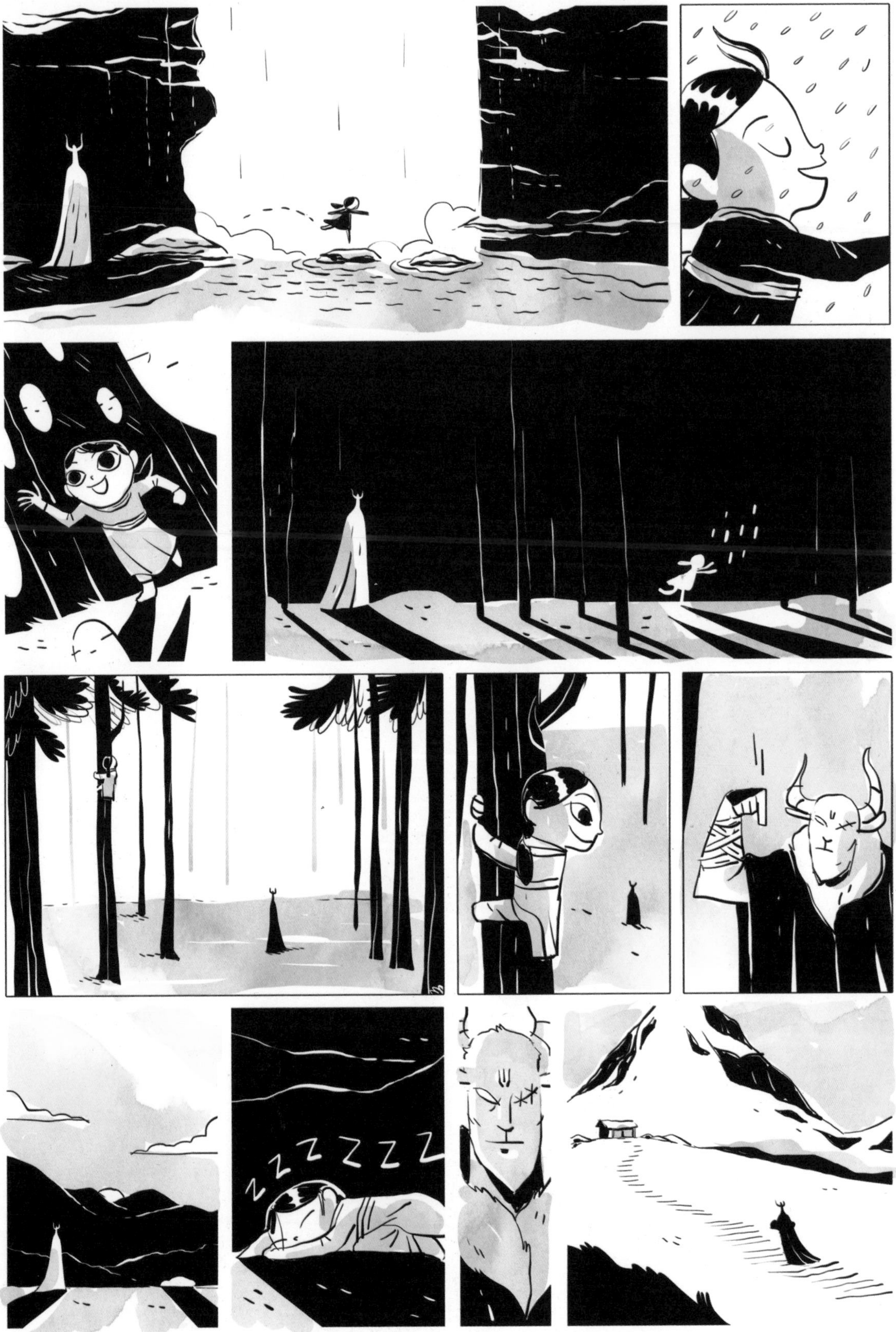
ZZZZZZ

ONE MONTH LATER ...

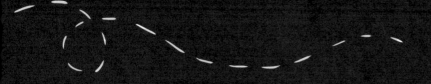

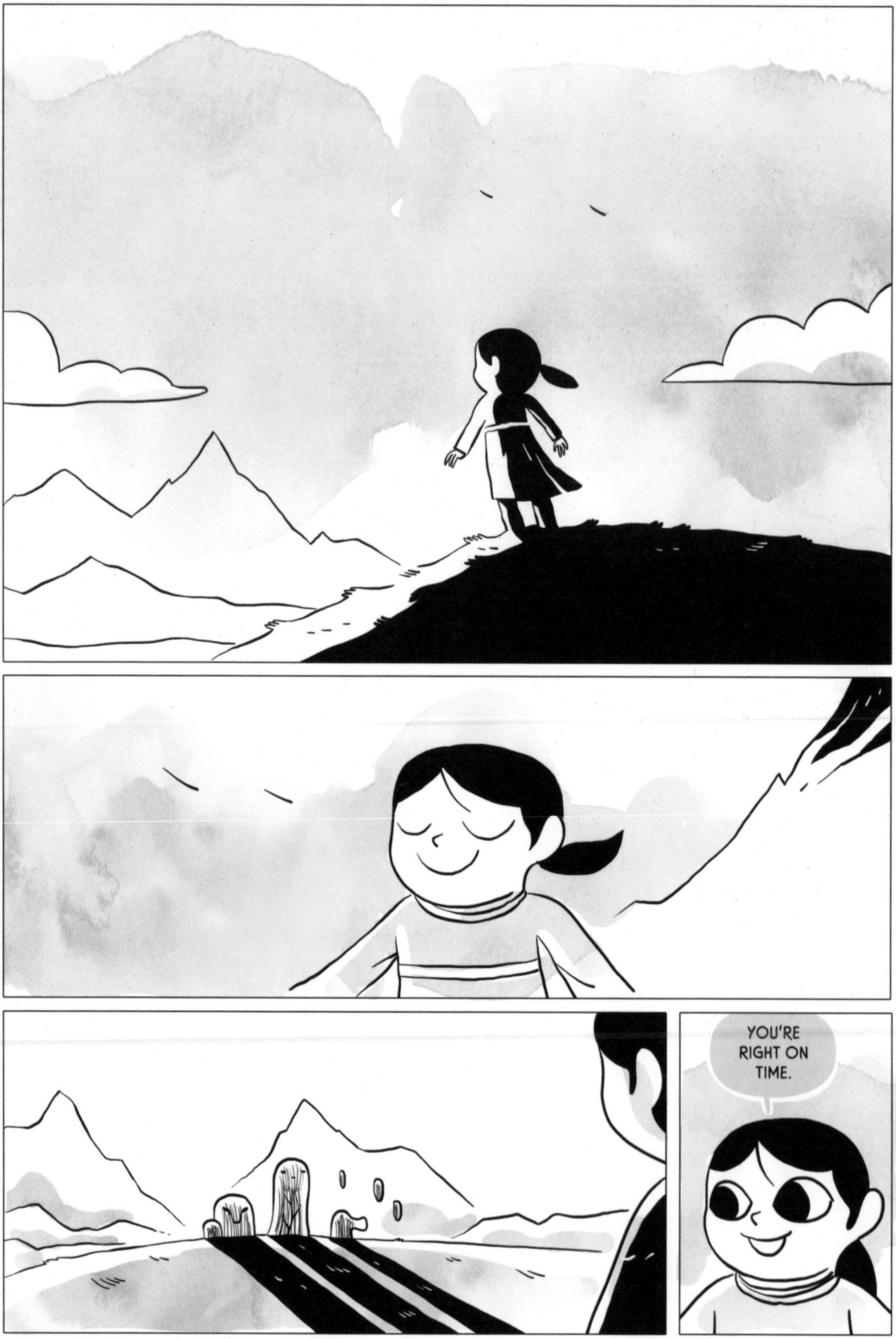
YOU'RE
RIGHT ON
TIME.

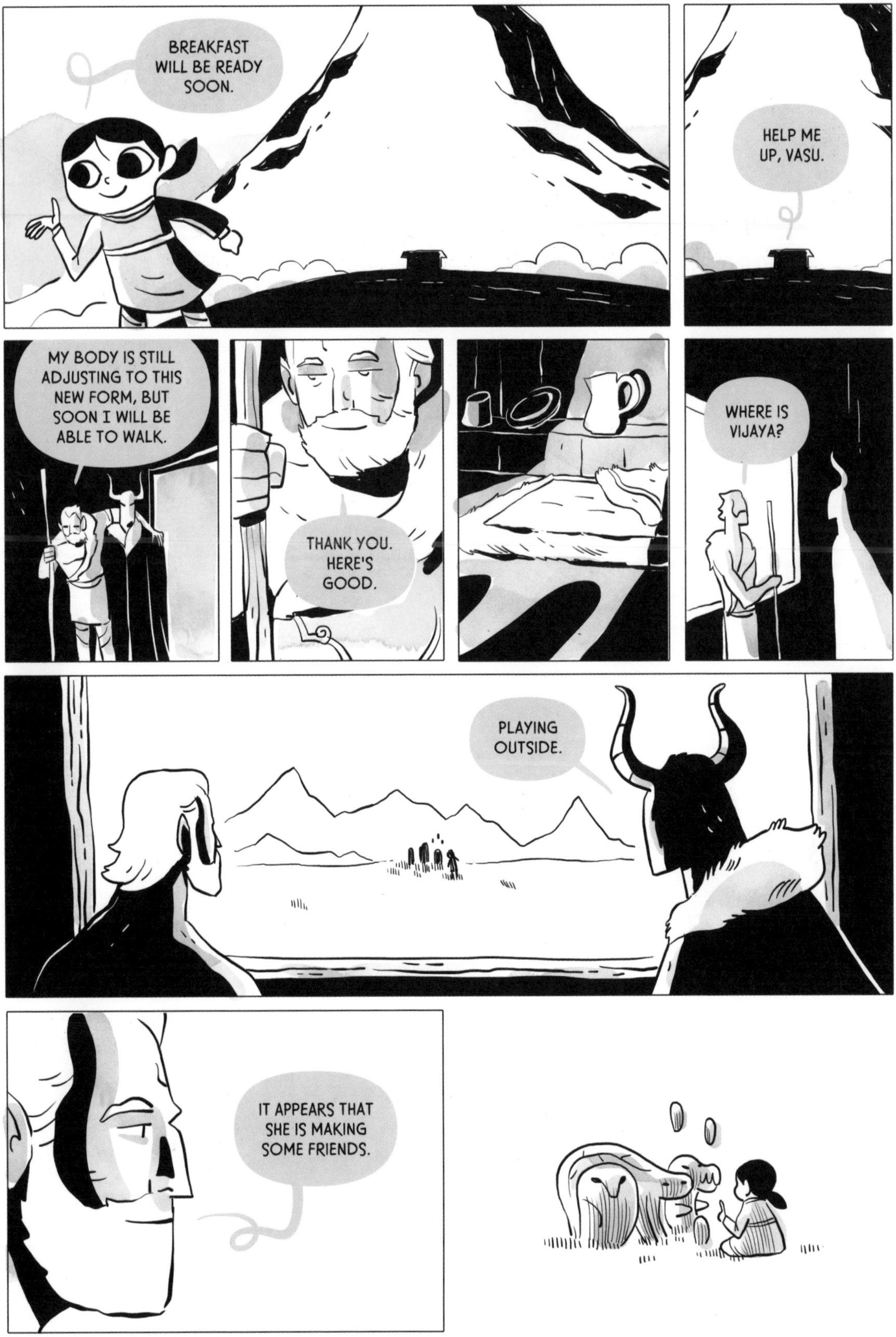

BREAKFAST WILL BE READY SOON.
HELP ME UP, VASU.
MY BODY IS STILL ADJUSTING TO THIS NEW FORM, BUT SOON I WILL BE ABLE TO WALK.
THANK YOU. HERE'S GOOD.
WHERE IS VIJAYA?
PLAYING OUTSIDE.
IT APPEARS THAT SHE IS MAKING SOME FRIENDS.

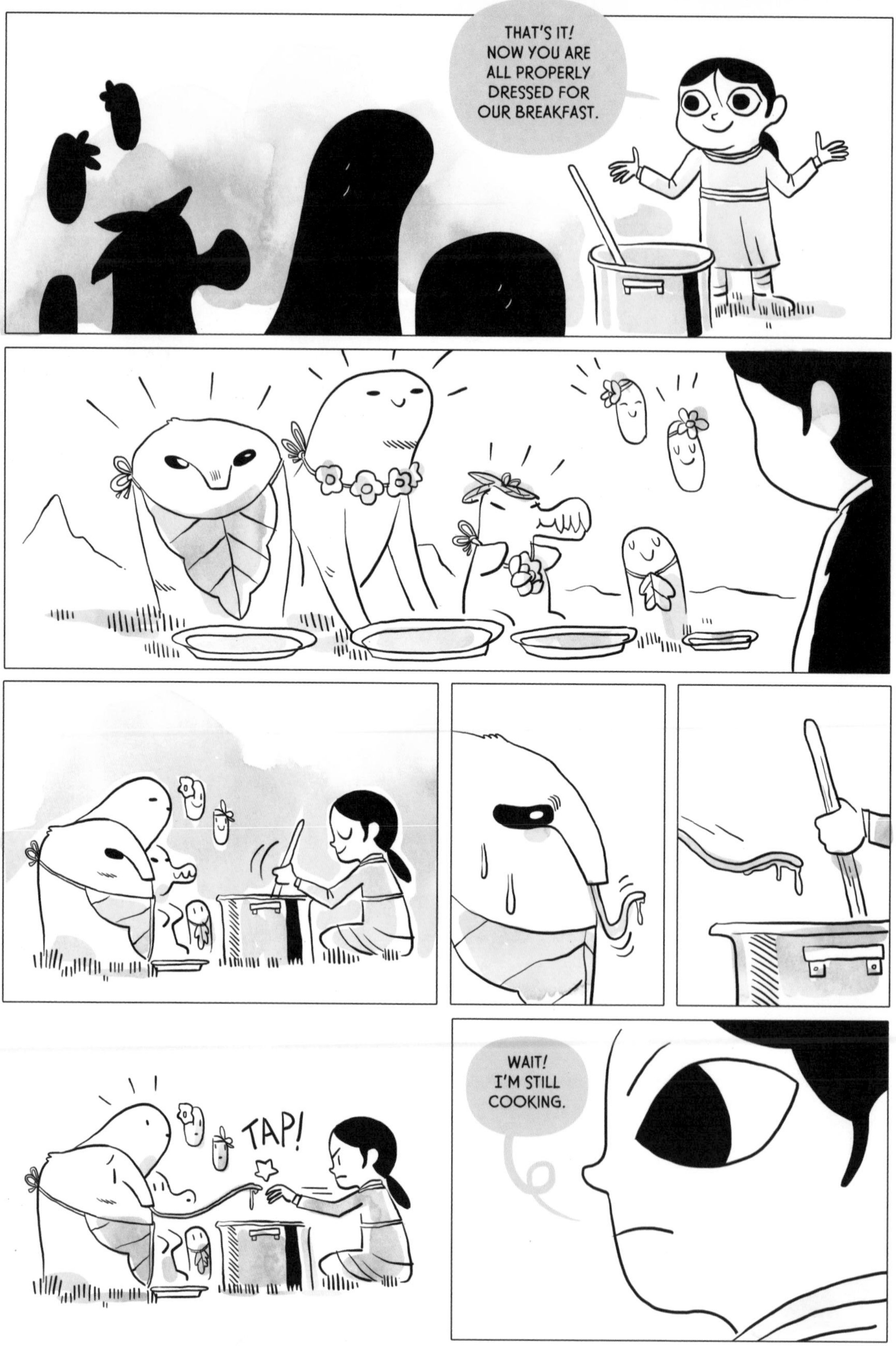
THAT'S IT! NOW YOU ARE ALL PROPERLY DRESSED FOR OUR BREAKFAST.
TAP!
WAIT! I'M STILL COOKING.

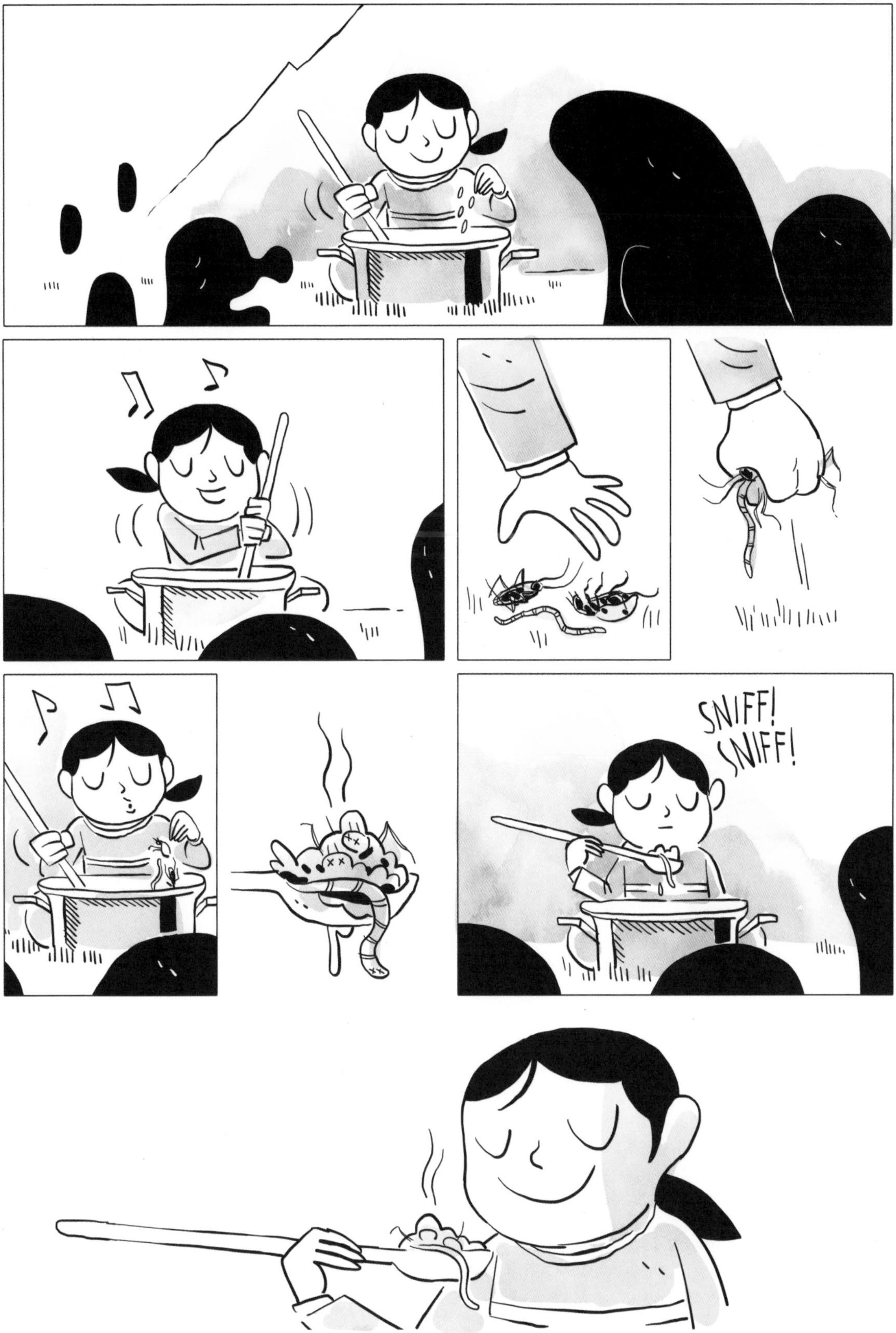
SNIFF!
SNIFF!

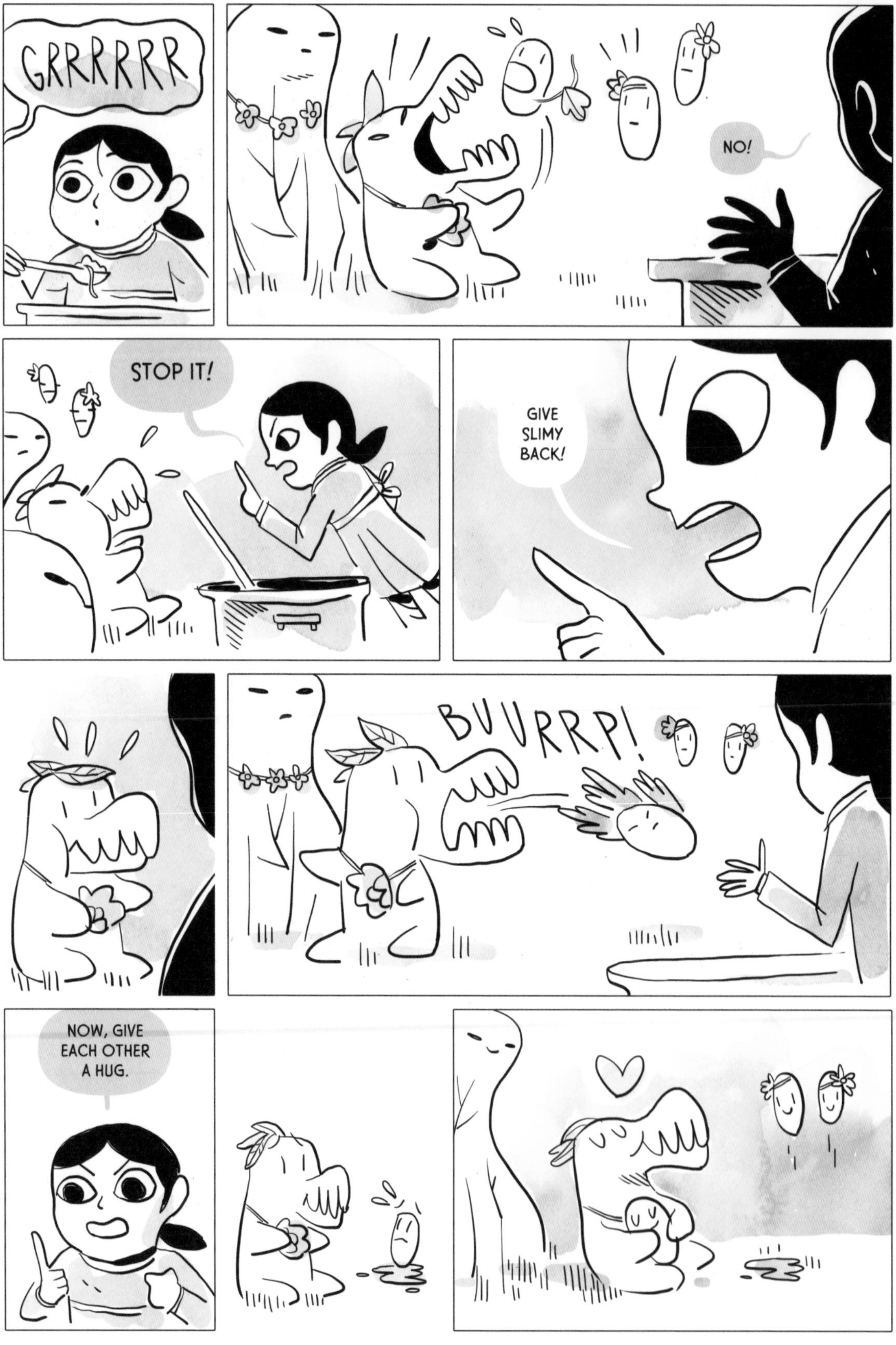
GRRRRRR
NO!
STOP IT!
GIVE SLIMY BACK!
BUURRP!
NOW, GIVE EACH OTHER A HUG.

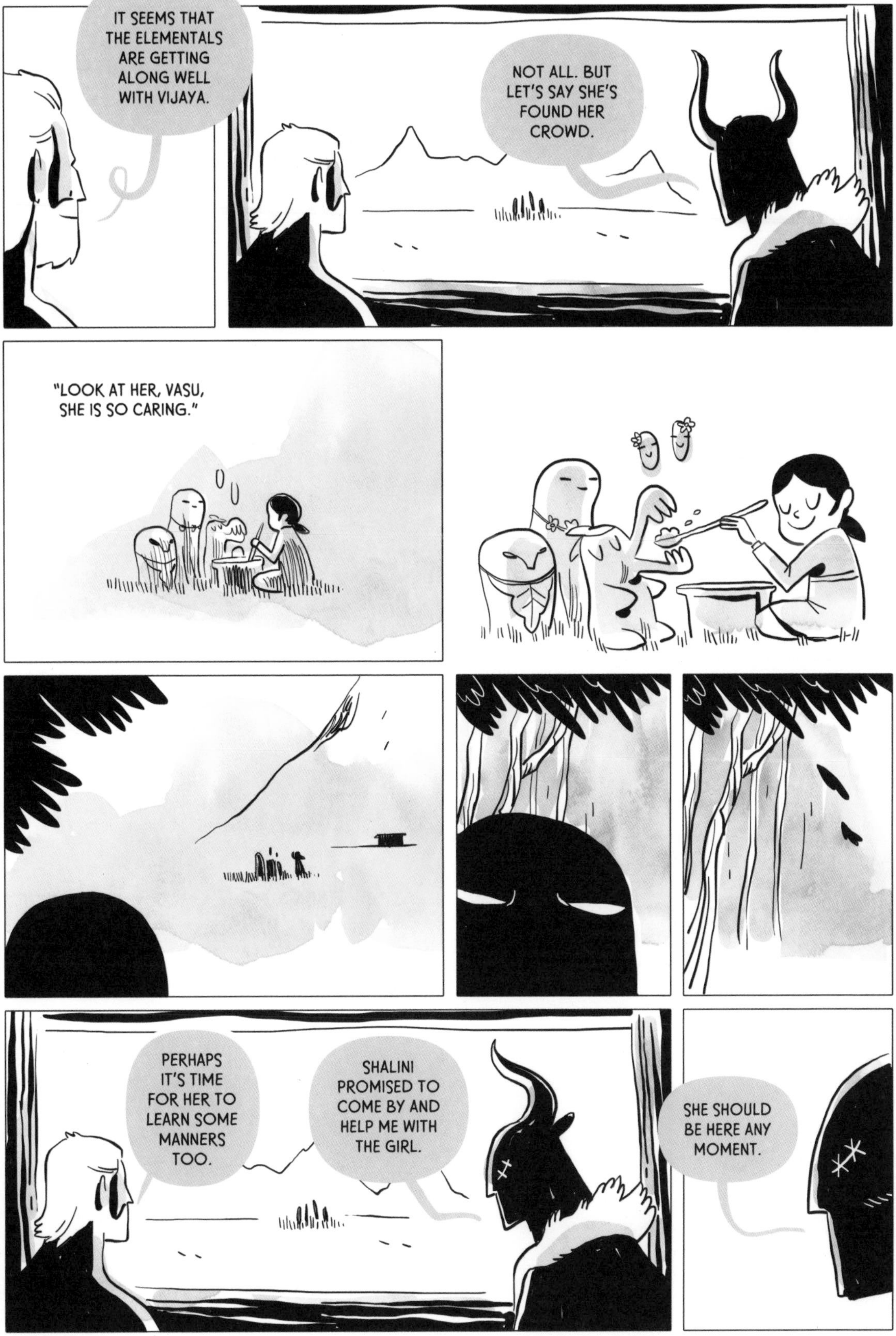
IT SEEMS THAT THE ELEMENTALS ARE GETTING ALONG WELL WITH VIJAYA.
NOT ALL. BUT LET'S SAY SHE'S FOUND HER CROWD.
"LOOK AT HER, VASU, SHE IS SO CARING."
PERHAPS IT'S TIME FOR HER TO LEARN SOME MANNERS TOO.
SHALINI PROMISED TO COME BY AND HELP ME WITH THE GIRL.
SHE SHOULD BE HERE ANY MOMENT.

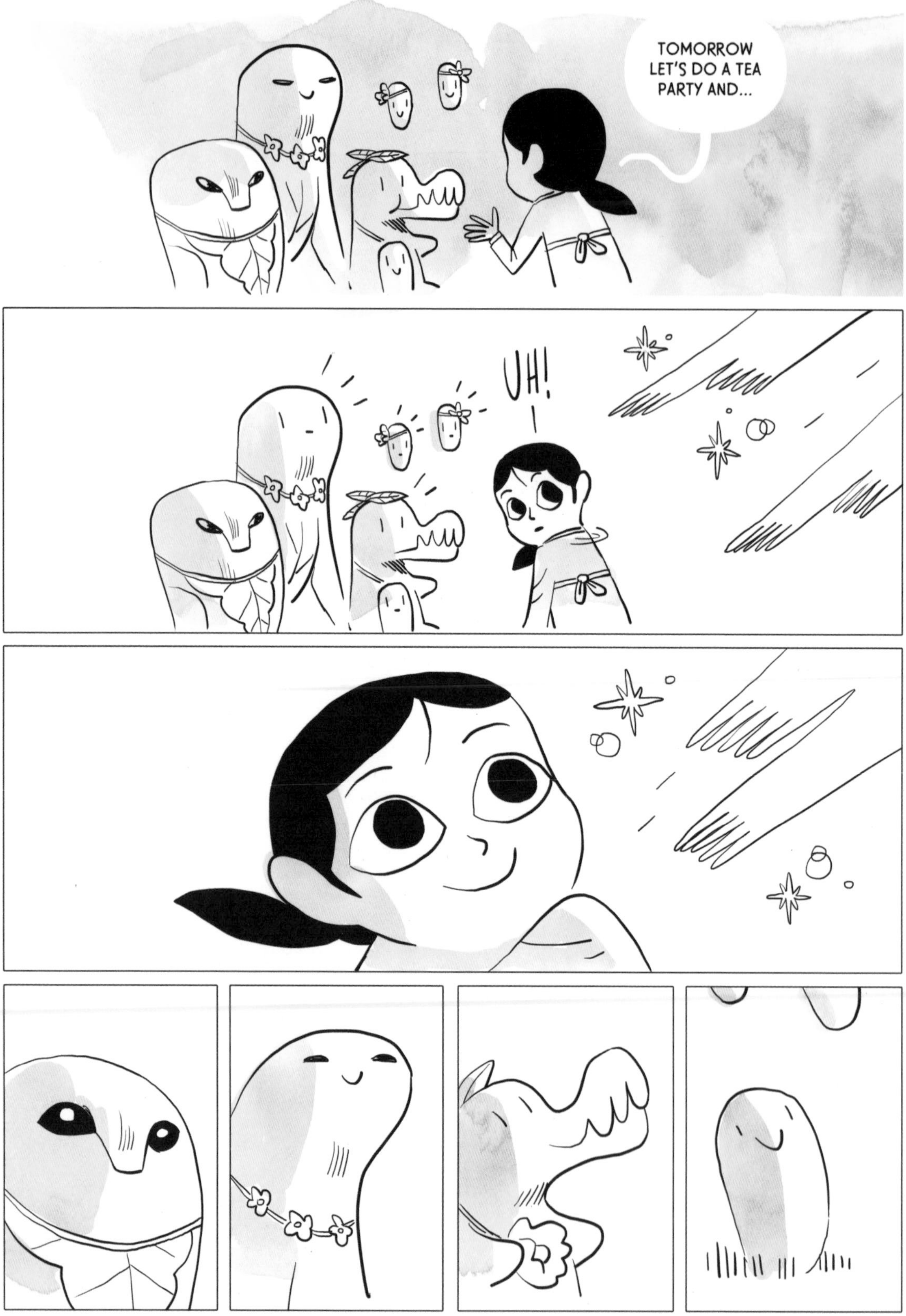
TOMORROW LET'S DO A TEA PARTY AND...
UH!

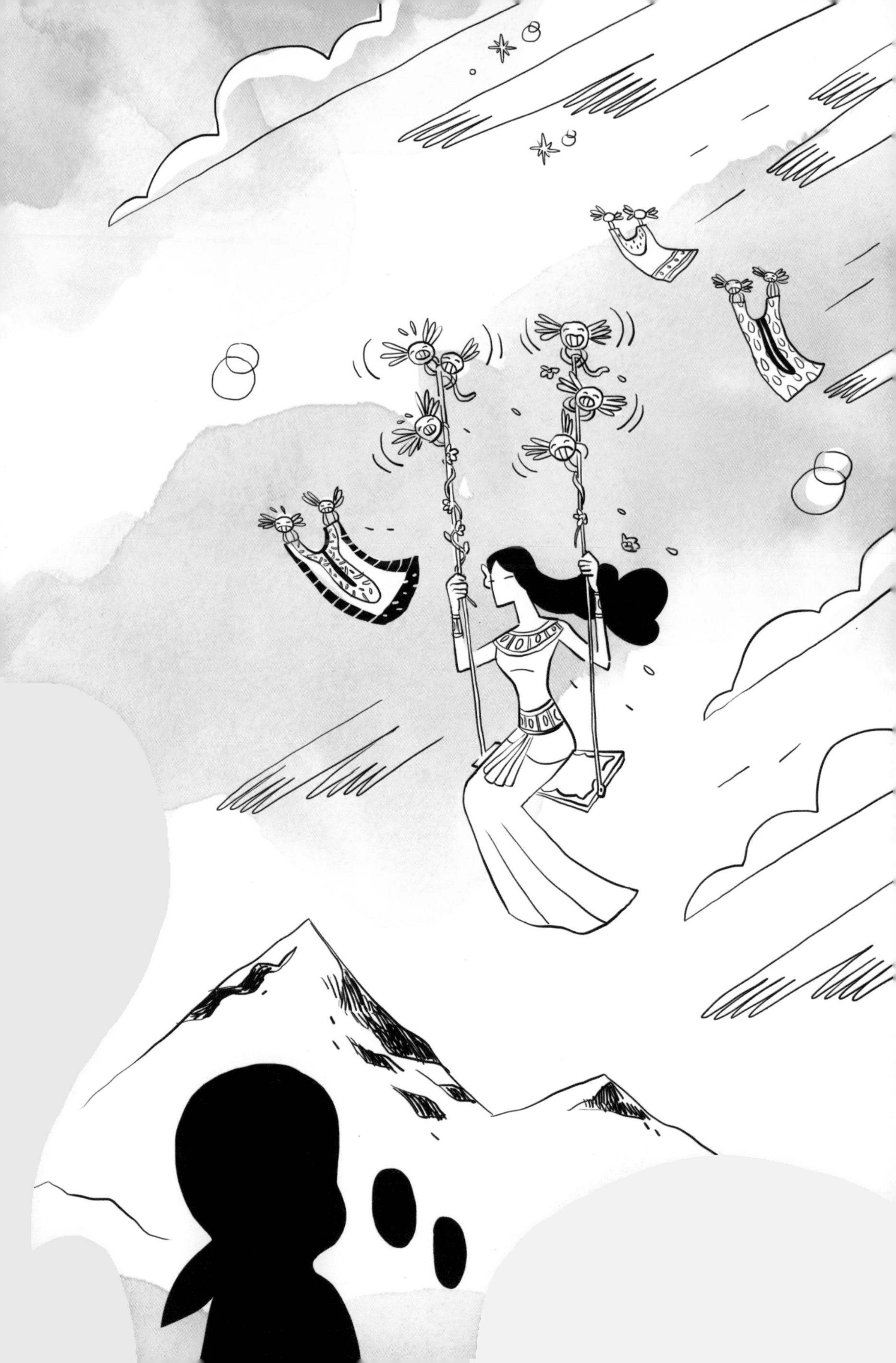

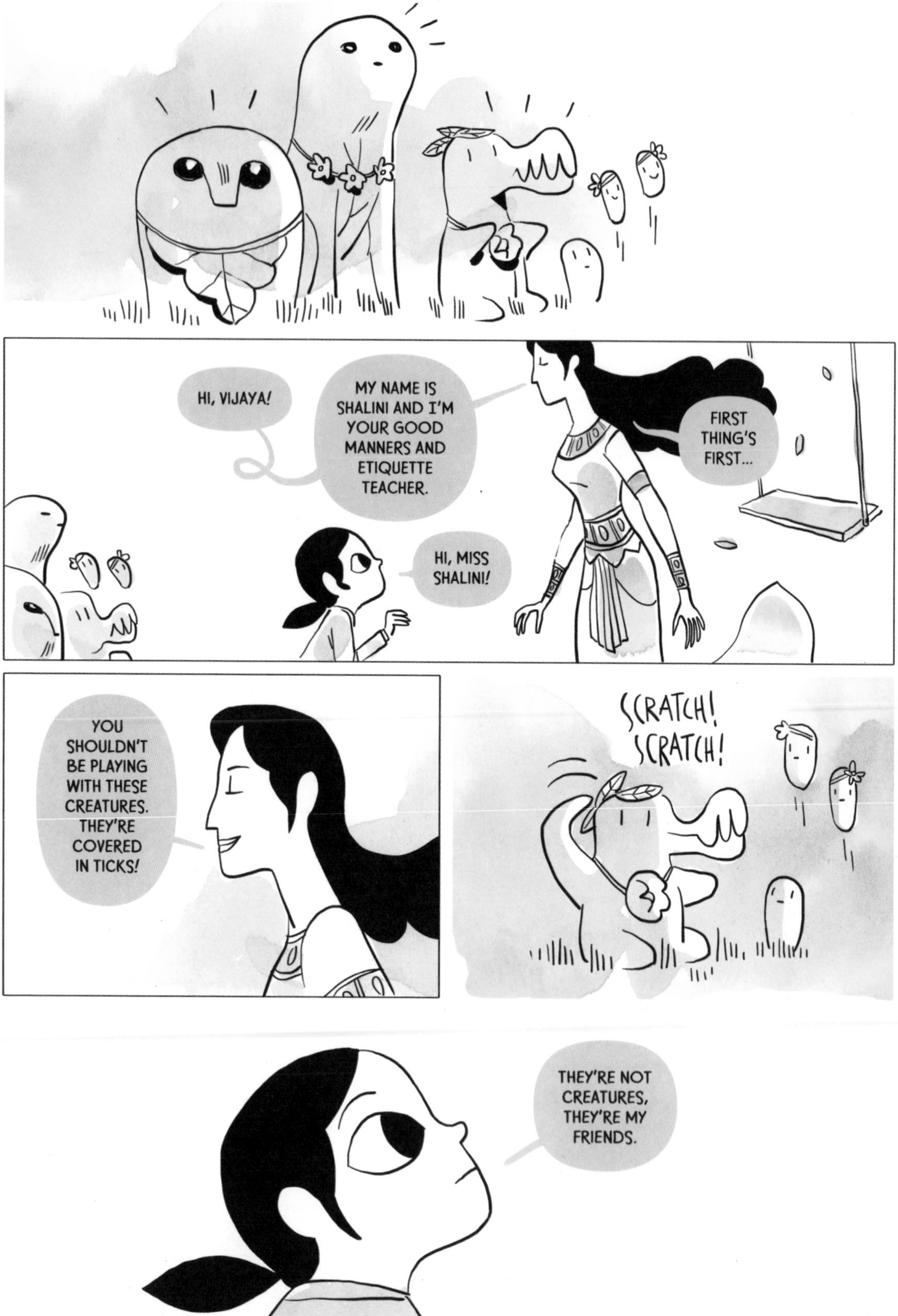

HI, VIJAYA!
MY NAME IS SHALINI AND I'M YOUR GOOD MANNERS AND ETIQUETTE TEACHER.
FIRST THING'S FIRST...
HI, MISS SHALINI!
YOU SHOULDN'T BE PLAYING WITH THESE CREATURES. THEY'RE COVERED IN TICKS!
SCRATCH! SCRATCH!
THEY'RE NOT CREATURES, THEY'RE MY FRIENDS.

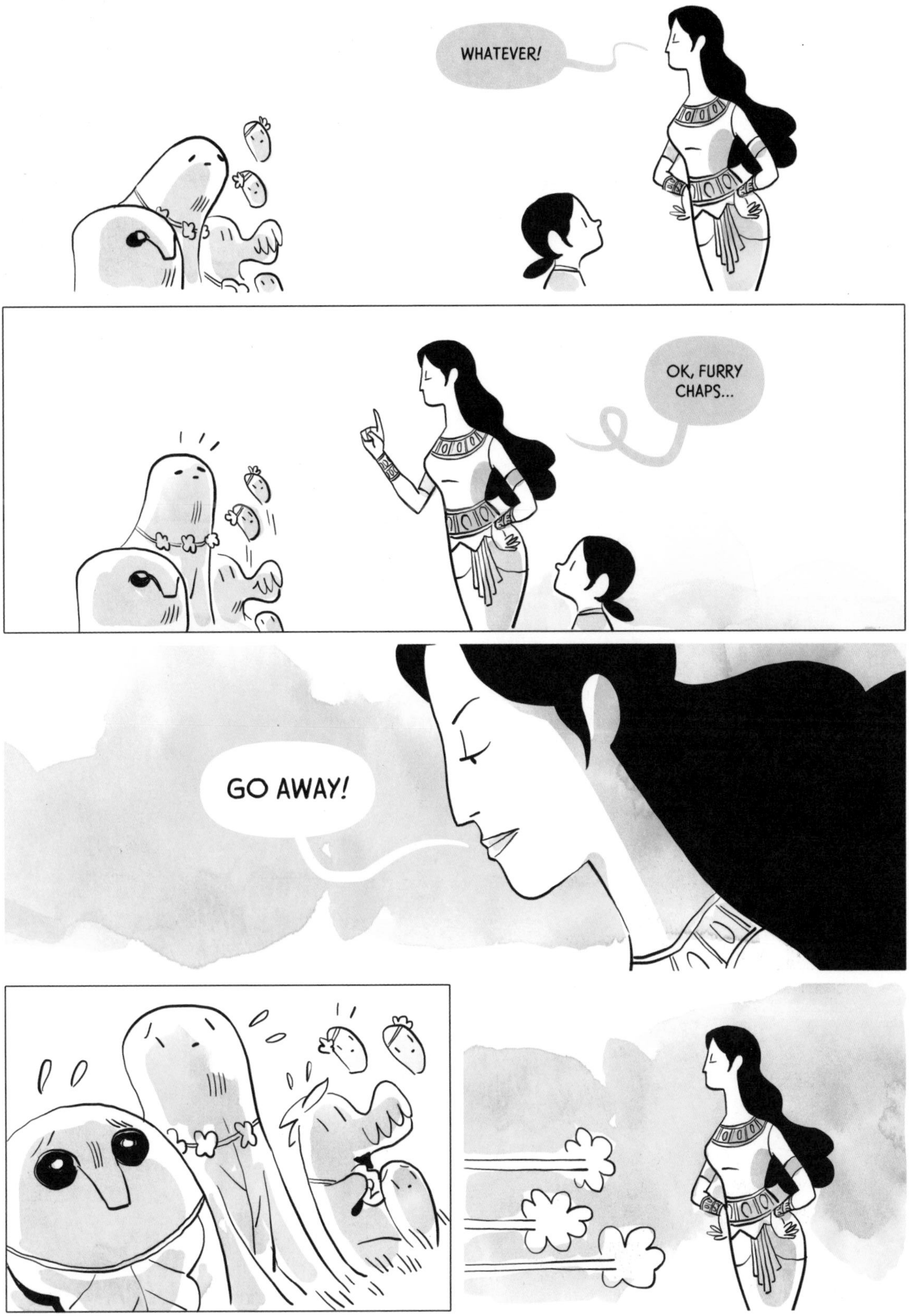
WHATEVER!
OK, FURRY CHAPS...
GO AWAY!

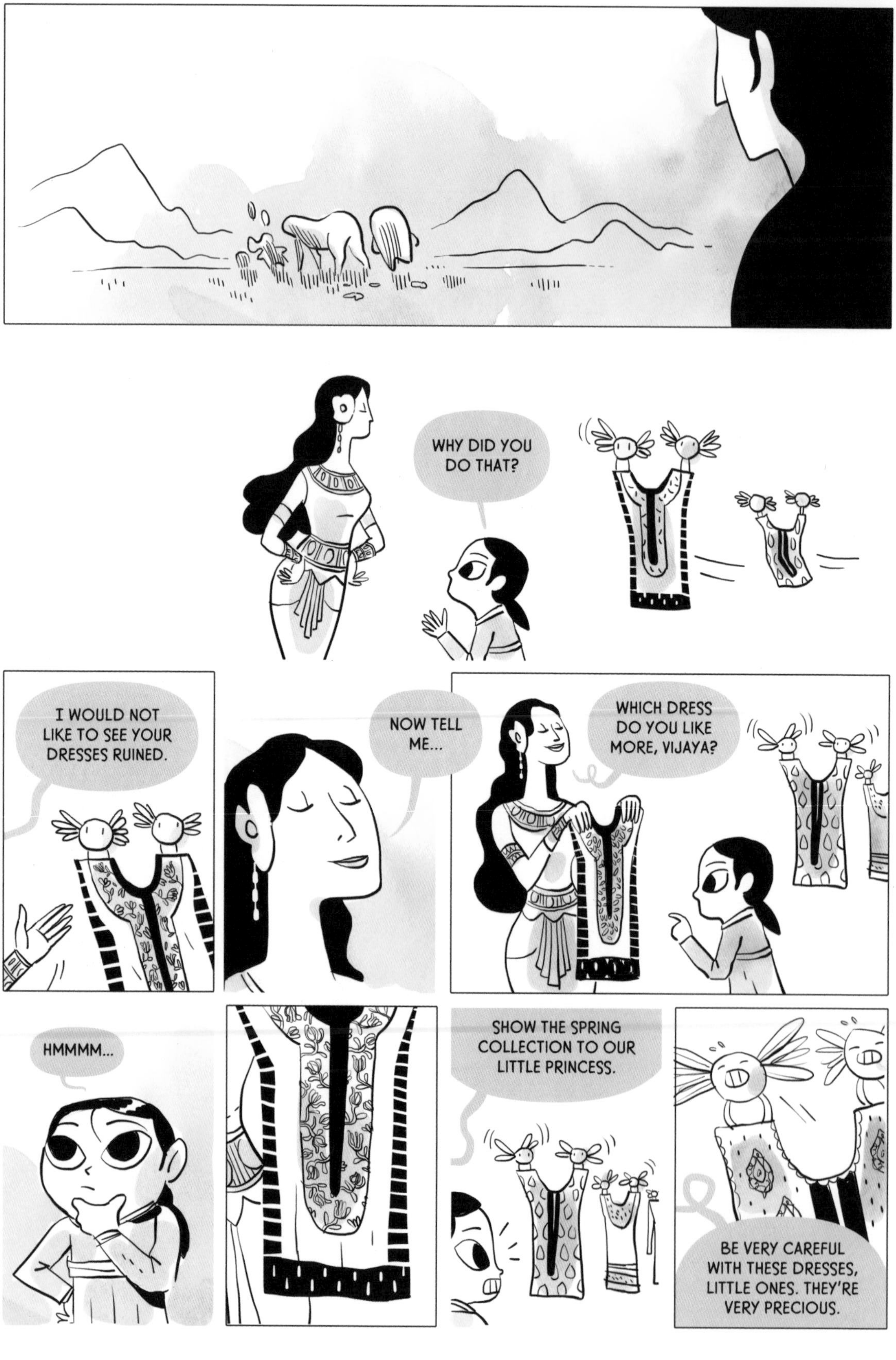
WHY DID YOU DO THAT?
I WOULD NOT LIKE TO SEE YOUR DRESSES RUINED.
NOW TELL ME...
WHICH DRESS DO YOU LIKE MORE, VIJAYA?
HMMMM...
SHOW THE SPRING COLLECTION TO OUR LITTLE PRINCESS.
BE VERY CAREFUL WITH THESE DRESSES, LITTLE ONES. THEY'RE VERY PRECIOUS.

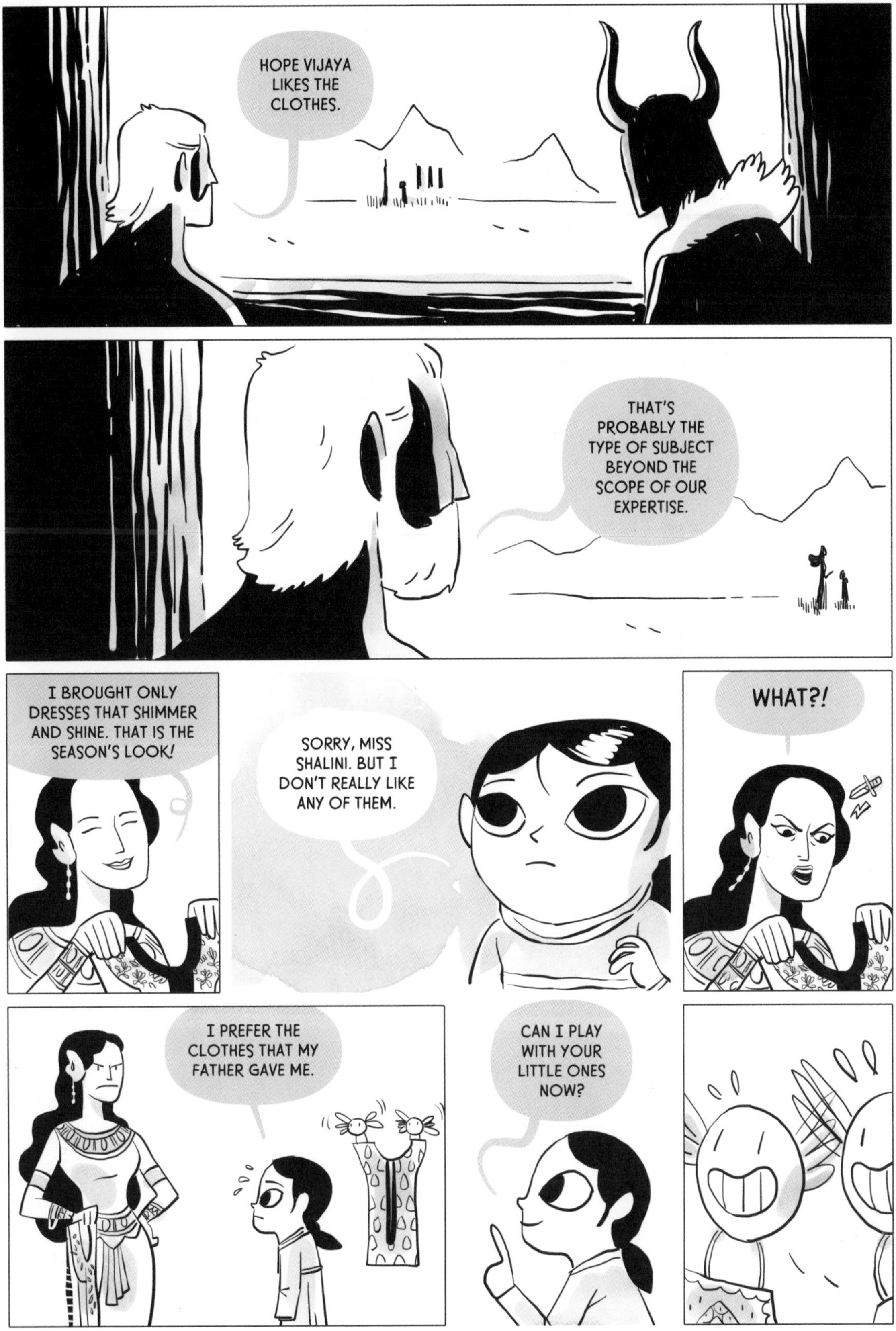
HOPE VIJAYA LIKES THE CLOTHES.
THAT'S PROBABLY THE TYPE OF SUBJECT BEYOND THE SCOPE OF OUR EXPERTISE.
I BROUGHT ONLY DRESSES THAT SHIMMER AND SHINE. THAT IS THE SEASON'S LOOK!
SORRY, MISS SHALINI. BUT I DON'T REALLY LIKE ANY OF THEM.
WHAT?!
I PREFER THE CLOTHES THAT MY FATHER GAVE ME.
CAN I PLAY WITH YOUR LITTLE ONES NOW?

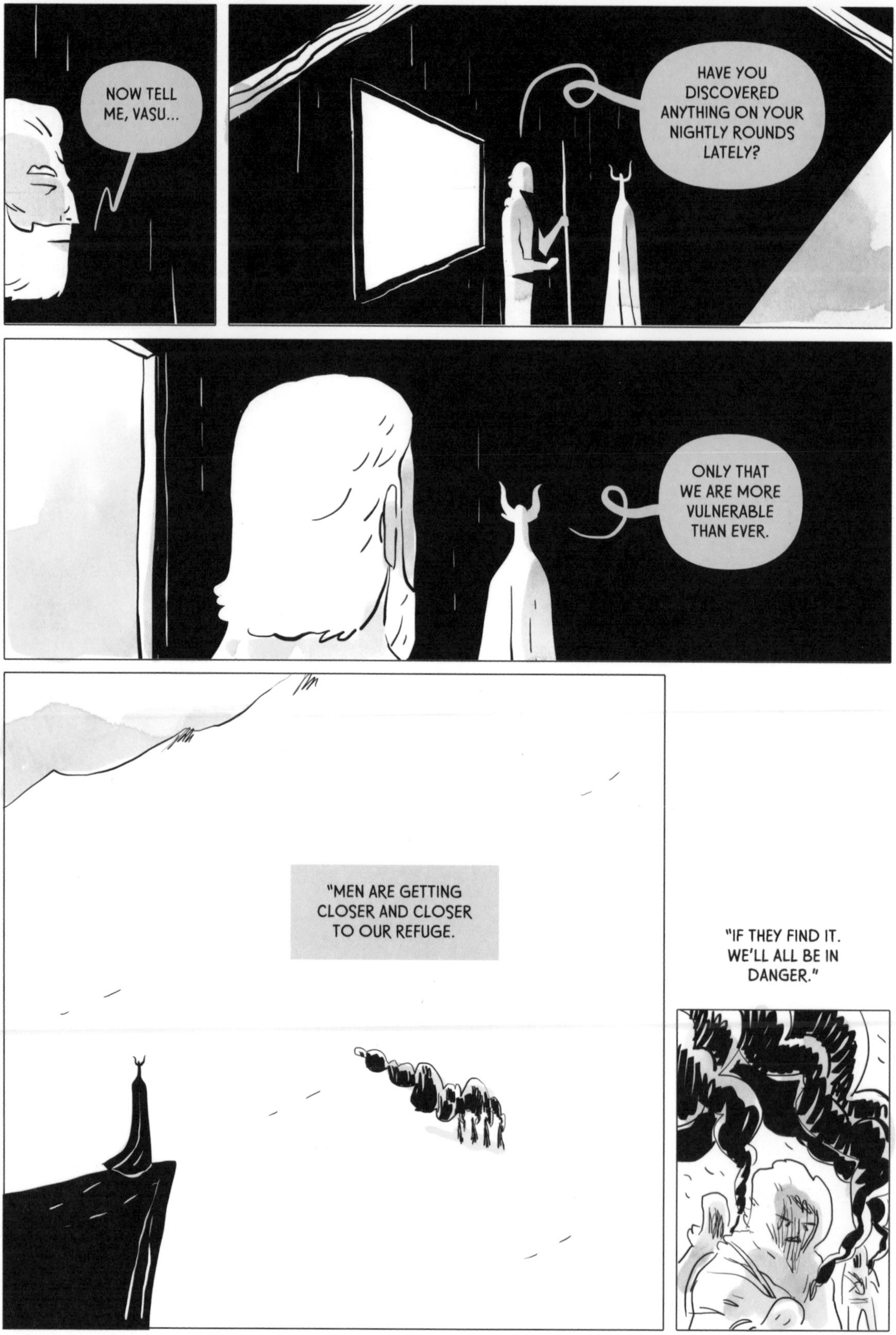
NOW TELL ME, VASU...
HAVE YOU DISCOVERED ANYTHING ON YOUR NIGHTLY ROUNDS LATELY?
ONLY THAT WE ARE MORE VULNERABLE THAN EVER.
"MEN ARE GETTING CLOSER AND CLOSER TO OUR REFUGE.
"IF THEY FIND IT. WE'LL ALL BE IN DANGER."

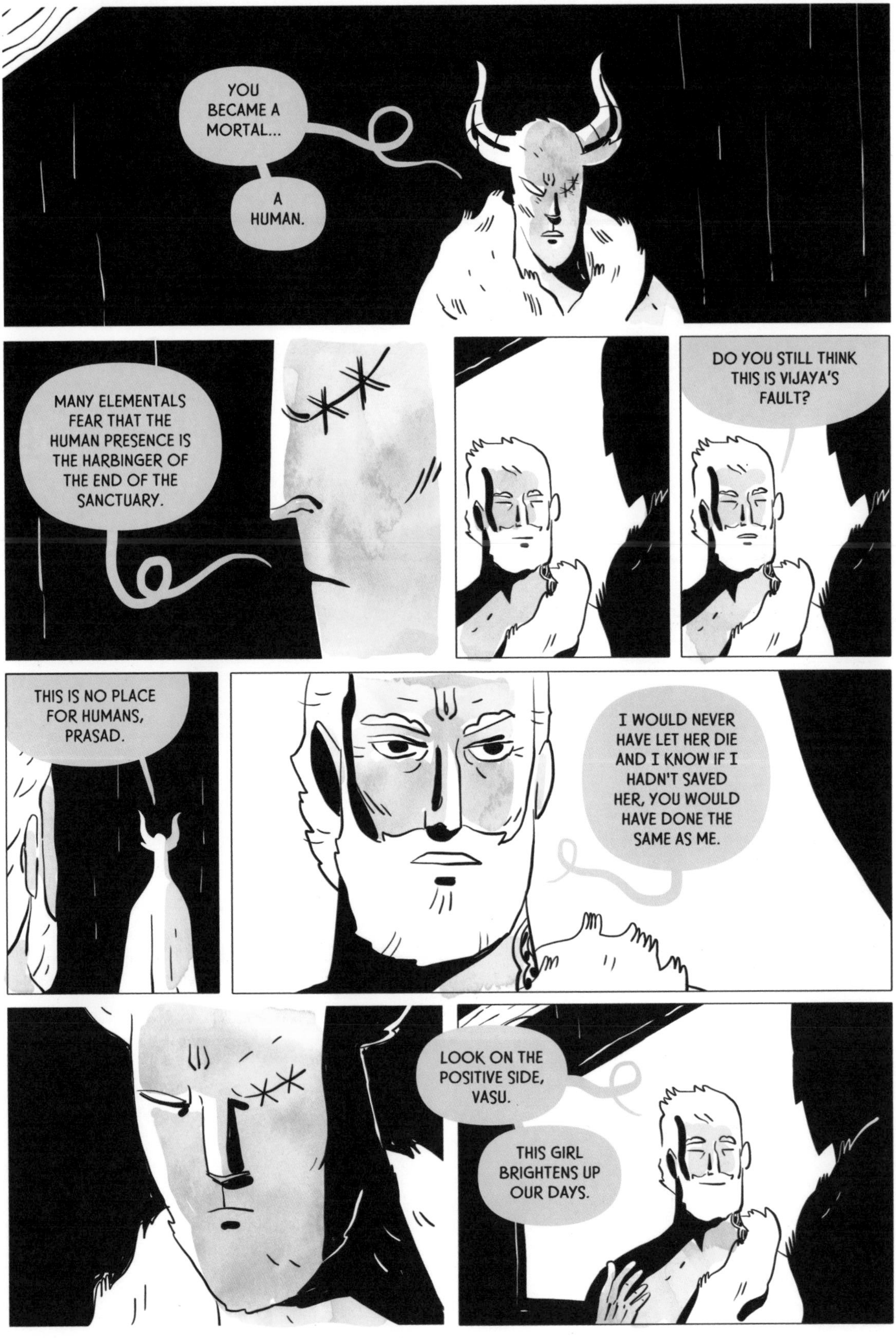
YOU BECAME A MORTAL...
A HUMAN.
MANY ELEMENTALS FEAR THAT THE HUMAN PRESENCE IS THE HARBINGER OF THE END OF THE SANCTUARY.
DO YOU STILL THINK THIS IS VIJAYA'S FAULT?
THIS IS NO PLACE FOR HUMANS, PRASAD.
I WOULD NEVER HAVE LET HER DIE AND I KNOW IF I HADN'T SAVED HER, YOU WOULD HAVE DONE THE SAME AS ME.
LOOK ON THE POSITIVE SIDE, VASU.
THIS GIRL BRIGHTENS UP OUR DAYS.

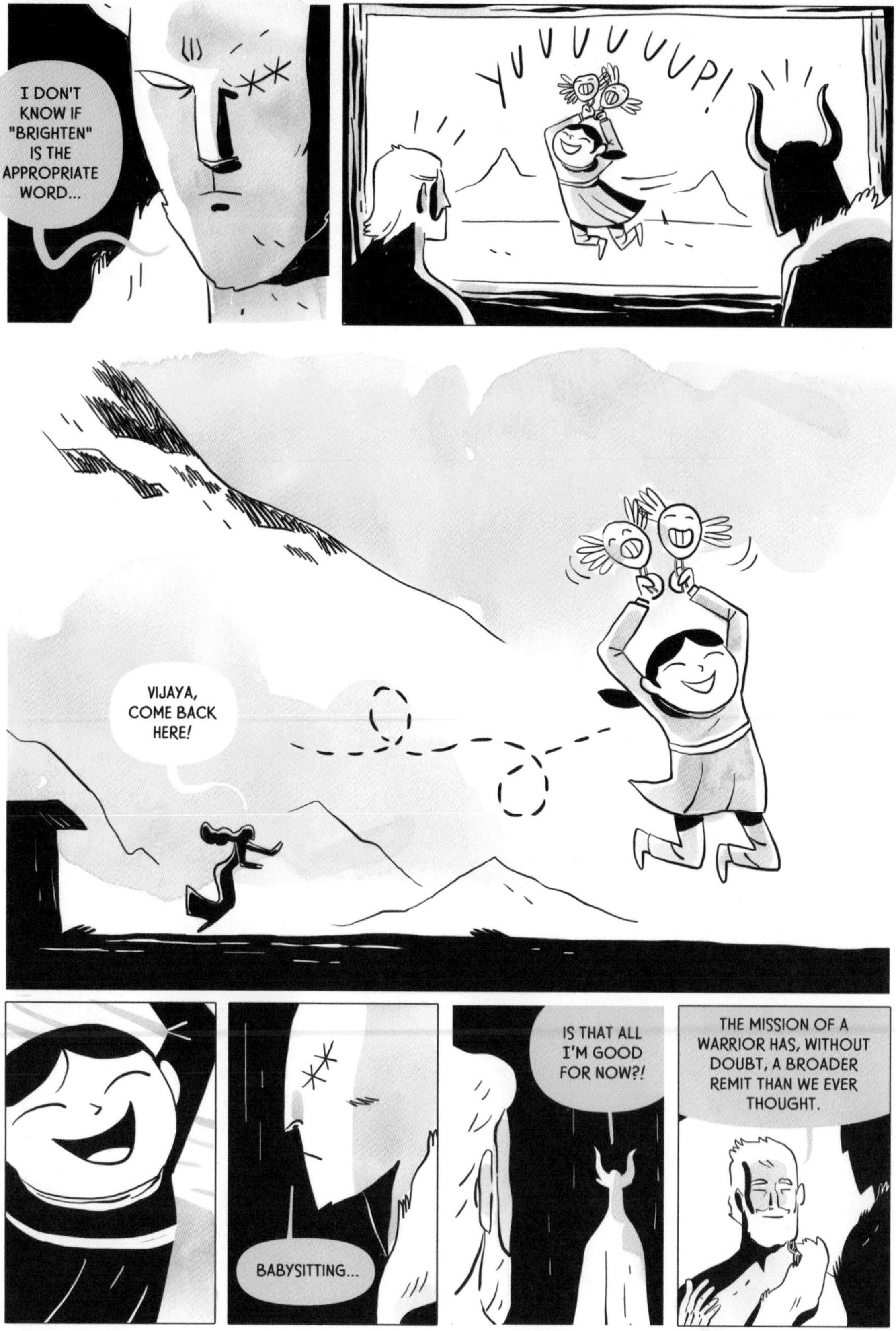
I DON'T KNOW IF "BRIGHTEN" IS THE APPROPRIATE WORD...
YUUUUUUUP!
VIJAYA, COME BACK HERE!
BABYSITTING...
IS THAT ALL I'M GOOD FOR NOW?!
THE MISSION OF A WARRIOR HAS, WITHOUT DOUBT, A BROADER REMIT THAN WE EVER THOUGHT.

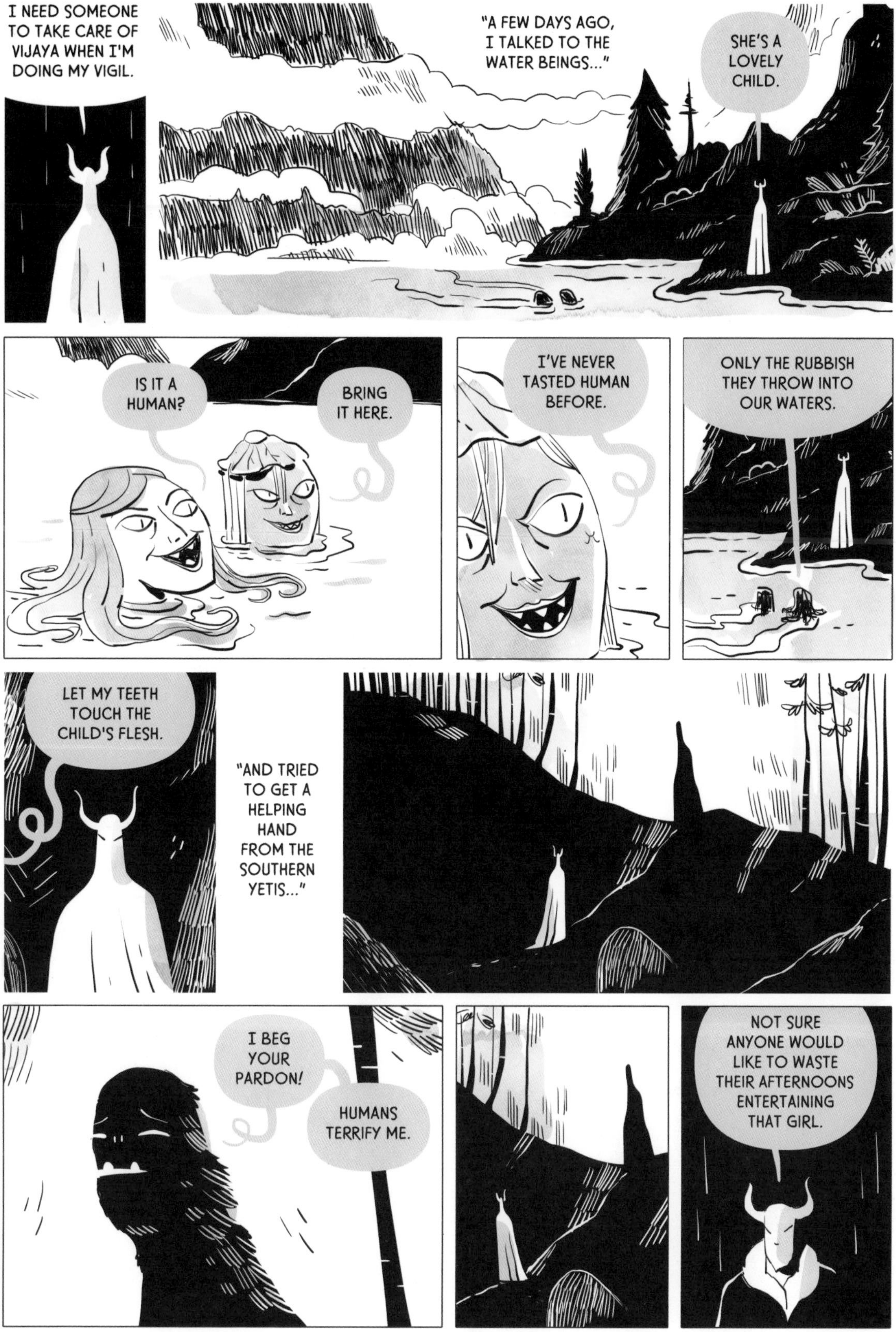
I NEED SOMEONE TO TAKE CARE OF VIJAYA WHEN I'M DOING MY VIGIL.
"A FEW DAYS AGO, I TALKED TO THE WATER BEINGS..."
SHE'S A LOVELY CHILD.
IS IT A HUMAN?
BRING IT HERE.
I'VE NEVER TASTED HUMAN BEFORE.
ONLY THE RUBBISH THEY THROW INTO OUR WATERS.
LET MY TEETH TOUCH THE CHILD'S FLESH.
"AND TRIED TO GET A HELPING HAND FROM THE SOUTHERN YETIS..."
I BEG YOUR PARDON!
HUMANS TERRIFY ME.
NOT SURE ANYONE WOULD LIKE TO WASTE THEIR AFTERNOONS ENTERTAINING THAT GIRL.

ENOUGH!

WHAT SORT OF MANNERS ARE YOU TEACHING THIS GIRL?

SHE IS BEHAVING LIKE A RASCAL.

IT WON'T HAPPEN AGAIN, SHALINI.

LOOK AT MY HAIR. MY NAILS ... ARGH! MY DRESS IS RUINED FROM CHASING HER.

AND POOR LITTLE ONES. THEY ARE TRAUMATISED.

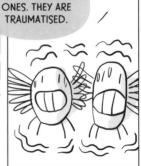

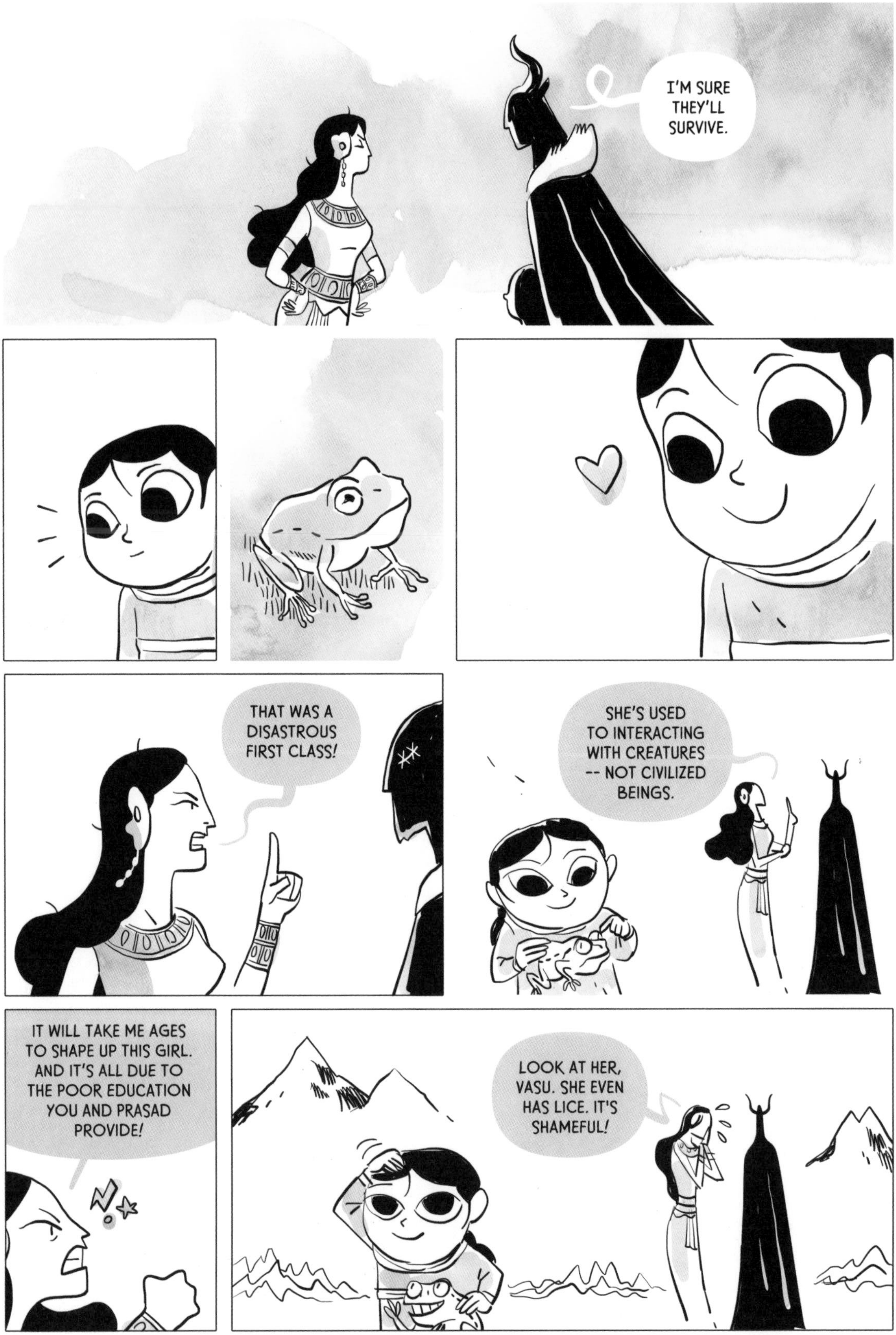
I'M SURE THEY'LL SURVIVE.
THAT WAS A DISASTROUS FIRST CLASS!
SHE'S USED TO INTERACTING WITH CREATURES -- NOT CIVILIZED BEINGS.
IT WILL TAKE ME AGES TO SHAPE UP THIS GIRL. AND IT'S ALL DUE TO THE POOR EDUCATION YOU AND PRASAD PROVIDE!
LOOK AT HER, VASU. SHE EVEN HAS LICE. IT'S SHAMEFUL!

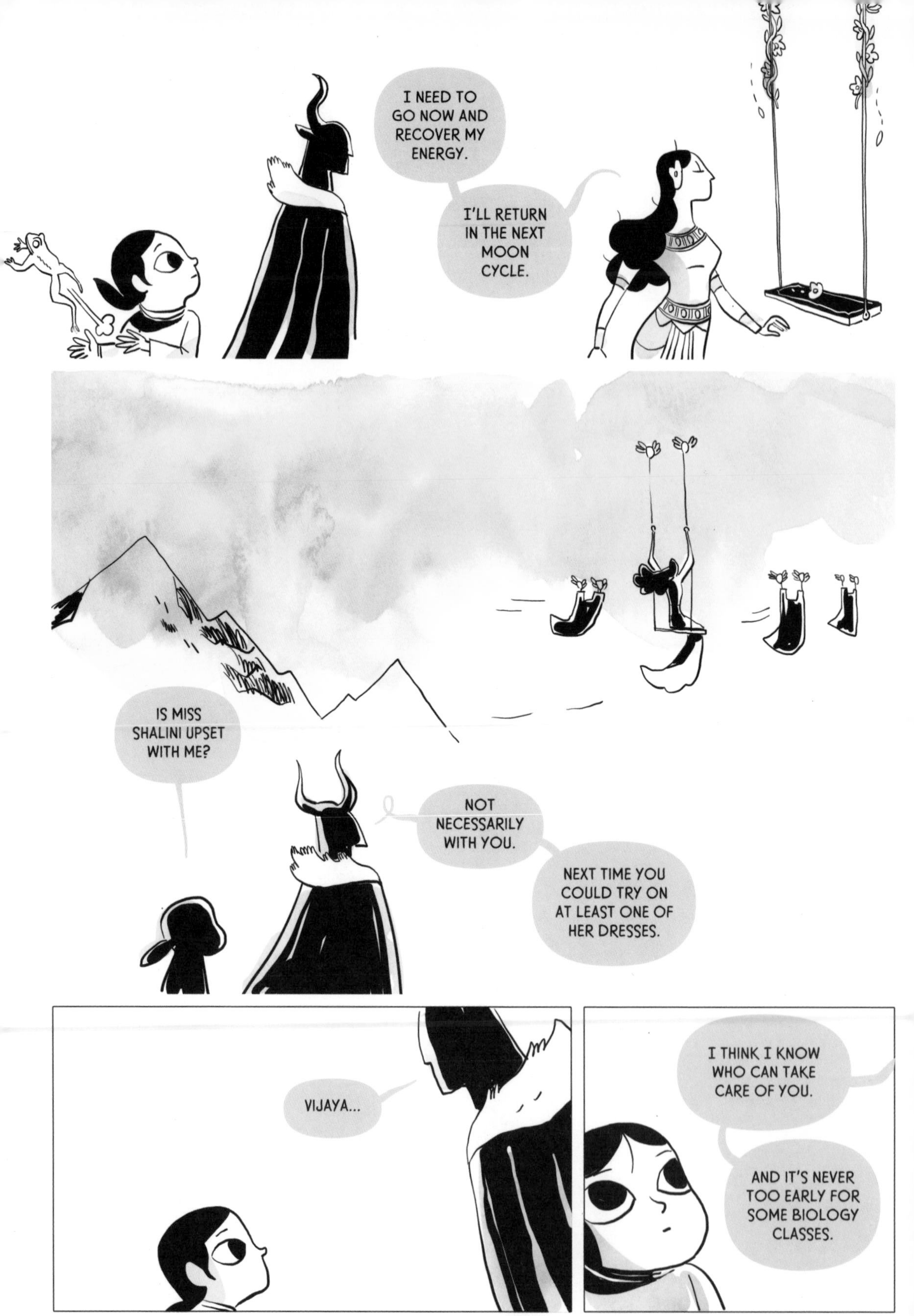
I NEED TO GO NOW AND RECOVER MY ENERGY.
I'LL RETURN IN THE NEXT MOON CYCLE.
IS MISS SHALINI UPSET WITH ME?
NOT NECESSARILY WITH YOU.
NEXT TIME YOU COULD TRY ON AT LEAST ONE OF HER DRESSES.
VIJAYA...
I THINK I KNOW WHO CAN TAKE CARE OF YOU.
AND IT'S NEVER TOO EARLY FOR SOME BIOLOGY CLASSES.

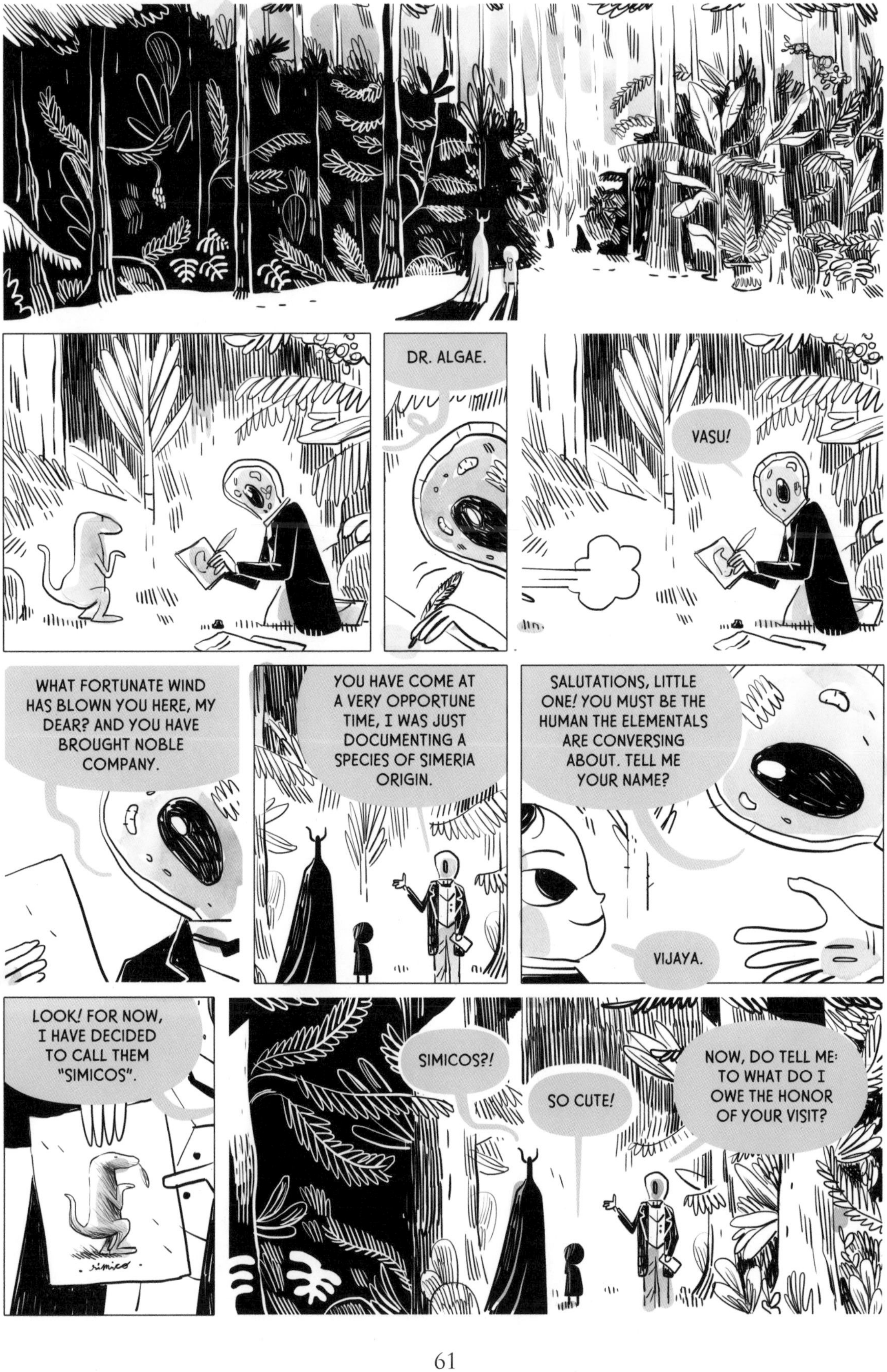
DR. ALGAE.
VASU!
WHAT FORTUNATE WIND HAS BLOWN YOU HERE, MY DEAR? AND YOU HAVE BROUGHT NOBLE COMPANY.
YOU HAVE COME AT A VERY OPPORTUNE TIME, I WAS JUST DOCUMENTING A SPECIES OF SIMERIA ORIGIN.
SALUTATIONS, LITTLE ONE! YOU MUST BE THE HUMAN THE ELEMENTALS ARE CONVERSING ABOUT. TELL ME YOUR NAME?
VIJAYA.
LOOK! FOR NOW, I HAVE DECIDED TO CALL THEM "SIMICOS".
SIMICOS?!
SO CUTE!
NOW, DO TELL ME: TO WHAT DO I OWE THE HONOR OF YOUR VISIT?

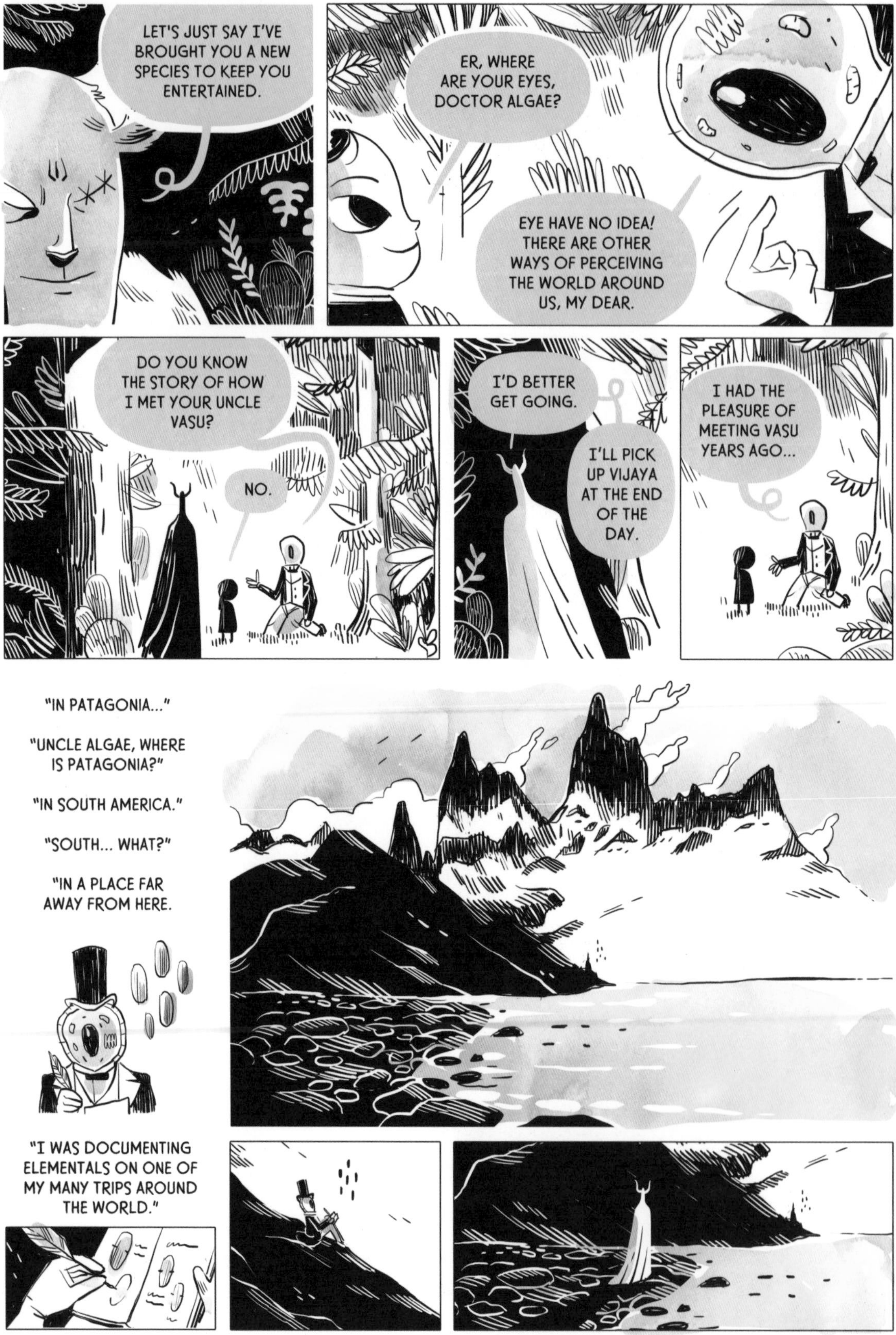
LET'S JUST SAY I'VE BROUGHT YOU A NEW SPECIES TO KEEP YOU ENTERTAINED.
ER, WHERE ARE YOUR EYES, DOCTOR ALGAE?
EYE HAVE NO IDEA! THERE ARE OTHER WAYS OF PERCEIVING THE WORLD AROUND US, MY DEAR.
DO YOU KNOW THE STORY OF HOW I MET YOUR UNCLE VASU?
NO.
I'D BETTER GET GOING.
I'LL PICK UP VIJAYA AT THE END OF THE DAY.
I HAD THE PLEASURE OF MEETING VASU YEARS AGO...
"IN PATAGONIA..."
"UNCLE ALGAE, WHERE IS PATAGONIA?"
"IN SOUTH AMERICA."
"SOUTH... WHAT?"
"IN A PLACE FAR AWAY FROM HERE.
"I WAS DOCUMENTING ELEMENTALS ON ONE OF MY MANY TRIPS AROUND THE WORLD."

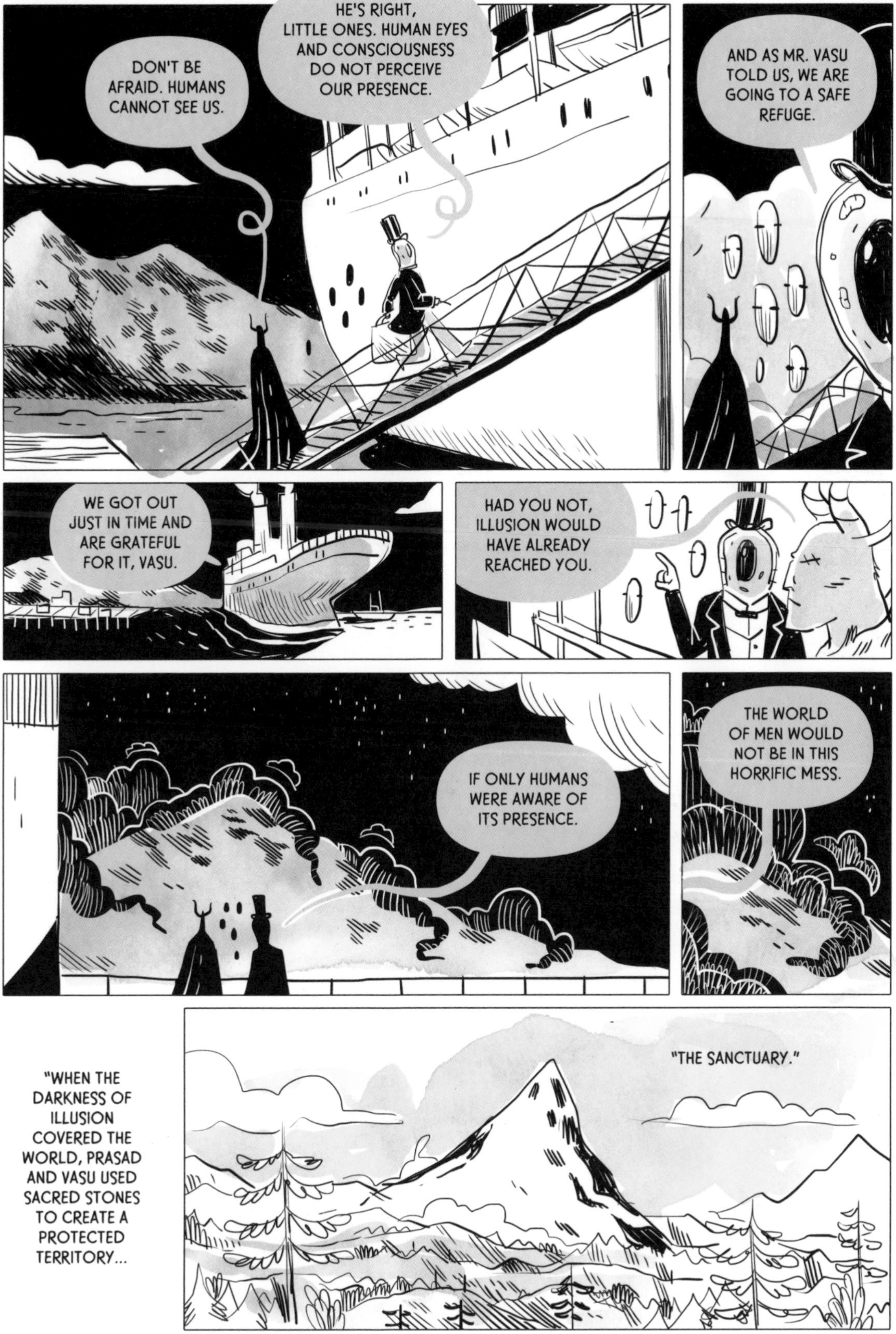
DON'T BE AFRAID. HUMANS CANNOT SEE US.
HE'S RIGHT, LITTLE ONES. HUMAN EYES AND CONSCIOUSNESS DO NOT PERCEIVE OUR PRESENCE.
AND AS MR. VASU TOLD US, WE ARE GOING TO A SAFE REFUGE.
WE GOT OUT JUST IN TIME AND ARE GRATEFUL FOR IT, VASU.
HAD YOU NOT, ILLUSION WOULD HAVE ALREADY REACHED YOU.
IF ONLY HUMANS WERE AWARE OF ITS PRESENCE.
THE WORLD OF MEN WOULD NOT BE IN THIS HORRIFIC MESS.
"WHEN THE DARKNESS OF ILLUSION COVERED THE WORLD, PRASAD AND VASU USED SACRED STONES TO CREATE A PROTECTED TERRITORY...
"THE SANCTUARY."

"HERE THE
ELEMENTALS
RENEW THEIR
ENERGIES AND
GET SOME
FRESH AIR.

"AND ONCE
RECOVERED...

"THEY RETURN TO THE
WORLD TO CONTINUE
THEIR WORK.

"THESE LOVELY BEINGS
COME AND GO, MY DEAR."

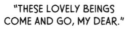

"WHY, UNCLE? IT'S SO
MUCH MORE FUN HERE."

"ELEMENTAL
BUSINESS,
VIJAYA.

"THEY ARE
INDEED
OF GREAT
IMPORTANCE
FOR THE
BALANCE OF
NATURE."

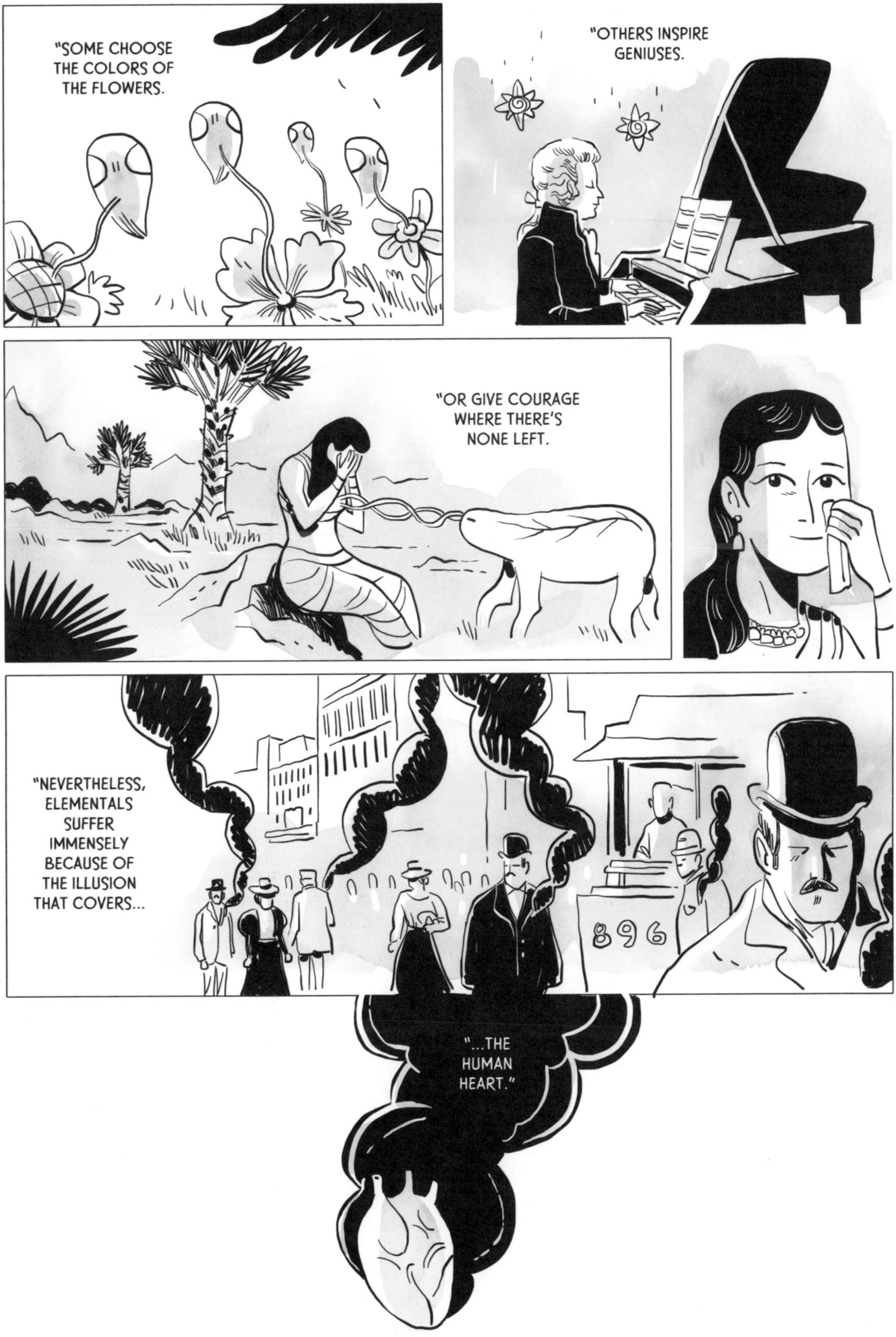
"SOME CHOOSE THE COLORS OF THE FLOWERS.
"OTHERS INSPIRE GENIUSES.
"OR GIVE COURAGE WHERE THERE'S NONE LEFT.
"NEVERTHELESS, ELEMENTALS SUFFER IMMENSELY BECAUSE OF THE ILLUSION THAT COVERS...
896
"...THE HUMAN HEART."

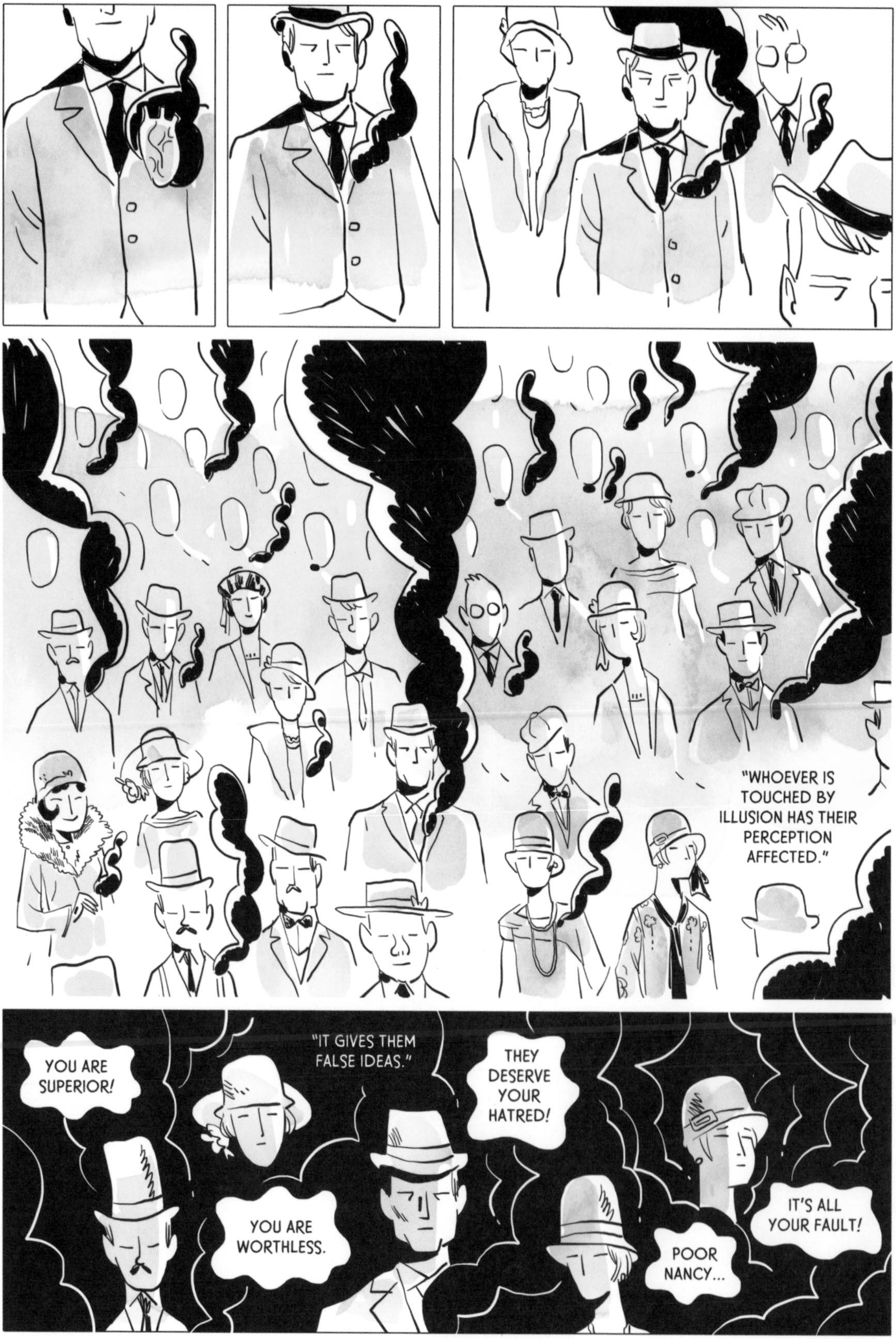
"WHOEVER IS TOUCHED BY ILLUSION HAS THEIR PERCEPTION AFFECTED."
YOU ARE SUPERIOR!
"IT GIVES THEM FALSE IDEAS."
THEY DESERVE YOUR HATRED!
YOU ARE WORTHLESS.
POOR NANCY...
IT'S ALL YOUR FAULT!

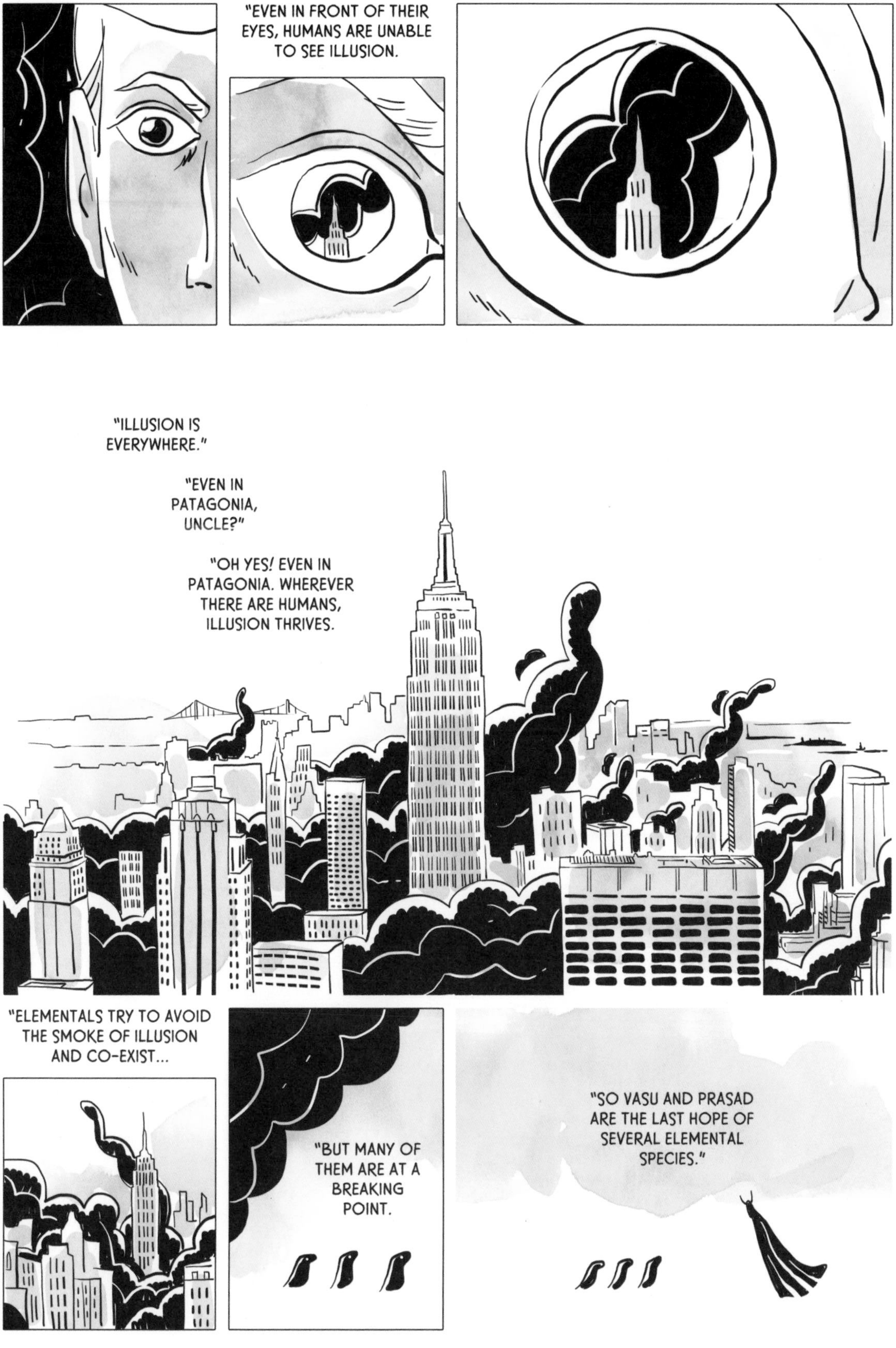
"EVEN IN FRONT OF THEIR EYES, HUMANS ARE UNABLE TO SEE ILLUSION.
"ILLUSION IS EVERYWHERE."
"EVEN IN PATAGONIA, UNCLE?"
"OH YES! EVEN IN PATAGONIA. WHEREVER THERE ARE HUMANS, ILLUSION THRIVES.
"ELEMENTALS TRY TO AVOID THE SMOKE OF ILLUSION AND CO-EXIST...
"BUT MANY OF THEM ARE AT A BREAKING POINT.
"SO VASU AND PRASAD ARE THE LAST HOPE OF SEVERAL ELEMENTAL SPECIES."

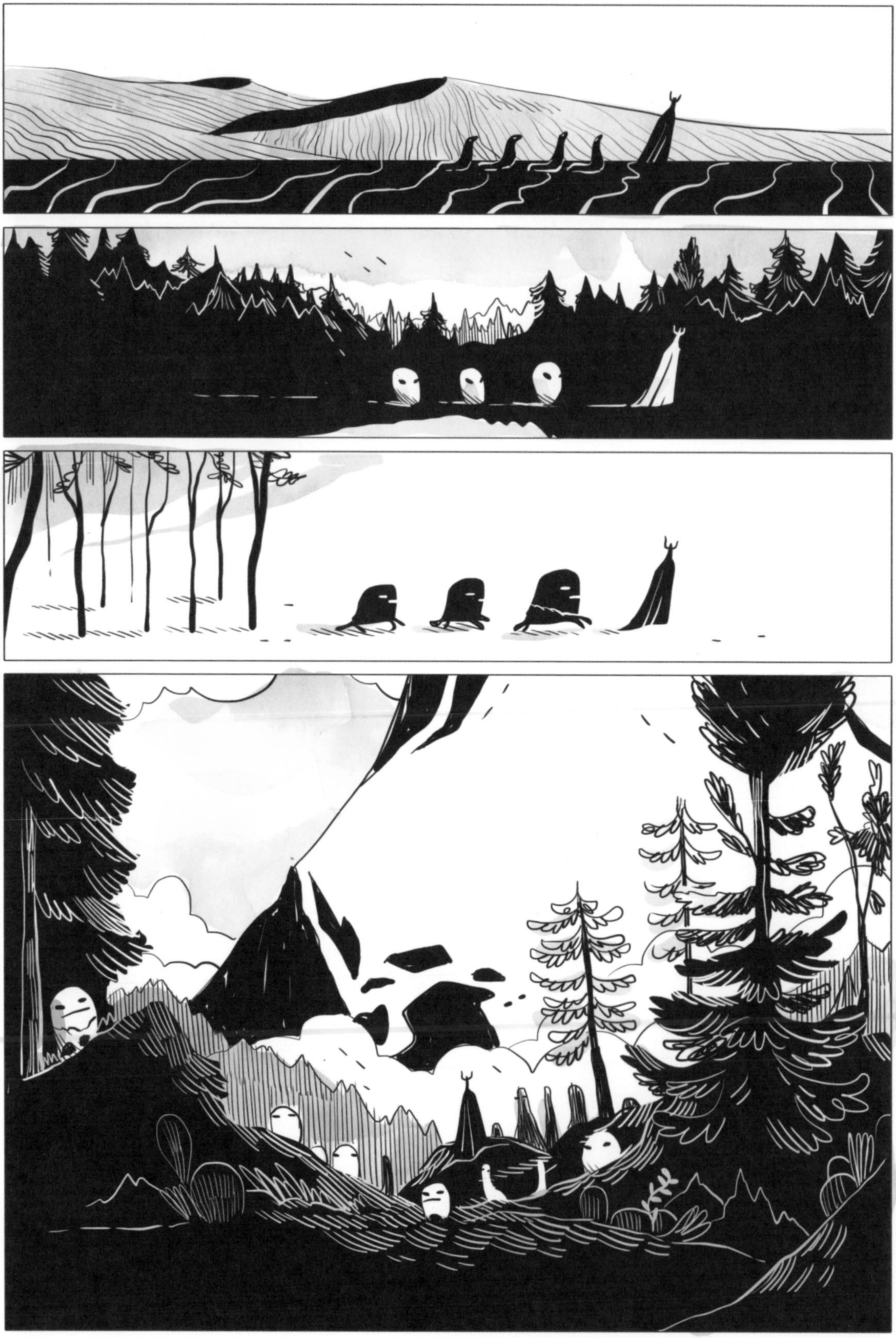

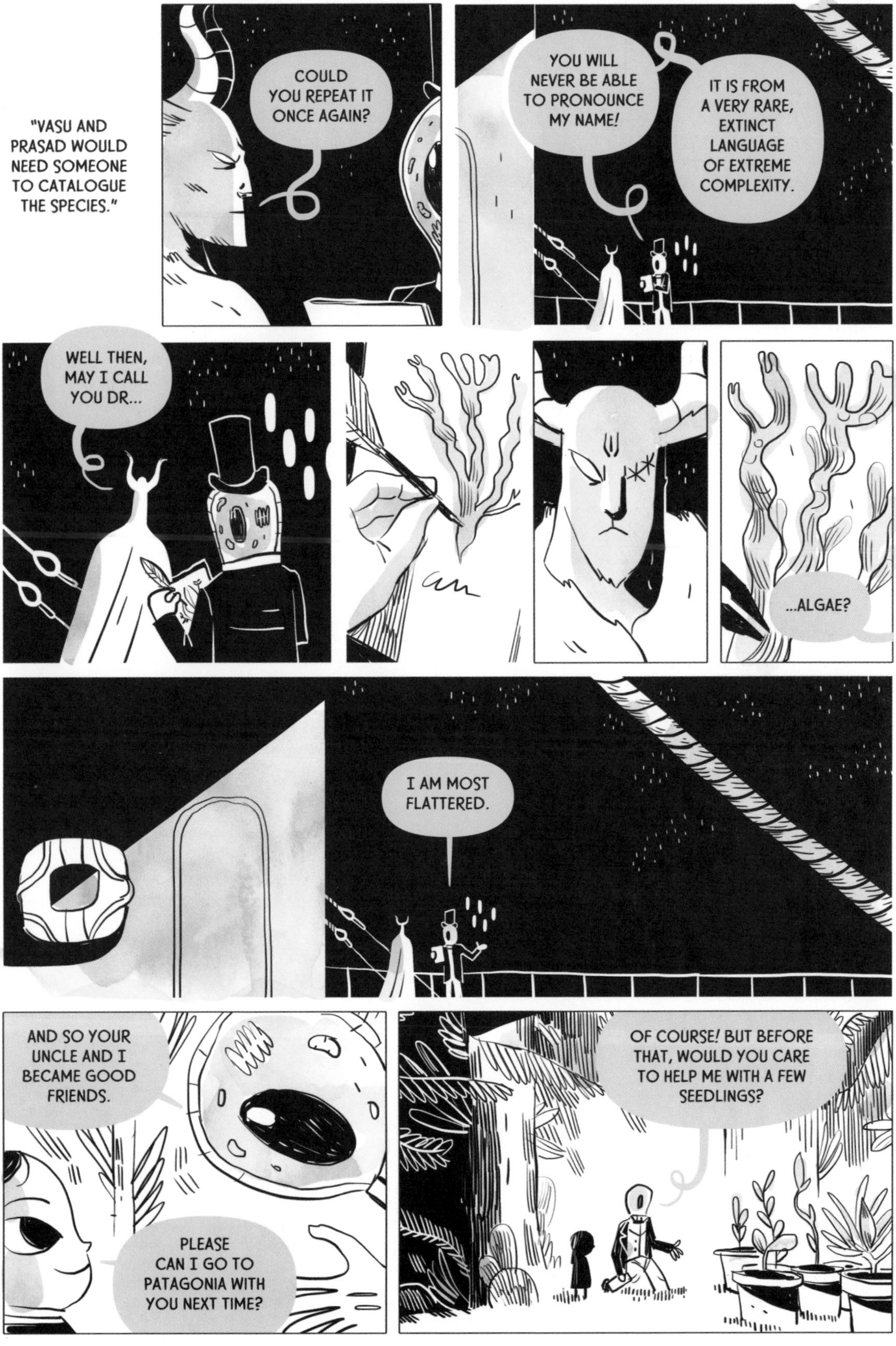
"VASU AND PRASAD WOULD NEED SOMEONE TO CATALOGUE THE SPECIES."
COULD YOU REPEAT IT ONCE AGAIN?
YOU WILL NEVER BE ABLE TO PRONOUNCE MY NAME!
IT IS FROM A VERY RARE, EXTINCT LANGUAGE OF EXTREME COMPLEXITY.
WELL THEN, MAY I CALL YOU DR...
...ALGAE?
I AM MOST FLATTERED.
AND SO YOUR UNCLE AND I BECAME GOOD FRIENDS.
PLEASE CAN I GO TO PATAGONIA WITH YOU NEXT TIME?
OF COURSE! BUT BEFORE THAT, WOULD YOU CARE TO HELP ME WITH A FEW SEEDLINGS?

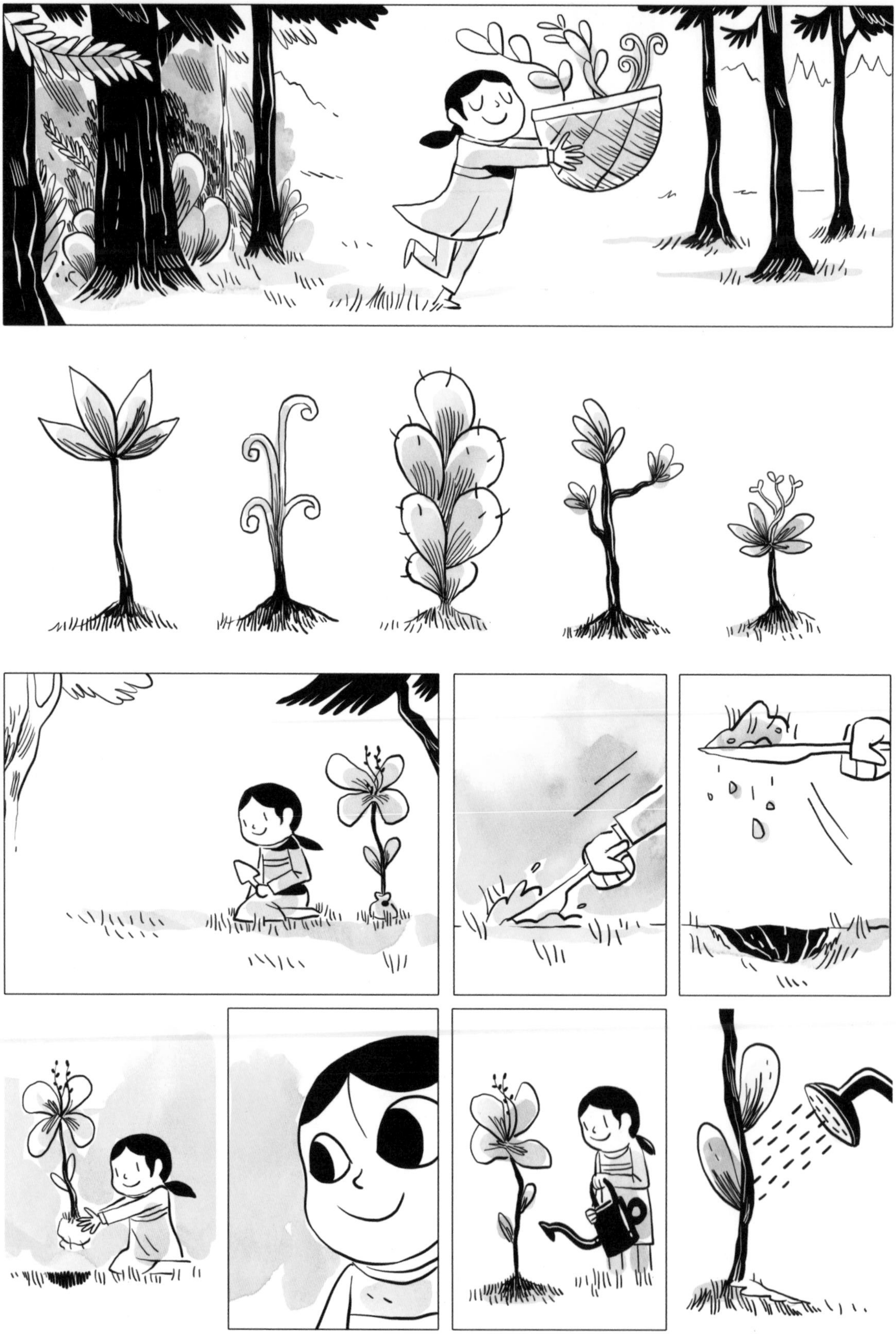

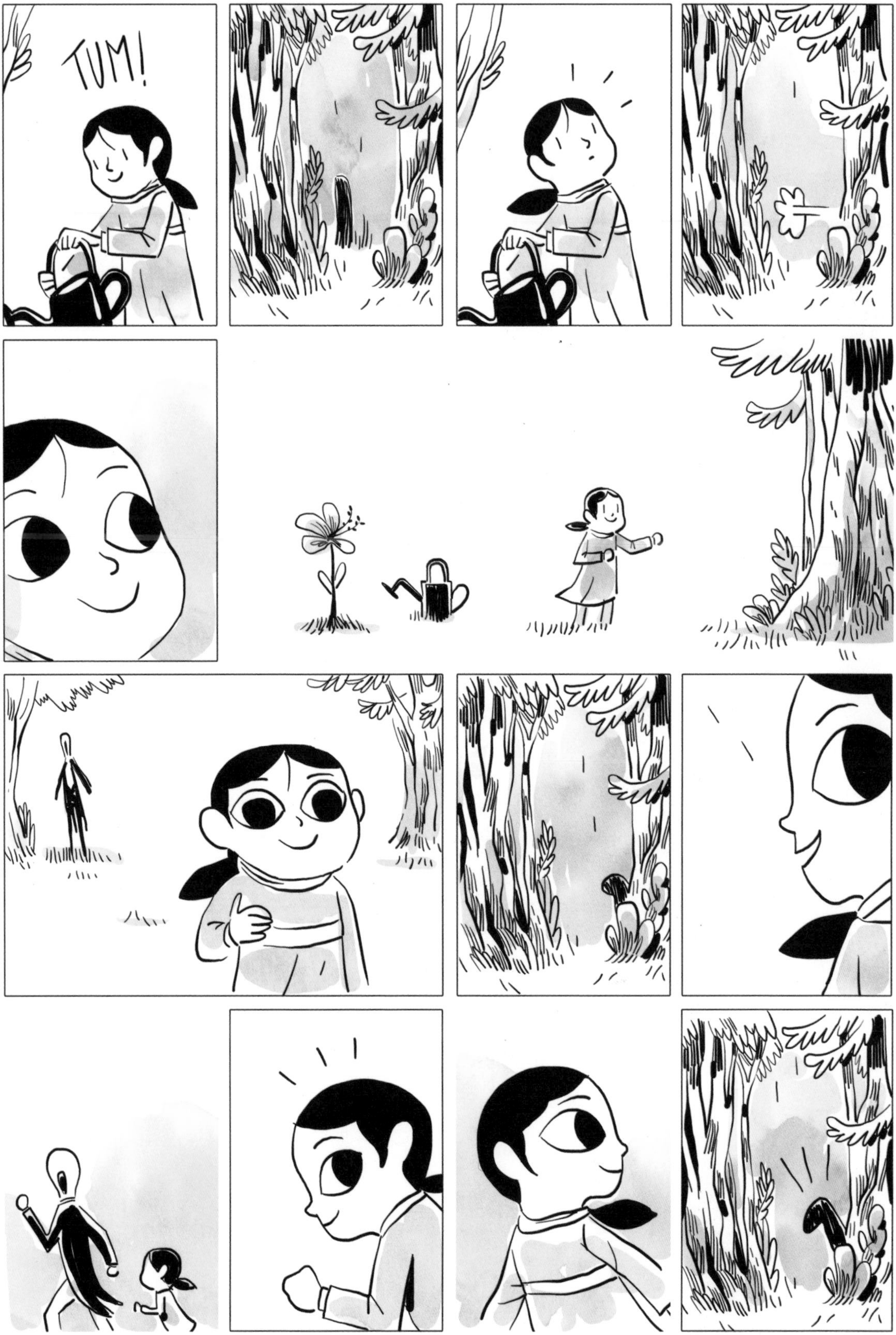
TUM!

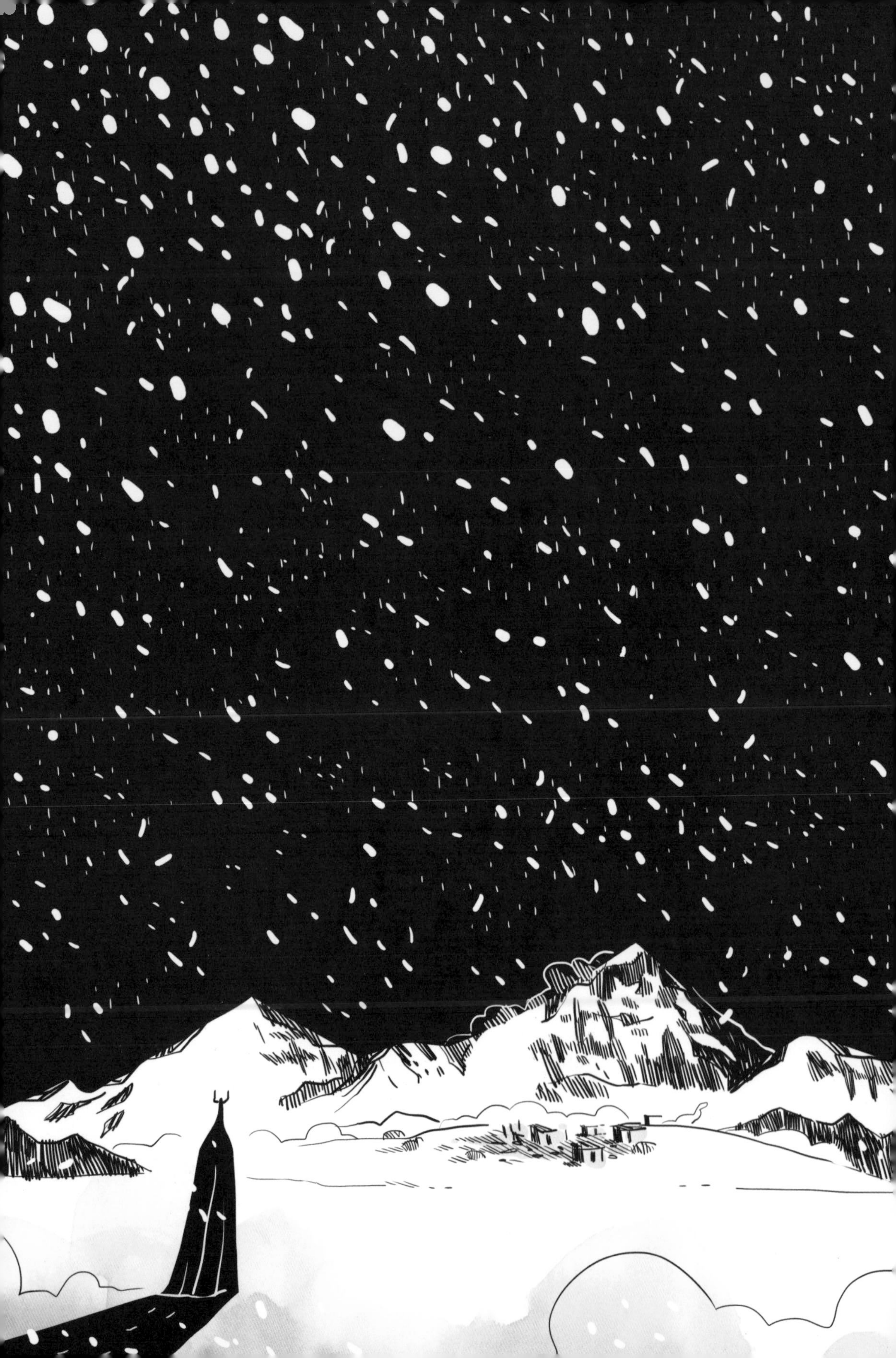

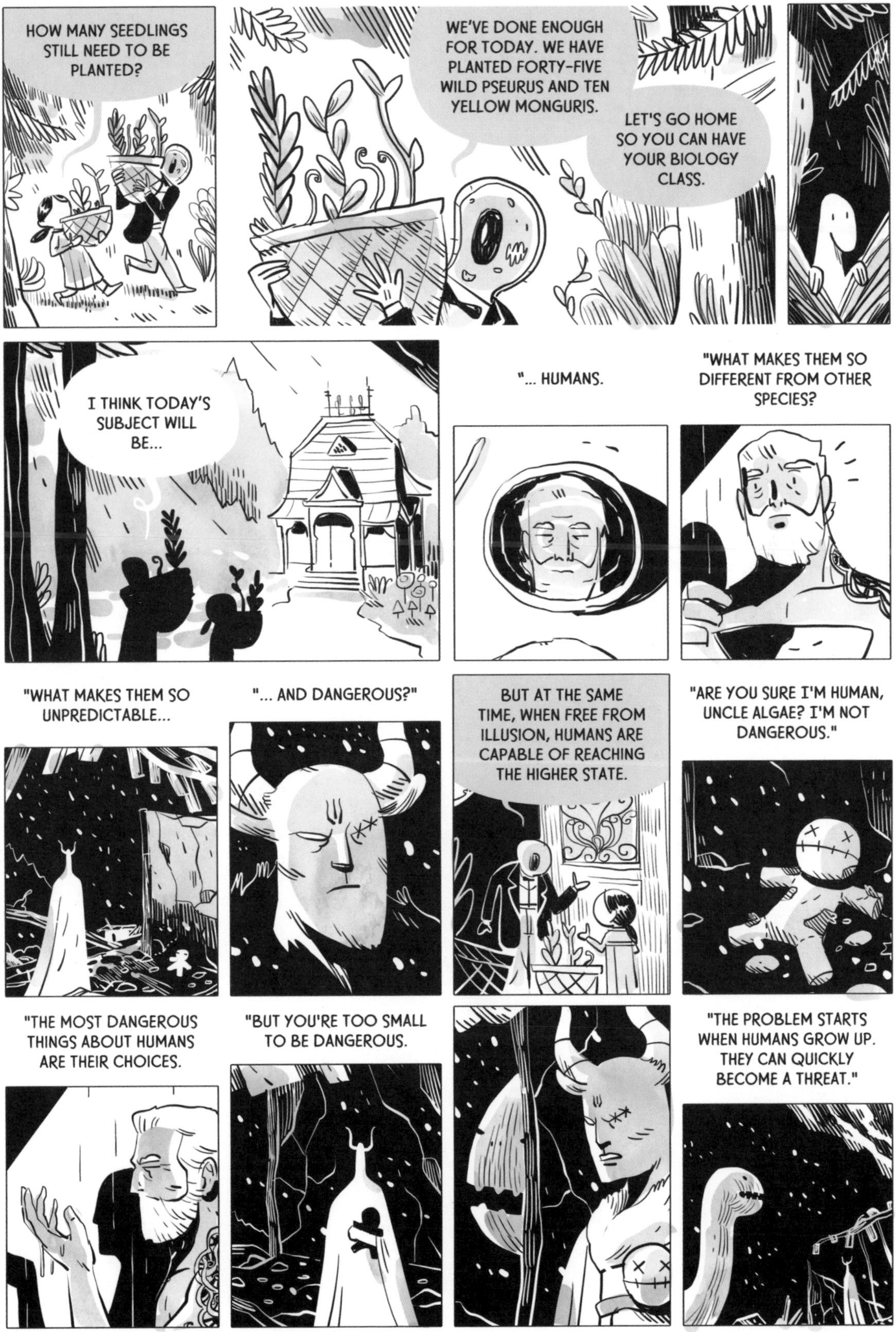
HOW MANY SEEDLINGS STILL NEED TO BE PLANTED?
WE'VE DONE ENOUGH FOR TODAY. WE HAVE PLANTED FORTY-FIVE WILD PSEURUS AND TEN YELLOW MONGURIS.
LET'S GO HOME SO YOU CAN HAVE YOUR BIOLOGY CLASS.
I THINK TODAY'S SUBJECT WILL BE...
"... HUMANS.
"WHAT MAKES THEM SO DIFFERENT FROM OTHER SPECIES?
"WHAT MAKES THEM SO UNPREDICTABLE...
"... AND DANGEROUS?"
BUT AT THE SAME TIME, WHEN FREE FROM ILLUSION, HUMANS ARE CAPABLE OF REACHING THE HIGHER STATE.
"ARE YOU SURE I'M HUMAN, UNCLE ALGAE? I'M NOT DANGEROUS."
"THE MOST DANGEROUS THINGS ABOUT HUMANS ARE THEIR CHOICES.
"BUT YOU'RE TOO SMALL TO BE DANGEROUS.
"THE PROBLEM STARTS WHEN HUMANS GROW UP. THEY CAN QUICKLY BECOME A THREAT."

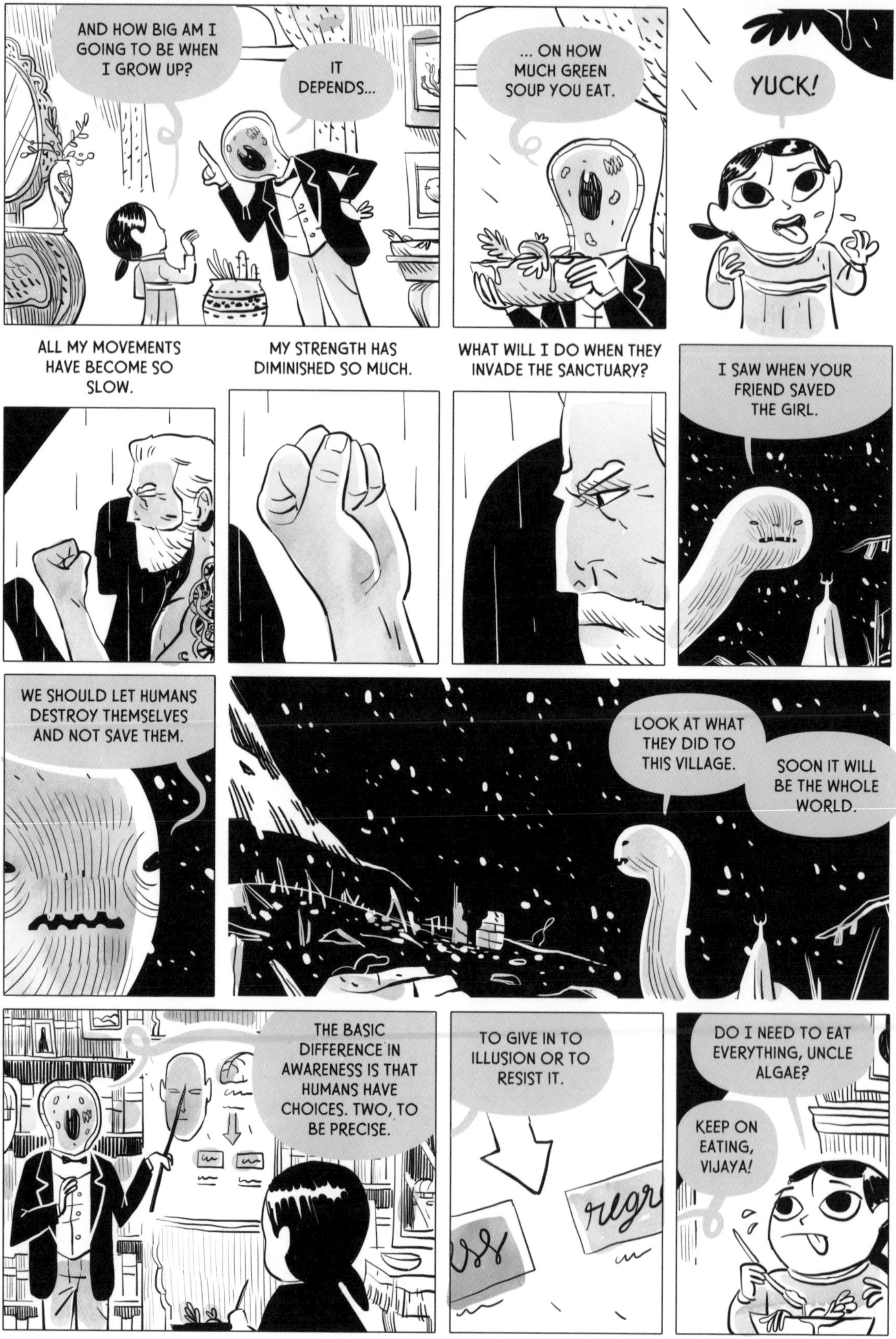
AND HOW BIG AM I GOING TO BE WHEN I GROW UP?
IT DEPENDS...
... ON HOW MUCH GREEN SOUP YOU EAT.
YUCK!
ALL MY MOVEMENTS HAVE BECOME SO SLOW.
MY STRENGTH HAS DIMINISHED SO MUCH.
WHAT WILL I DO WHEN THEY INVADE THE SANCTUARY?
I SAW WHEN YOUR FRIEND SAVED THE GIRL.
WE SHOULD LET HUMANS DESTROY THEMSELVES AND NOT SAVE THEM.
LOOK AT WHAT THEY DID TO THIS VILLAGE.
SOON IT WILL BE THE WHOLE WORLD.
THE BASIC DIFFERENCE IN AWARENESS IS THAT HUMANS HAVE CHOICES. TWO, TO BE PRECISE.
TO GIVE IN TO ILLUSION OR TO RESIST IT.
DO I NEED TO EAT EVERYTHING, UNCLE ALGAE?
KEEP ON EATING, VIJAYA!

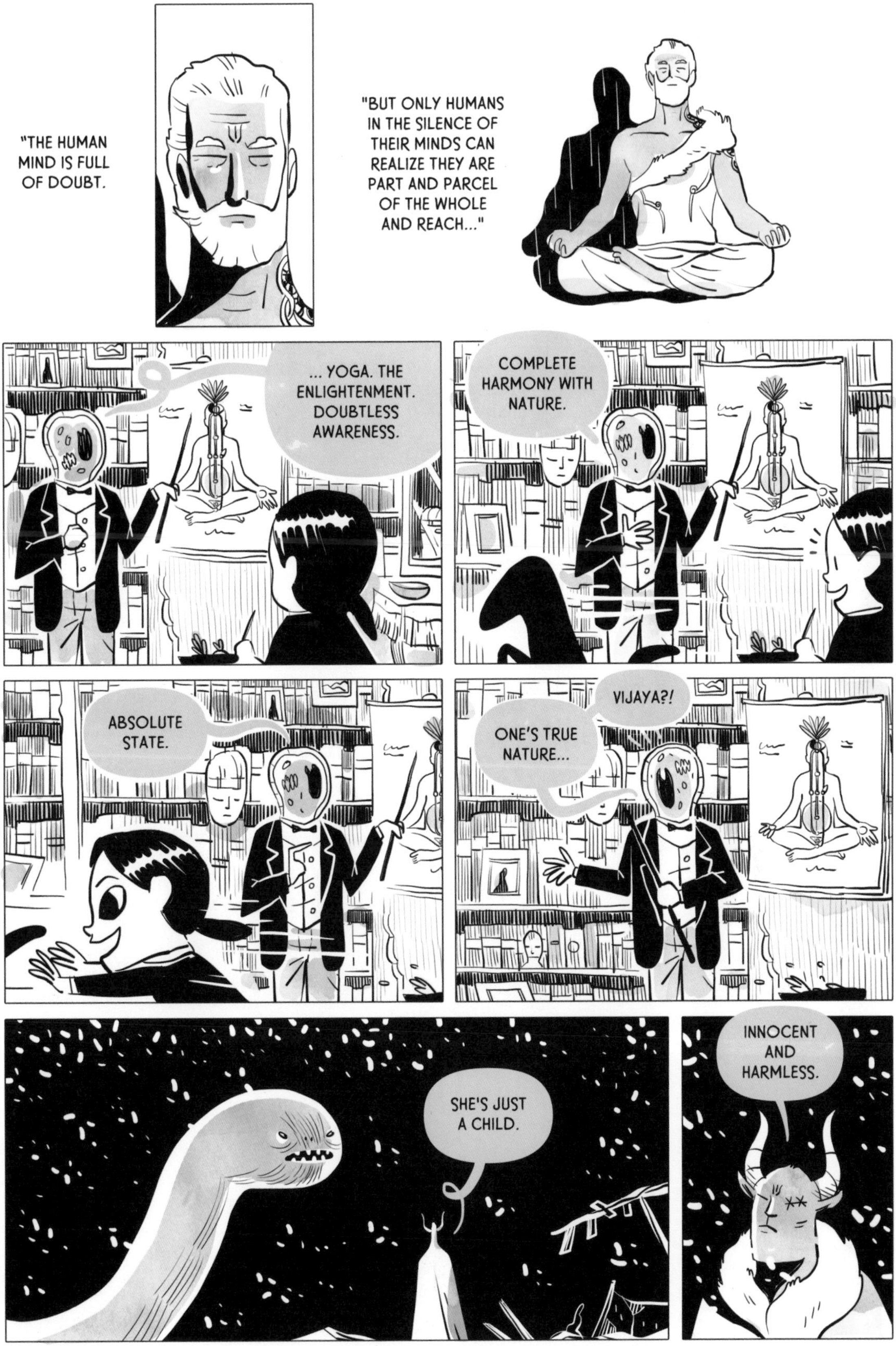
"THE HUMAN MIND IS FULL OF DOUBT.
"BUT ONLY HUMANS IN THE SILENCE OF THEIR MINDS CAN REALIZE THEY ARE PART AND PARCEL OF THE WHOLE AND REACH..."
... YOGA. THE ENLIGHTENMENT. DOUBTLESS AWARENESS.
COMPLETE HARMONY WITH NATURE.
ABSOLUTE STATE.
ONE'S TRUE NATURE...
VIJAYA?!
SHE'S JUST A CHILD.
INNOCENT AND HARMLESS.

VIJAYA!

"BUT SHE WILL GROW UP..."

COME HERE, SIMICO!

"YOUR HOUSE WILL TREMBLE."

AND WHEN YOU LEAST EXPECT IT...

"WILL SHATTER INTO PIECES."

THAT WAS A RARE ITEM.

SIGH!

EXCUSE ME, I BETTER GO.

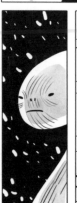

GOTCHA!

UNCLE ALGAE, I CAUGHT HIM!

76

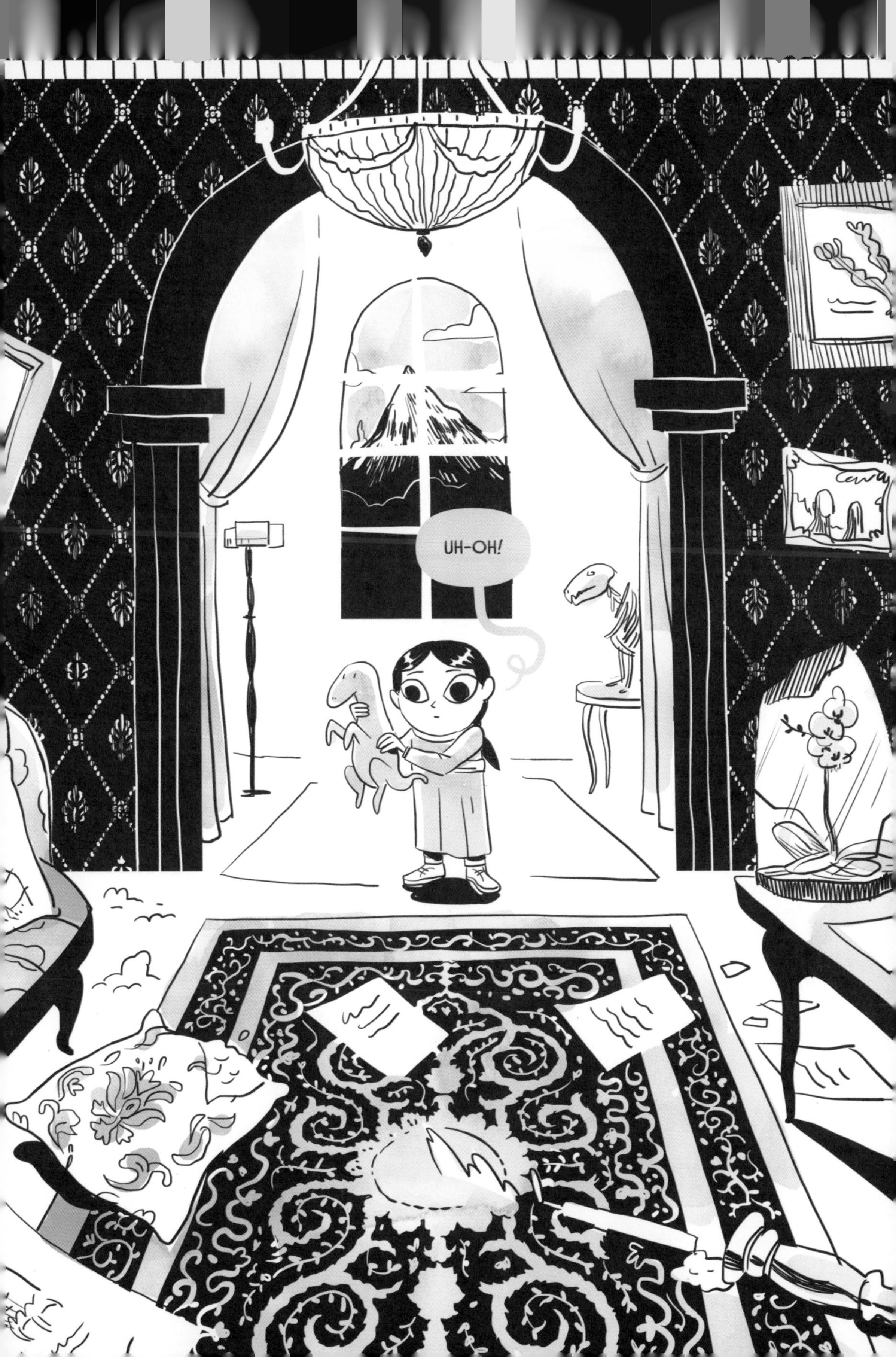
UH-OH!

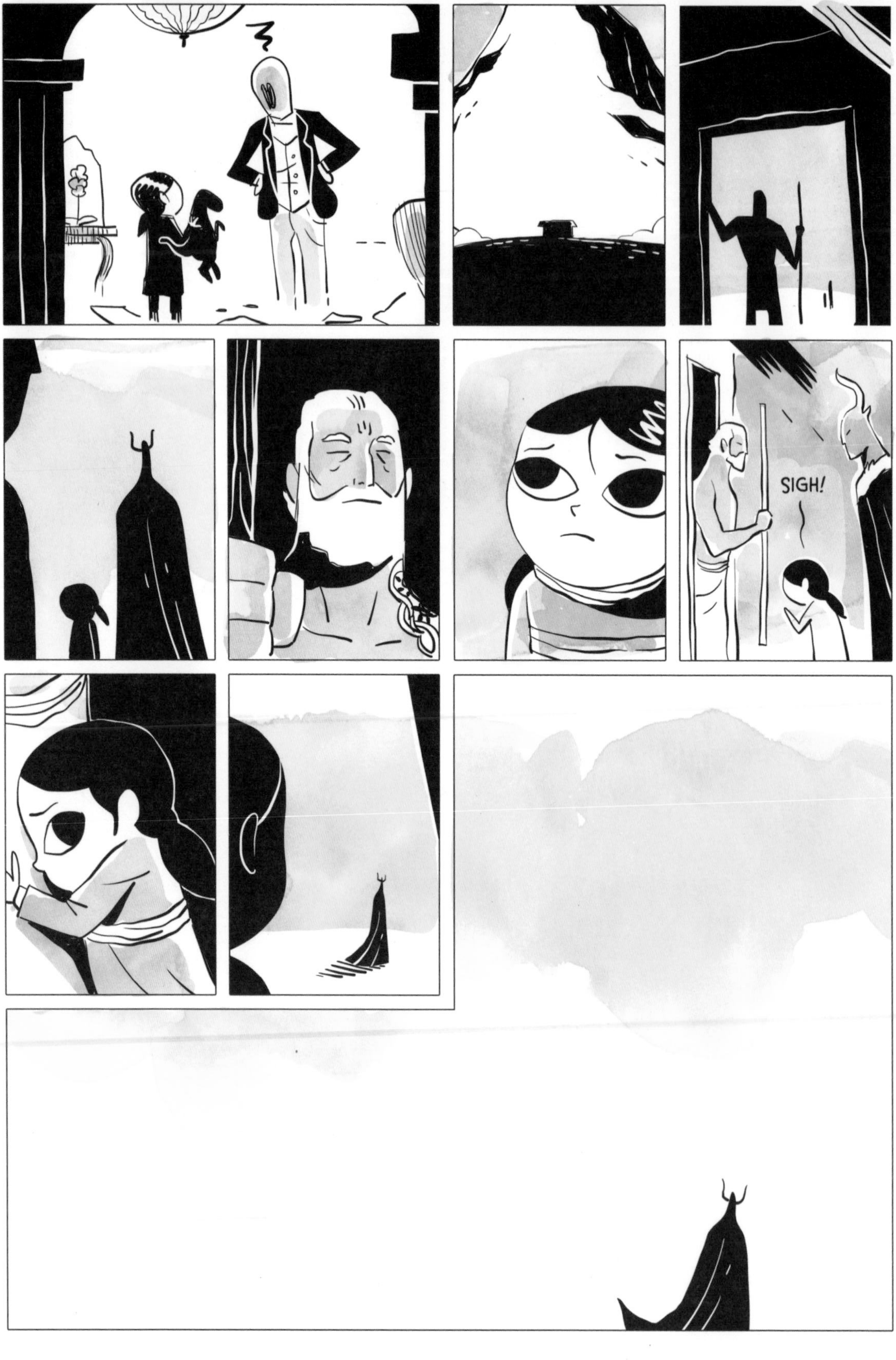
SIGH!

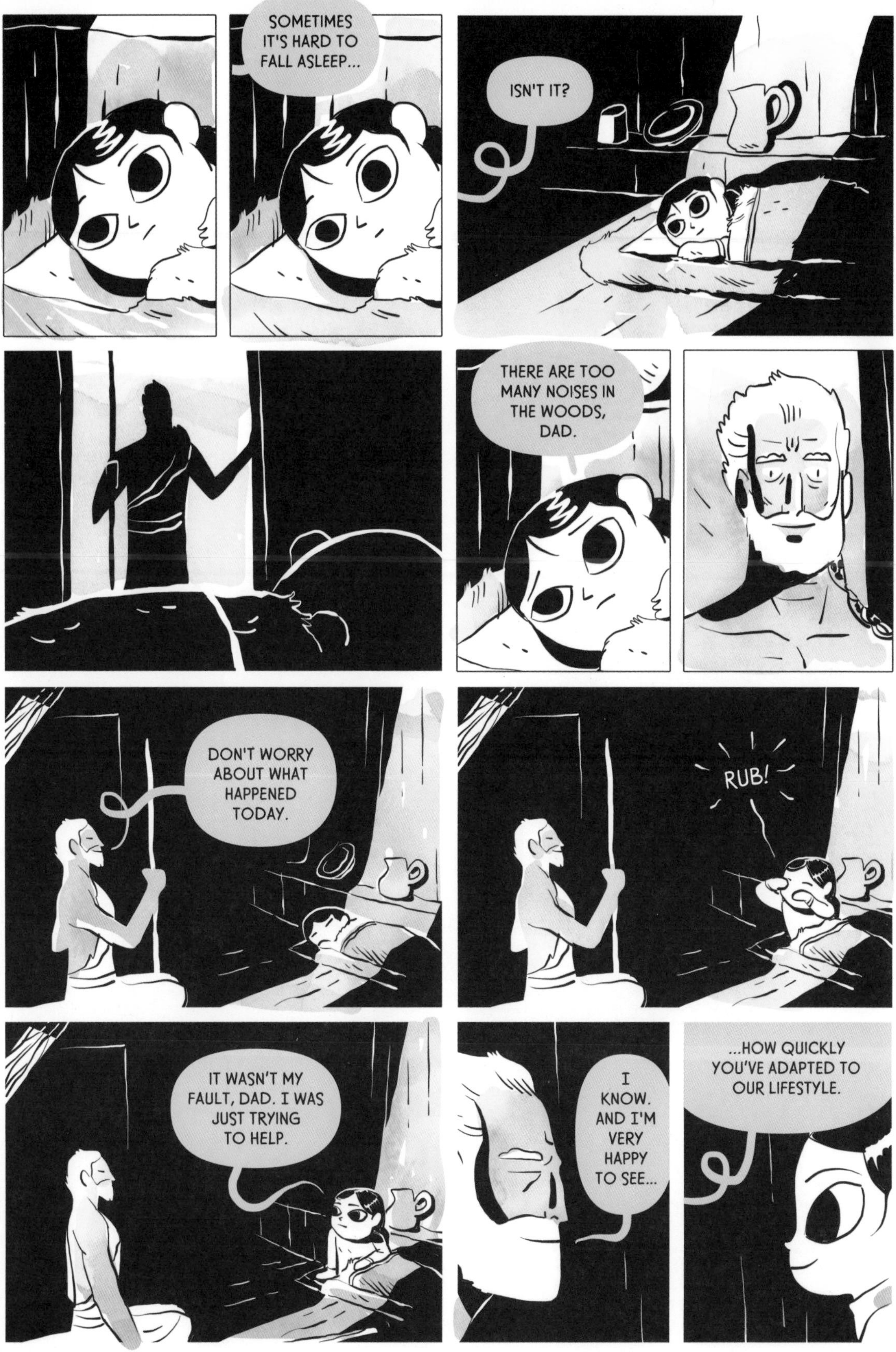
SOMETIMES IT'S HARD TO FALL ASLEEP...
ISN'T IT?
THERE ARE TOO MANY NOISES IN THE WOODS, DAD.
DON'T WORRY ABOUT WHAT HAPPENED TODAY.
RUB!
IT WASN'T MY FAULT, DAD. I WAS JUST TRYING TO HELP.
I KNOW. AND I'M VERY HAPPY TO SEE...
...HOW QUICKLY YOU'VE ADAPTED TO OUR LIFESTYLE.

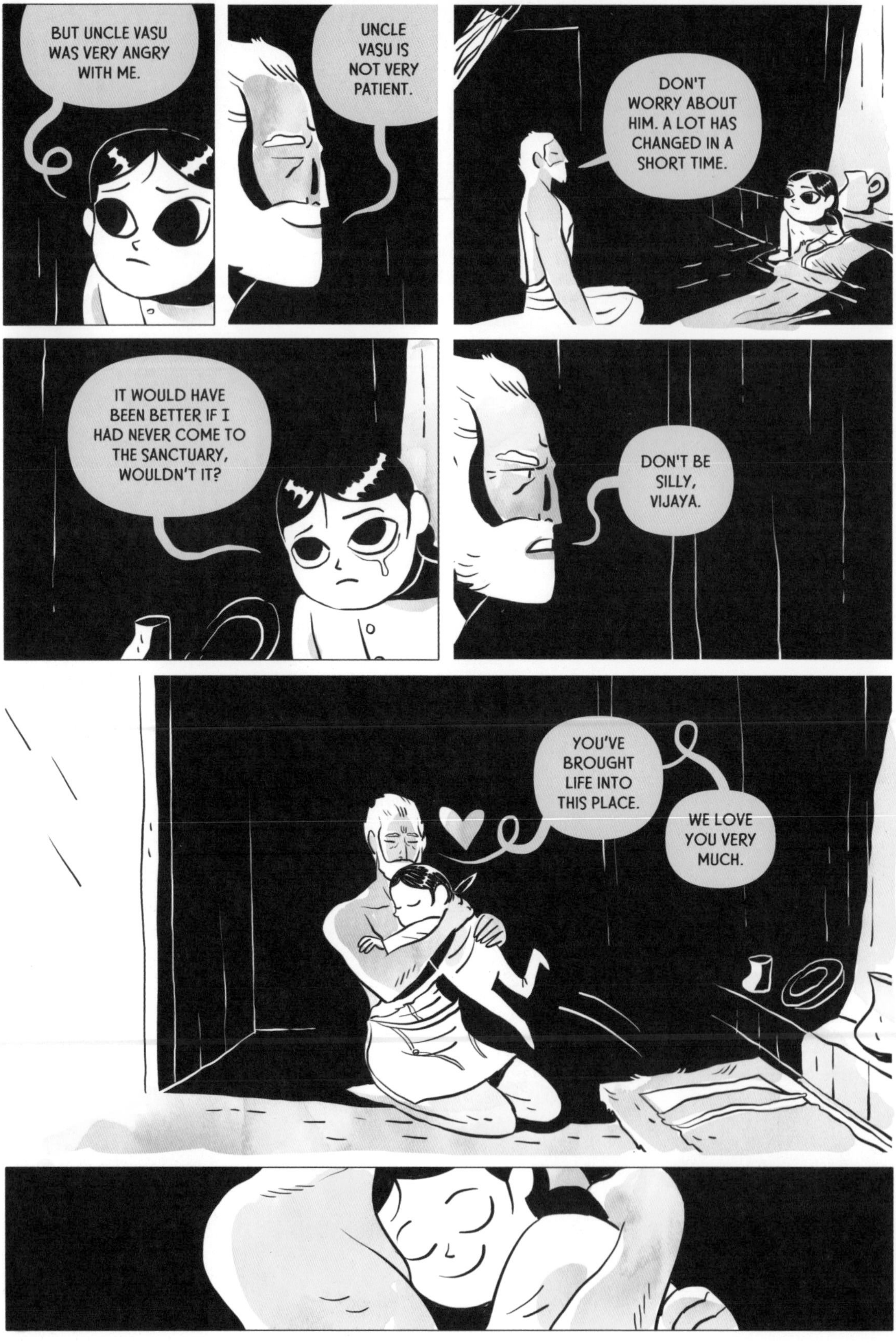
BUT UNCLE VASU WAS VERY ANGRY WITH ME.
UNCLE VASU IS NOT VERY PATIENT.
DON'T WORRY ABOUT HIM. A LOT HAS CHANGED IN A SHORT TIME.
IT WOULD HAVE BEEN BETTER IF I HAD NEVER COME TO THE SANCTUARY, WOULDN'T IT?
DON'T BE SILLY, VIJAYA.
YOU'VE BROUGHT LIFE INTO THIS PLACE.
WE LOVE YOU VERY MUCH.

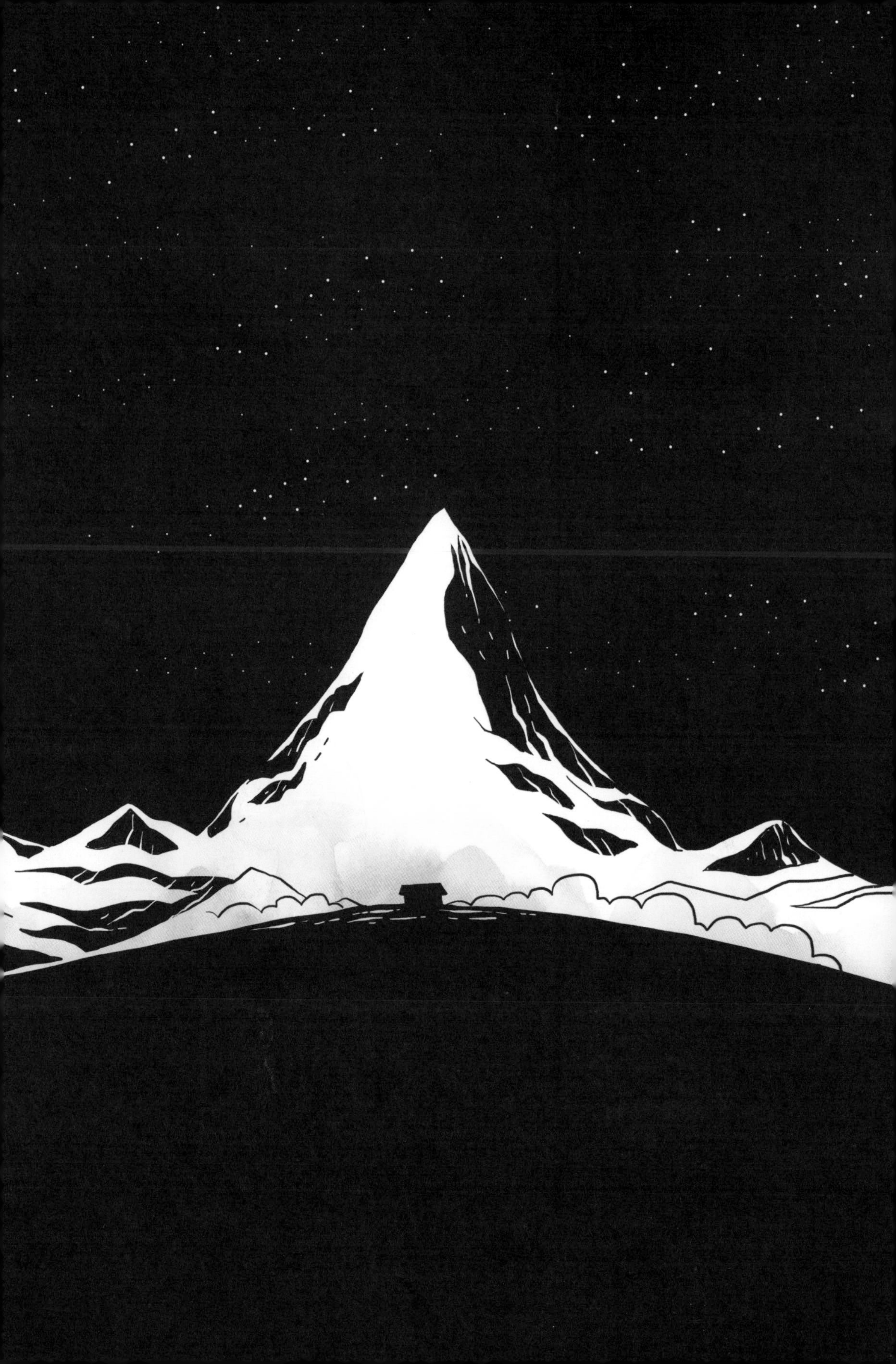

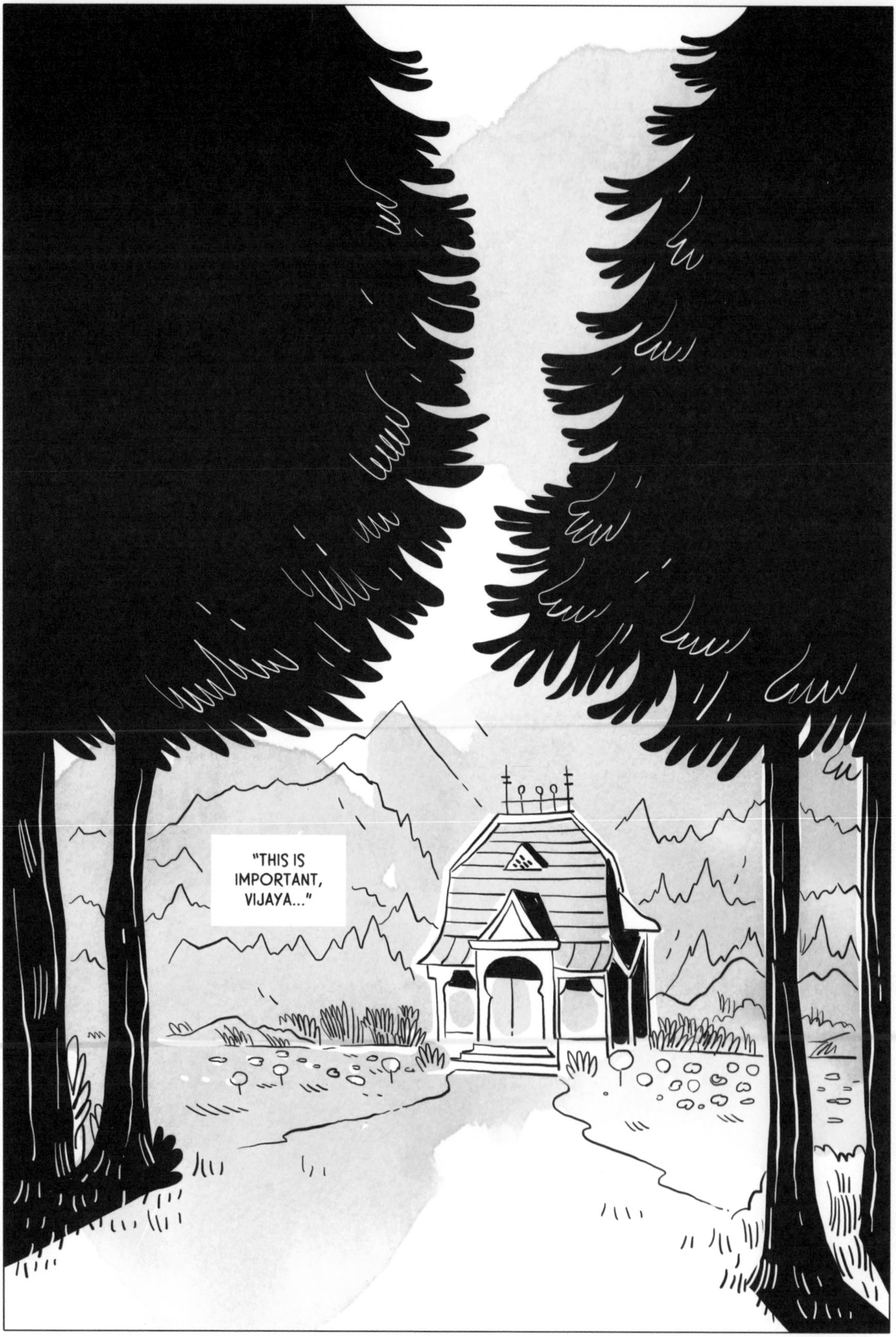
"THIS IS IMPORTANT, VIJAYA..."

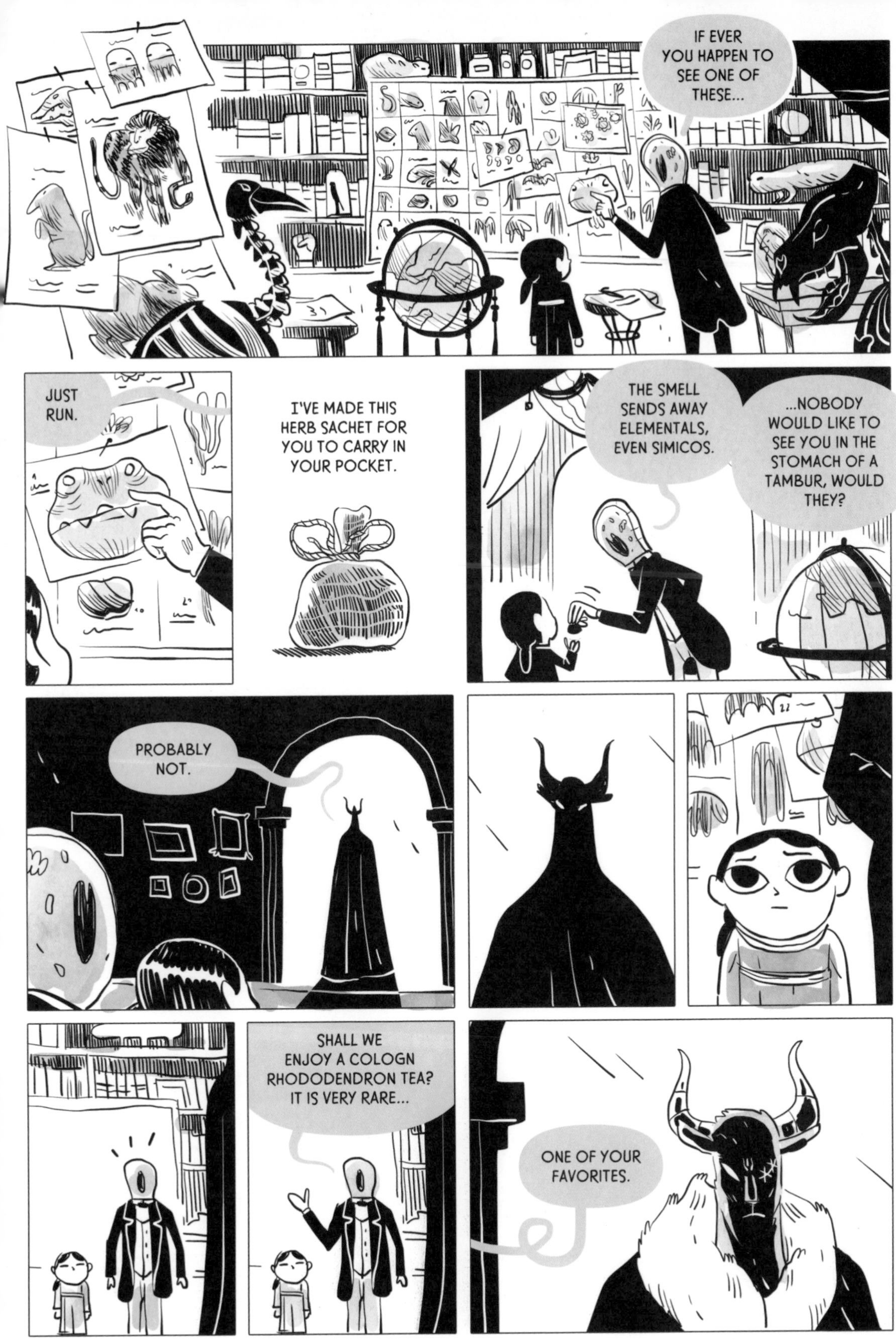
IF EVER YOU HAPPEN TO SEE ONE OF THESE...
JUST RUN.
I'VE MADE THIS HERB SACHET FOR YOU TO CARRY IN YOUR POCKET.
THE SMELL SENDS AWAY ELEMENTALS, EVEN SIMICOS.
...NOBODY WOULD LIKE TO SEE YOU IN THE STOMACH OF A TAMBUR, WOULD THEY?
PROBABLY NOT.
SHALL WE ENJOY A COLOGN RHODODENDRON TEA? IT IS VERY RARE...
ONE OF YOUR FAVORITES.

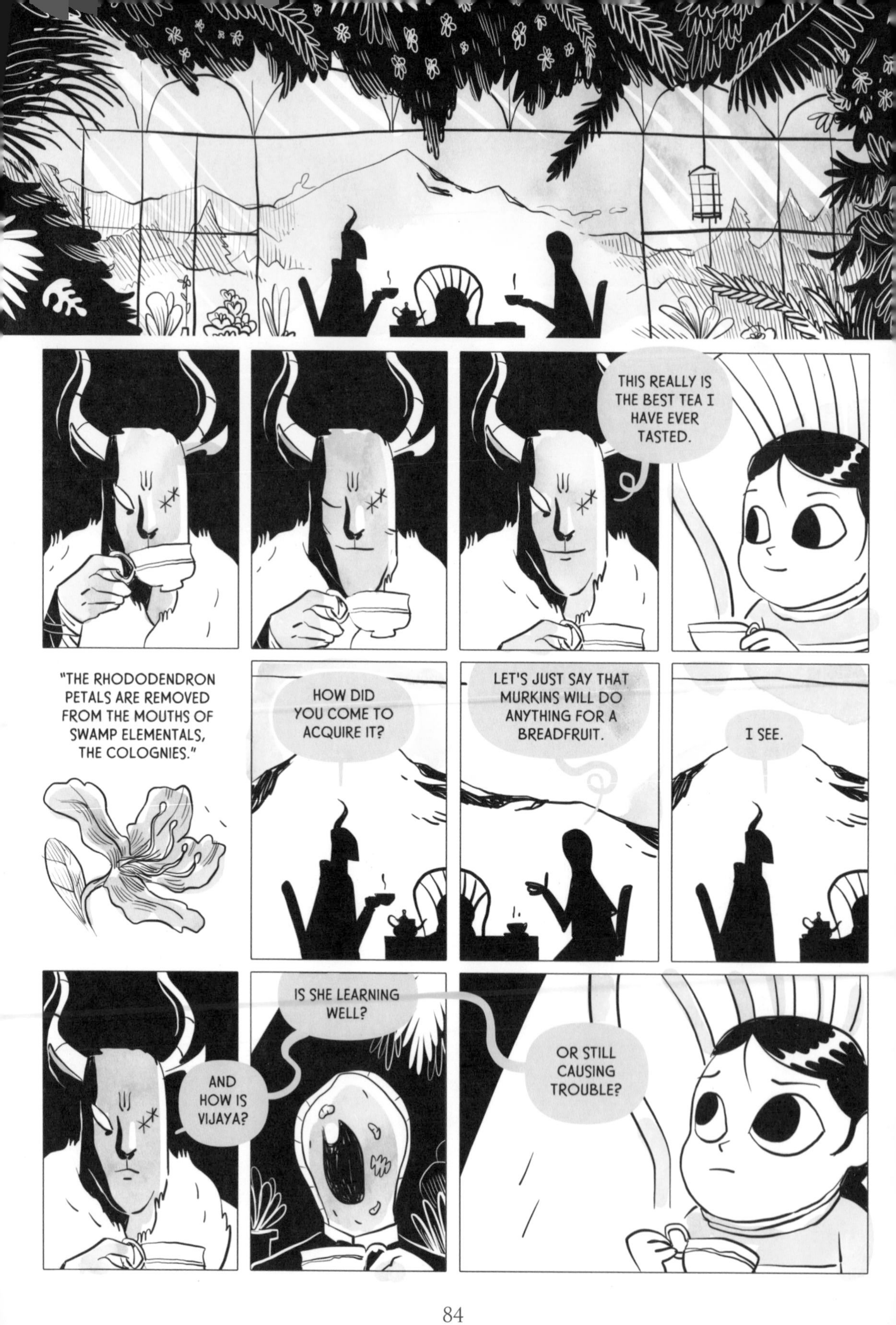
THIS REALLY IS THE BEST TEA I HAVE EVER TASTED.
"THE RHODODENDRON PETALS ARE REMOVED FROM THE MOUTHS OF SWAMP ELEMENTALS, THE COLOGNIES."
HOW DID YOU COME TO ACQUIRE IT?
LET'S JUST SAY THAT MURKINS WILL DO ANYTHING FOR A BREADFRUIT.
I SEE.
AND HOW IS VIJAYA?
IS SHE LEARNING WELL?
OR STILL CAUSING TROUBLE?

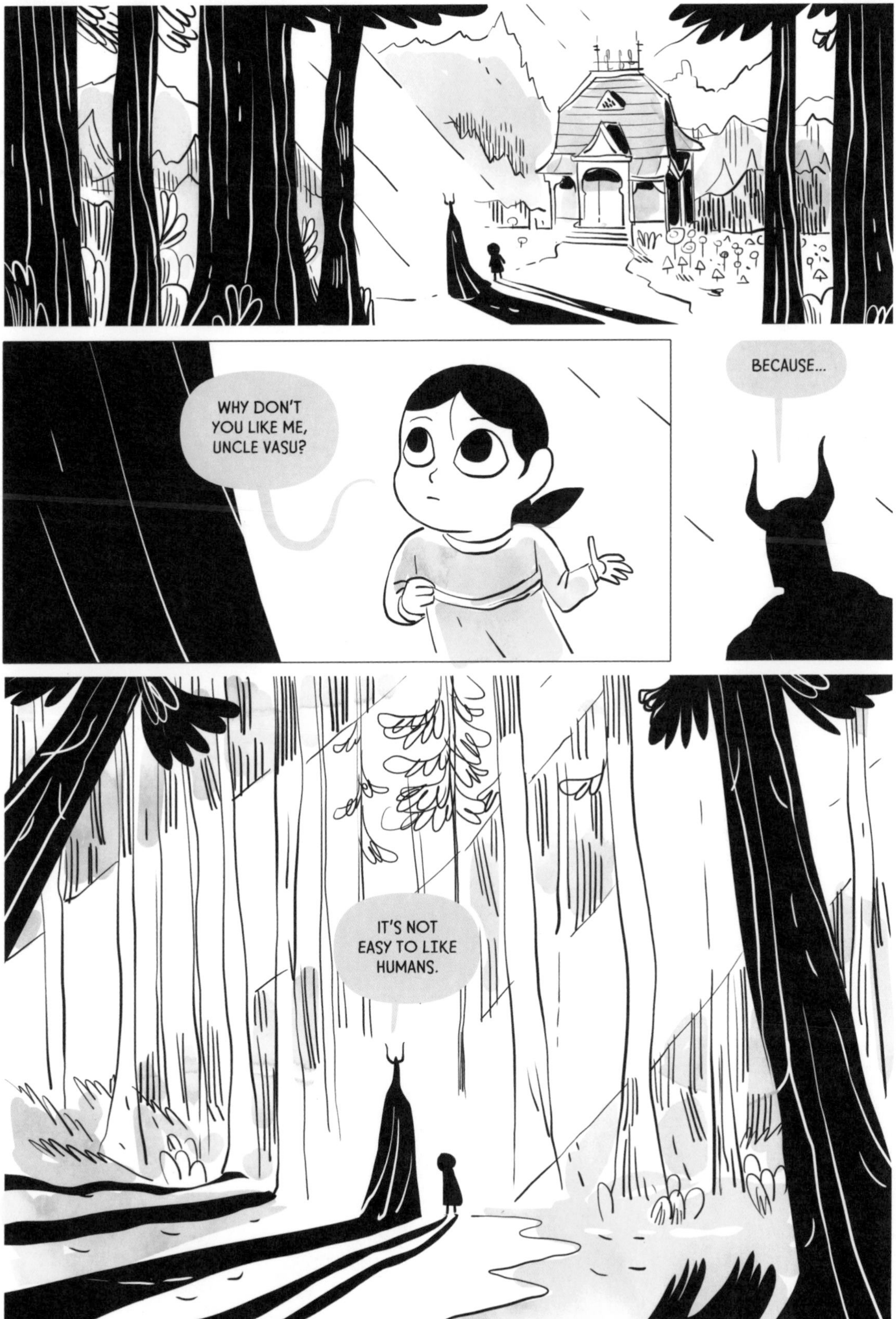
WHY DON'T YOU LIKE ME, UNCLE VASU?
BECAUSE...
IT'S NOT EASY TO LIKE HUMANS.

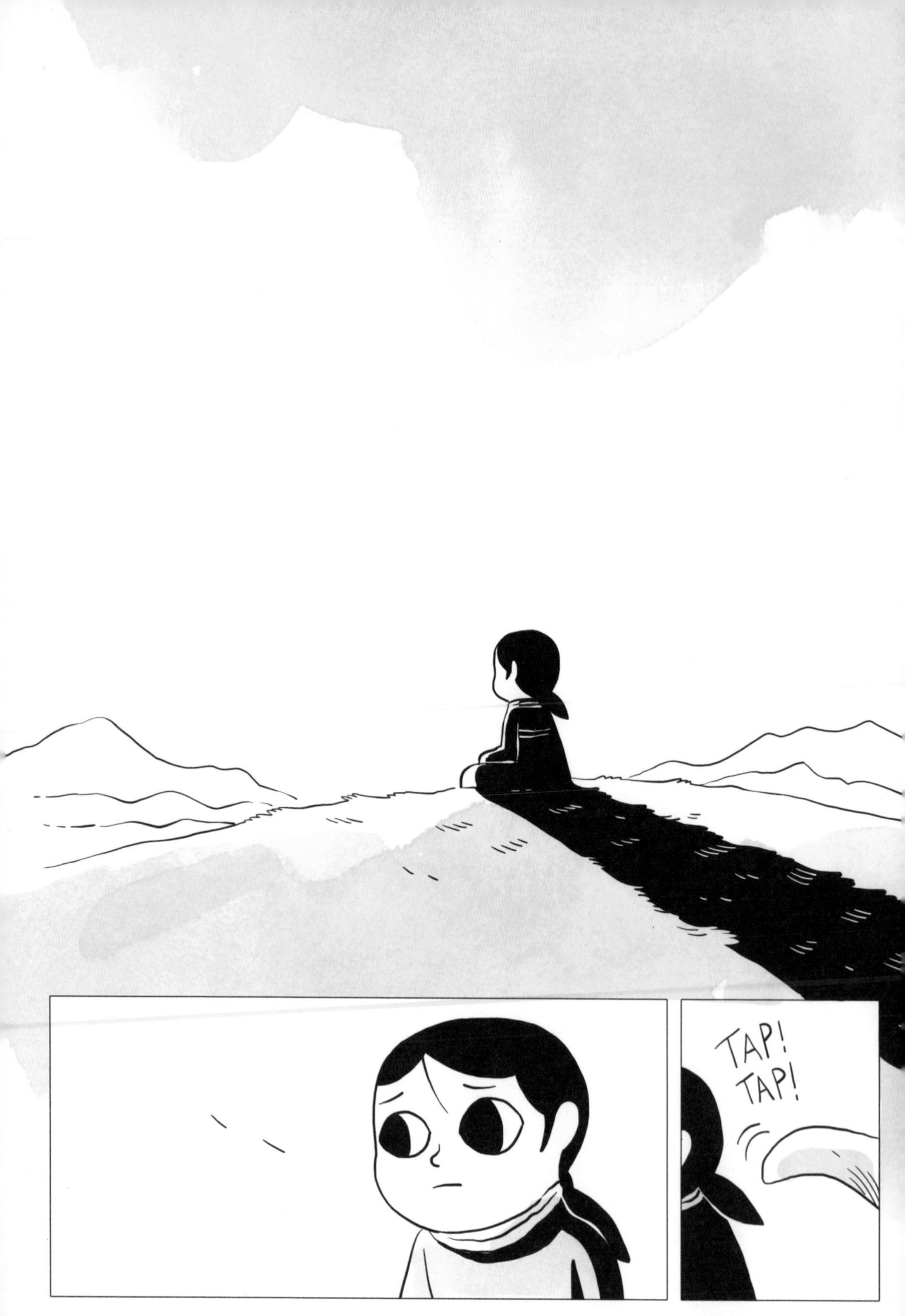
TAP!
TAP!

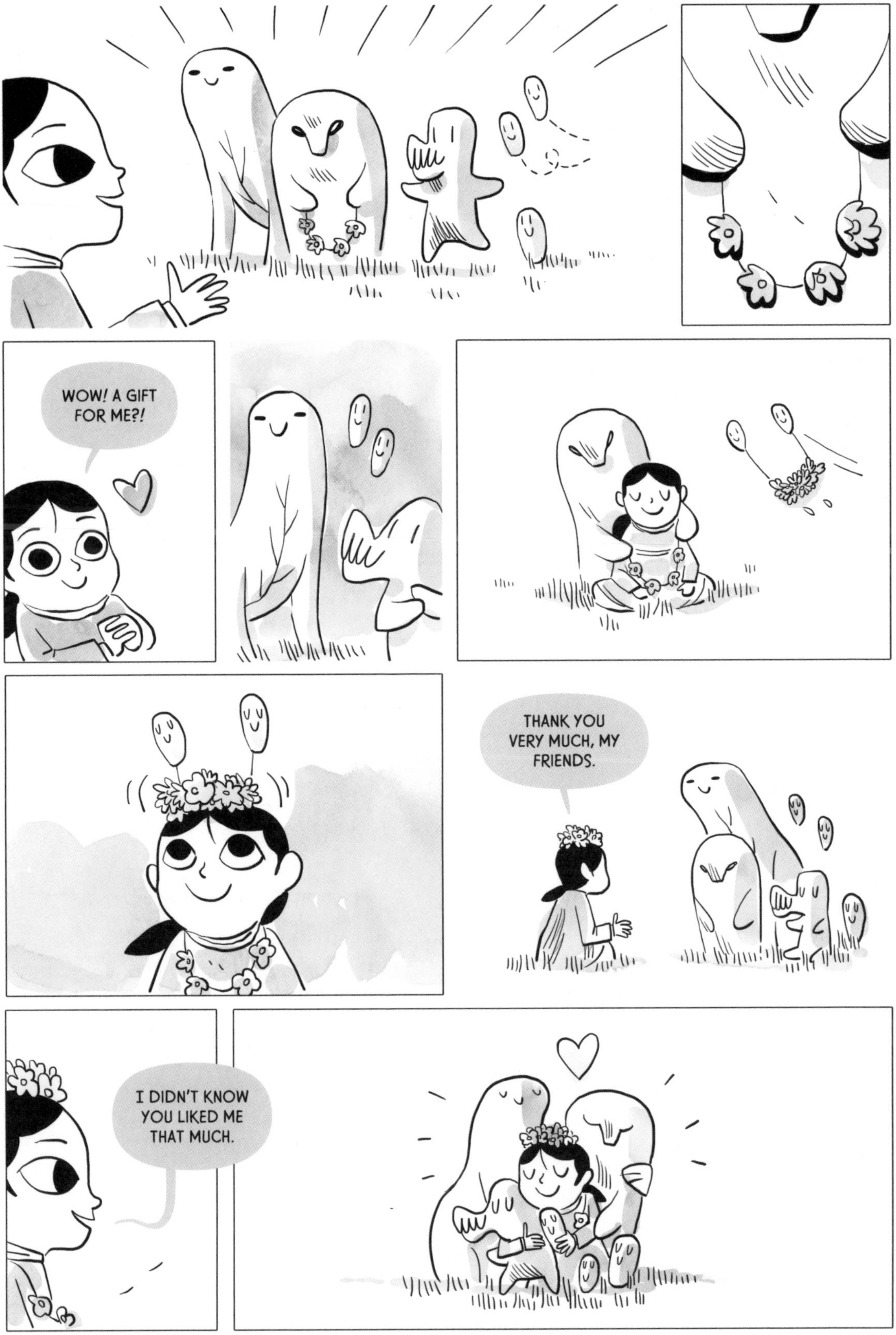
WOW! A GIFT FOR ME?!
THANK YOU VERY MUCH, MY FRIENDS.
I DIDN'T KNOW YOU LIKED ME THAT MUCH.

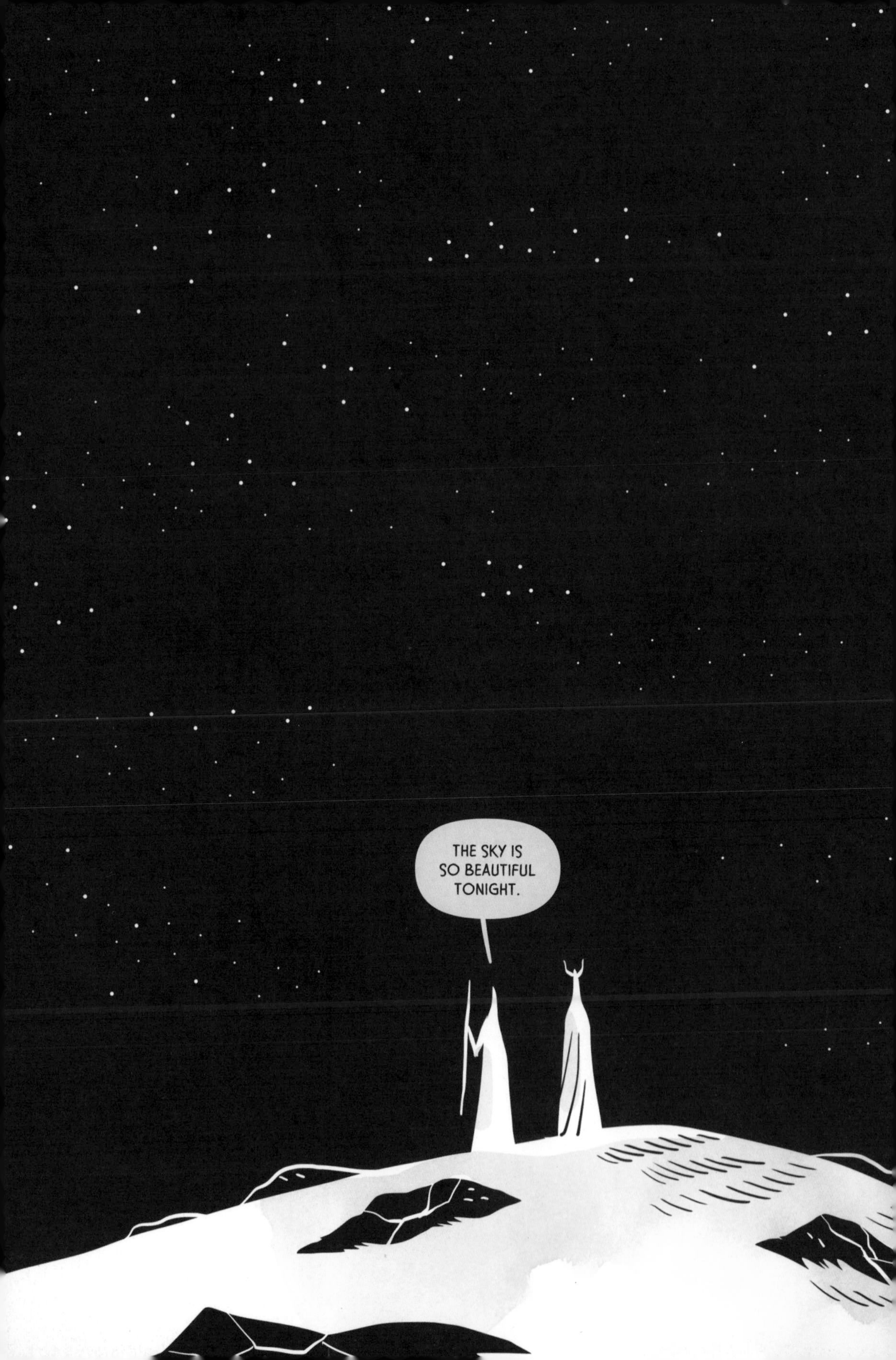
THE SKY IS SO BEAUTIFUL TONIGHT.

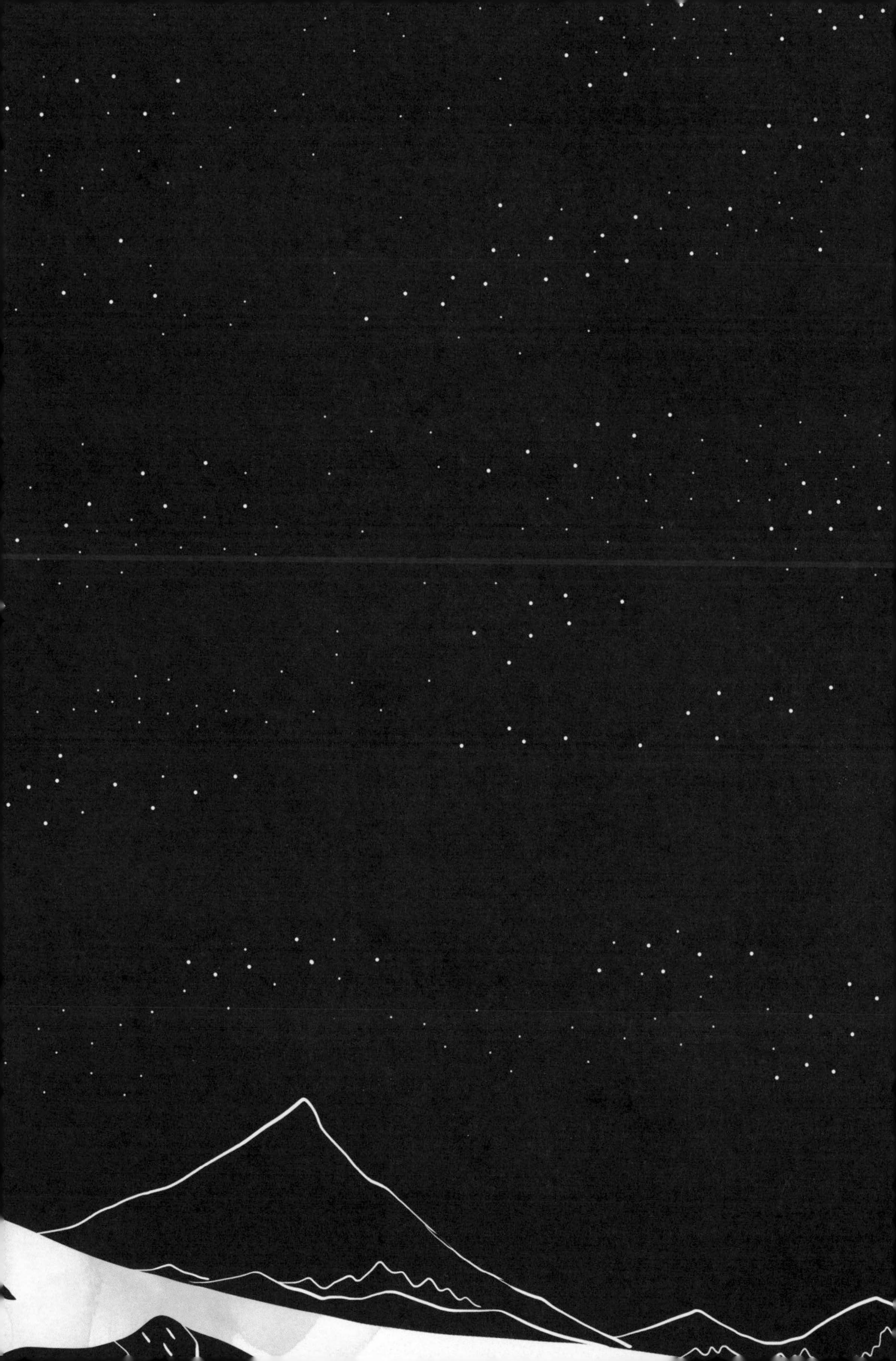

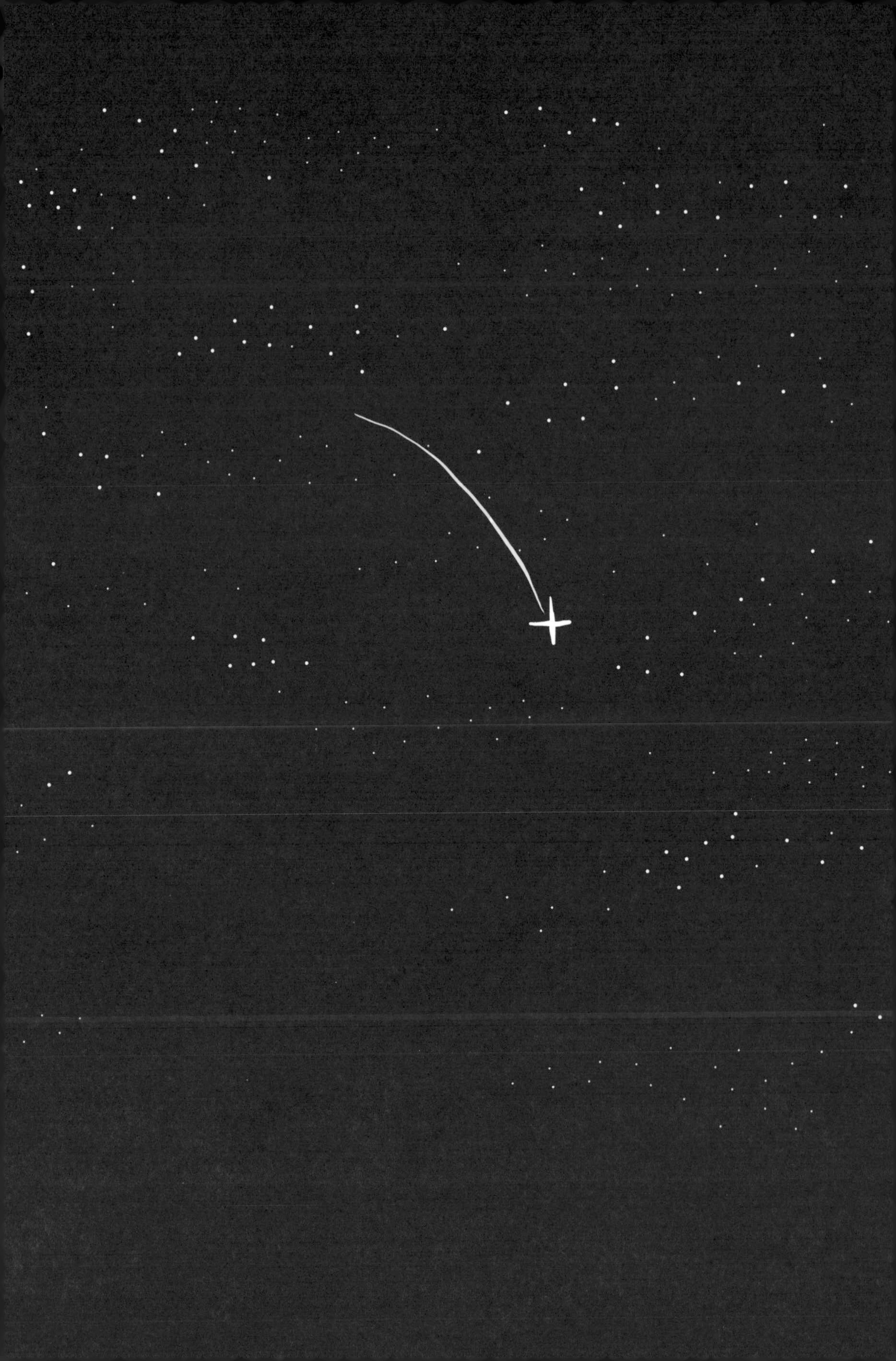

IT FEELS GOOD TO AT LAST BE ABLE TO WALK UP HERE.

YOU MUST BE RELIEVED TO BE DOING AT LEAST ONE OF THE THINGS YOU WERE CAPABLE OF BEFORE.

BEING HUMAN IS NOT AS BAD AS IT SEEMS, VASU

DO YOU REMEMBER THE LAST TIME I WAS IN ALBION?

ELEMENTALS THERE WERE SUFFERING...

"HUMANS DESTROYED THE FORESTS WHERE THE ELEMENTALS LIVED AND BUILT MACHINES.

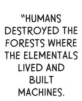

"HUMANITY DISCONNECTED ITSELF FROM NATURE...

"AND PERVERTED ITS OWN INNOCENCE."

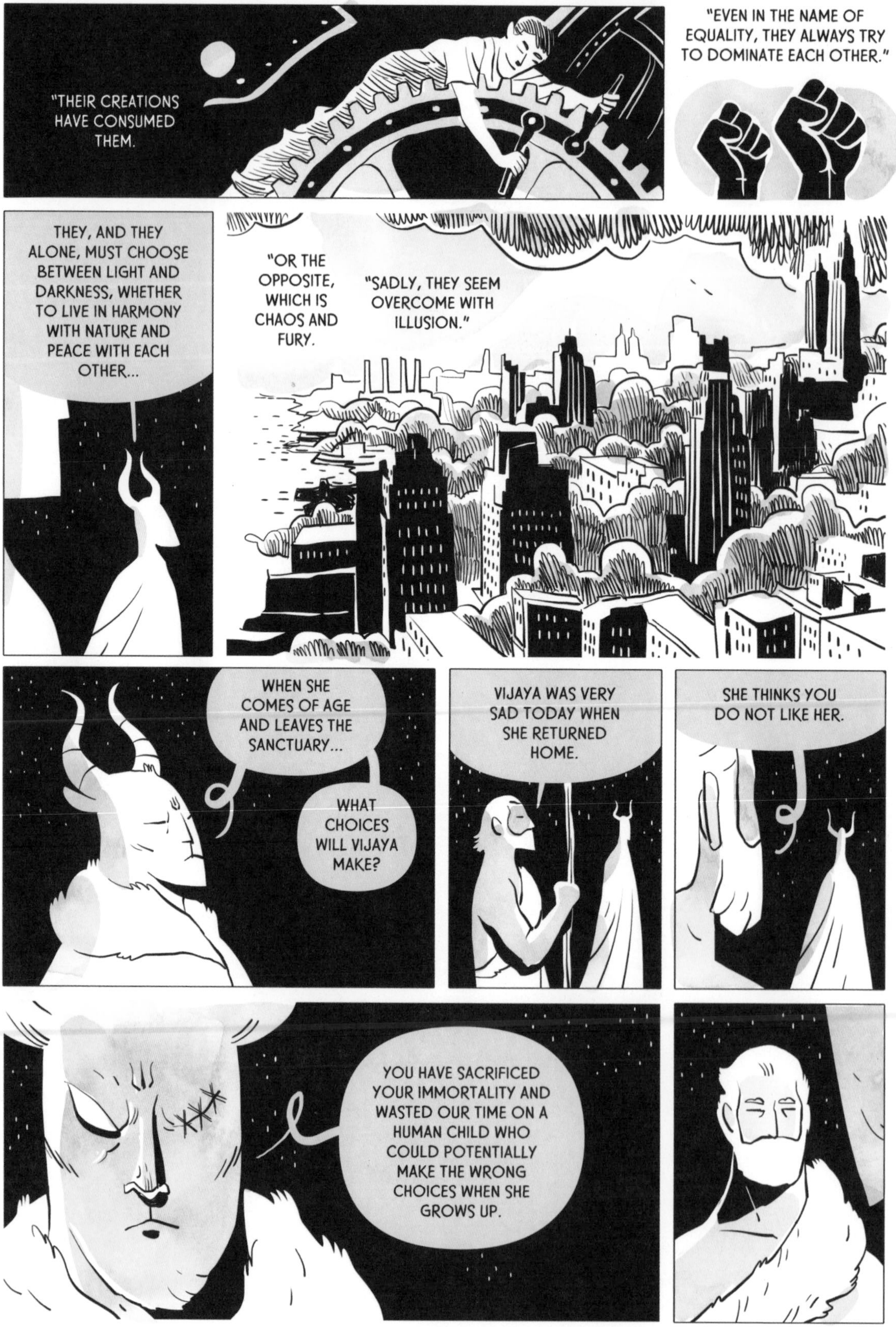
"THEIR CREATIONS HAVE CONSUMED THEM.
"EVEN IN THE NAME OF EQUALITY, THEY ALWAYS TRY TO DOMINATE EACH OTHER."
THEY, AND THEY ALONE, MUST CHOOSE BETWEEN LIGHT AND DARKNESS, WHETHER TO LIVE IN HARMONY WITH NATURE AND PEACE WITH EACH OTHER...
"OR THE OPPOSITE, WHICH IS CHAOS AND FURY.
"SADLY, THEY SEEM OVERCOME WITH ILLUSION."
WHEN SHE COMES OF AGE AND LEAVES THE SANCTUARY...
WHAT CHOICES WILL VIJAYA MAKE?
VIJAYA WAS VERY SAD TODAY WHEN SHE RETURNED HOME.
SHE THINKS YOU DO NOT LIKE HER.
YOU HAVE SACRIFICED YOUR IMMORTALITY AND WASTED OUR TIME ON A HUMAN CHILD WHO COULD POTENTIALLY MAKE THE WRONG CHOICES WHEN SHE GROWS UP.

HUMANS WILL REACH THEIR EVOLUTIONARY APEX WHEN THEY START MAKING THE RIGHT CHOICES.

WE HAVE TO BELIEVE THAT WHEN VIJAYA RETURNS TO THE WORLD OF MEN, SHE WILL BE A FORCE FOR GOOD.

AND SHE WILL HELP OTHERS TO MAKE THE RIGHT DECISIONS.

ARE YOU JUST SAYING THAT BECAUSE YOU ARE NOW HUMAN?

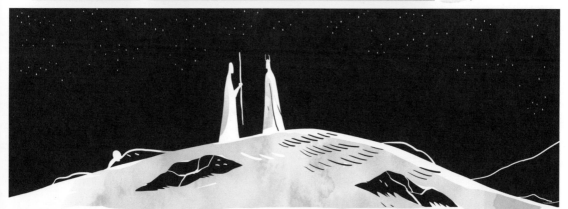

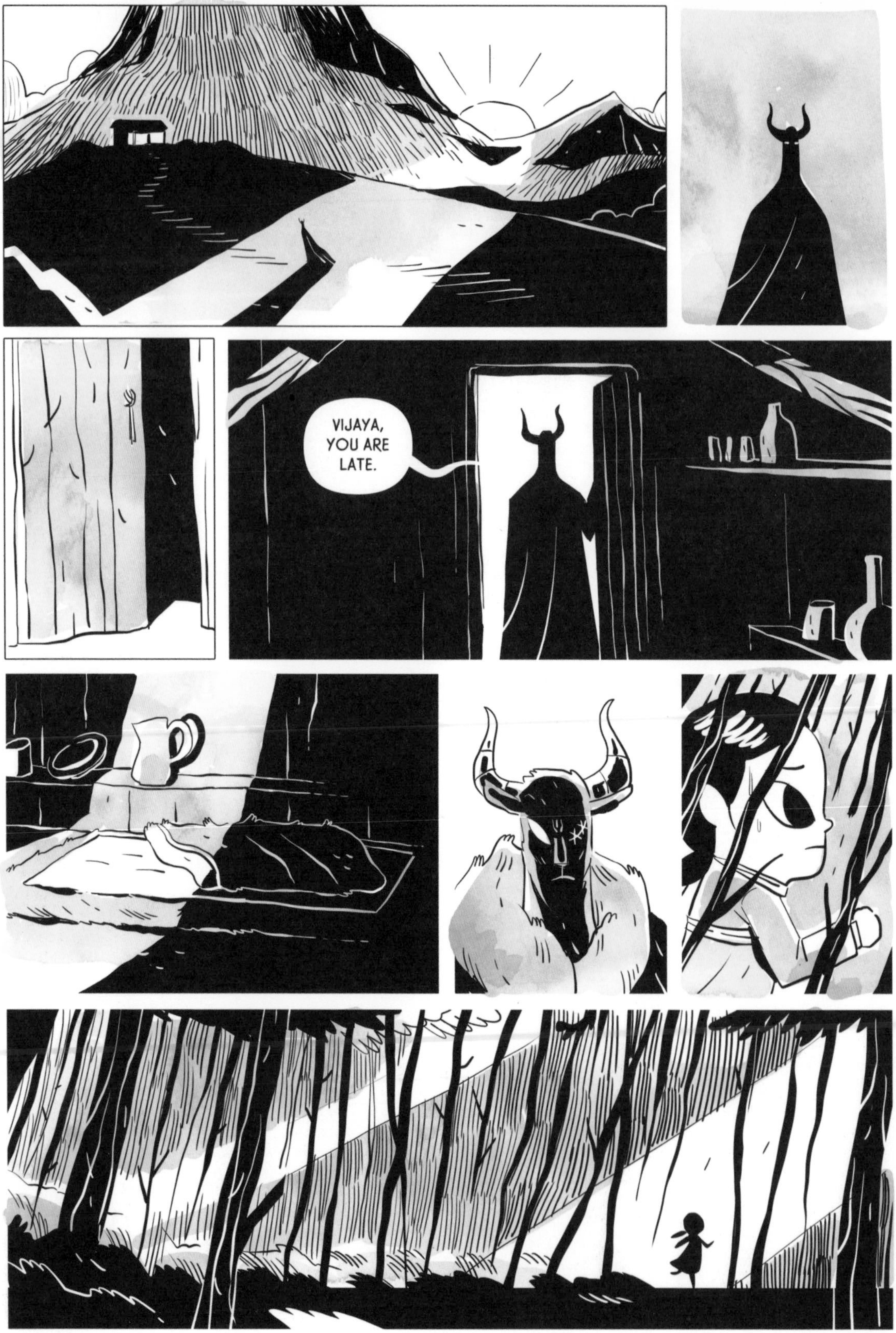
VIJAYA, YOU ARE LATE.

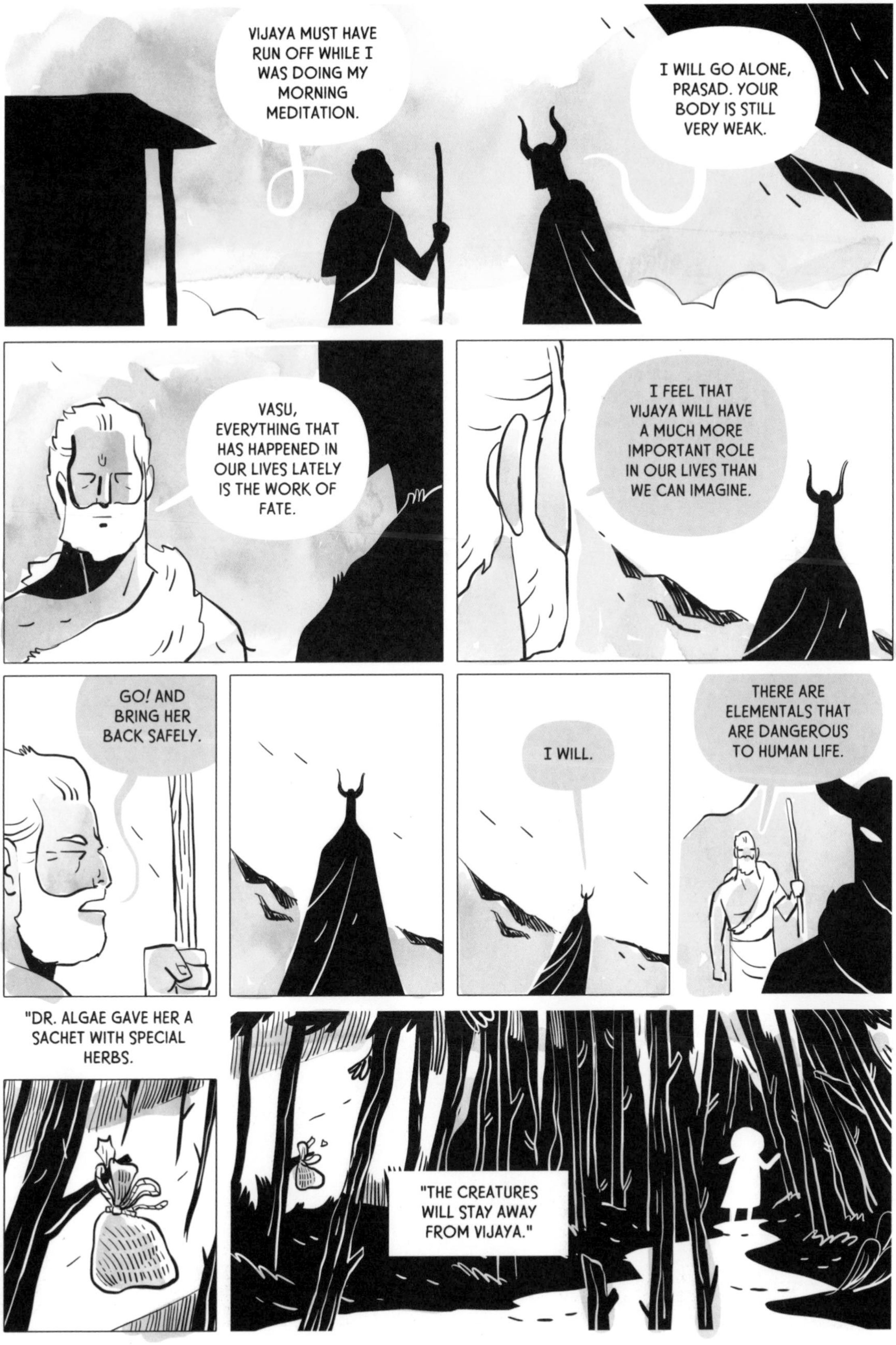
VIJAYA MUST HAVE RUN OFF WHILE I WAS DOING MY MORNING MEDITATION.
I WILL GO ALONE, PRASAD. YOUR BODY IS STILL VERY WEAK.
VASU, EVERYTHING THAT HAS HAPPENED IN OUR LIVES LATELY IS THE WORK OF FATE.
I FEEL THAT VIJAYA WILL HAVE A MUCH MORE IMPORTANT ROLE IN OUR LIVES THAN WE CAN IMAGINE.
GO! AND BRING HER BACK SAFELY.
I WILL.
THERE ARE ELEMENTALS THAT ARE DANGEROUS TO HUMAN LIFE.
"DR. ALGAE GAVE HER A SACHET WITH SPECIAL HERBS.
"THE CREATURES WILL STAY AWAY FROM VIJAYA."

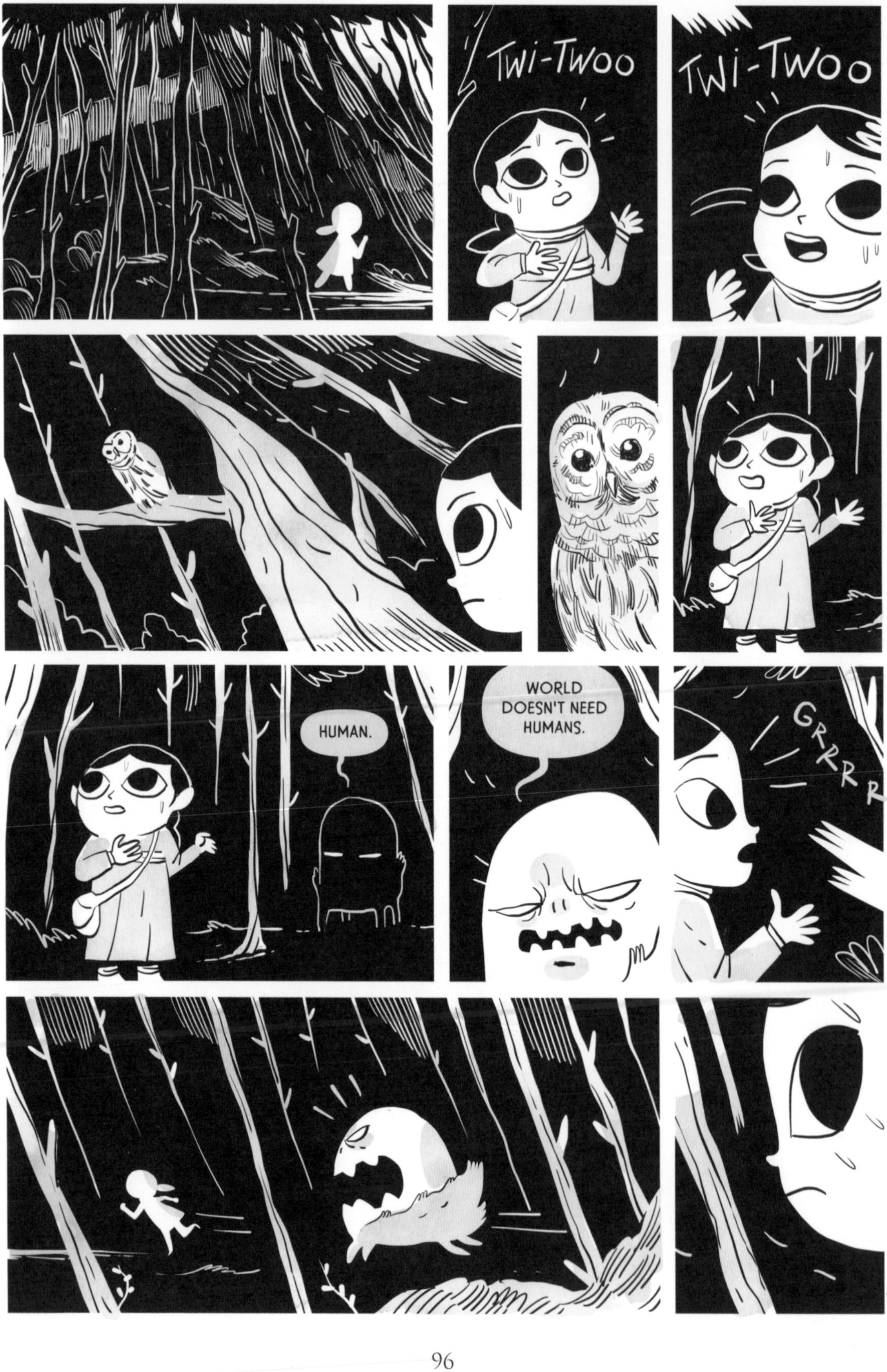

TWI-TWOO
TWI-TWOO
HUMAN.
WORLD DOESN'T NEED HUMANS.
GRRRRR

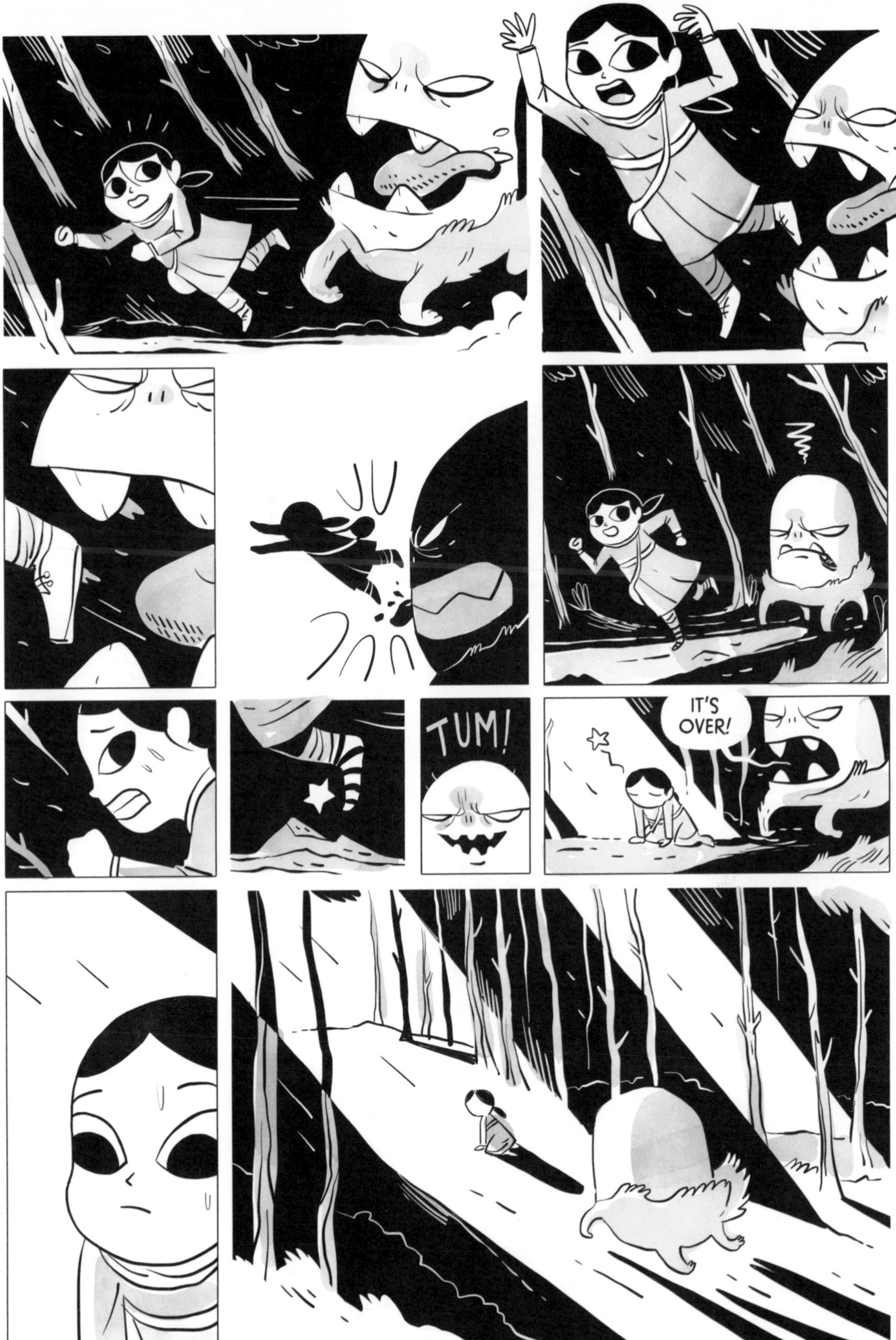
TUM!
IT'S OVER!

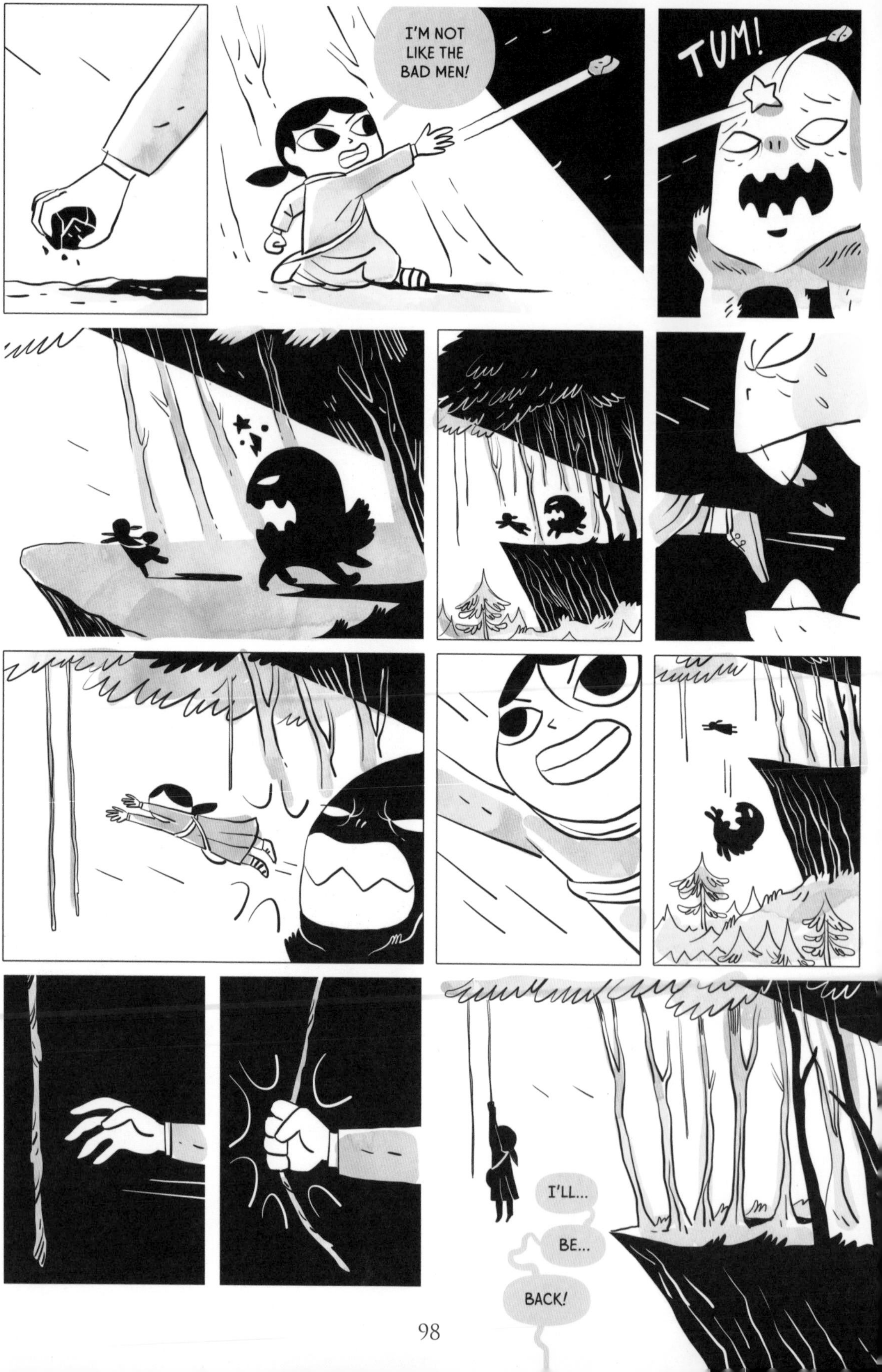
I'M NOT LIKE THE BAD MEN!
TUM!
I'LL...
BE...
BACK!

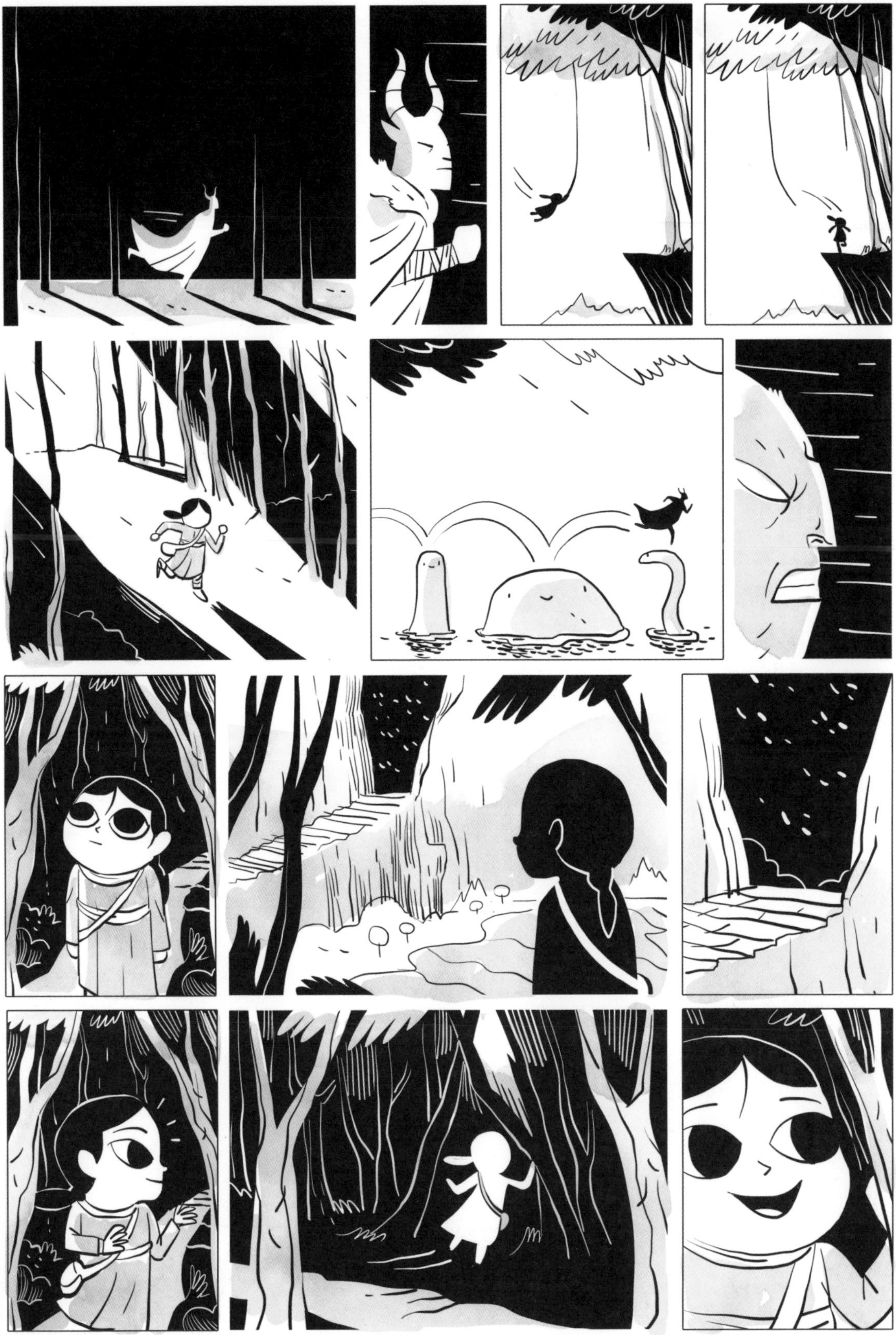

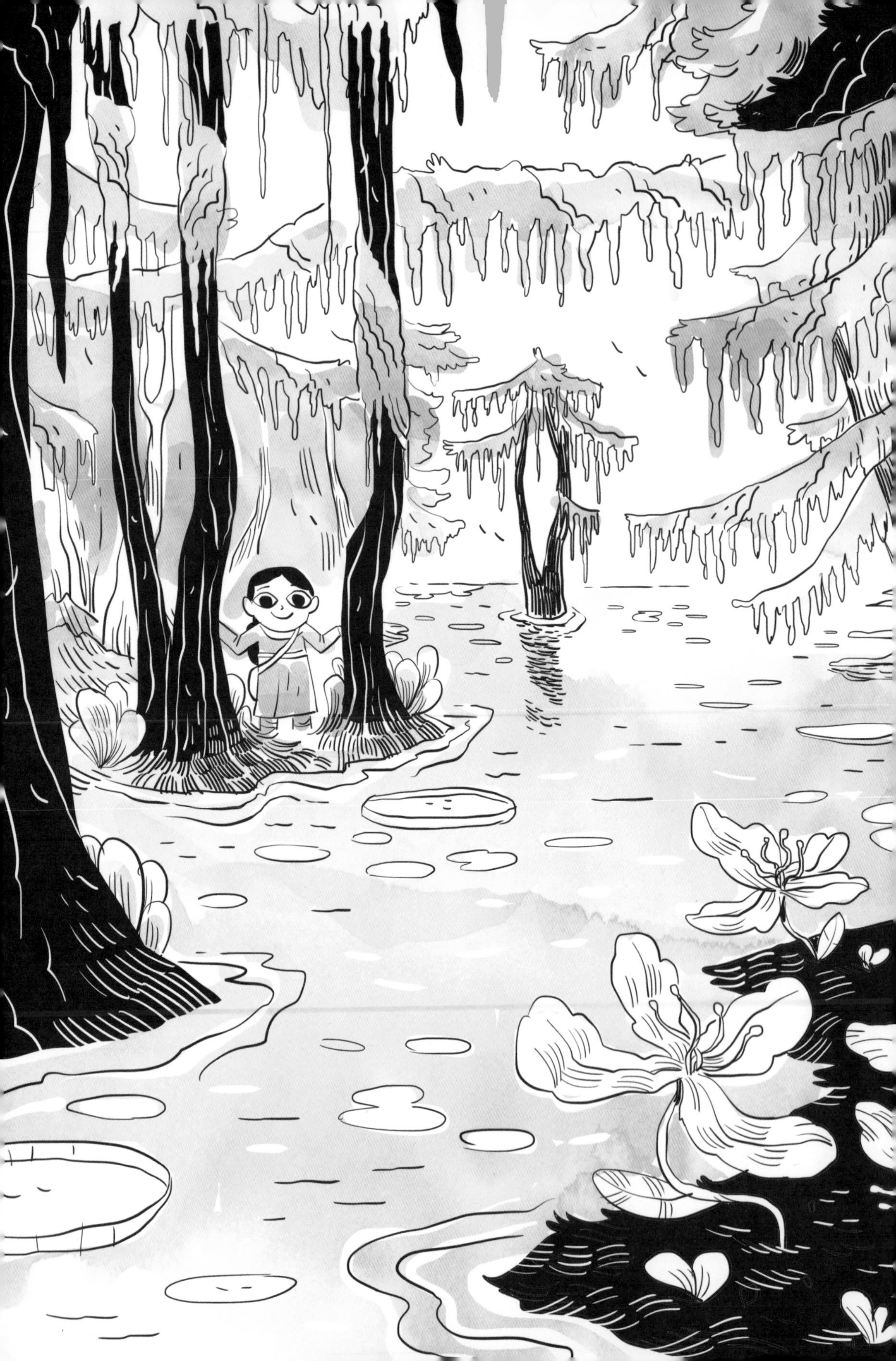

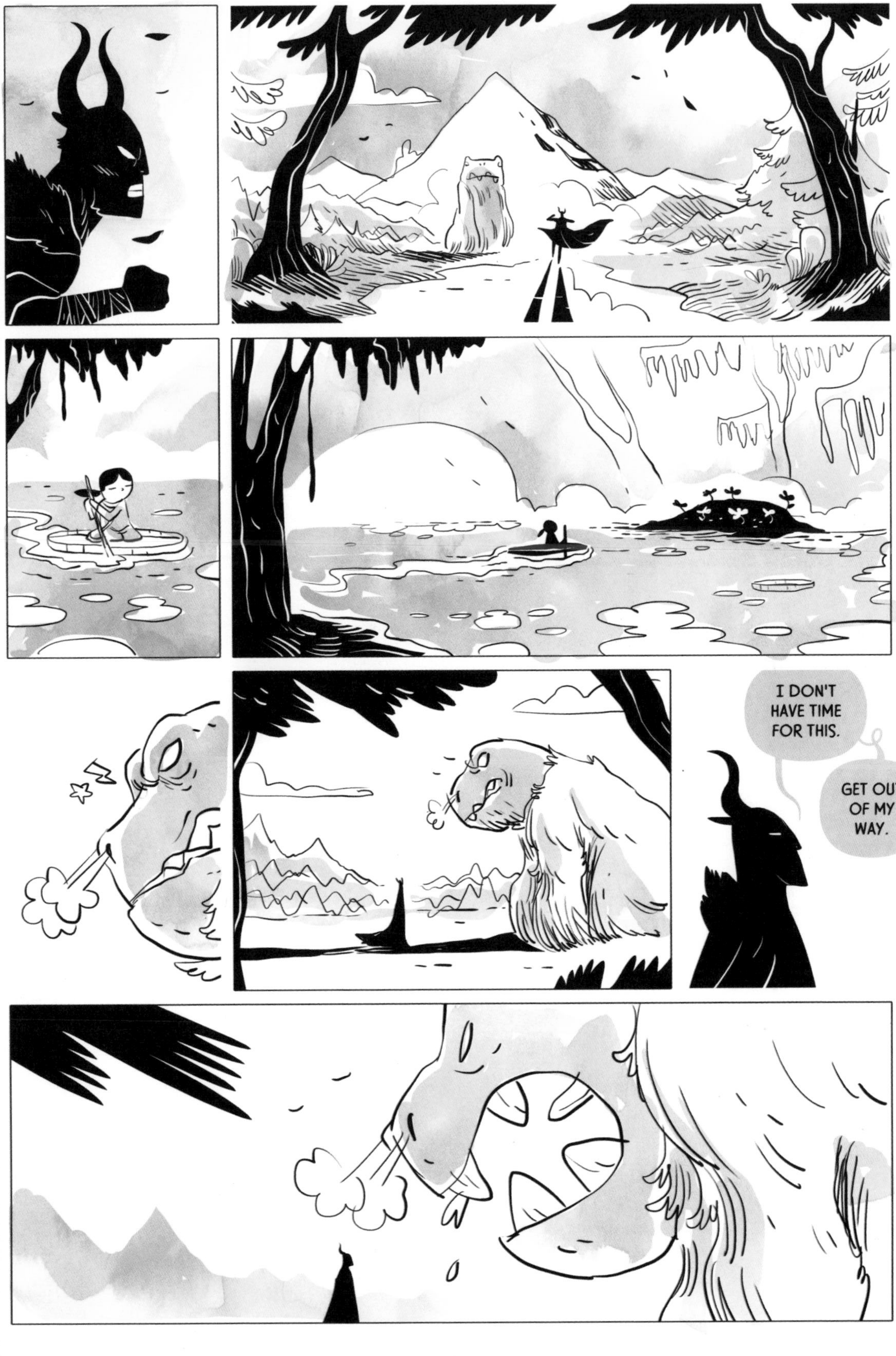

I DON'T HAVE TIME FOR THIS.
GET OUT OF MY WAY.

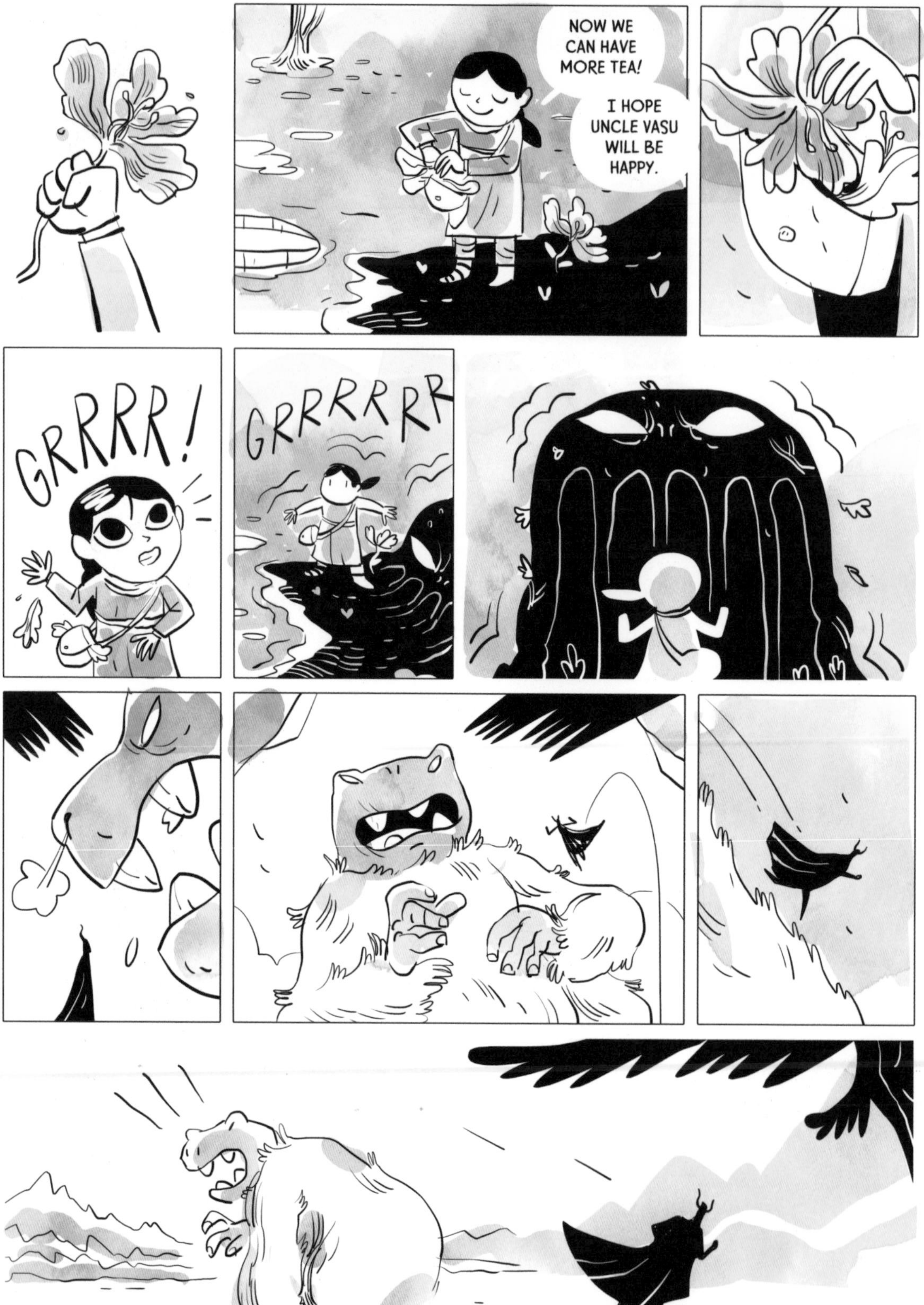
NOW WE CAN HAVE MORE TEA!
I HOPE UNCLE VASU WILL BE HAPPY.
GRRRR!
GRRRRRR

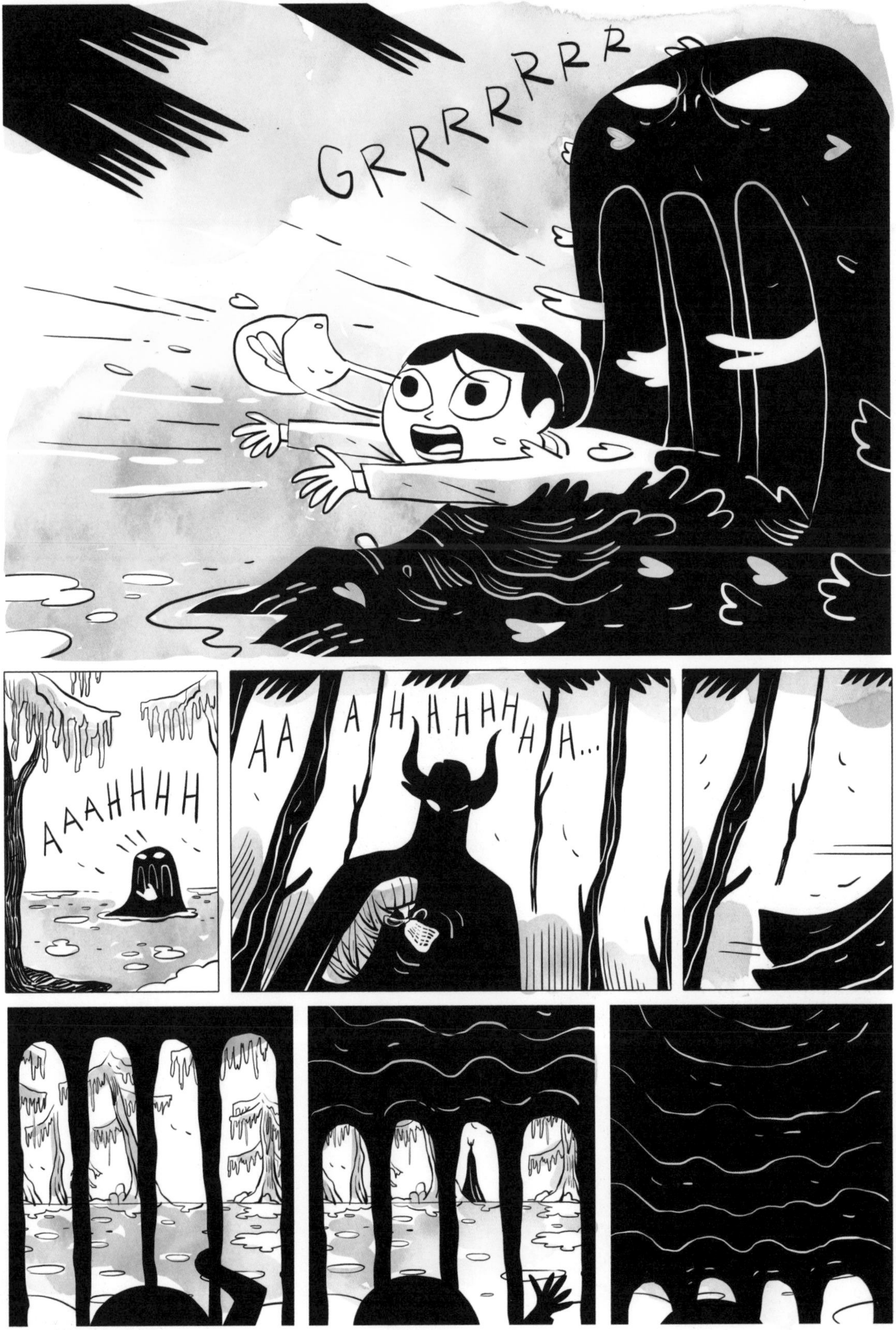
GRRRRRRRR
AAAHHHH
AA A HHHHHHH...

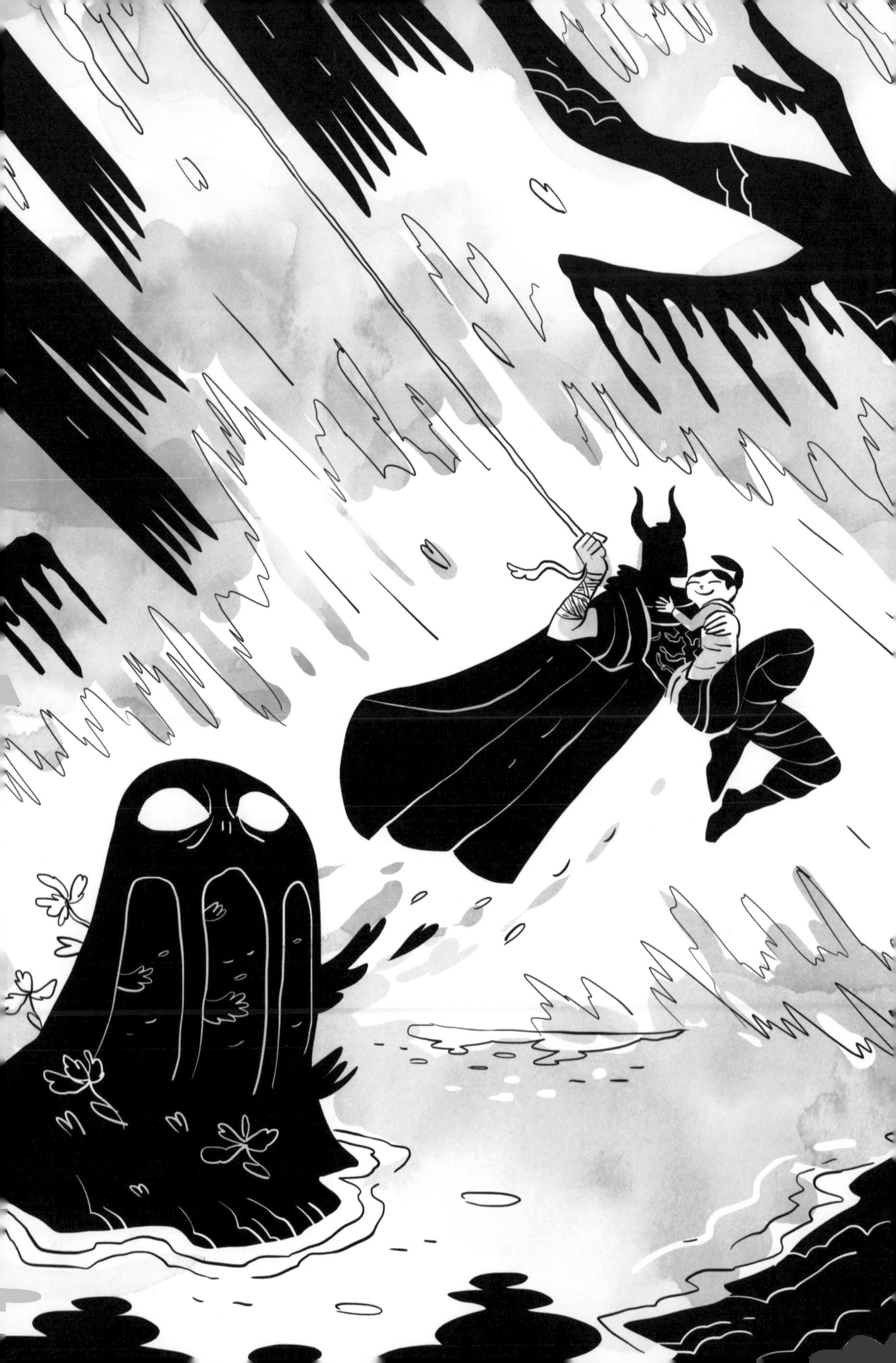

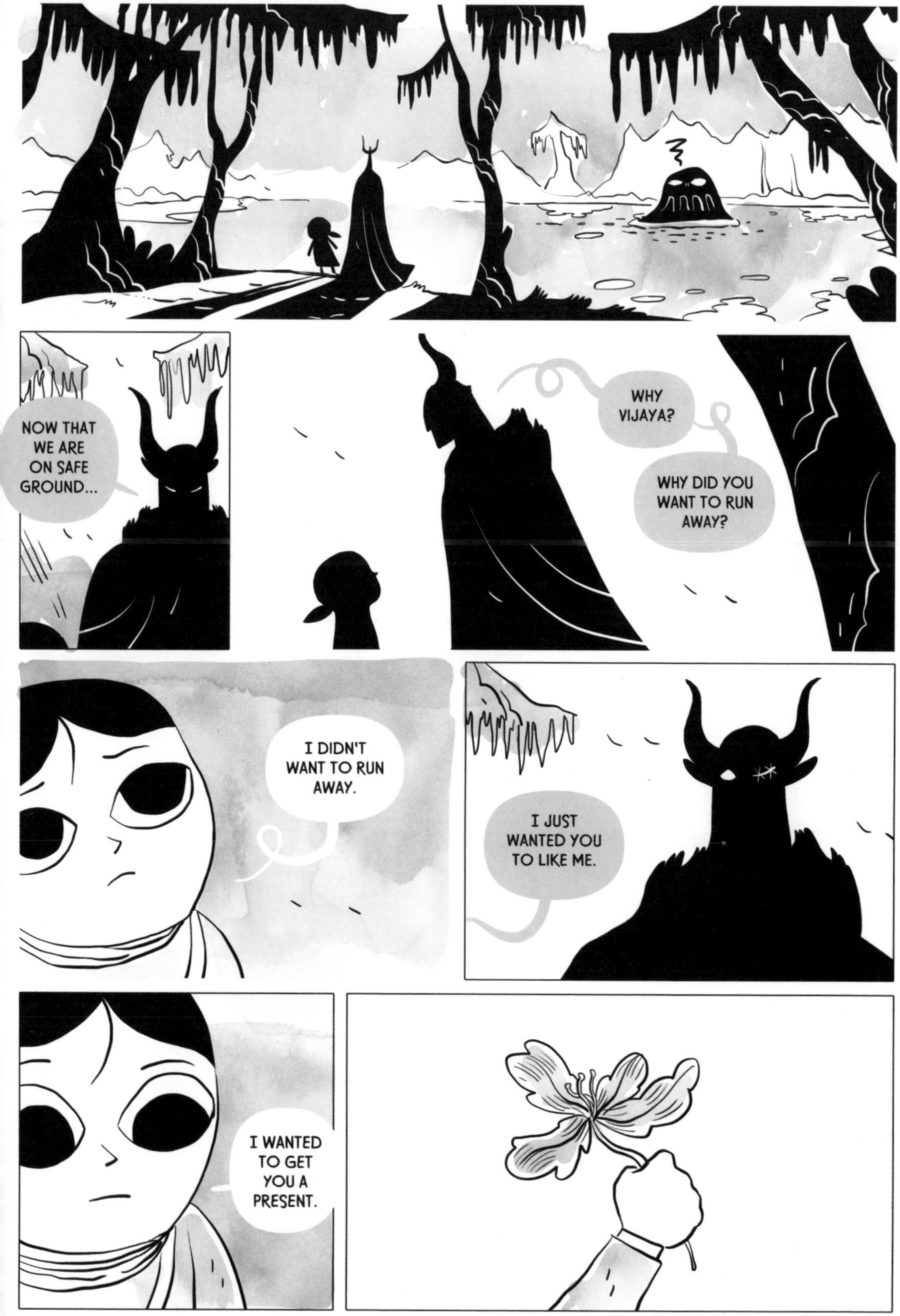
NOW THAT WE ARE ON SAFE GROUND...
WHY VIJAYA?
WHY DID YOU WANT TO RUN AWAY?
I DIDN'T WANT TO RUN AWAY.
I JUST WANTED YOU TO LIKE ME.
I WANTED TO GET YOU A PRESENT.

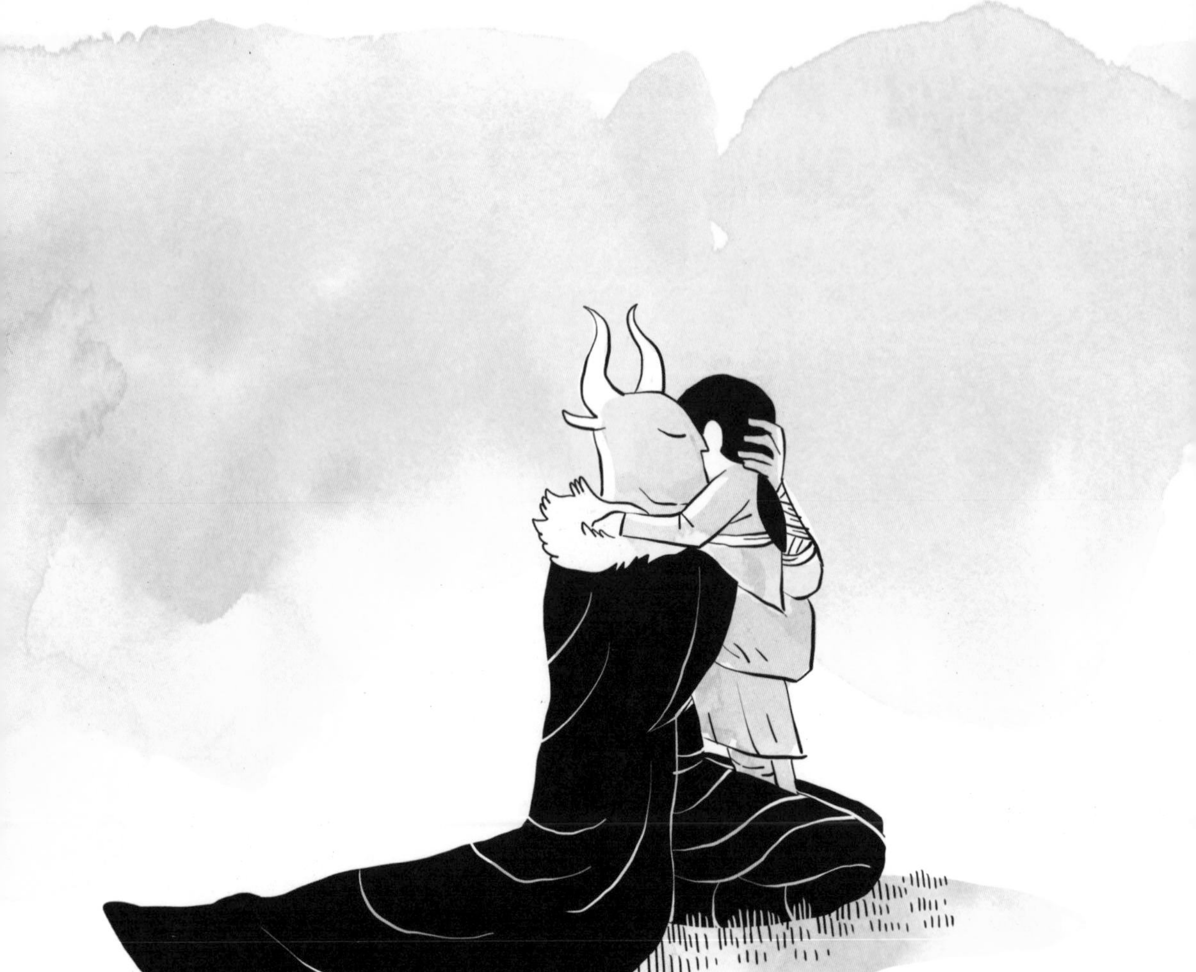

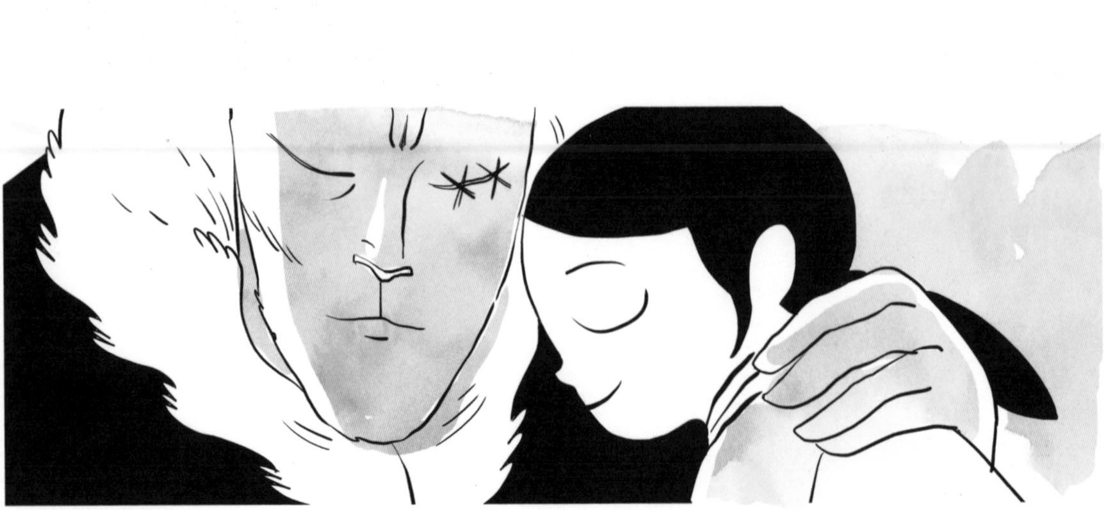

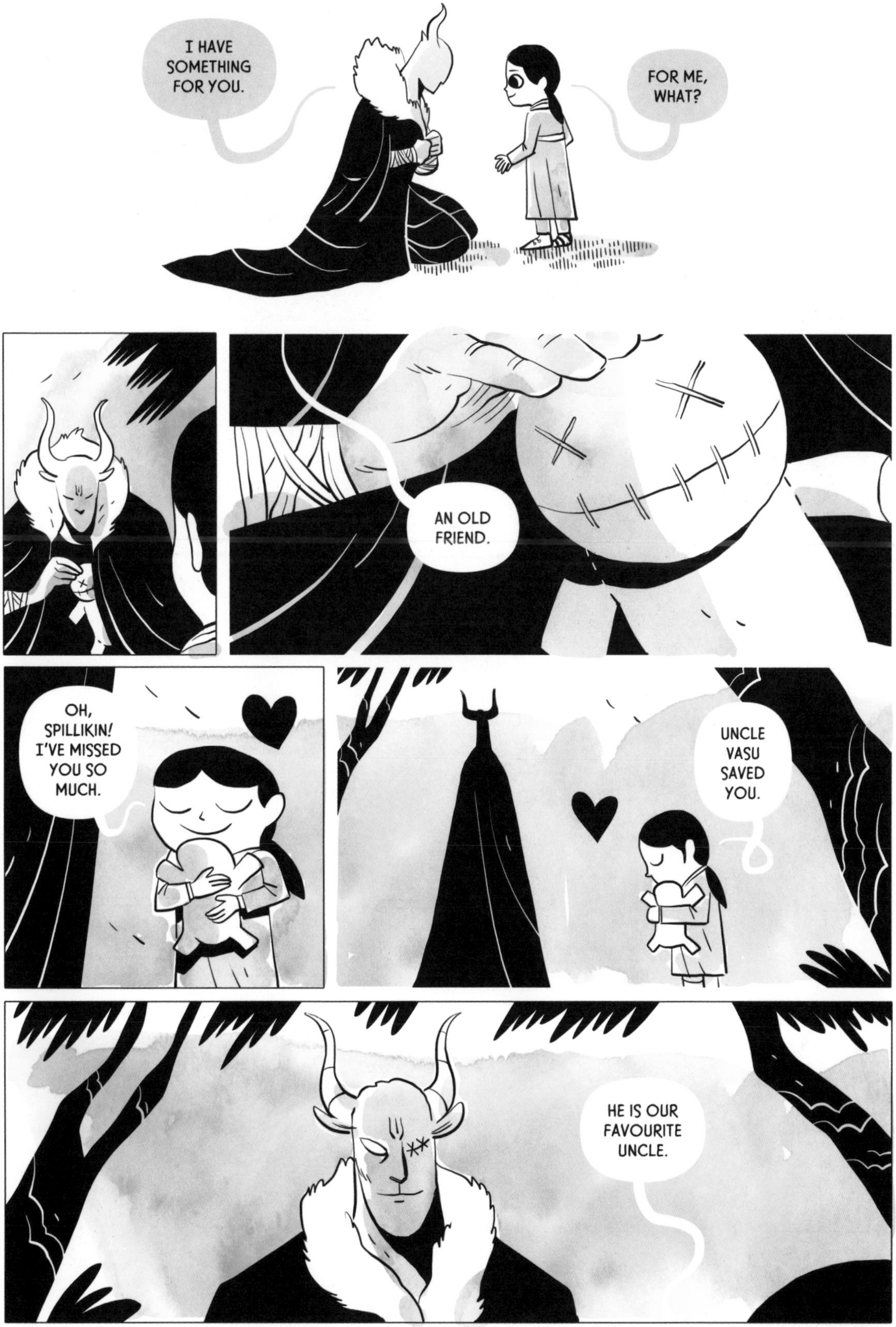
I HAVE SOMETHING FOR YOU.
FOR ME, WHAT?
AN OLD FRIEND.
OH, SPILLIKIN! I'VE MISSED YOU SO MUCH.
UNCLE VASU SAVED YOU.
HE IS OUR FAVOURITE UNCLE.

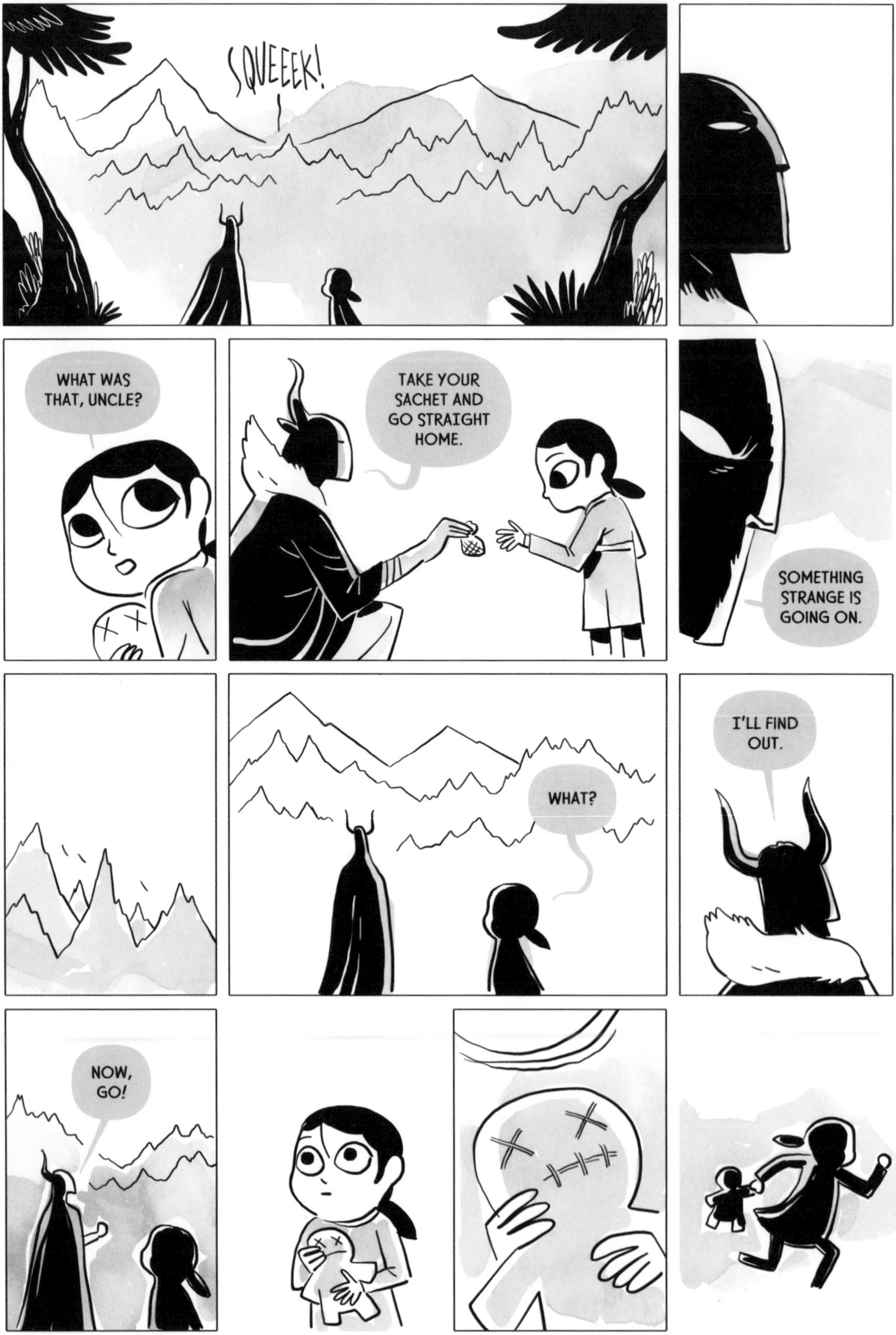
SQUEEEK!
WHAT WAS THAT, UNCLE?
TAKE YOUR SACHET AND GO STRAIGHT HOME.
SOMETHING STRANGE IS GOING ON.
WHAT?
I'LL FIND OUT.
NOW, GO!

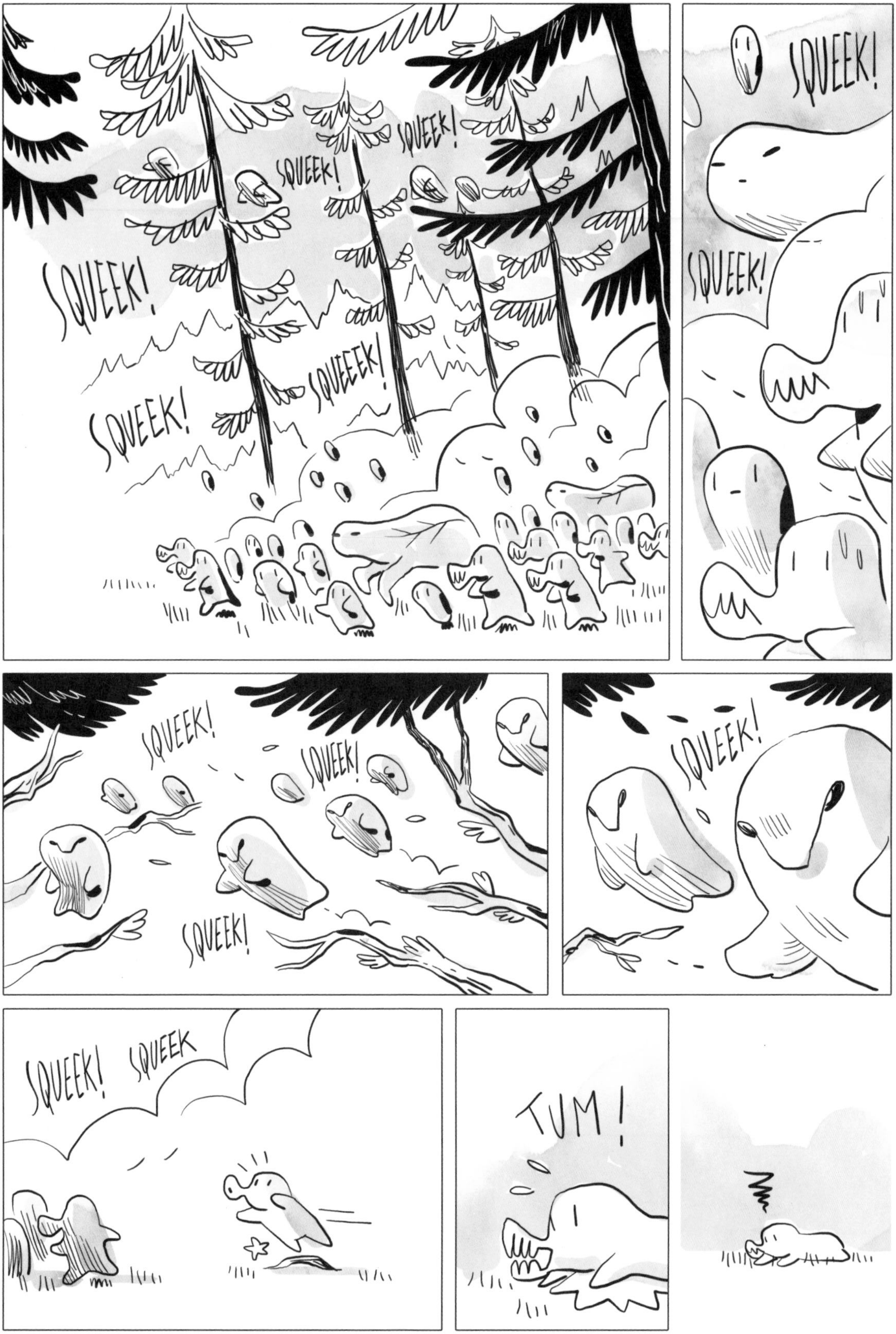
SQUEEK!
SQUEEK!
SQUEEK!
SQUEEK!
SQUEEEK!
SQUEEK!
SQUEEK!
SQUEEK!
SQUEEK!
SQUEEK!
SQUEEK!
SQUEEK!
SQUEEK
TUM!

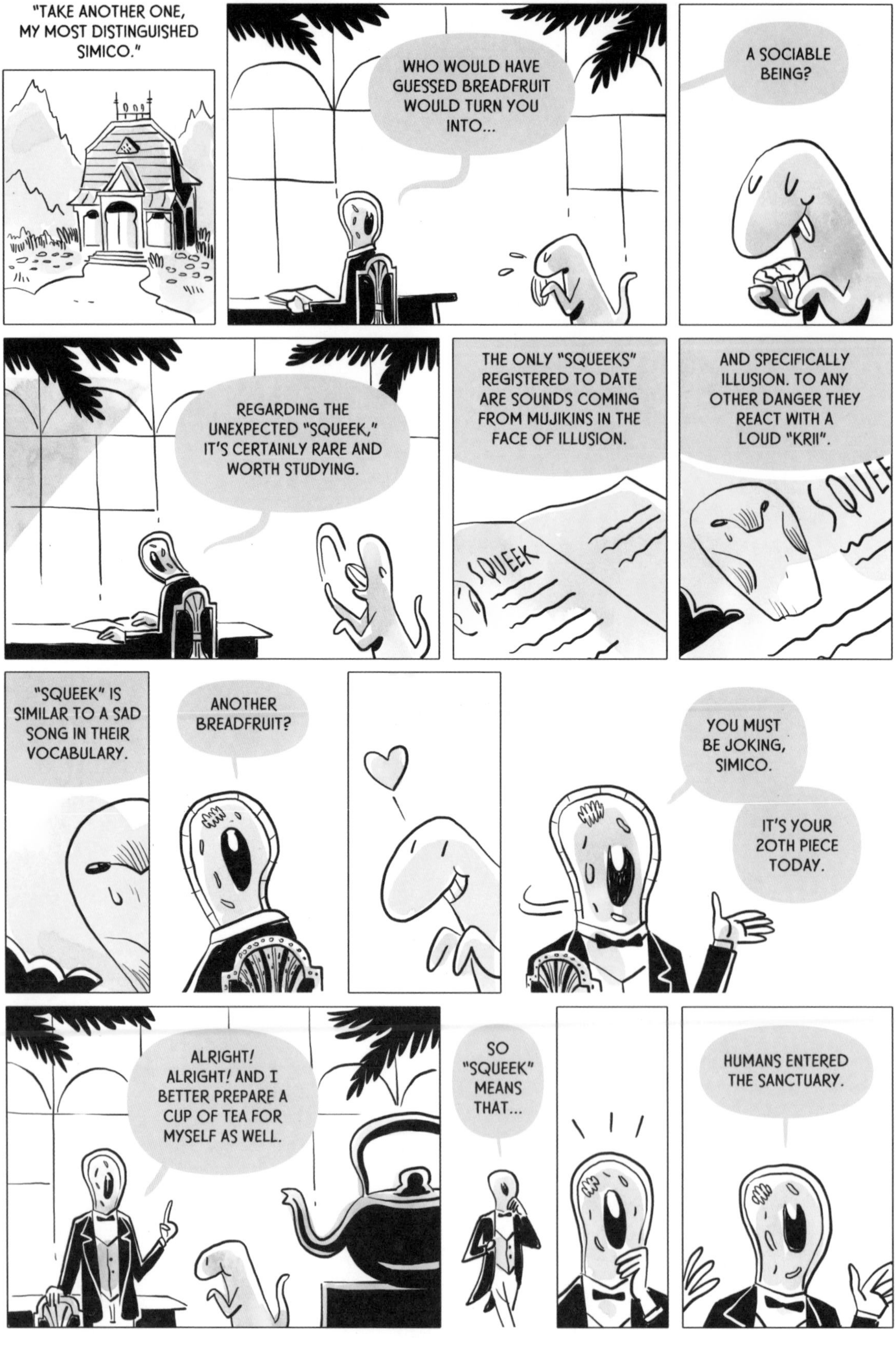
"TAKE ANOTHER ONE, MY MOST DISTINGUISHED SIMICO."
WHO WOULD HAVE GUESSED BREADFRUIT WOULD TURN YOU INTO...
A SOCIABLE BEING?
REGARDING THE UNEXPECTED "SQUEEK," IT'S CERTAINLY RARE AND WORTH STUDYING.
THE ONLY "SQUEEKS" REGISTERED TO DATE ARE SOUNDS COMING FROM MUJIKINS IN THE FACE OF ILLUSION.
SQUEEK
AND SPECIFICALLY ILLUSION. TO ANY OTHER DANGER THEY REACT WITH A LOUD "KRII".
"SQUEEK" IS SIMILAR TO A SAD SONG IN THEIR VOCABULARY.
ANOTHER BREADFRUIT?
YOU MUST BE JOKING, SIMICO.
IT'S YOUR 20TH PIECE TODAY.
ALRIGHT! ALRIGHT! AND I BETTER PREPARE A CUP OF TEA FOR MYSELF AS WELL.
SO "SQUEEK" MEANS THAT...
HUMANS ENTERED THE SANCTUARY.

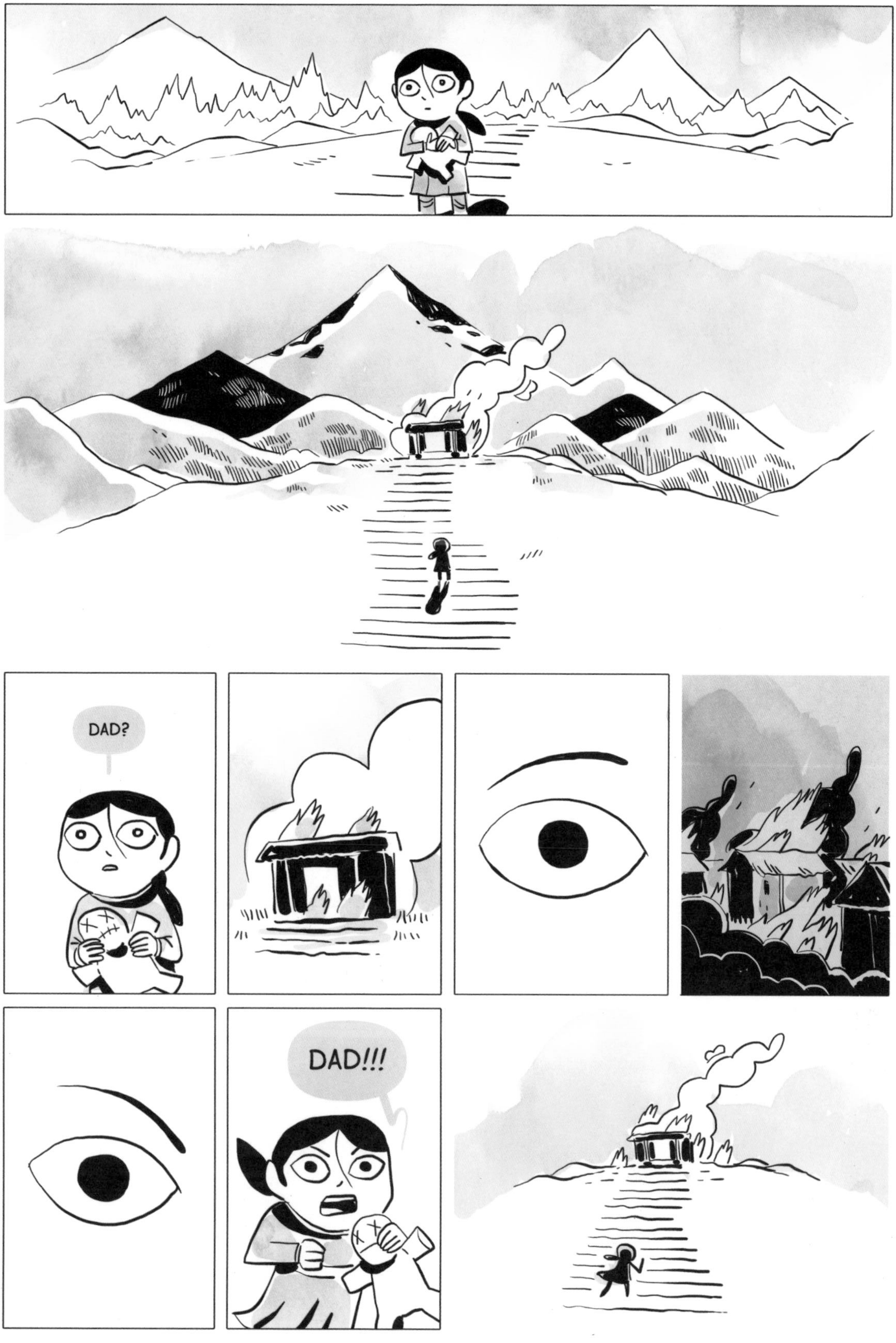
DAD?
DAD!!!

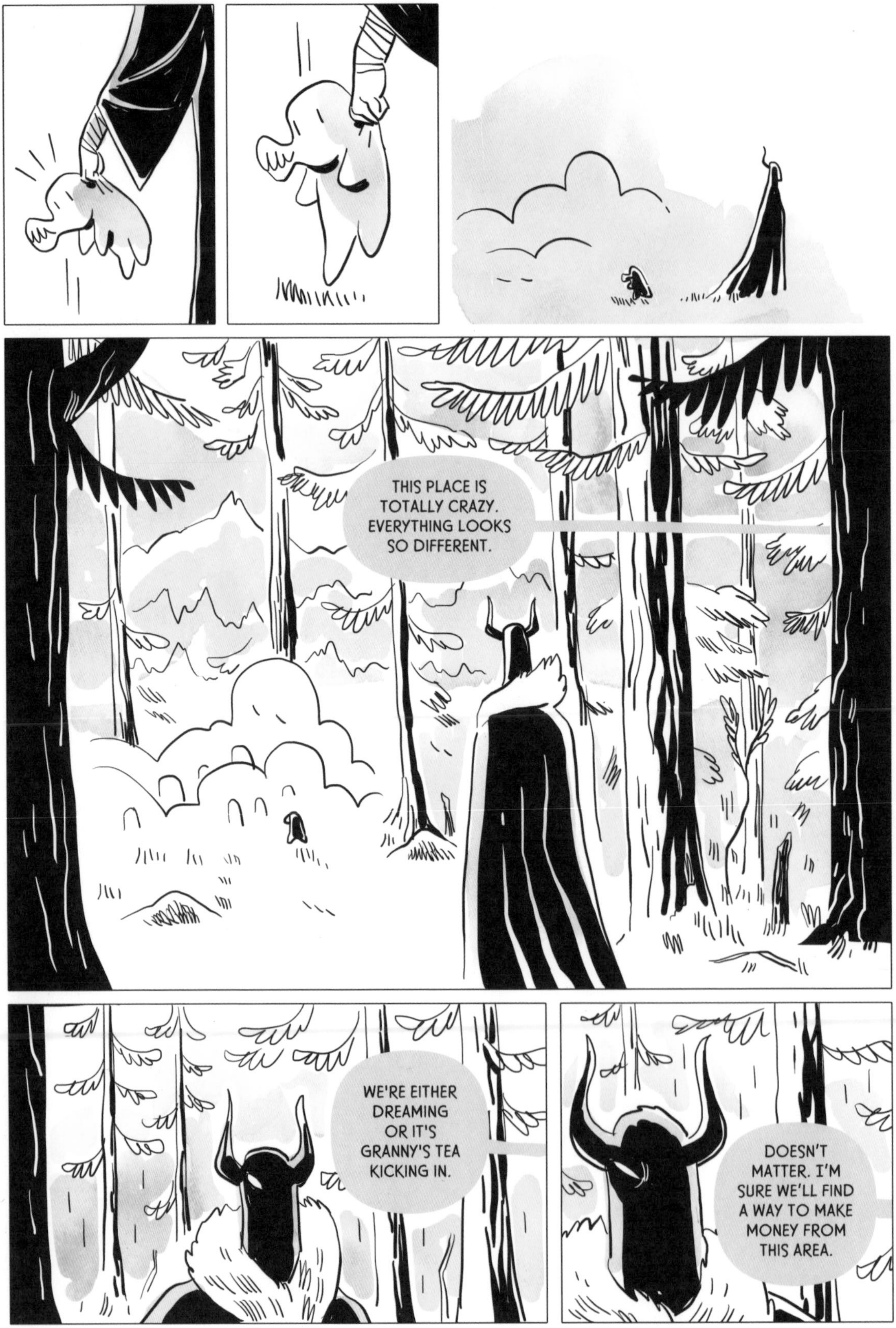
THIS PLACE IS TOTALLY CRAZY. EVERYTHING LOOKS SO DIFFERENT.
WE'RE EITHER DREAMING OR IT'S GRANNY'S TEA KICKING IN.
DOESN'T MATTER. I'M SURE WE'LL FIND A WAY TO MAKE MONEY FROM THIS AREA.

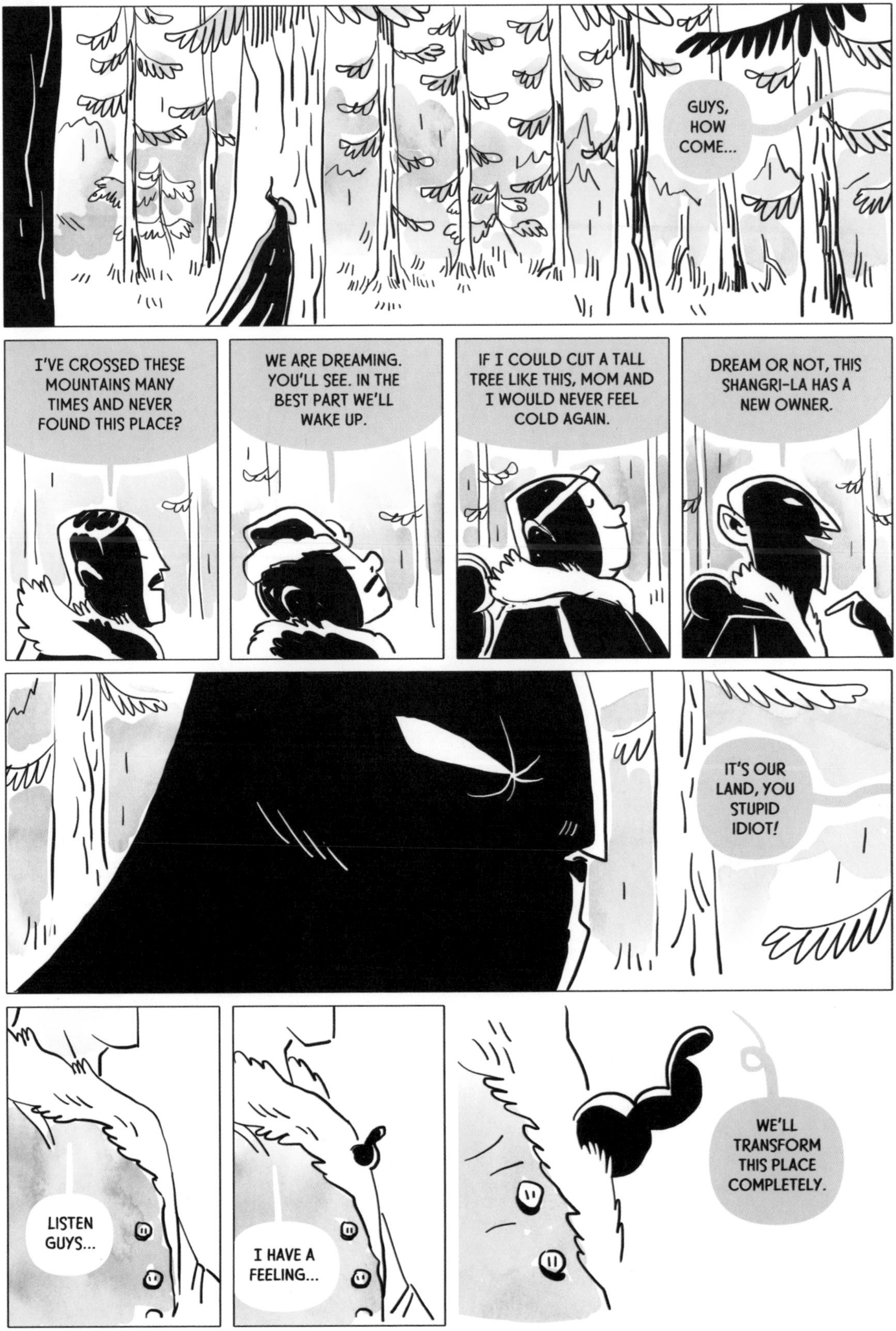
GUYS, HOW COME...
I'VE CROSSED THESE MOUNTAINS MANY TIMES AND NEVER FOUND THIS PLACE?
WE ARE DREAMING. YOU'LL SEE. IN THE BEST PART WE'LL WAKE UP.
IF I COULD CUT A TALL TREE LIKE THIS, MOM AND I WOULD NEVER FEEL COLD AGAIN.
DREAM OR NOT, THIS SHANGRI-LA HAS A NEW OWNER.
IT'S OUR LAND, YOU STUPID IDIOT!
LISTEN GUYS...
I HAVE A FEELING...
WE'LL TRANSFORM THIS PLACE COMPLETELY.

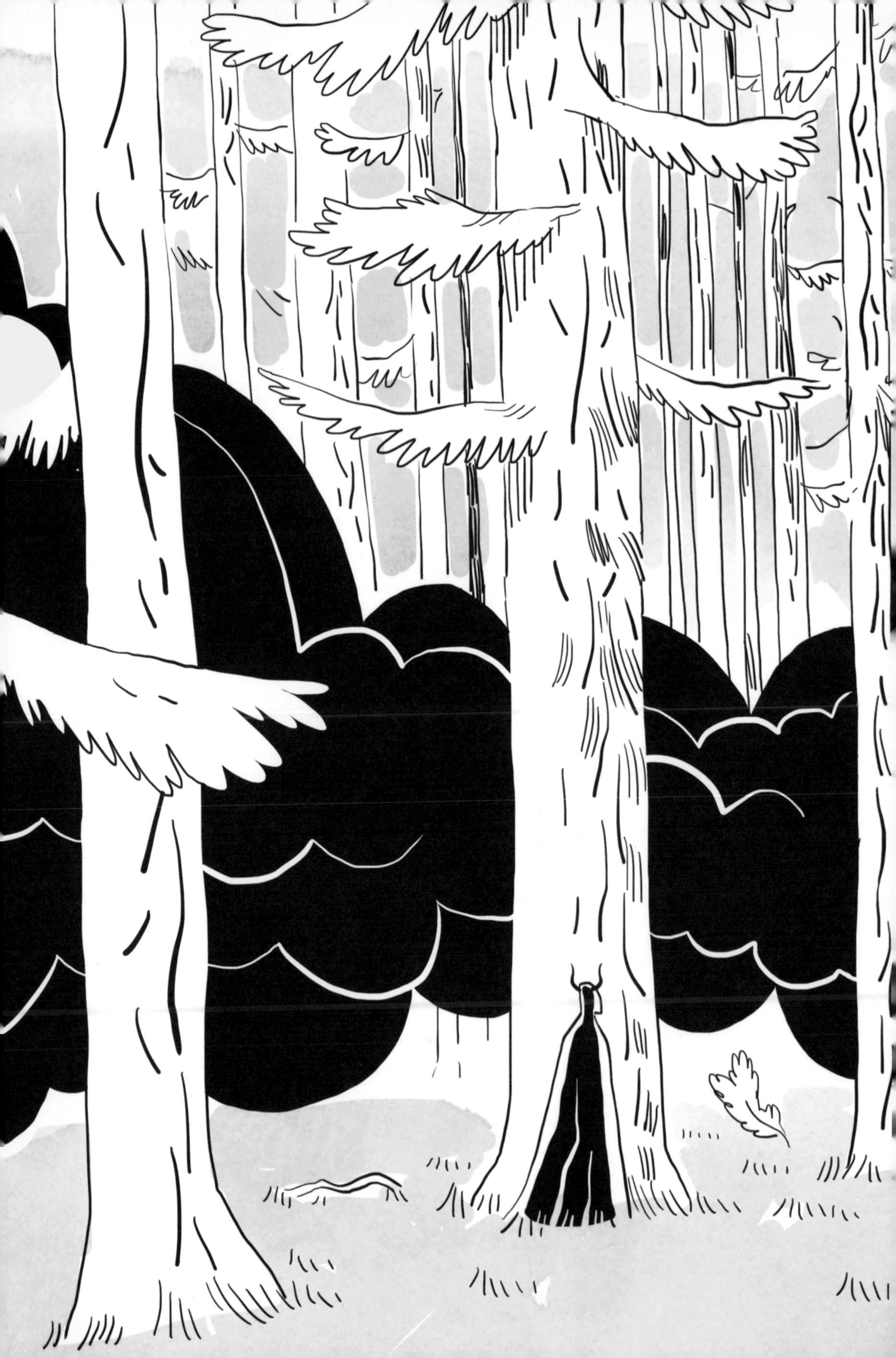

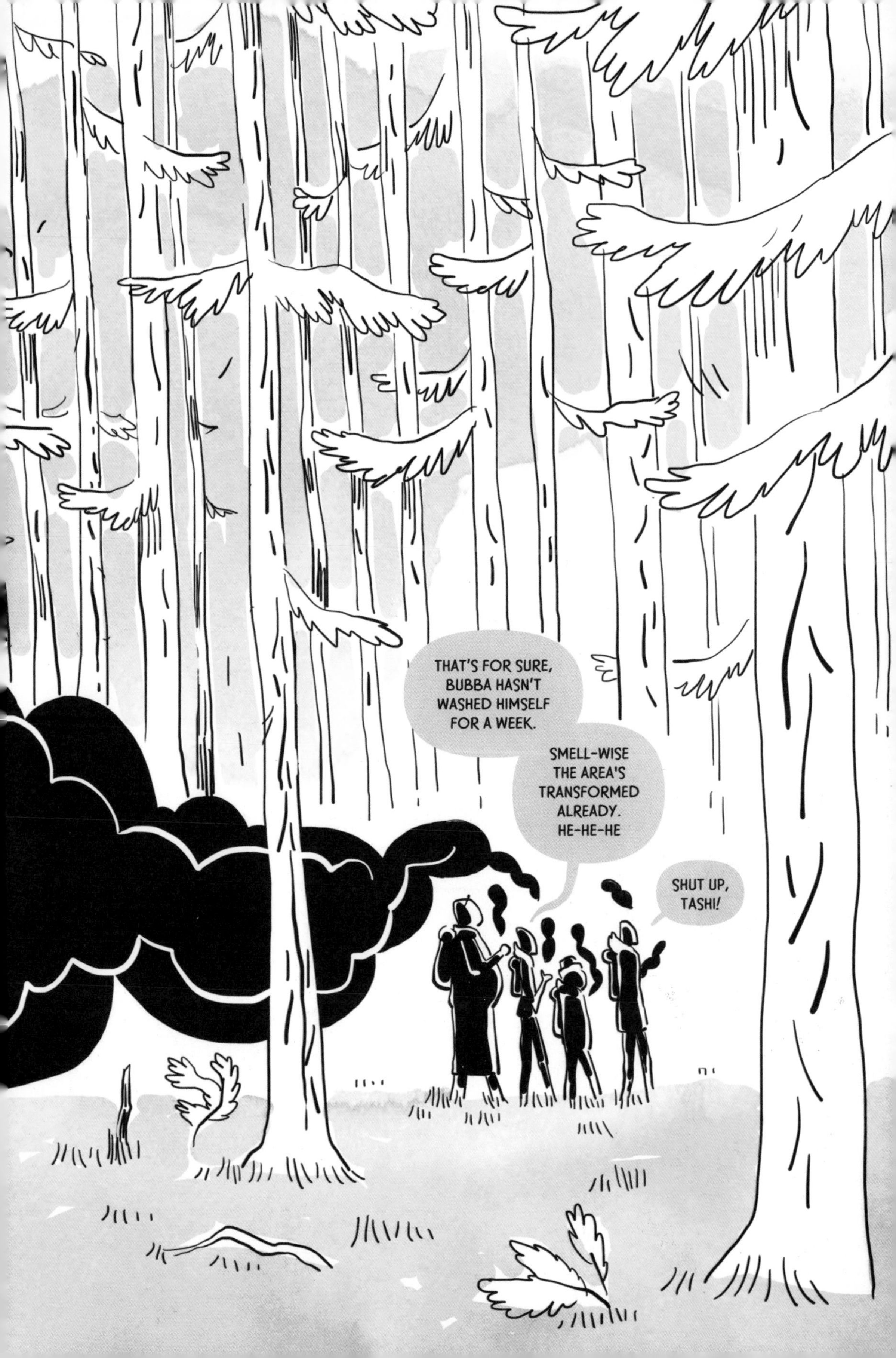
THAT'S FOR SURE, BUBBA HASN'T WASHED HIMSELF FOR A WEEK.
SMELL-WISE THE AREA'S TRANSFORMED ALREADY. HE-HE-HE
SHUT UP, TASHI!

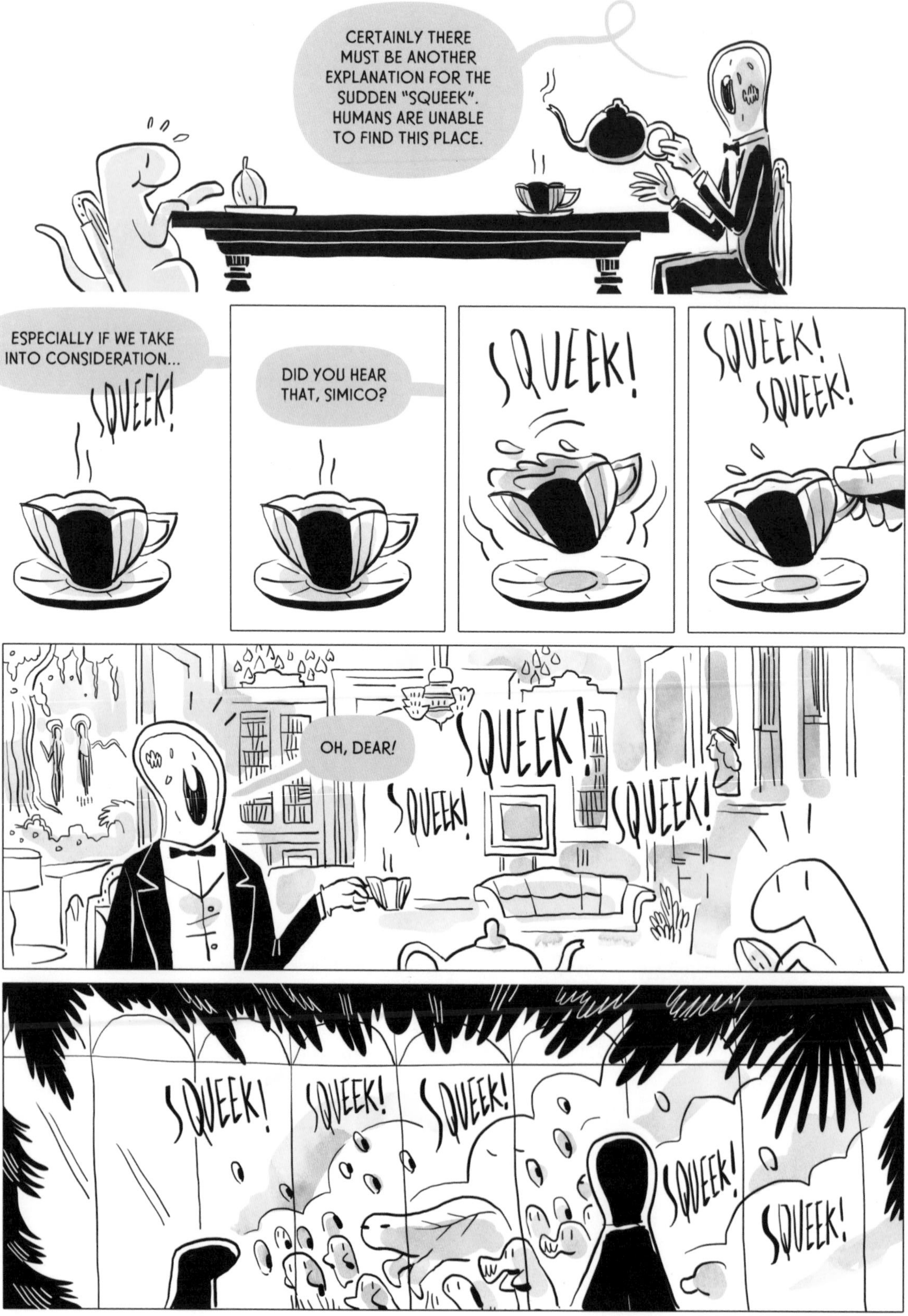
CERTAINLY THERE MUST BE ANOTHER EXPLANATION FOR THE SUDDEN "SQUEEK". HUMANS ARE UNABLE TO FIND THIS PLACE.
ESPECIALLY IF WE TAKE INTO CONSIDERATION...
SQUEEK!
DID YOU HEAR THAT, SIMICO?
SQUEEK!
SQUEEK! SQUEEK!
OH, DEAR!
SQUEEK!
SQUEEK!
SQUEEK!
SQUEEK!
SQUEEK!
SQUEEK!
SQUEEK!
SQUEEK!

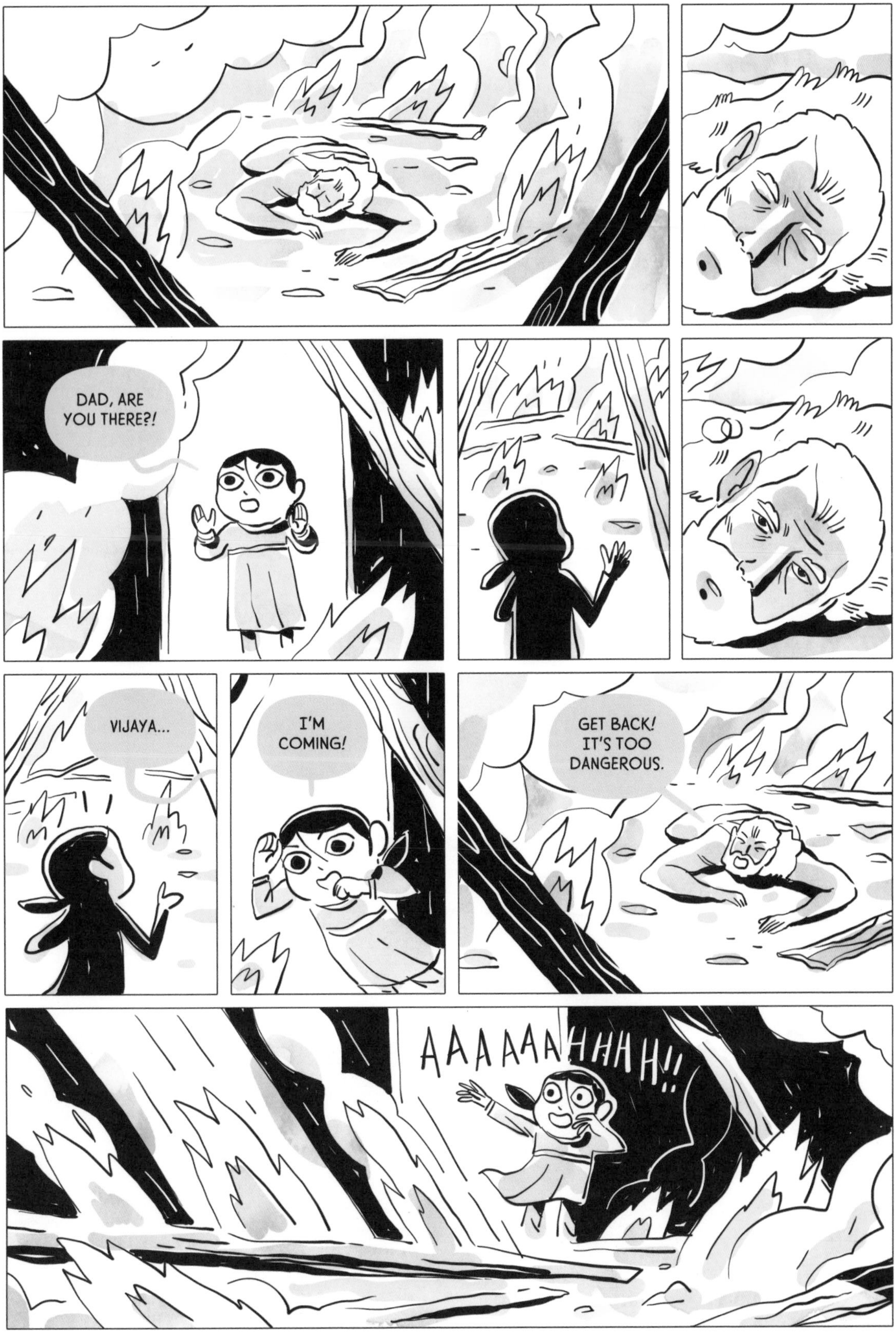
DAD, ARE YOU THERE?!
VIJAYA...
I'M COMING!
GET BACK! IT'S TOO DANGEROUS.
AAAAAAHHHH!!!

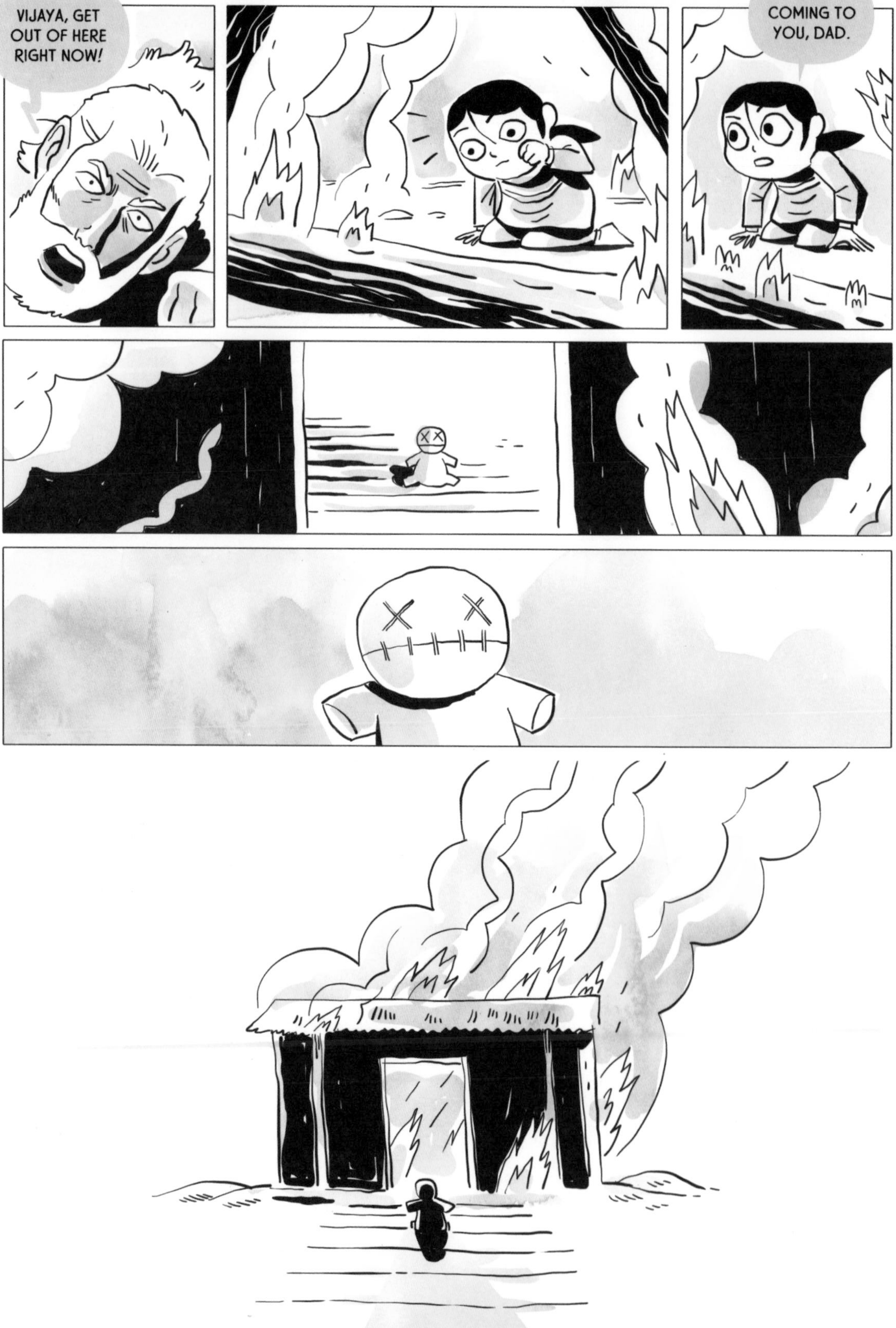
VIJAYA, GET OUT OF HERE RIGHT NOW!
I'M COMING TO YOU, DAD.

THIS PLACE IS GOING TO MAKE US SO RICH.

MOM WOULD LOVE IT HERE!

MRS. SHANTI WOULD BE HAPPY ANYWHERE AWAY FROM HER NEIGHBORS. HE-HE-HE

SO TRUE.

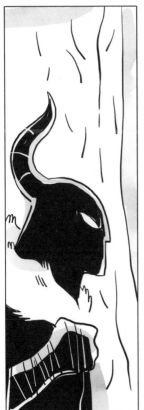

I'LL BE GLAD WHEN WE FIND A WAY OUT OF HERE.

I HAVE A BAD FEELING ABOUT THIS PLACE.

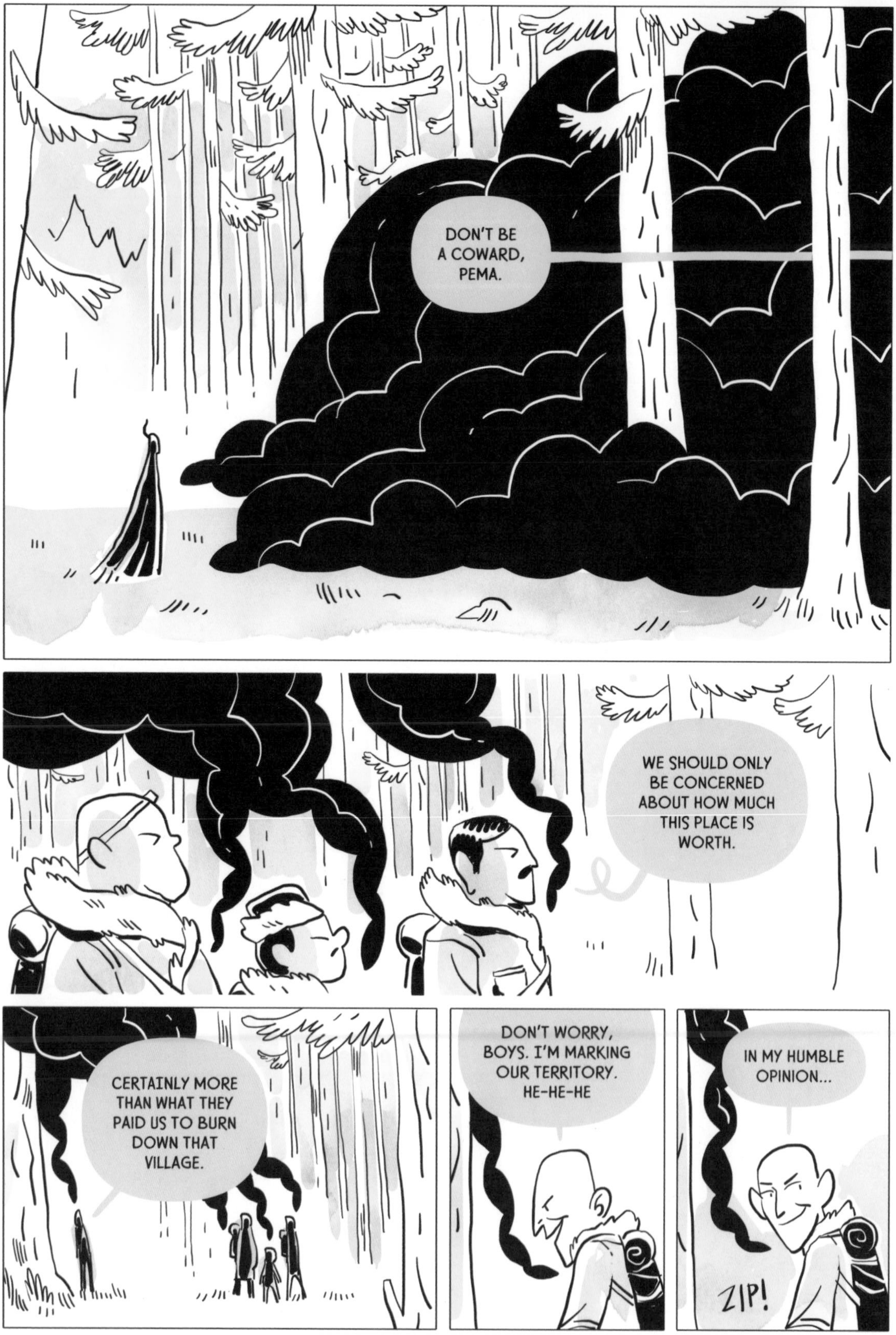
DON'T BE A COWARD, PEMA.
WE SHOULD ONLY BE CONCERNED ABOUT HOW MUCH THIS PLACE IS WORTH.
CERTAINLY MORE THAN WHAT THEY PAID US TO BURN DOWN THAT VILLAGE.
DON'T WORRY, BOYS. I'M MARKING OUR TERRITORY. HE-HE-HE
IN MY HUMBLE OPINION...
ZIP!

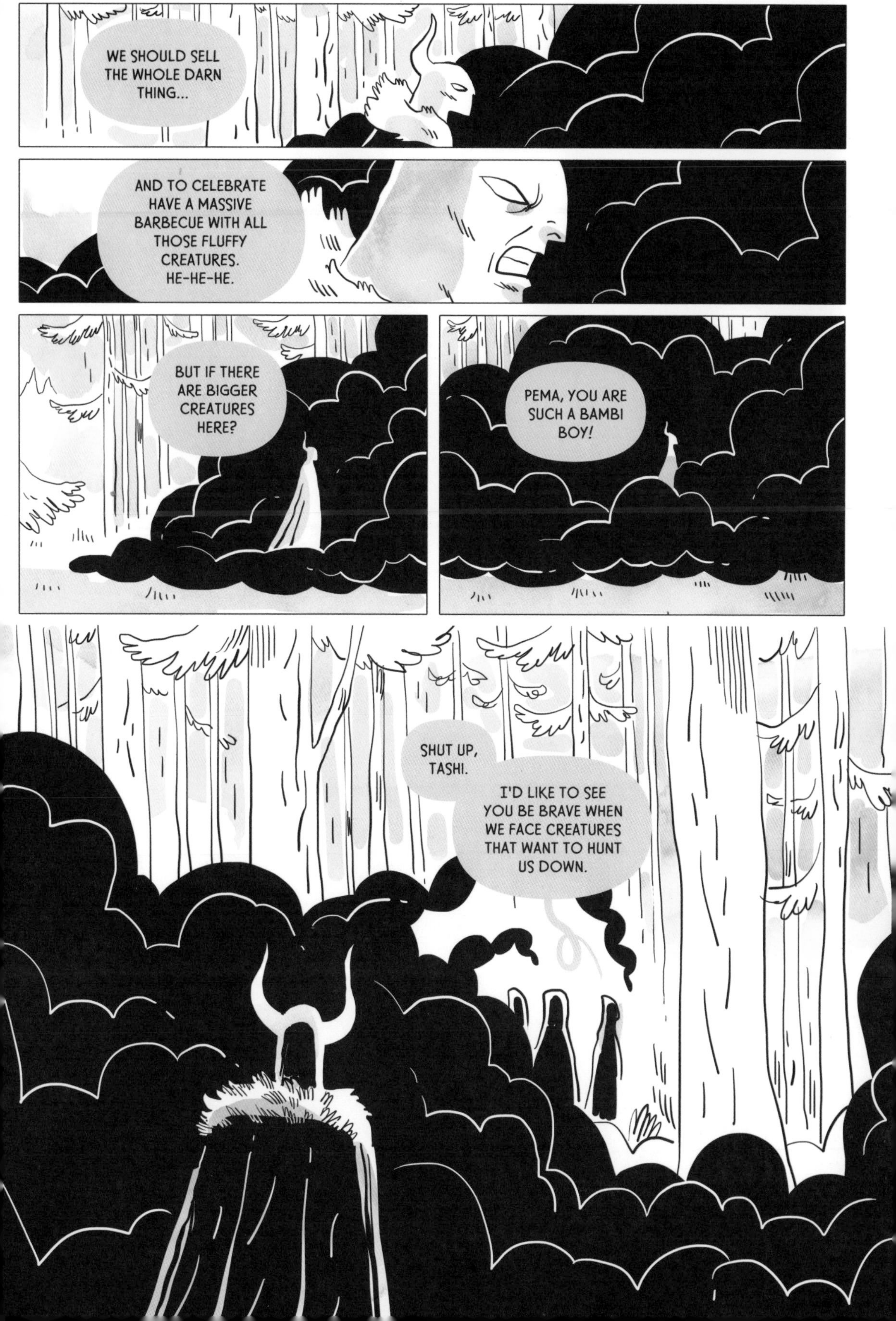
WE SHOULD SELL THE WHOLE DARN THING...
AND TO CELEBRATE HAVE A MASSIVE BARBECUE WITH ALL THOSE FLUFFY CREATURES. HE-HE-HE.
BUT IF THERE ARE BIGGER CREATURES HERE?
PEMA, YOU ARE SUCH A BAMBI BOY!
SHUT UP, TASHI.
I'D LIKE TO SEE YOU BE BRAVE WHEN WE FACE CREATURES THAT WANT TO HUNT US DOWN.

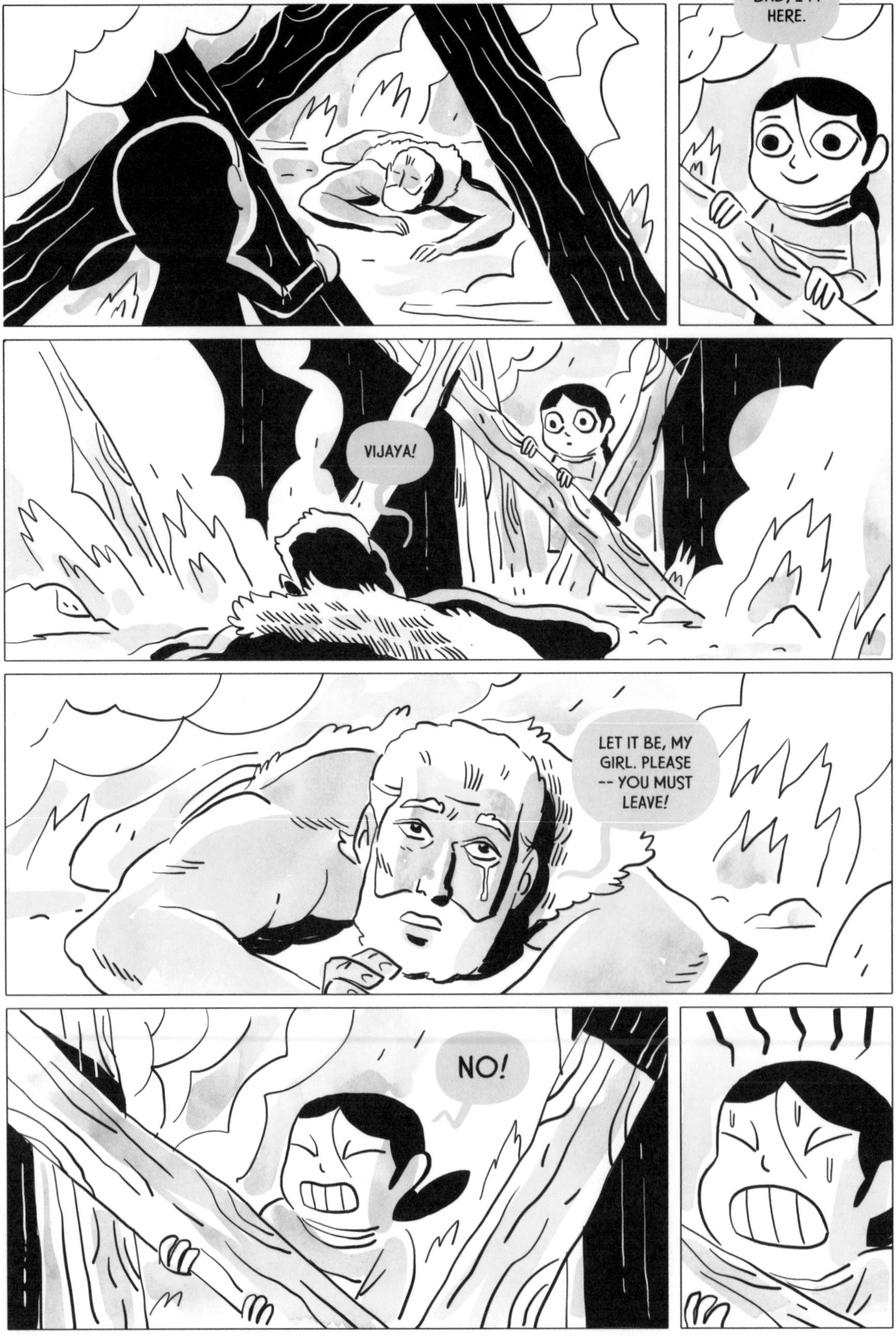
DAD, I'M HERE.
VIJAYA!
LET IT BE, MY GIRL. PLEASE -- YOU MUST LEAVE!
NO!

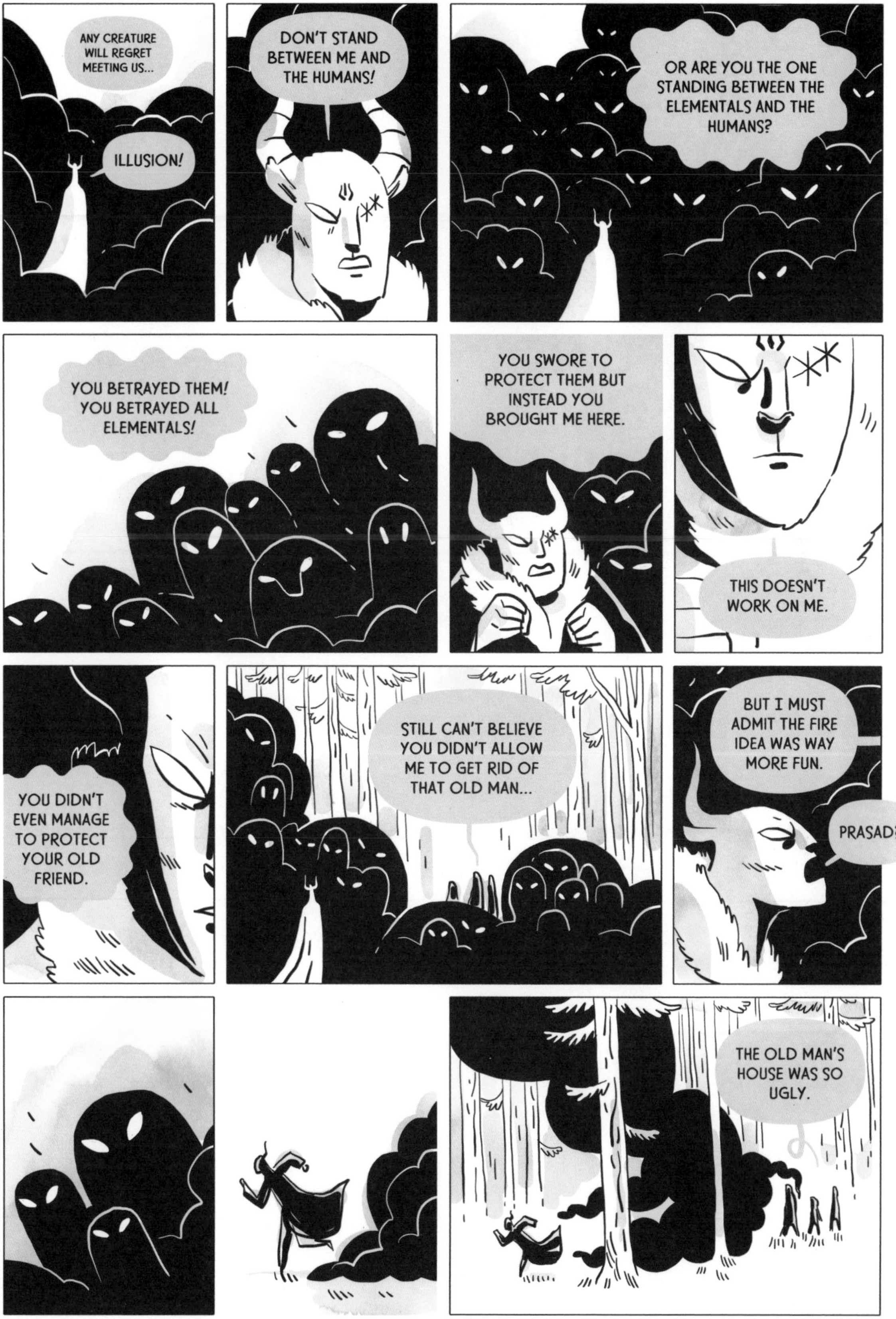
ANY CREATURE WILL REGRET MEETING US...
ILLUSION!
DON'T STAND BETWEEN ME AND THE HUMANS!
OR ARE YOU THE ONE STANDING BETWEEN THE ELEMENTALS AND THE HUMANS?
YOU BETRAYED THEM! YOU BETRAYED ALL ELEMENTALS!
YOU SWORE TO PROTECT THEM BUT INSTEAD YOU BROUGHT ME HERE.
THIS DOESN'T WORK ON ME.
YOU DIDN'T EVEN MANAGE TO PROTECT YOUR OLD FRIEND.
STILL CAN'T BELIEVE YOU DIDN'T ALLOW ME TO GET RID OF THAT OLD MAN...
BUT I MUST ADMIT THE FIRE IDEA WAS WAY MORE FUN.
PRASAD?!
THE OLD MAN'S HOUSE WAS SO UGLY.

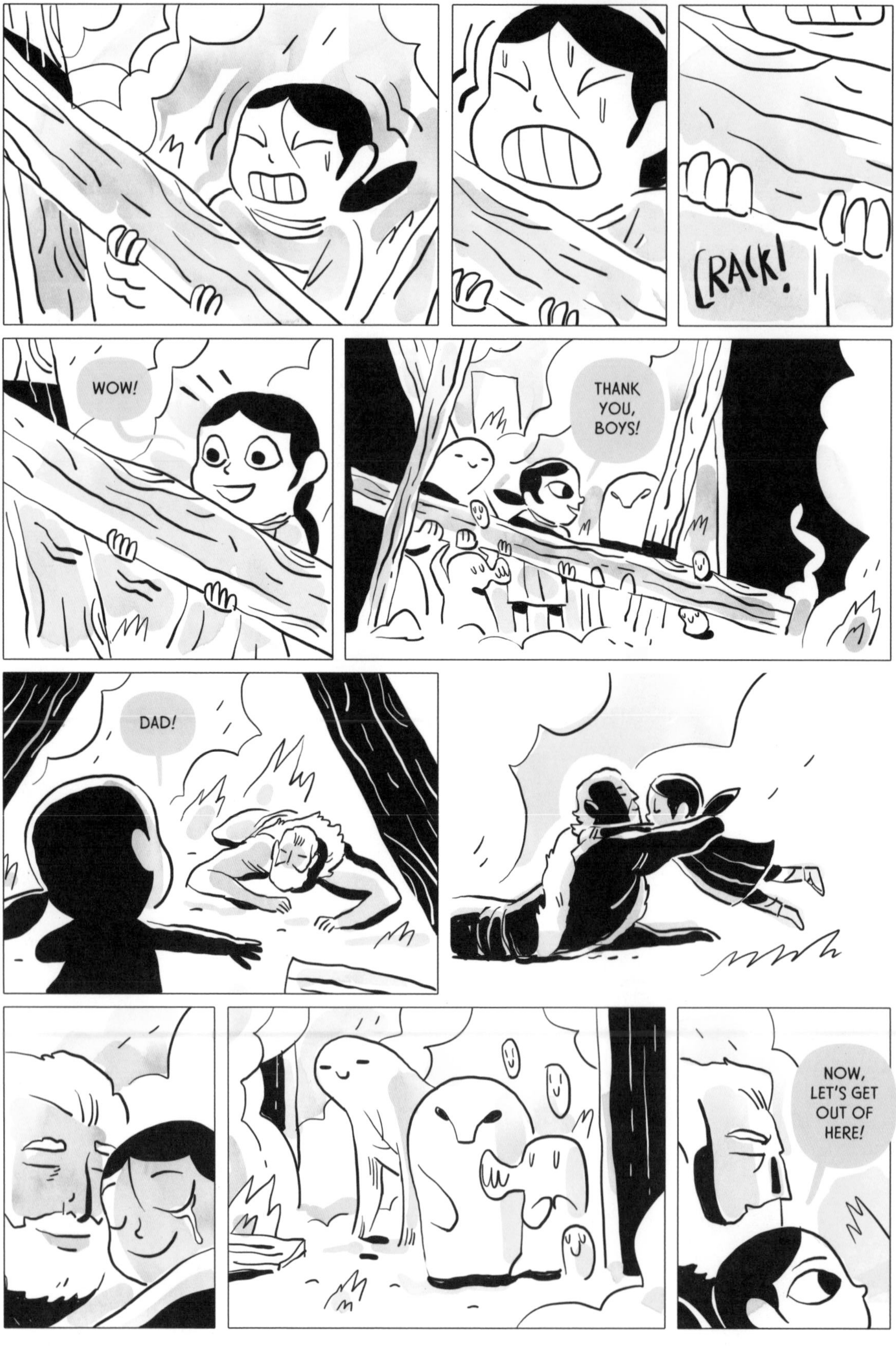
CRACK!
WOW!
THANK YOU, BOYS!
DAD!
NOW, LET'S GET OUT OF HERE!

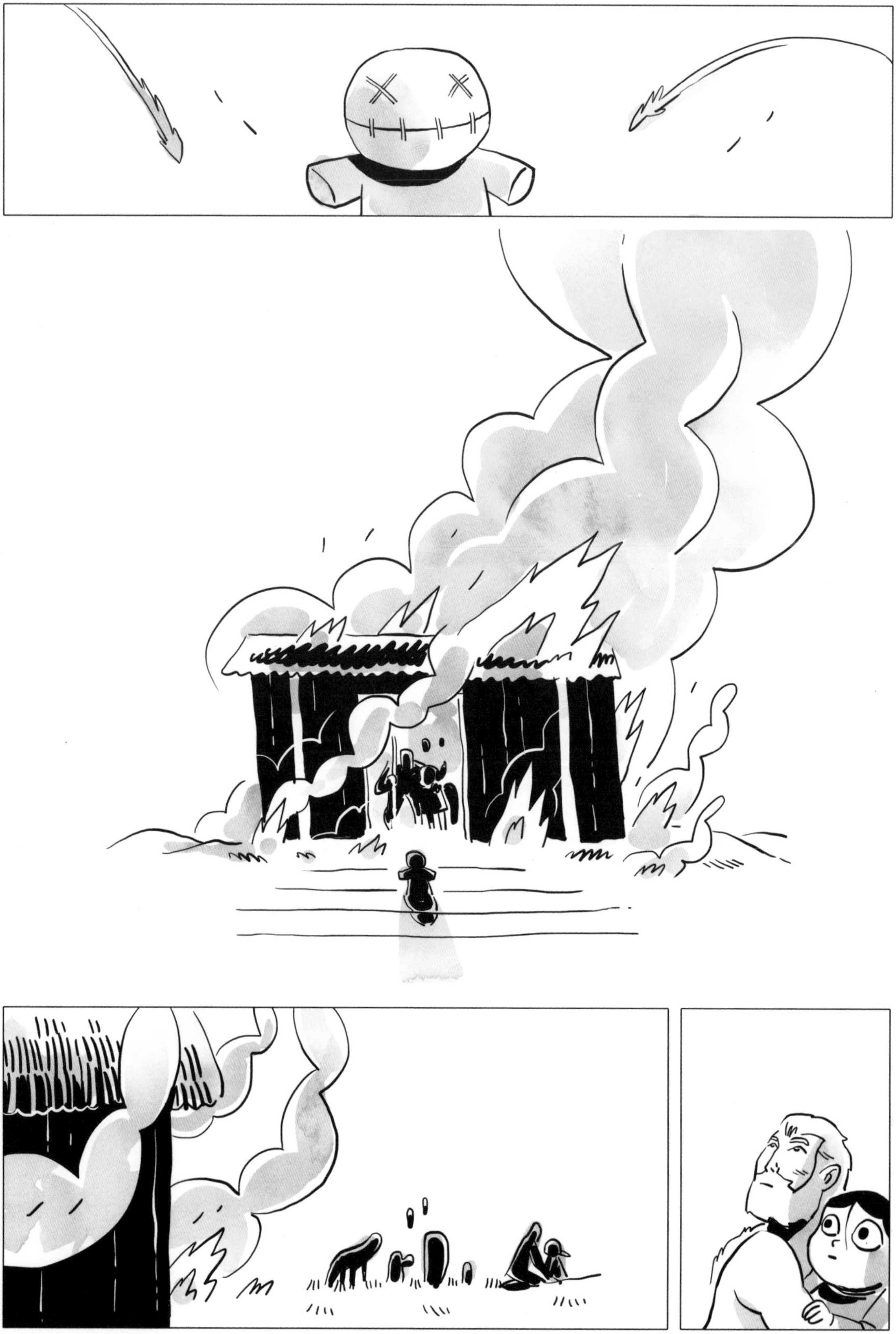

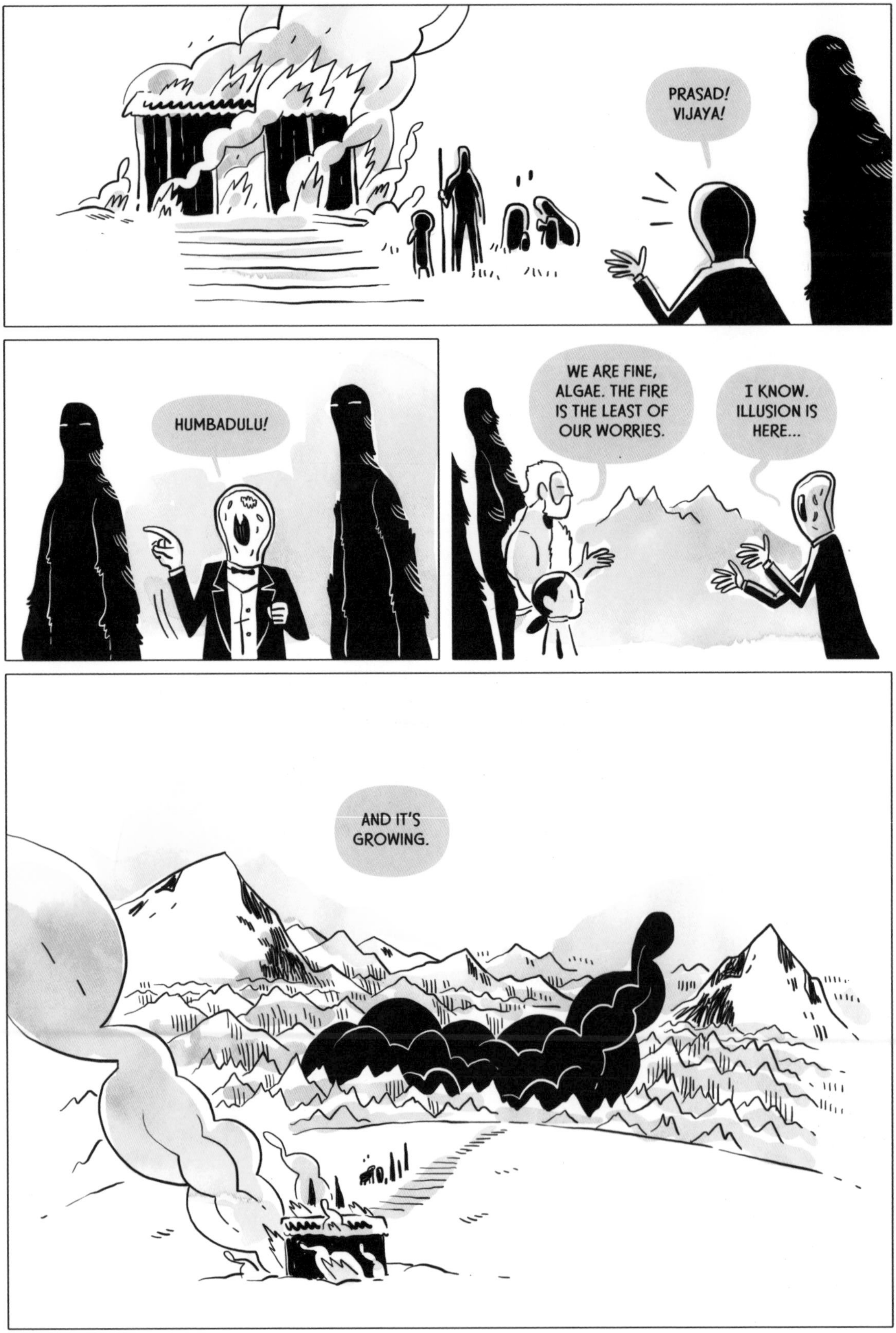
PRASAD! VIJAYA!
HUMBADULU!
WE ARE FINE, ALGAE. THE FIRE IS THE LEAST OF OUR WORRIES.
I KNOW. ILLUSION IS HERE...
AND IT'S GROWING.

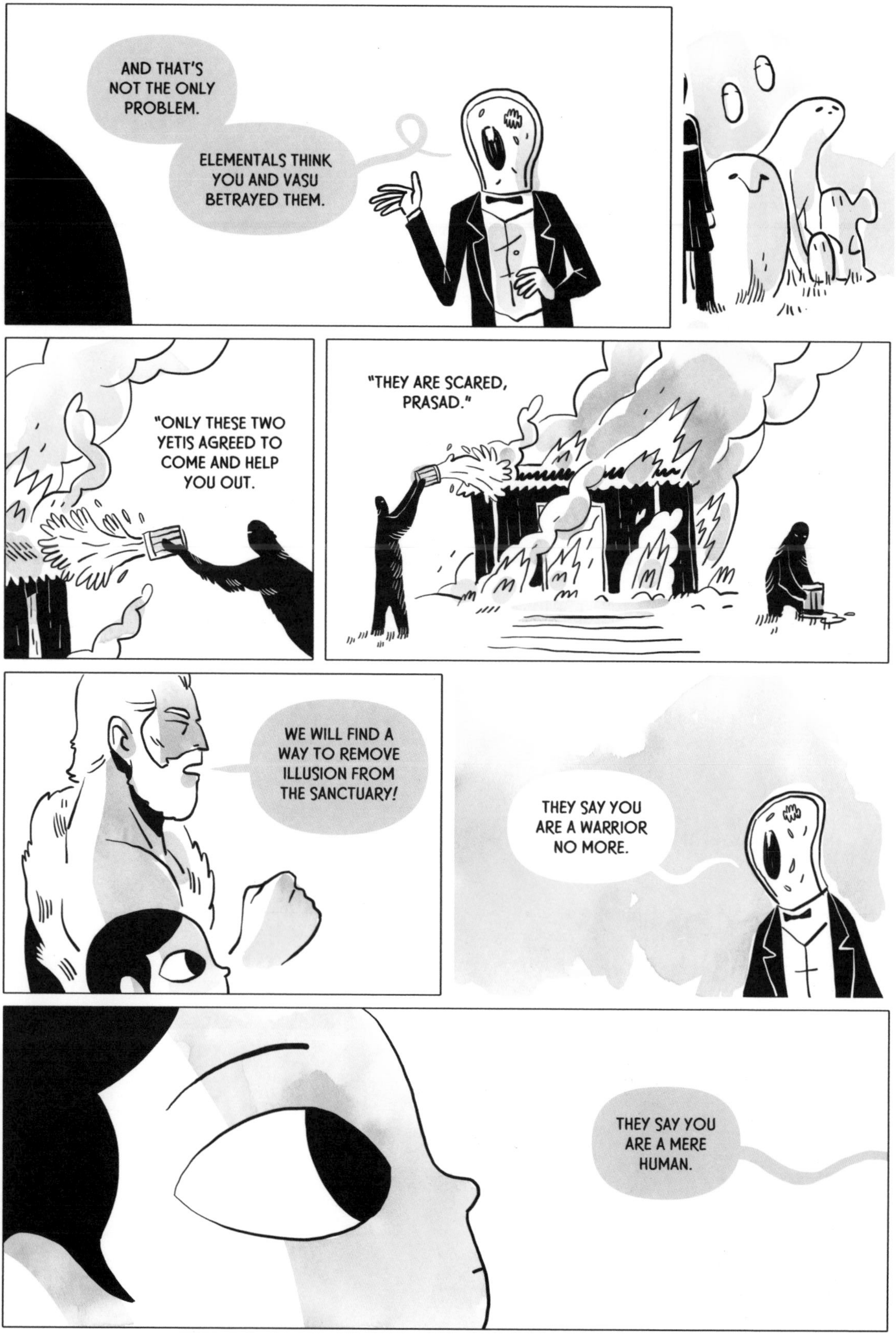
AND THAT'S NOT THE ONLY PROBLEM.
ELEMENTALS THINK YOU AND VASU BETRAYED THEM.
"ONLY THESE TWO YETIS AGREED TO COME AND HELP YOU OUT.
"THEY ARE SCARED, PRASAD."
WE WILL FIND A WAY TO REMOVE ILLUSION FROM THE SANCTUARY!
THEY SAY YOU ARE A WARRIOR NO MORE.
THEY SAY YOU ARE A MERE HUMAN.

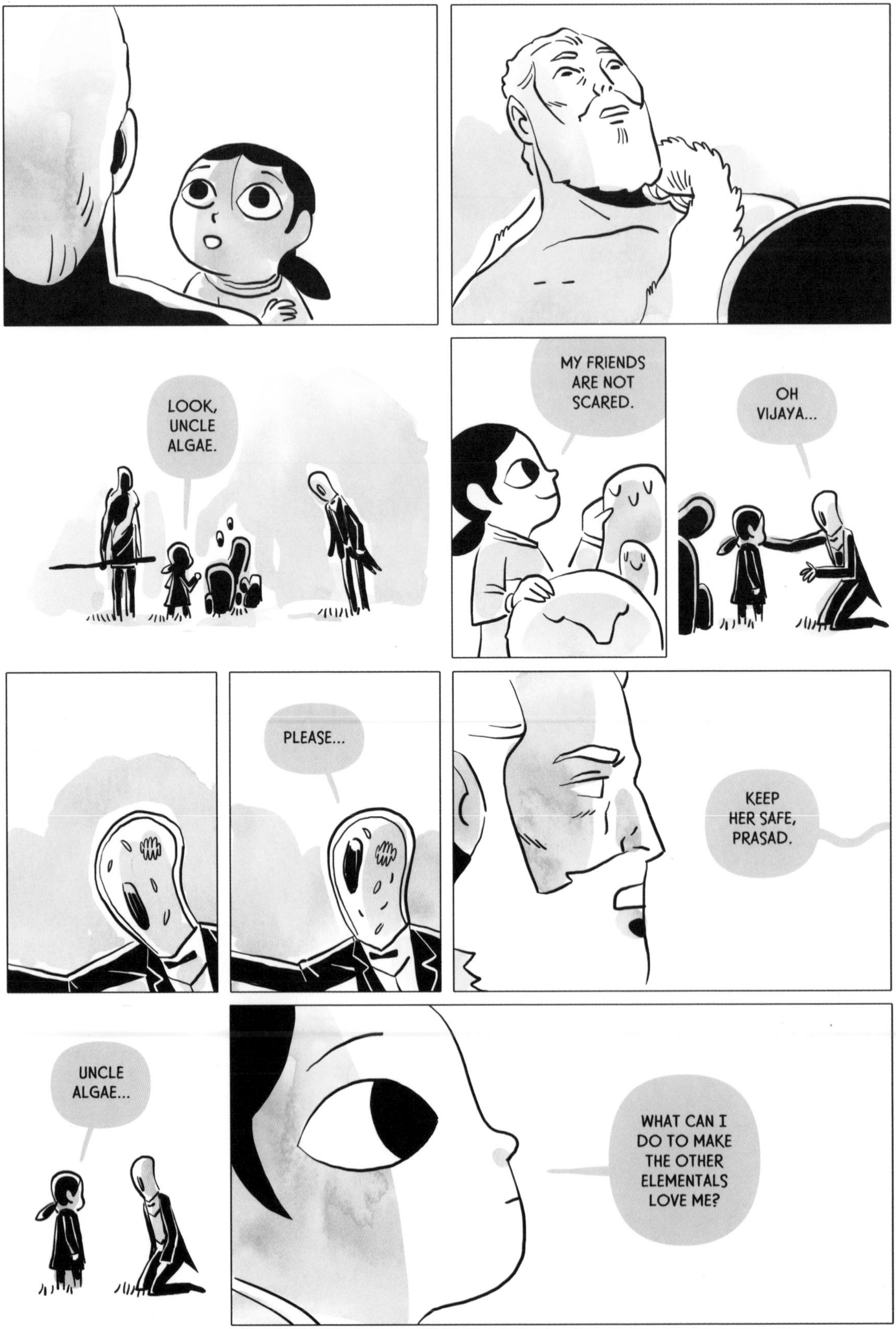
LOOK, UNCLE ALGAE.
MY FRIENDS ARE NOT SCARED.
OH VIJAYA...
PLEASE...
KEEP HER SAFE, PRASAD.
UNCLE ALGAE...
WHAT CAN I DO TO MAKE THE OTHER ELEMENTALS LOVE ME?

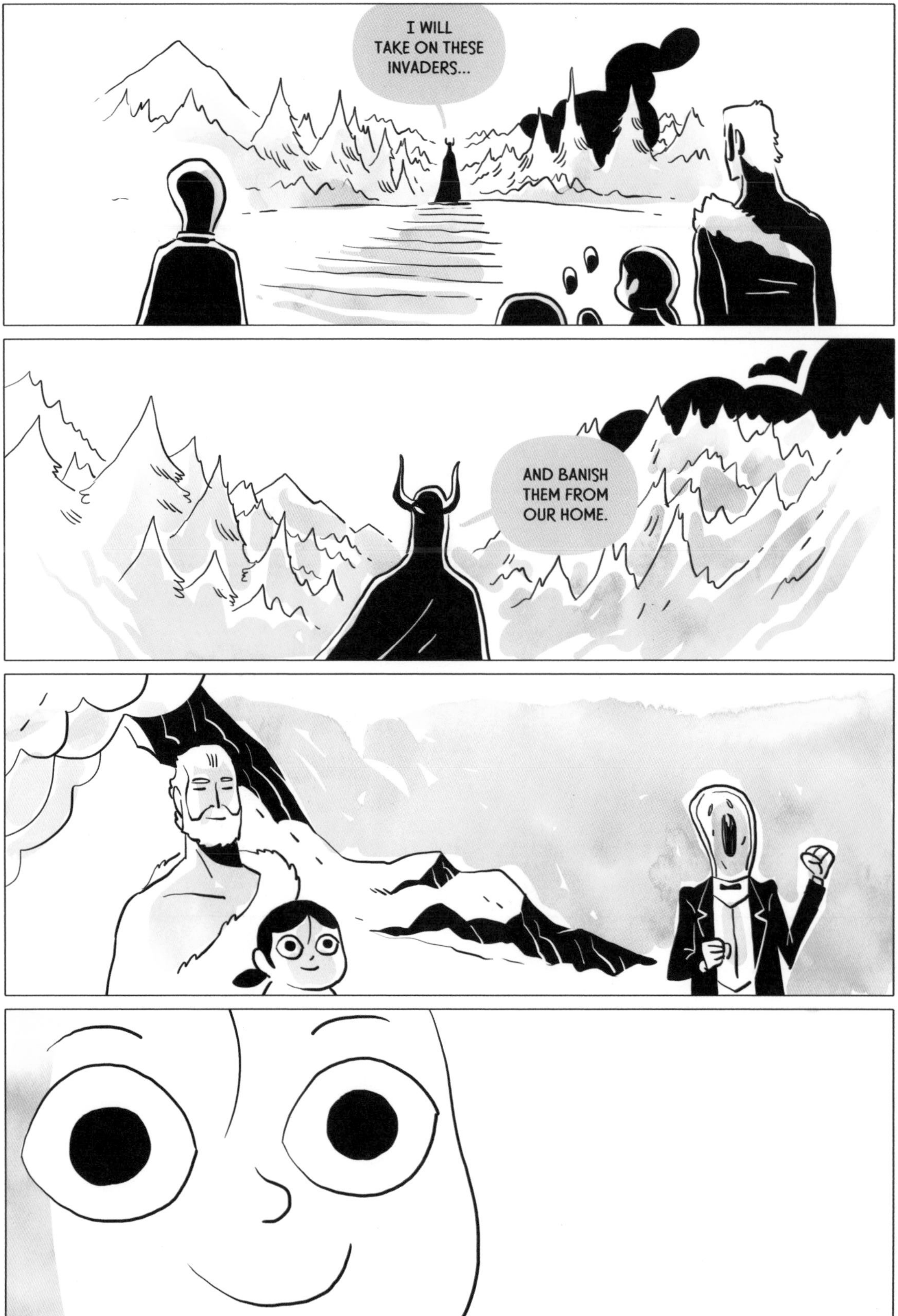
I WILL TAKE ON THESE INVADERS...
AND BANISH THEM FROM OUR HOME.

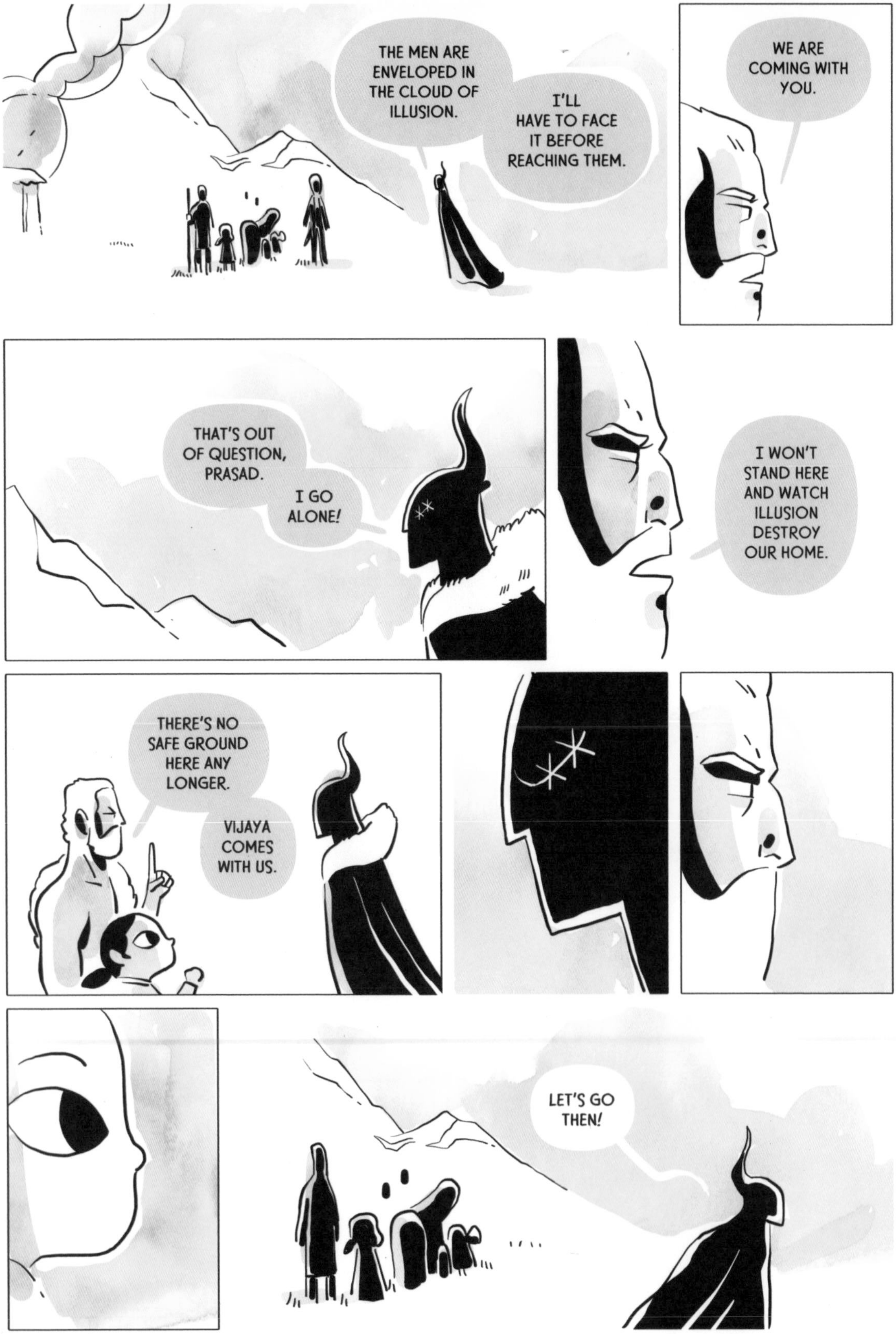

THE MEN ARE ENVELOPED IN THE CLOUD OF ILLUSION.
I'LL HAVE TO FACE IT BEFORE REACHING THEM.
WE ARE COMING WITH YOU.
THAT'S OUT OF QUESTION, PRASAD.
I GO ALONE!
I WON'T STAND HERE AND WATCH ILLUSION DESTROY OUR HOME.
THERE'S NO SAFE GROUND HERE ANY LONGER.
VIJAYA COMES WITH US.
LET'S GO THEN!

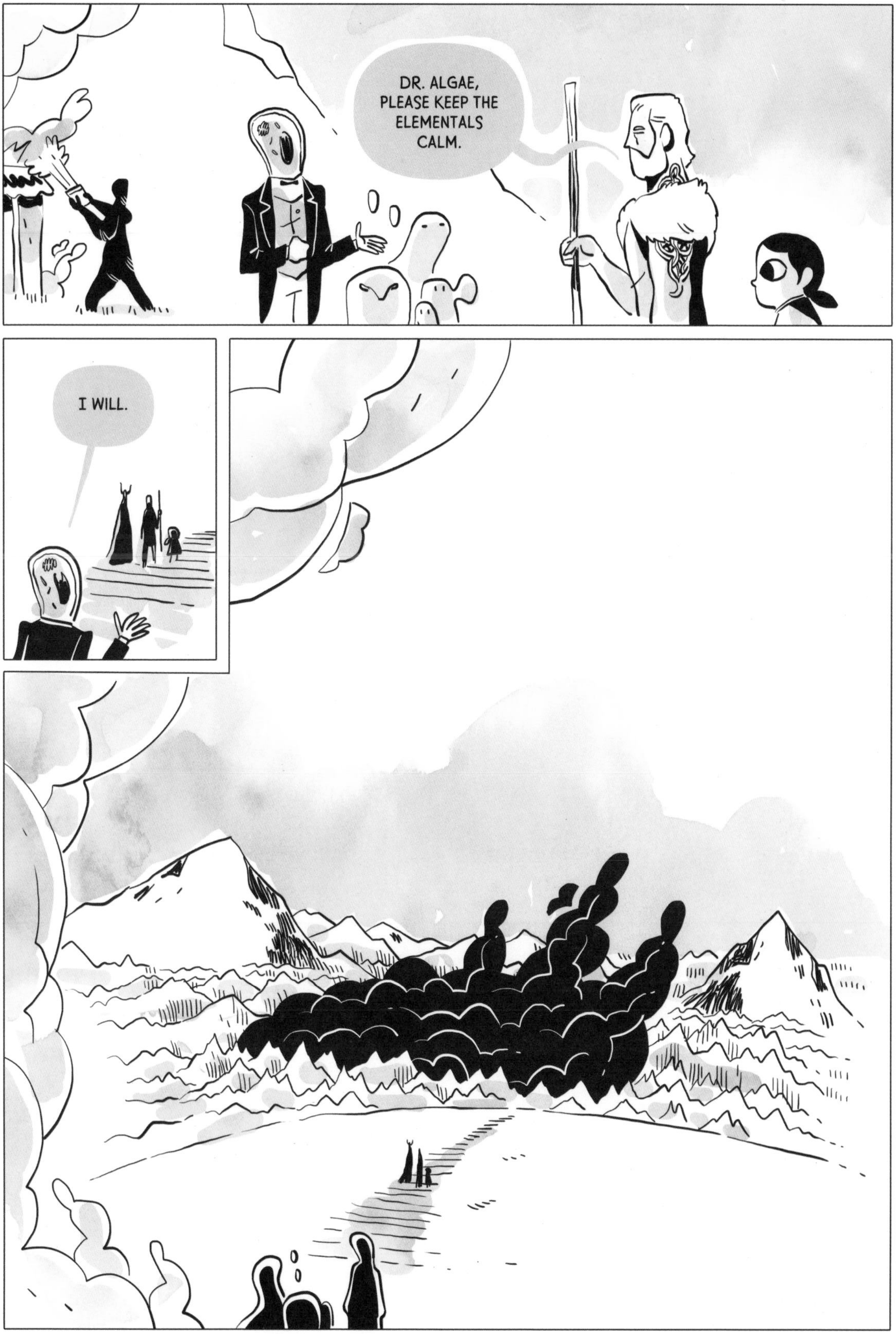
DR. ALGAE, PLEASE KEEP THE ELEMENTALS CALM.
I WILL.

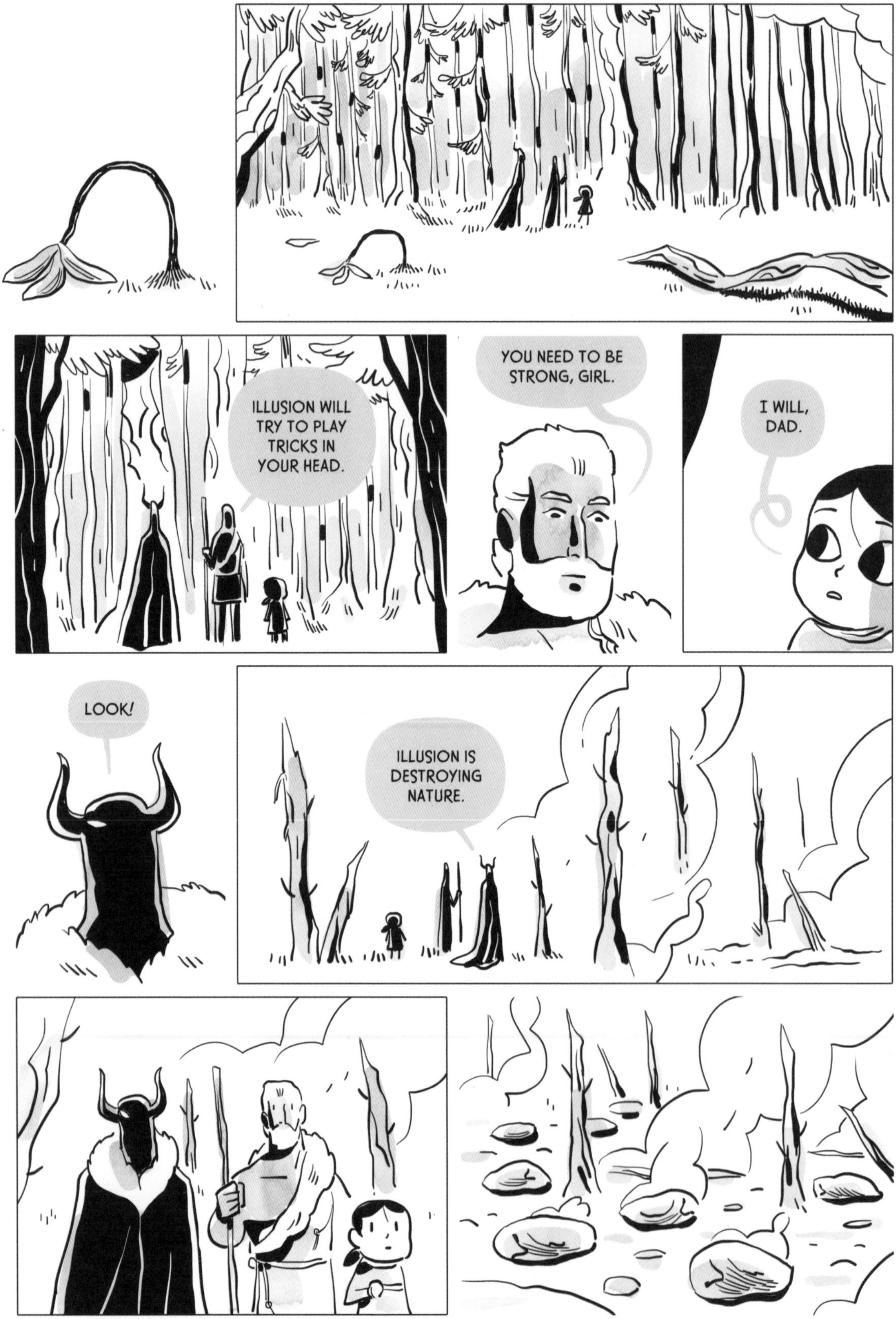
ILLUSION WILL TRY TO PLAY TRICKS IN YOUR HEAD.
YOU NEED TO BE STRONG, GIRL.
I WILL, DAD.
LOOK!
ILLUSION IS DESTROYING NATURE.

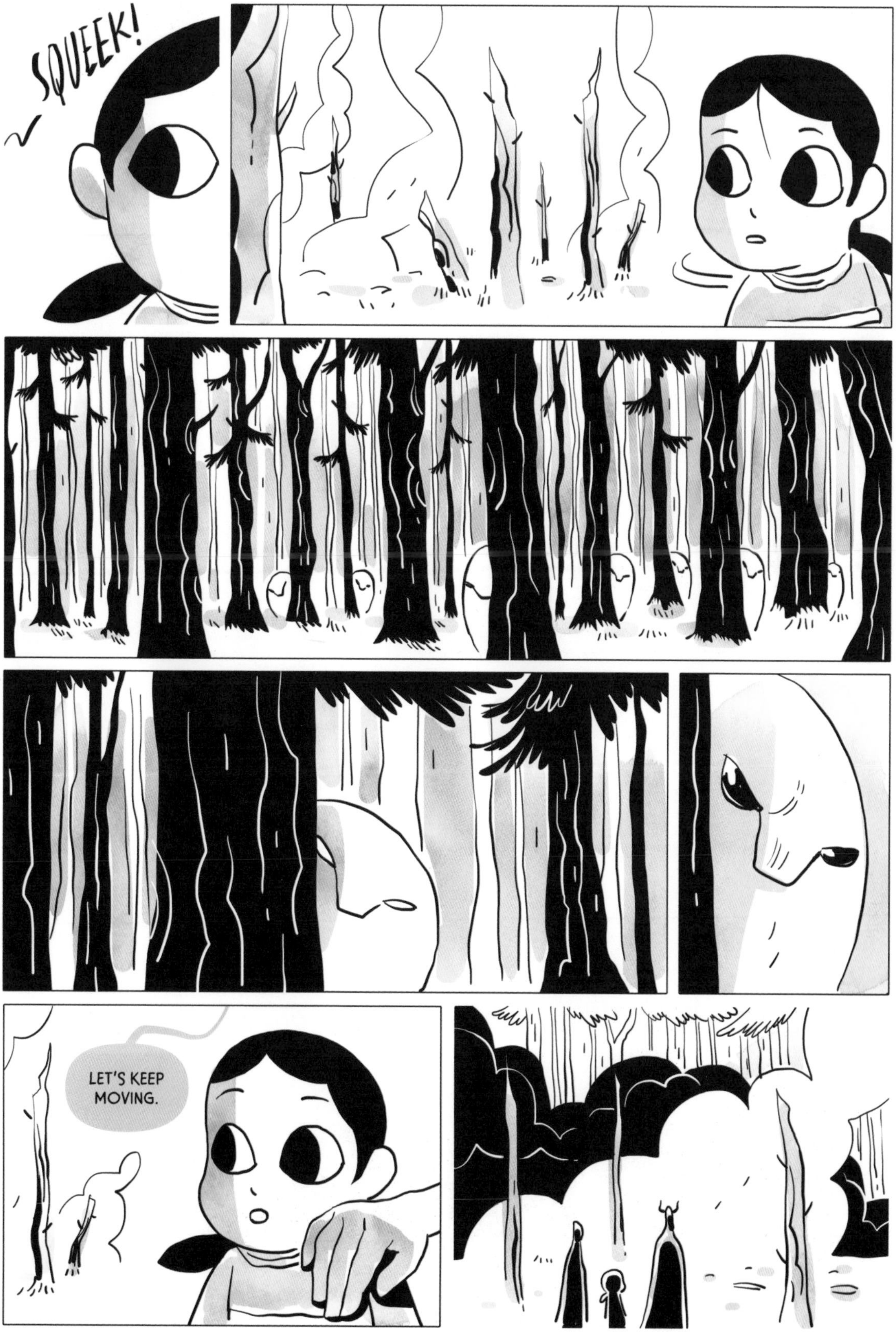
SQUEEK!
LET'S KEEP MOVING.

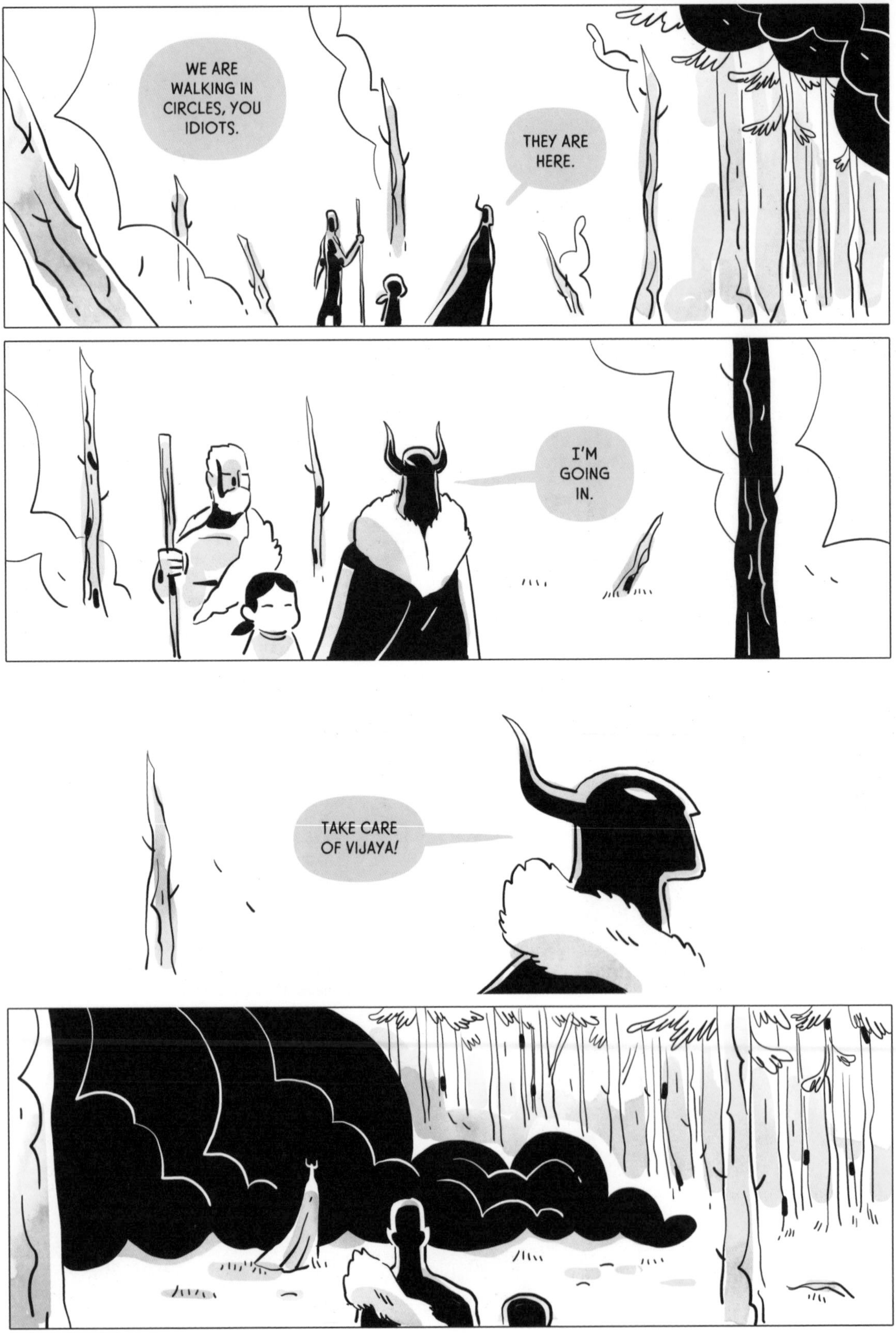
WE ARE WALKING IN CIRCLES, YOU IDIOTS.
THEY ARE HERE.
I'M GOING IN.
TAKE CARE OF VIJAYA!

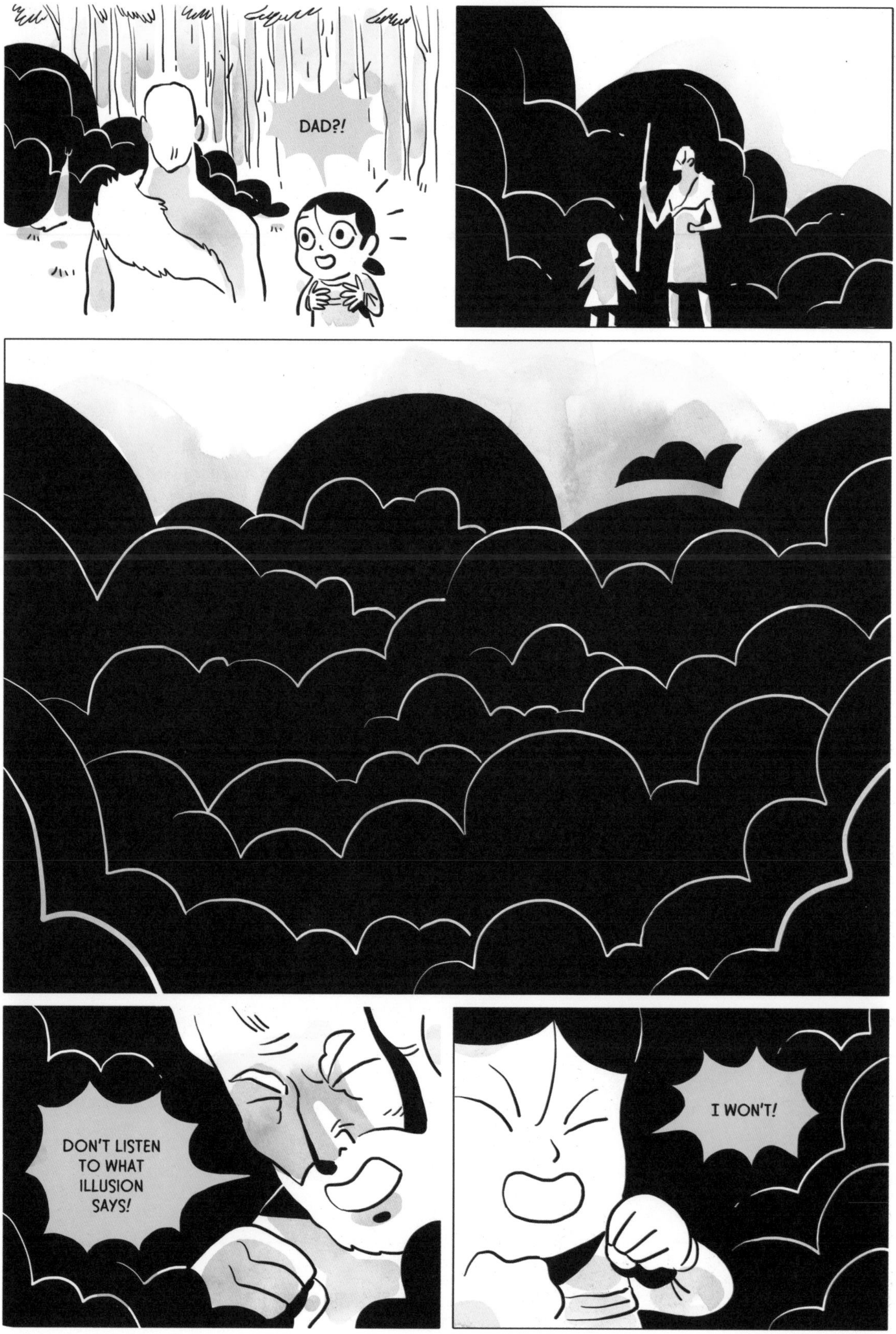
DAD?!
DON'T LISTEN TO WHAT ILLUSION SAYS!
I WON'T!

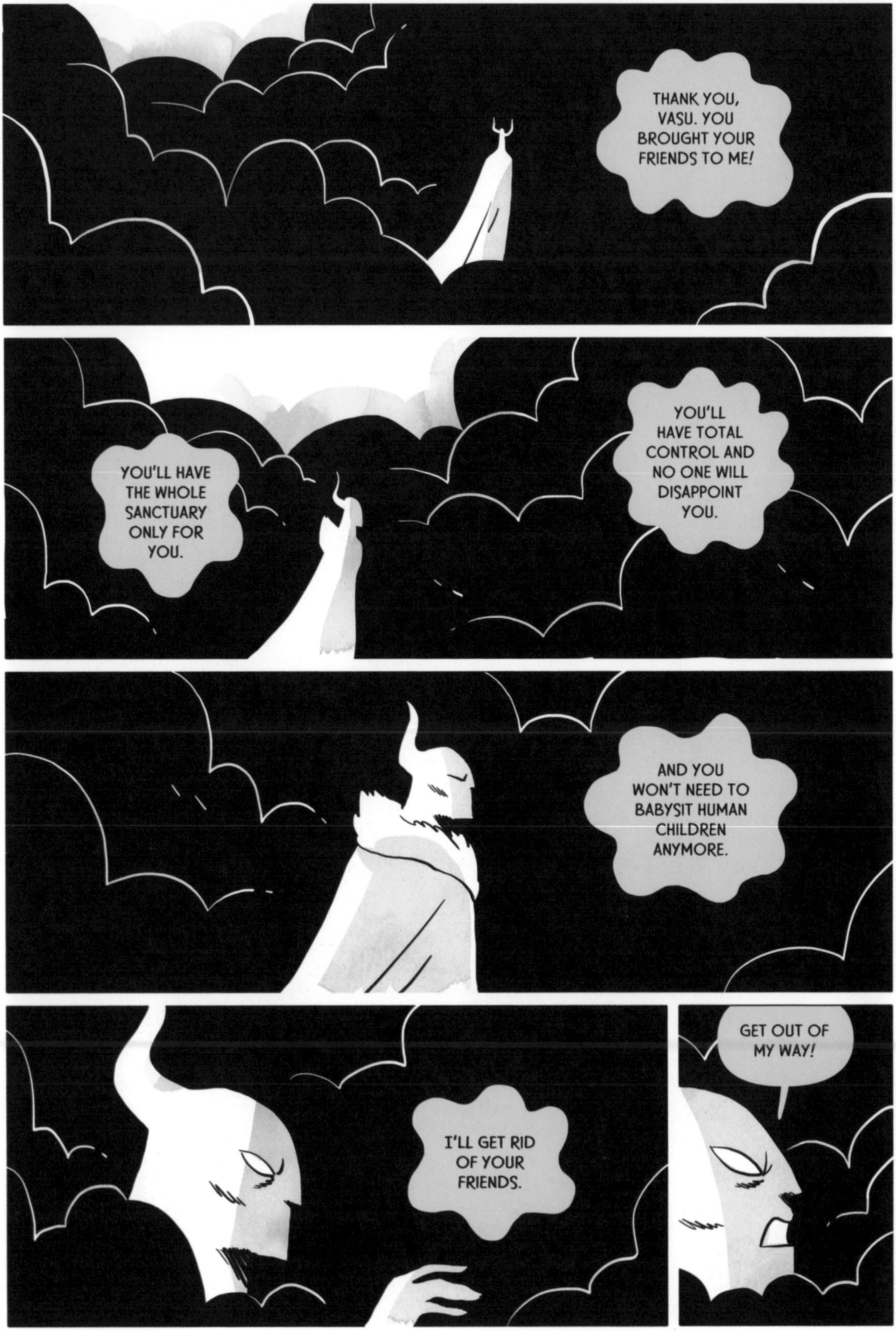
THANK YOU, VASU. YOU BROUGHT YOUR FRIENDS TO ME!
YOU'LL HAVE THE WHOLE SANCTUARY ONLY FOR YOU.
YOU'LL HAVE TOTAL CONTROL AND NO ONE WILL DISAPPOINT YOU.
AND YOU WON'T NEED TO BABYSIT HUMAN CHILDREN ANYMORE.
I'LL GET RID OF YOUR FRIENDS.
GET OUT OF MY WAY!

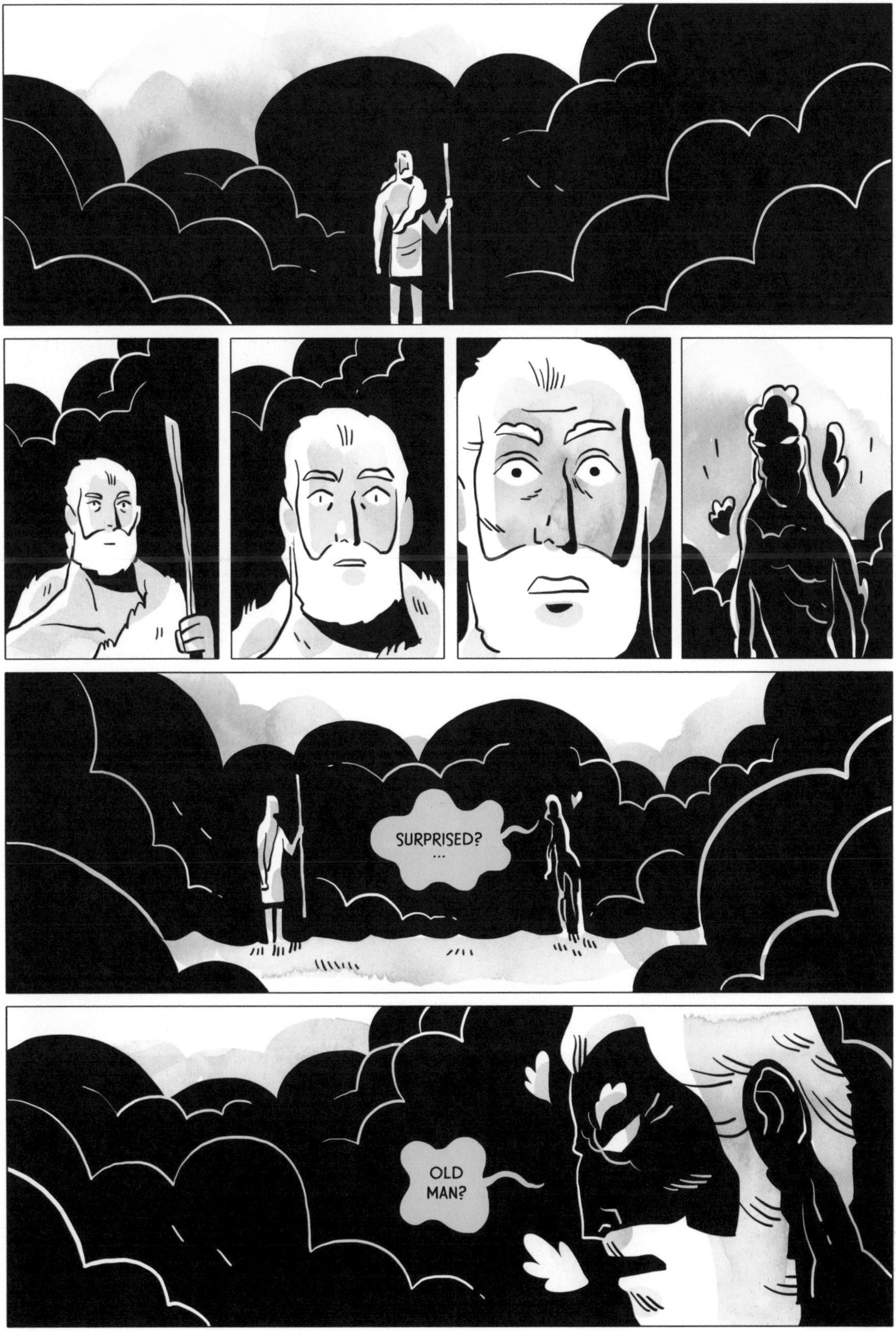
SURPRISED?
...
OLD
MAN?

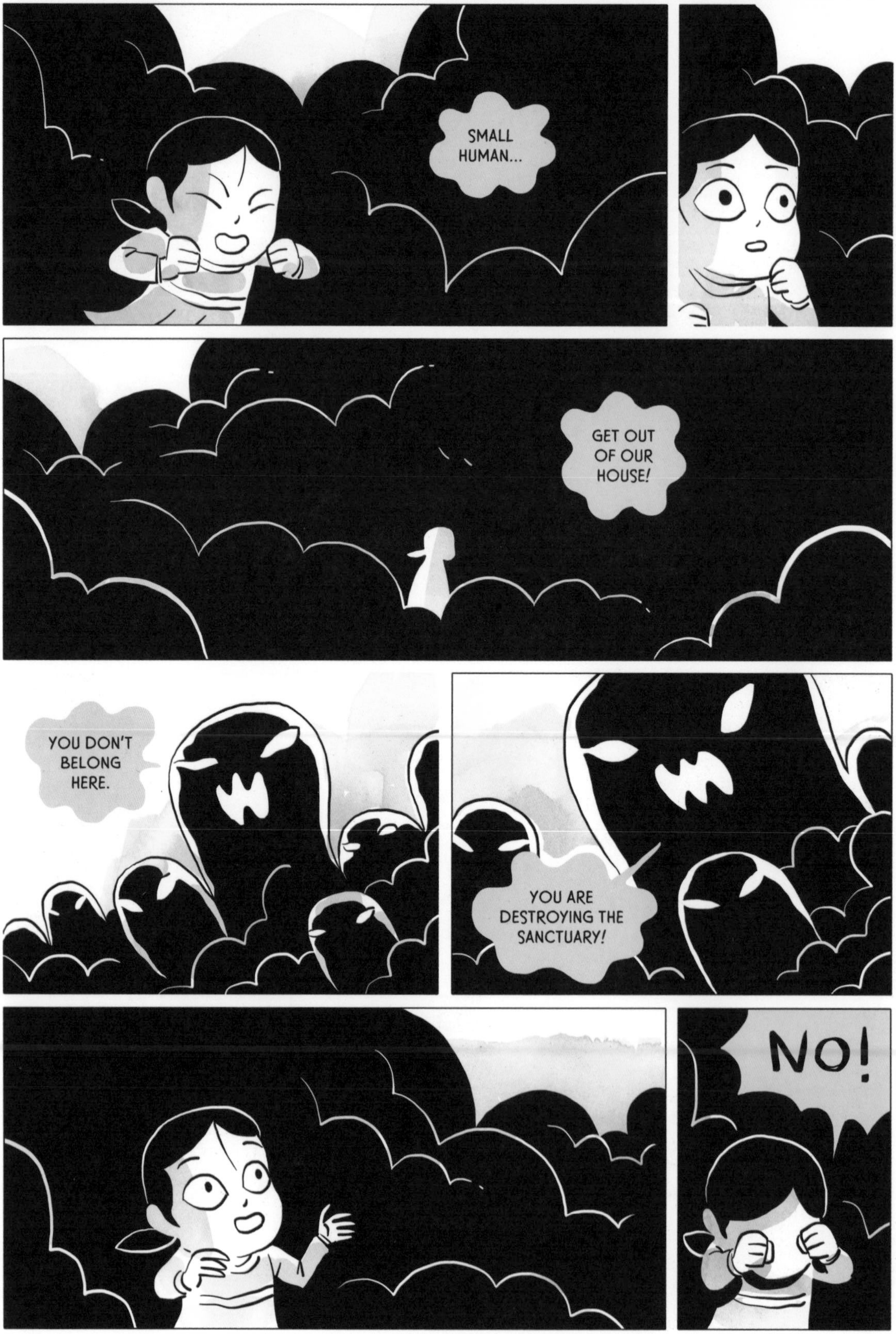
SMALL HUMAN...
GET OUT OF OUR HOUSE!
YOU DON'T BELONG HERE.
YOU ARE DESTROYING THE SANCTUARY!
NO!

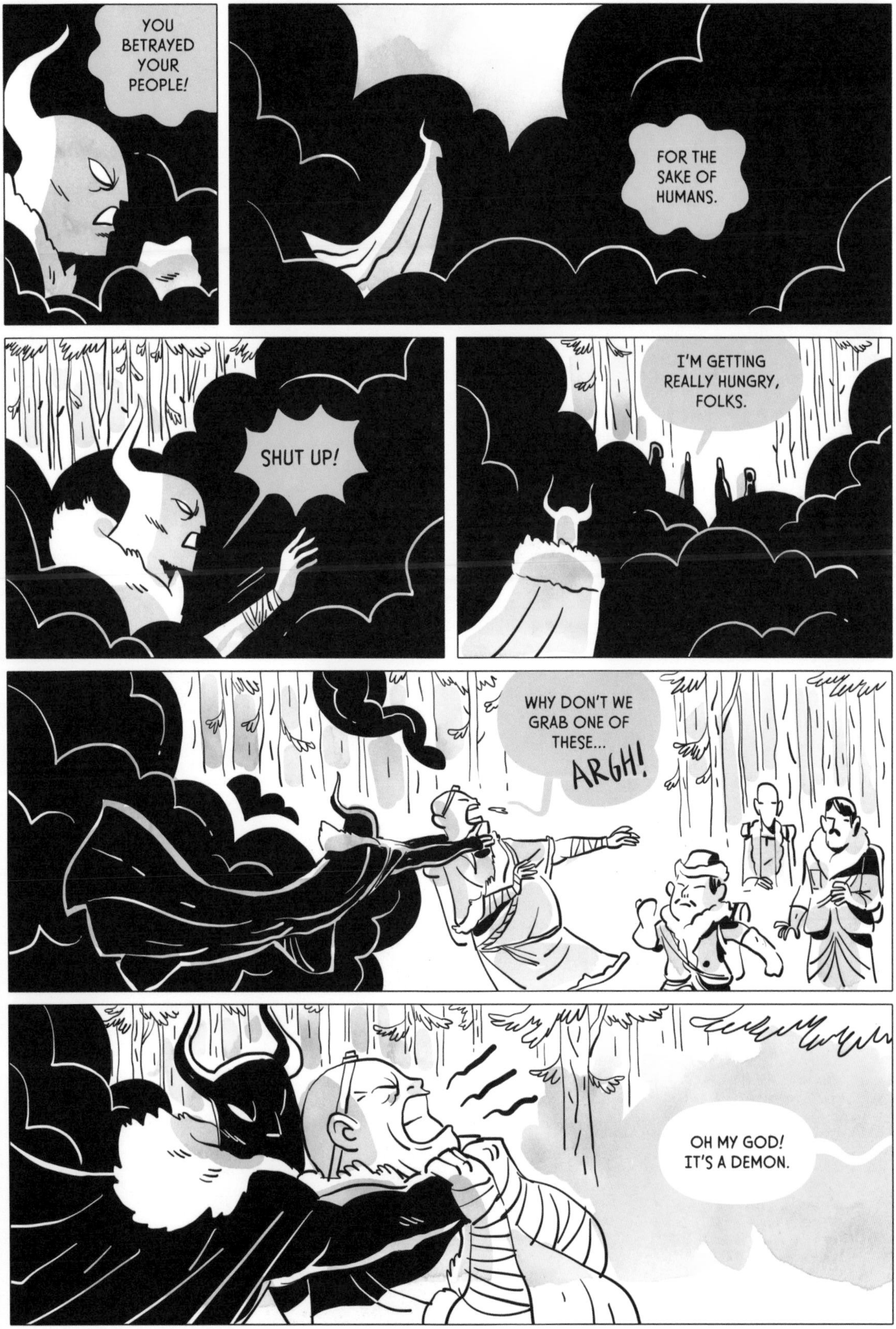
YOU BETRAYED YOUR PEOPLE!
FOR THE SAKE OF HUMANS.
SHUT UP!
I'M GETTING REALLY HUNGRY, FOLKS.
WHY DON'T WE GRAB ONE OF THESE... ARGH!
OH MY GOD! IT'S A DEMON.

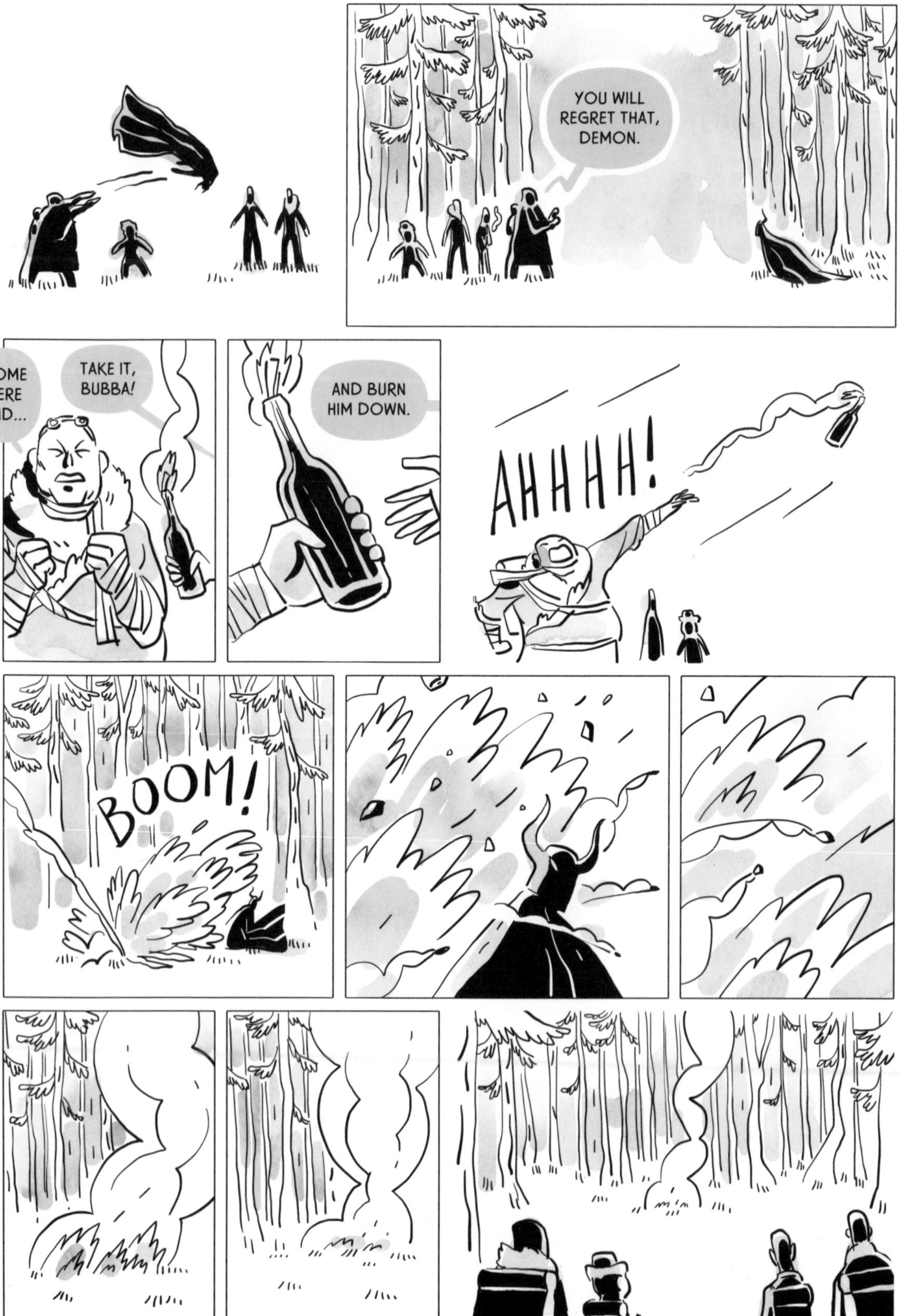
YOU WILL REGRET THAT, DEMON.
COME HERE AND...
TAKE IT, BUBBA!
AND BURN HIM DOWN.
AHHHH!
BOOM!

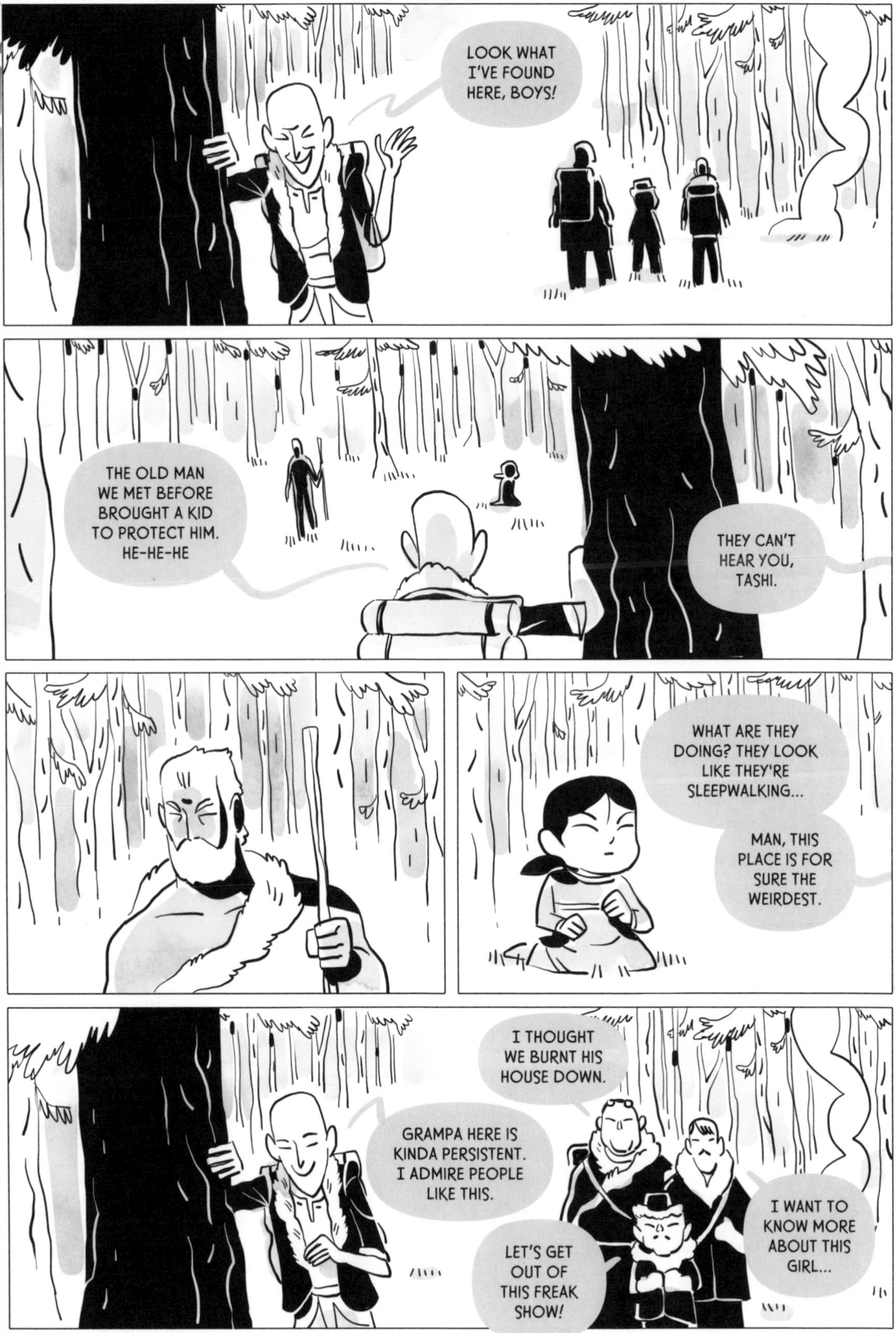
LOOK WHAT I'VE FOUND HERE, BOYS!
THE OLD MAN WE MET BEFORE BROUGHT A KID TO PROTECT HIM. HE-HE-HE
THEY CAN'T HEAR YOU, TASHI.
WHAT ARE THEY DOING? THEY LOOK LIKE THEY'RE SLEEPWALKING...
MAN, THIS PLACE IS FOR SURE THE WEIRDEST.
I THOUGHT WE BURNT HIS HOUSE DOWN.
GRAMPA HERE IS KINDA PERSISTENT. I ADMIRE PEOPLE LIKE THIS.
I WANT TO KNOW MORE ABOUT THIS GIRL...
LET'S GET OUT OF THIS FREAK SHOW!

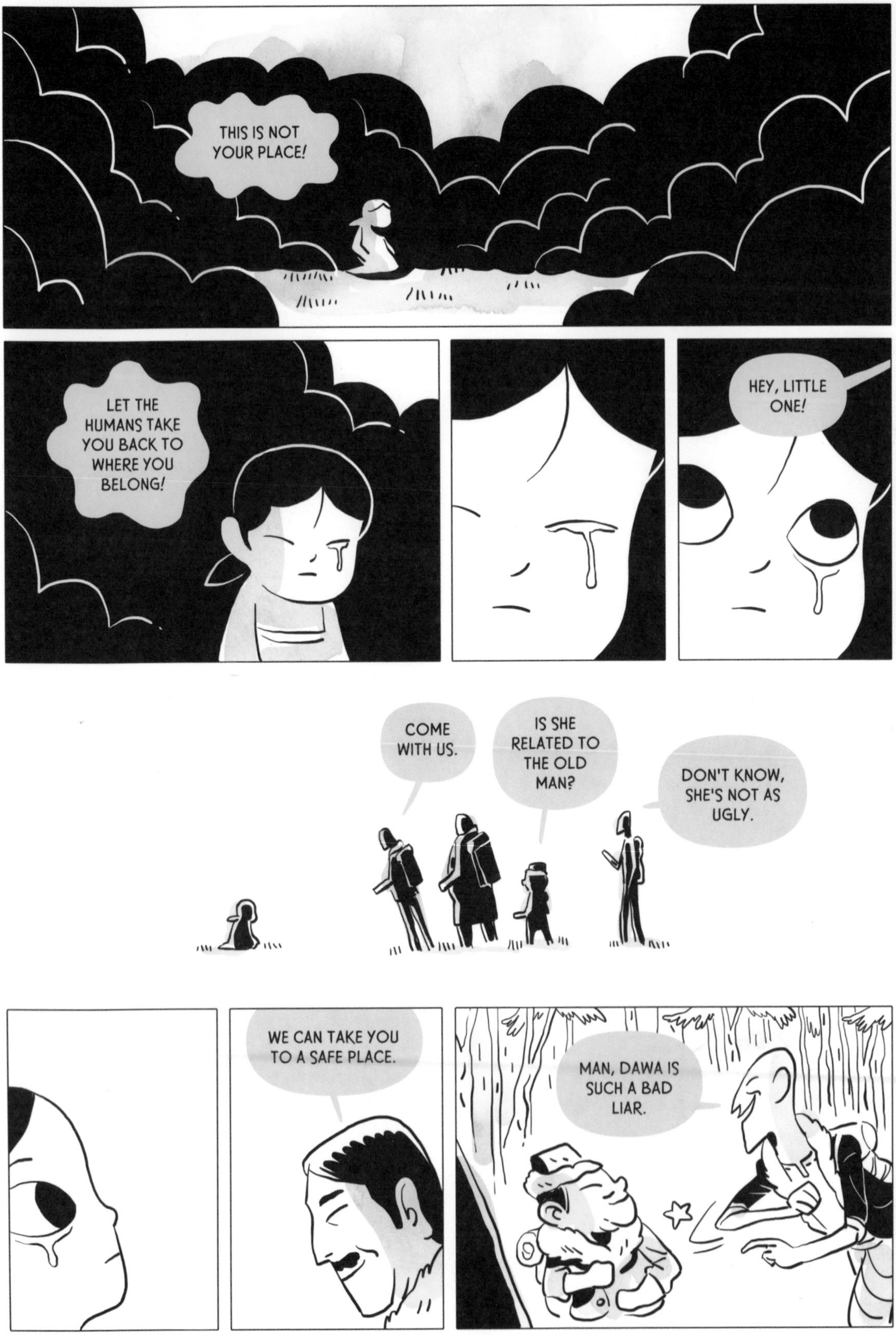

THIS IS NOT YOUR PLACE!
LET THE HUMANS TAKE YOU BACK TO WHERE YOU BELONG!
HEY, LITTLE ONE!
COME WITH US.
IS SHE RELATED TO THE OLD MAN?
DON'T KNOW, SHE'S NOT AS UGLY.
WE CAN TAKE YOU TO A SAFE PLACE.
MAN, DAWA IS SUCH A BAD LIAR.

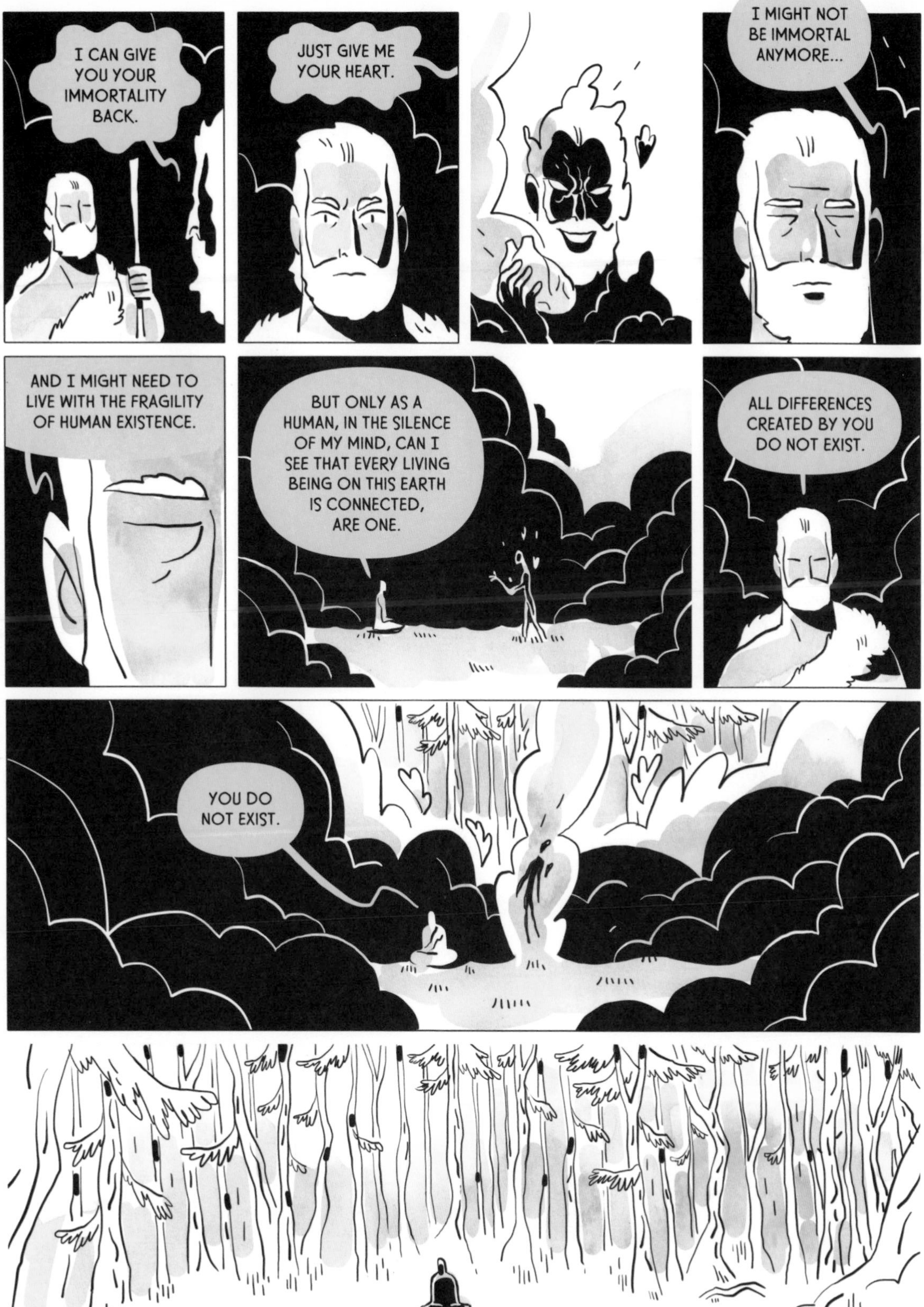
I CAN GIVE YOU YOUR IMMORTALITY BACK.
JUST GIVE ME YOUR HEART.
I MIGHT NOT BE IMMORTAL ANYMORE...
AND I MIGHT NEED TO LIVE WITH THE FRAGILITY OF HUMAN EXISTENCE.
BUT ONLY AS A HUMAN, IN THE SILENCE OF MY MIND, CAN I SEE THAT EVERY LIVING BEING ON THIS EARTH IS CONNECTED, ARE ONE.
ALL DIFFERENCES CREATED BY YOU DO NOT EXIST.
YOU DO NOT EXIST.

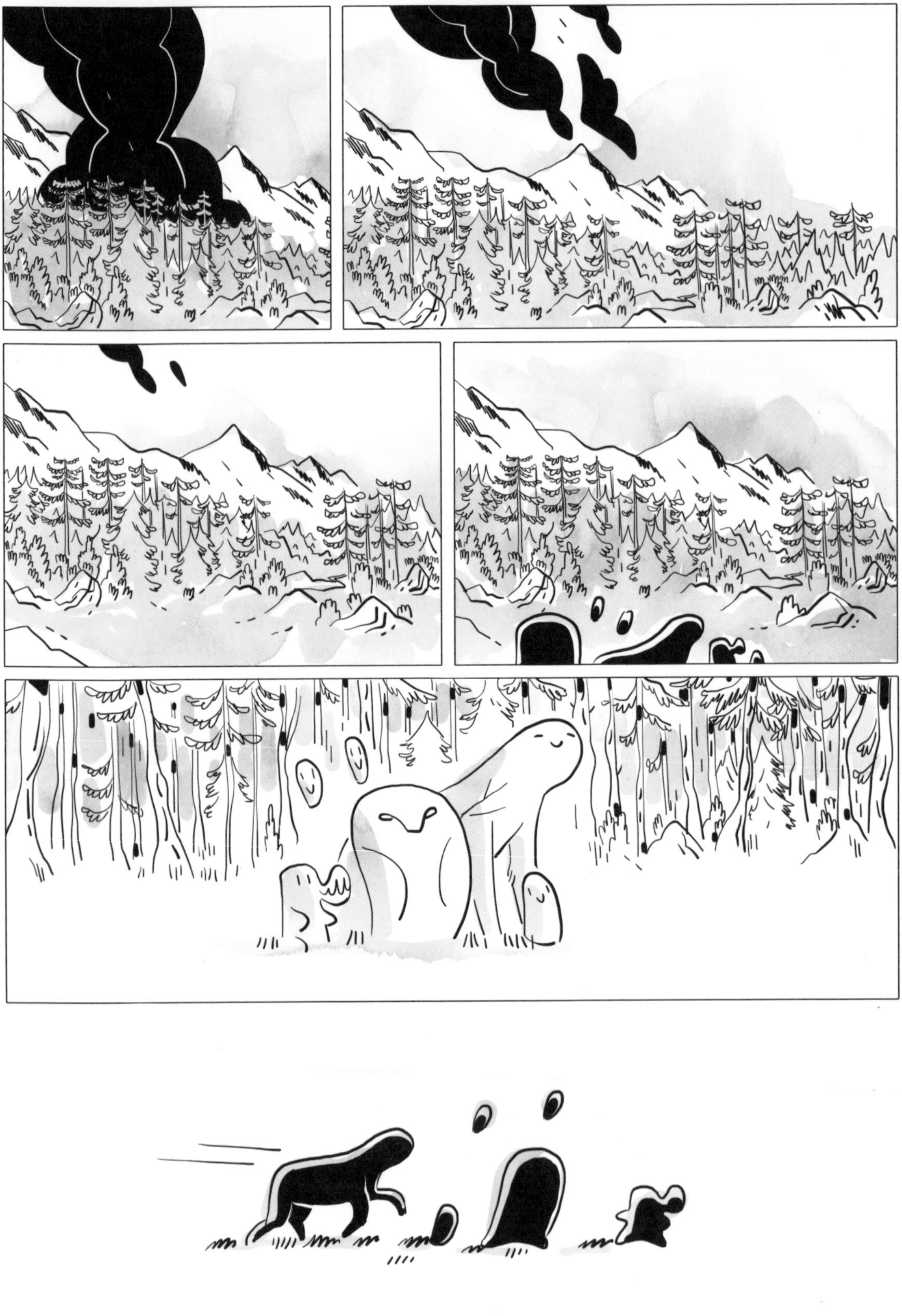

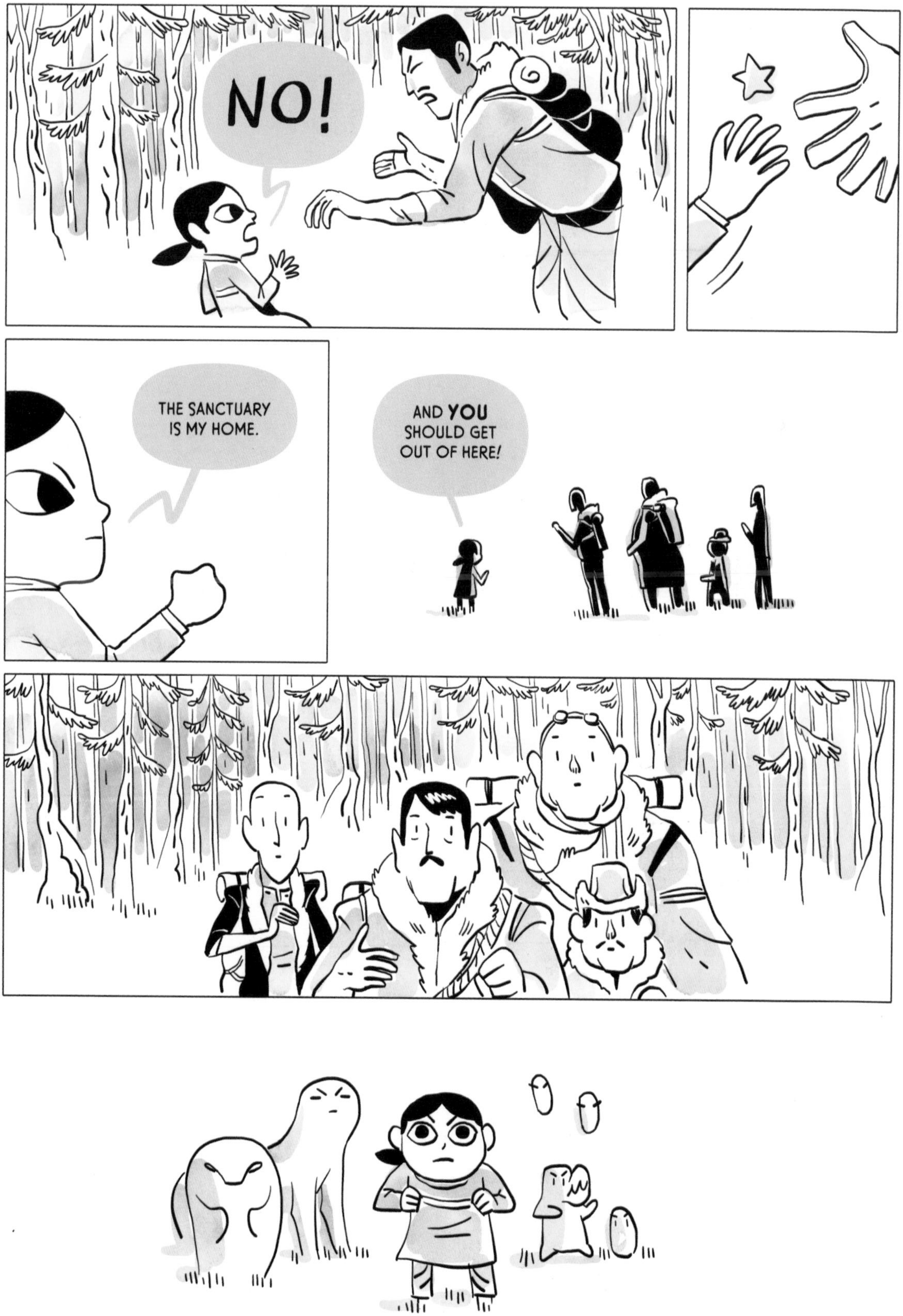
NO!
THE SANCTUARY IS MY HOME.
AND **YOU** SHOULD GET OUT OF HERE!

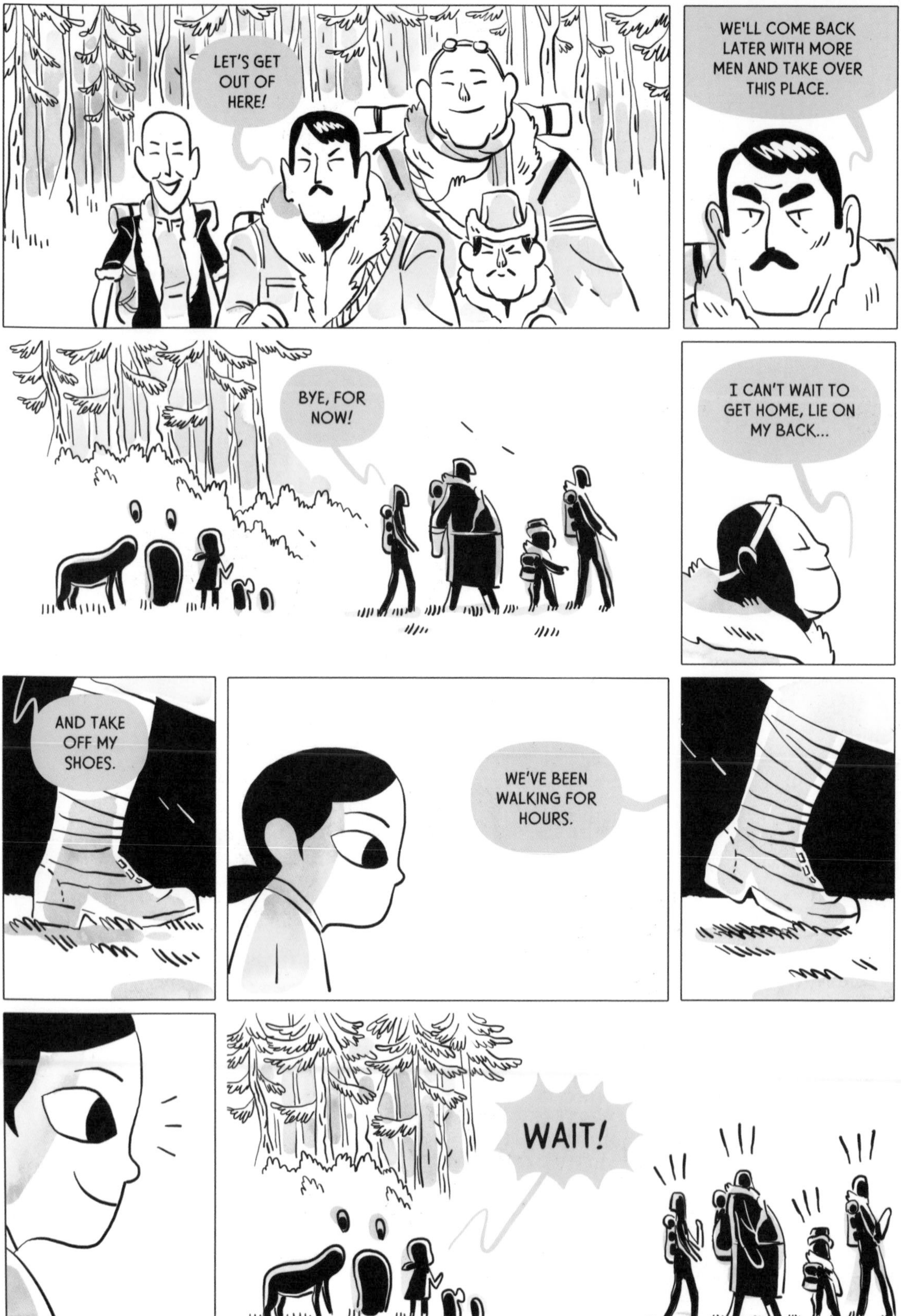
LET'S GET OUT OF HERE!
WE'LL COME BACK LATER WITH MORE MEN AND TAKE OVER THIS PLACE.
BYE, FOR NOW!
I CAN'T WAIT TO GET HOME, LIE ON MY BACK...
AND TAKE OFF MY SHOES.
WE'VE BEEN WALKING FOR HOURS.
WAIT!

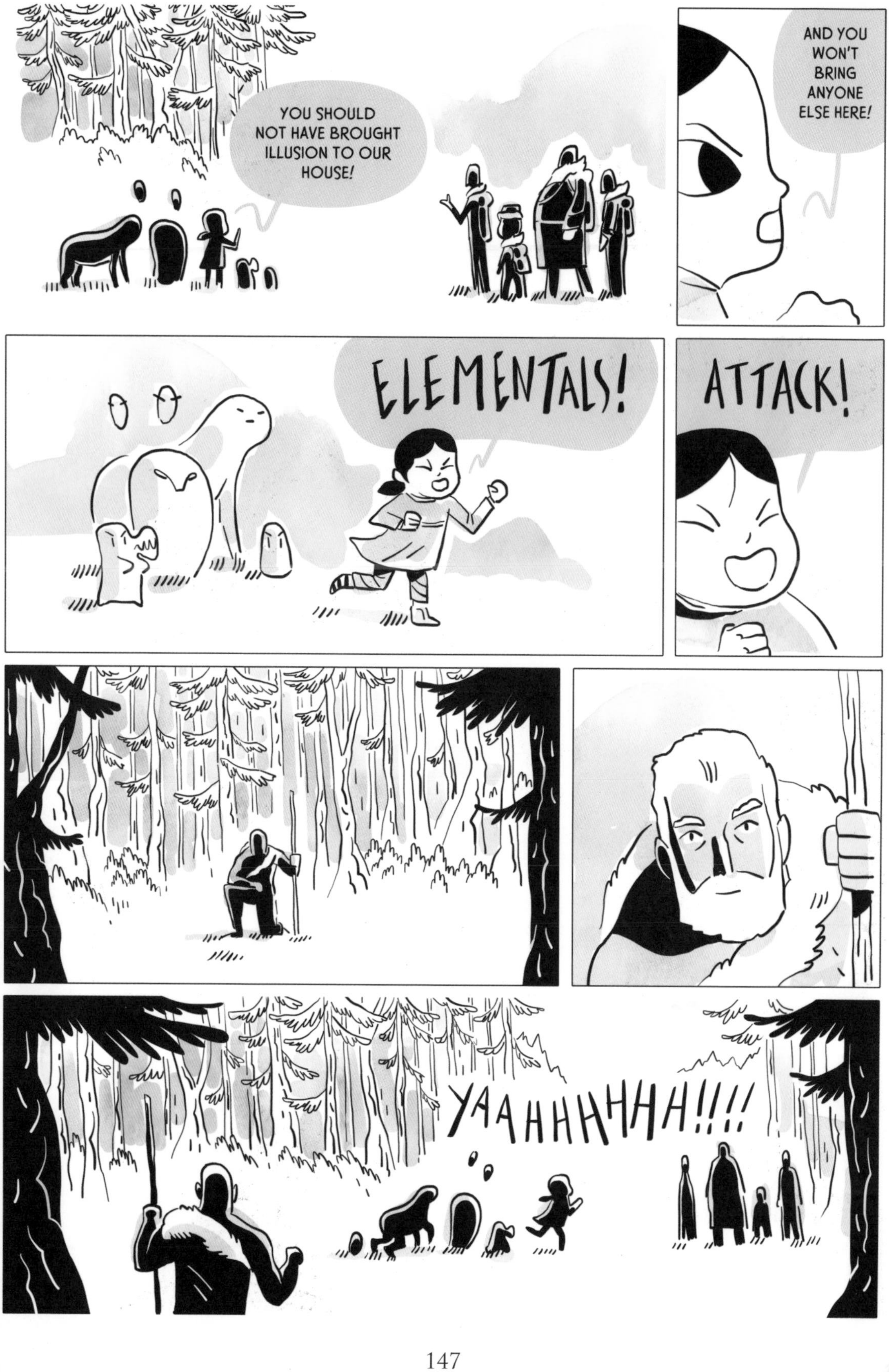
YOU SHOULD NOT HAVE BROUGHT ILLUSION TO OUR HOUSE!
AND YOU WON'T BRING ANYONE ELSE HERE!
ELEMENTALS!
ATTACK!
YAAHHHHHHA!!!!

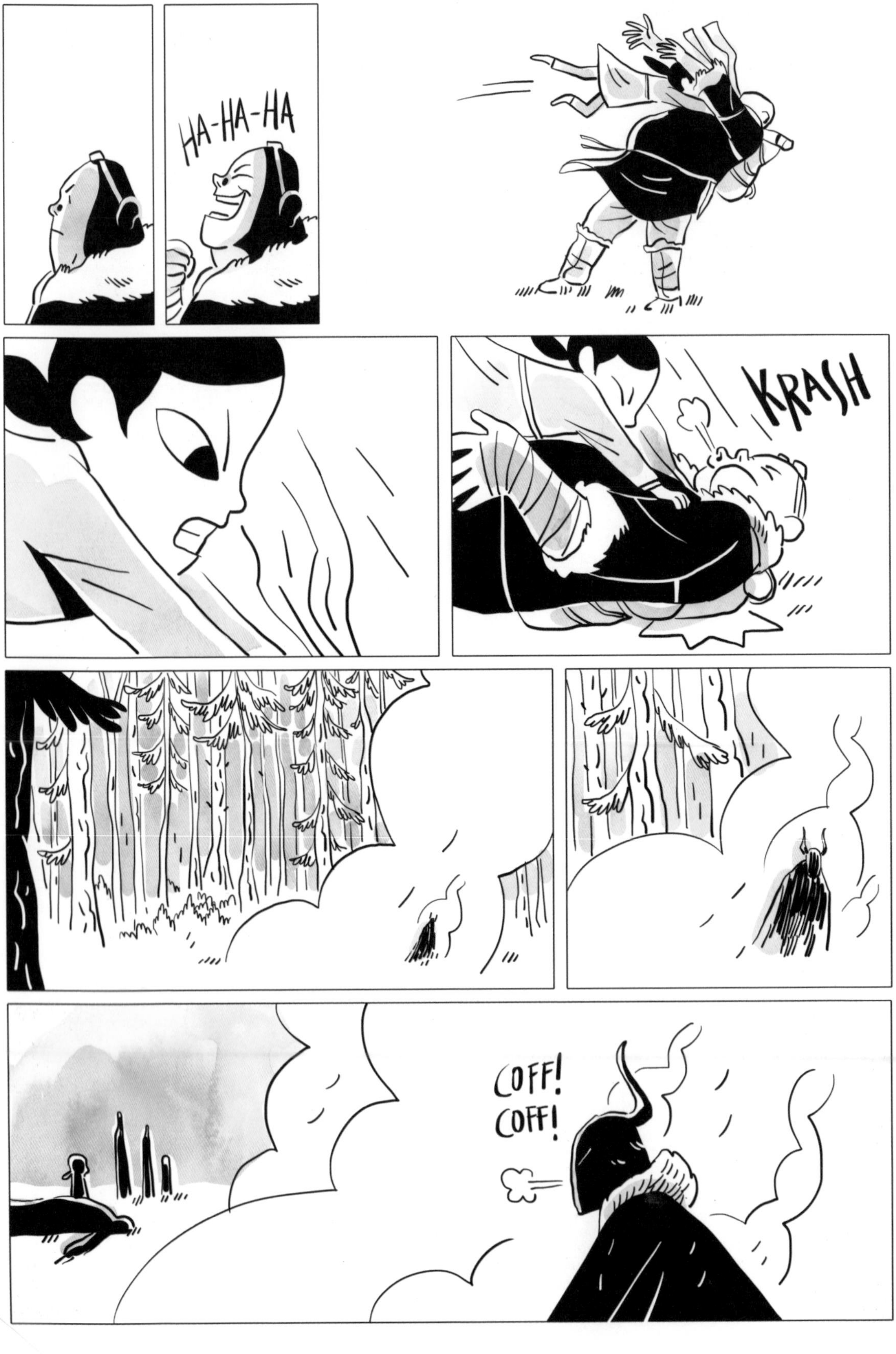
HA-HA-HA
KRASH
COFF!
COFF!

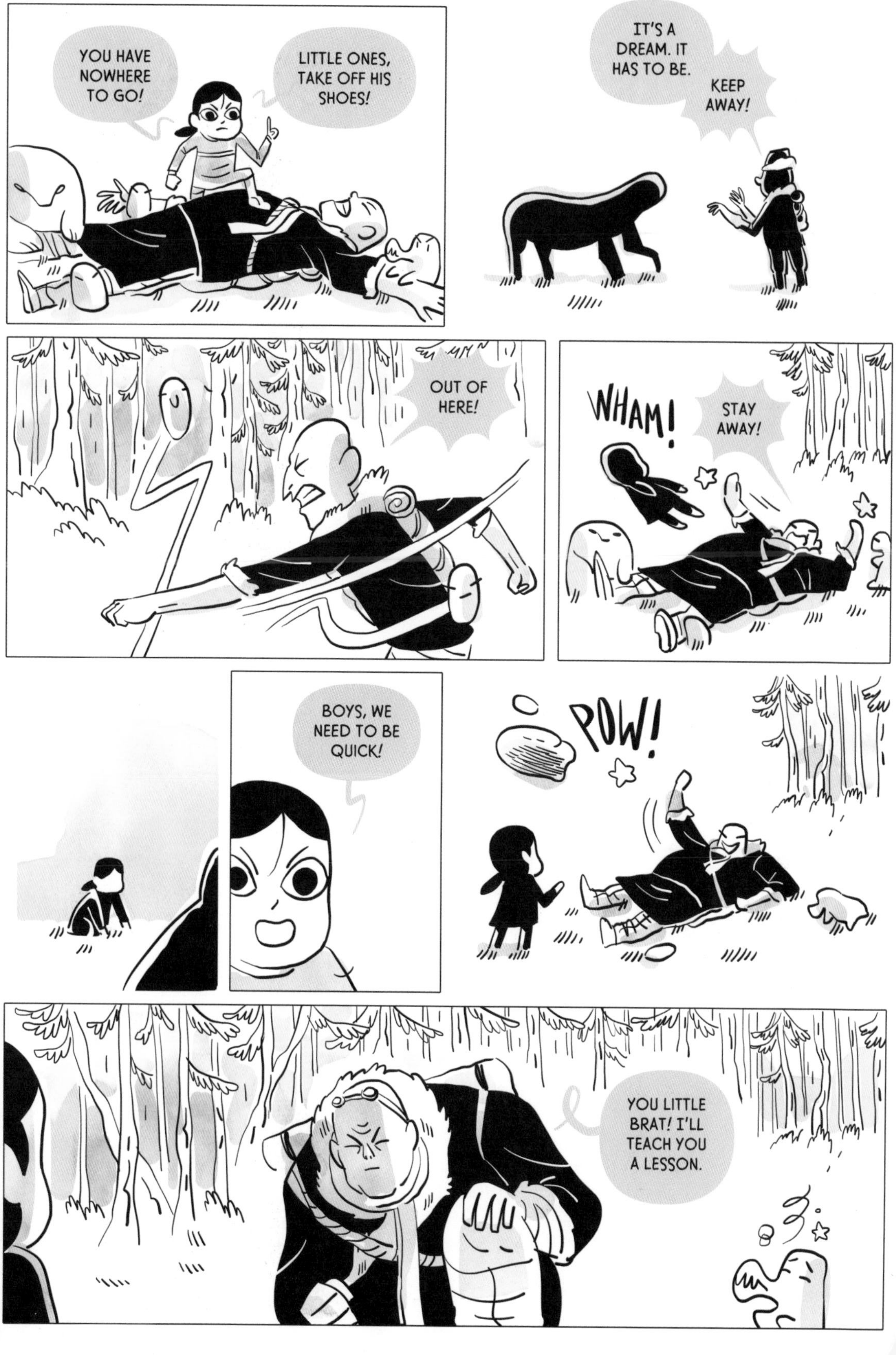
YOU HAVE NOWHERE TO GO!
LITTLE ONES, TAKE OFF HIS SHOES!
IT'S A DREAM. IT HAS TO BE.
KEEP AWAY!
OUT OF HERE!
WHAM!
STAY AWAY!
BOYS, WE NEED TO BE QUICK!
POW!
YOU LITTLE BRAT! I'LL TEACH YOU A LESSON.

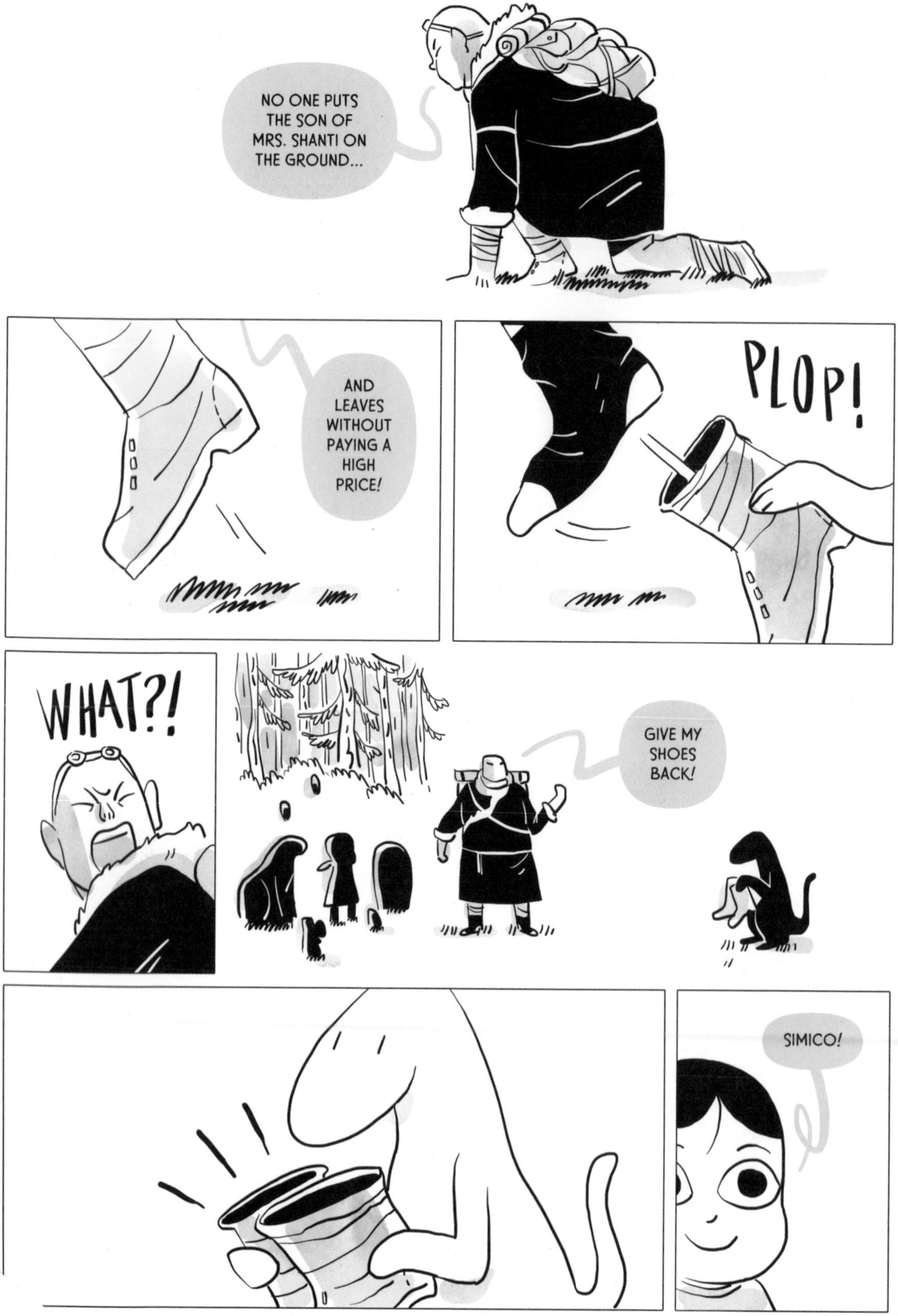
NO ONE PUTS THE SON OF MRS. SHANTI ON THE GROUND...
AND LEAVES WITHOUT PAYING A HIGH PRICE!
PLOP!
WHAT?!
GIVE MY SHOES BACK!
SIMICO!

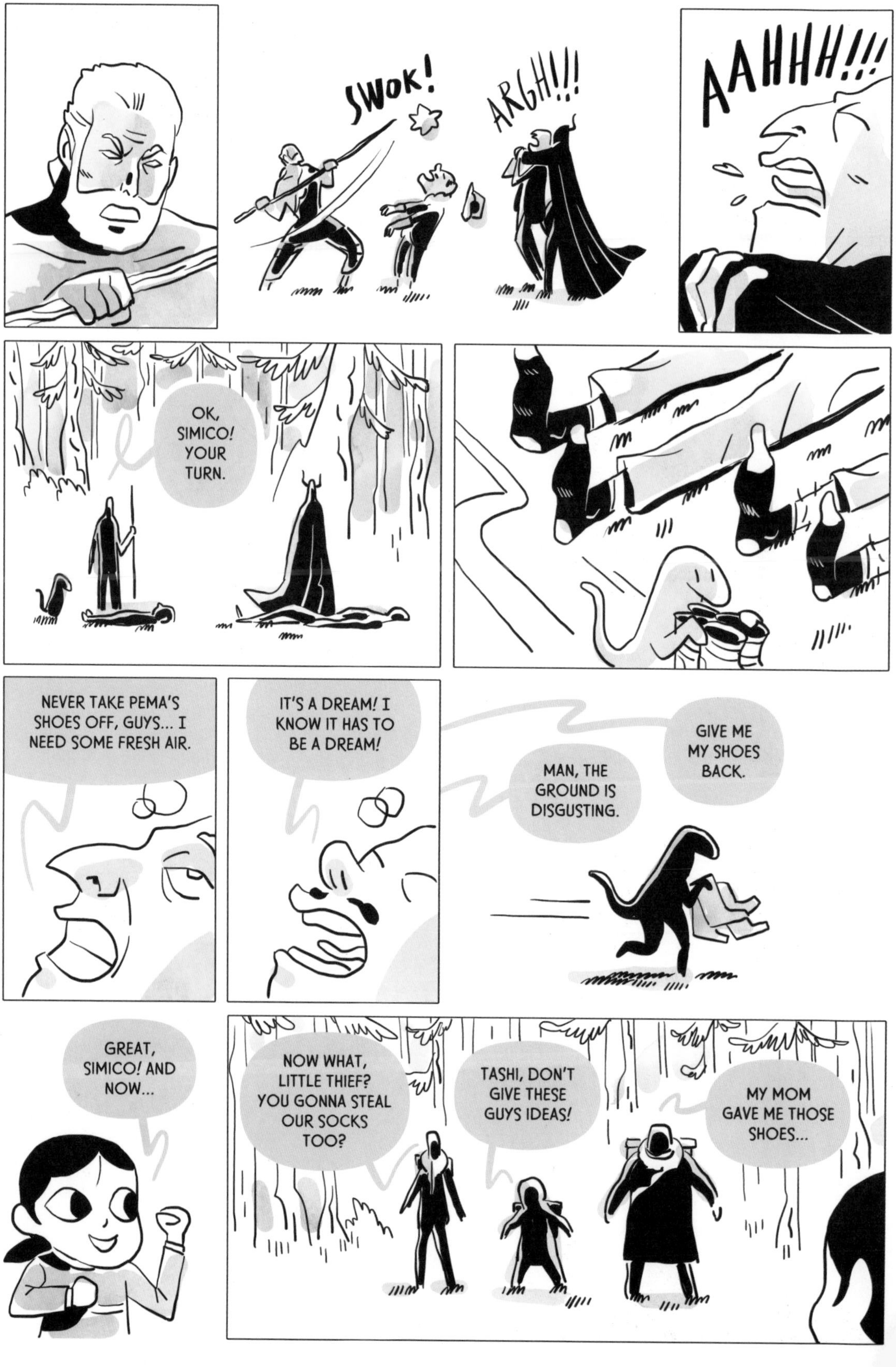
SWOK!
ARGH!!!
AAHHH!!!
OK, SIMICO! YOUR TURN.
NEVER TAKE PEMA'S SHOES OFF, GUYS... I NEED SOME FRESH AIR.
IT'S A DREAM! I KNOW IT HAS TO BE A DREAM!
MAN, THE GROUND IS DISGUSTING.
GIVE ME MY SHOES BACK.
GREAT, SIMICO! AND NOW...
NOW WHAT, LITTLE THIEF? YOU GONNA STEAL OUR SOCKS TOO?
TASHI, DON'T GIVE THESE GUYS IDEAS!
MY MOM GAVE ME THOSE SHOES...

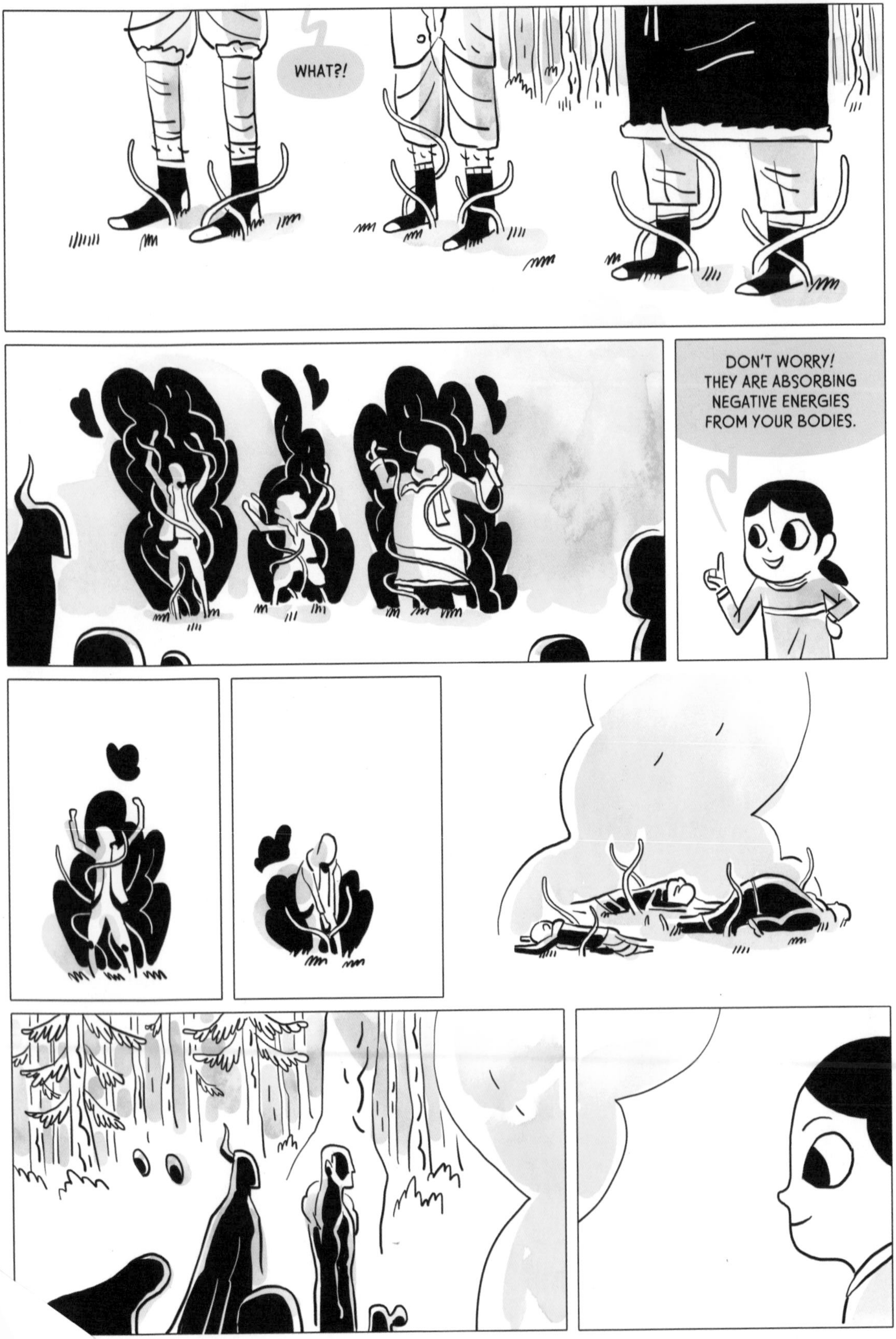
WHAT?!
DON'T WORRY! THEY ARE ABSORBING NEGATIVE ENERGIES FROM YOUR BODIES.

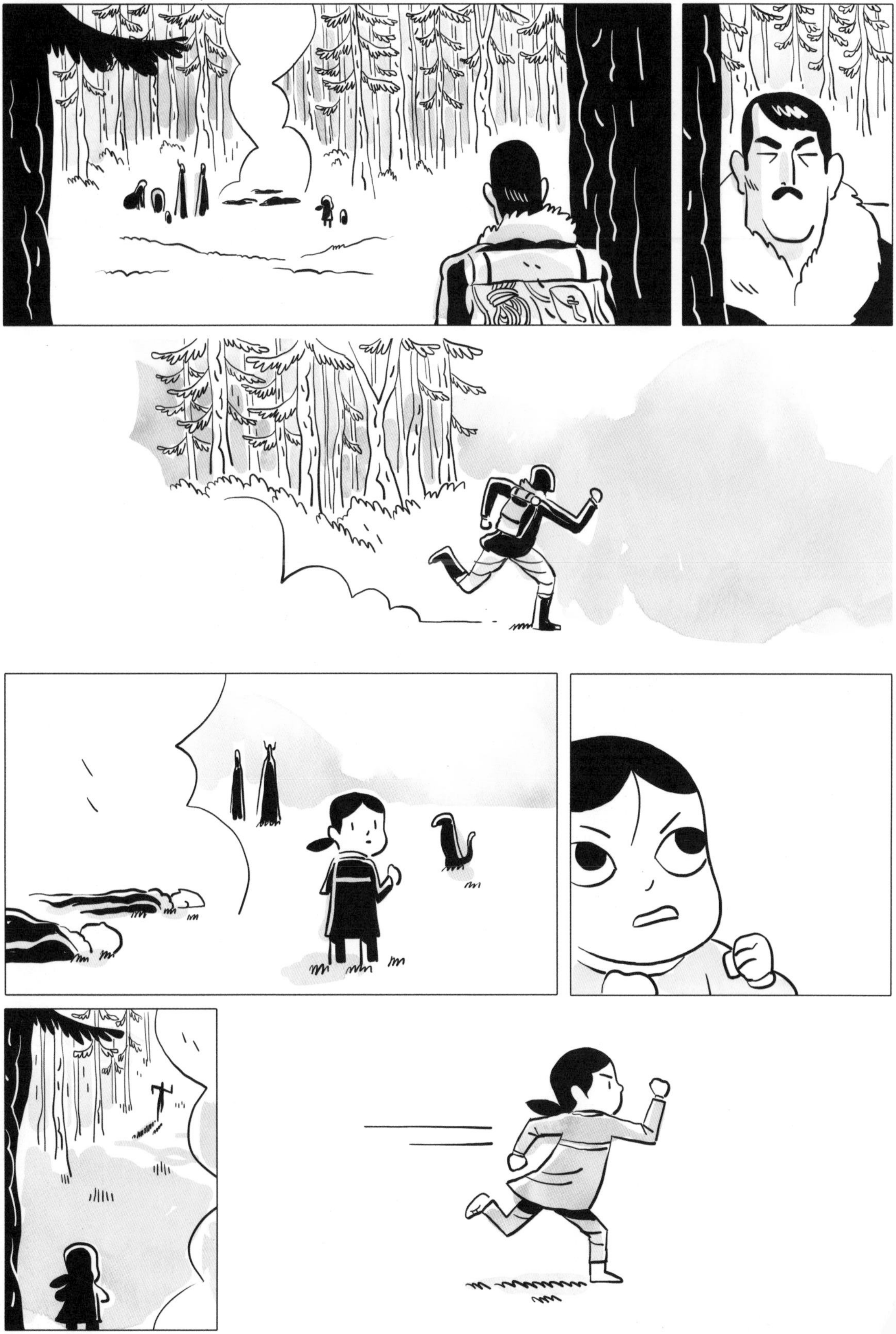

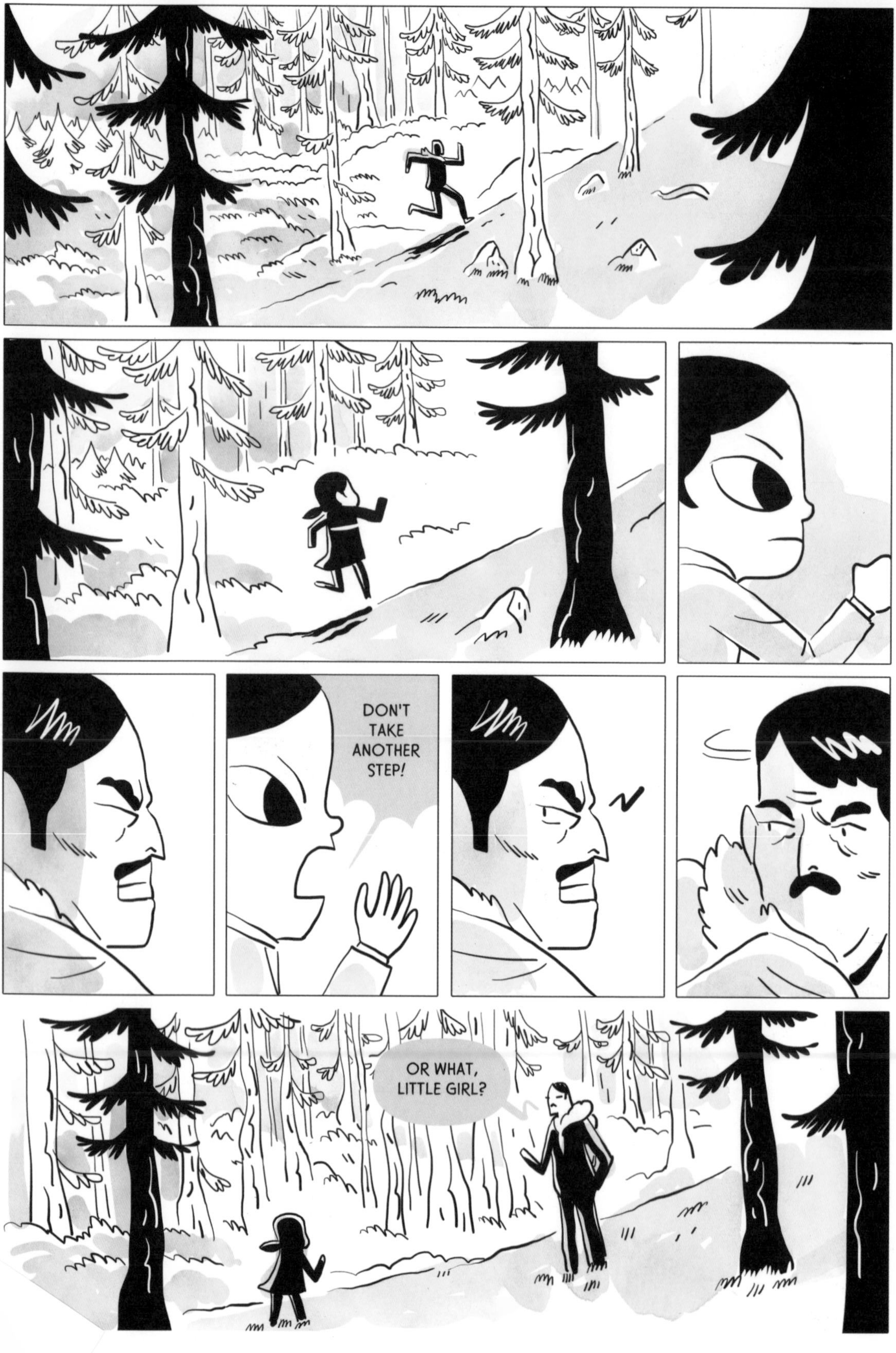
DON'T TAKE ANOTHER STEP!
OR WHAT, LITTLE GIRL?

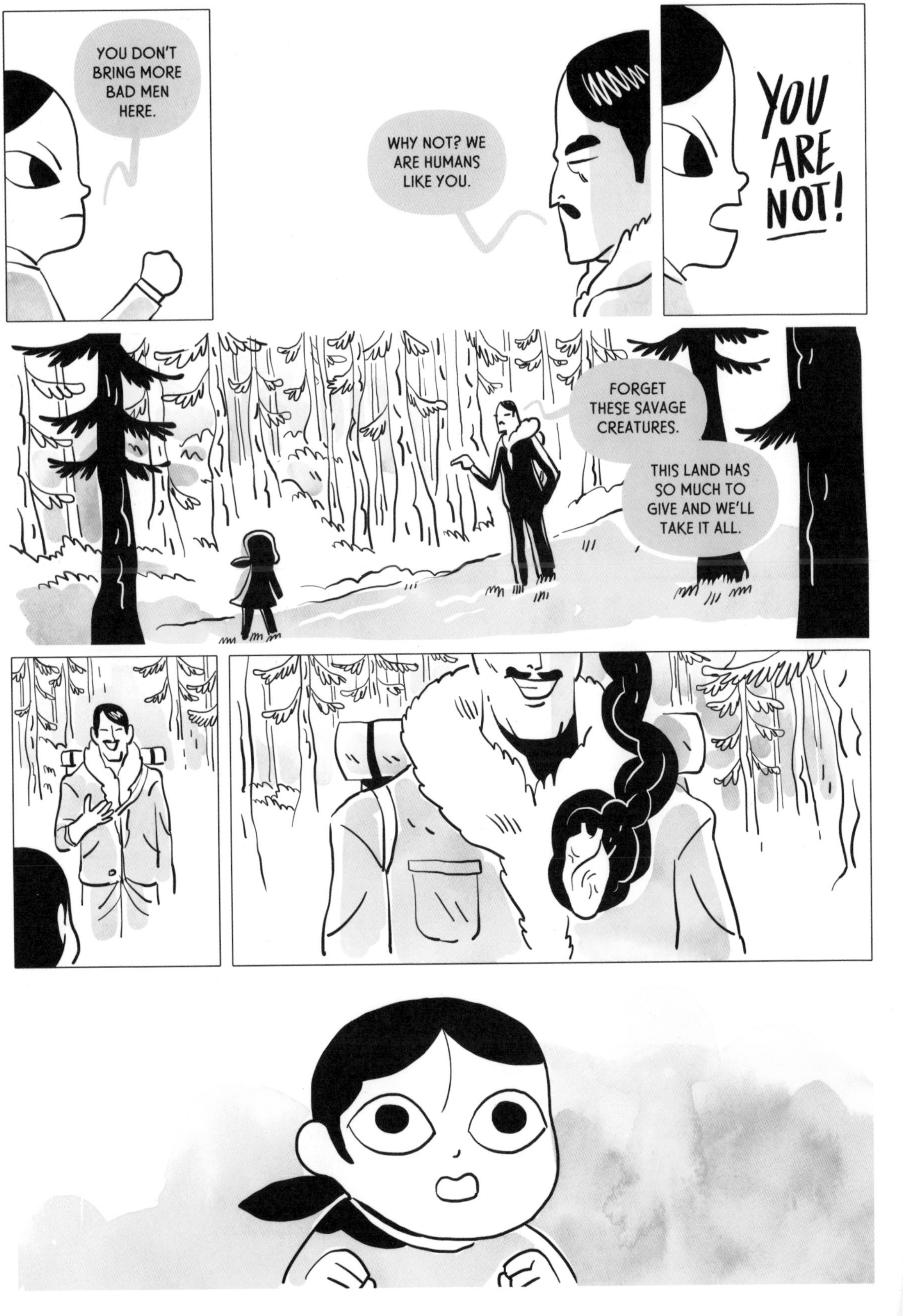
YOU DON'T BRING MORE BAD MEN HERE.
WHY NOT? WE ARE HUMANS LIKE YOU.
YOU ARE NOT!
FORGET THESE SAVAGE CREATURES.
THIS LAND HAS SO MUCH TO GIVE AND WE'LL TAKE IT ALL.

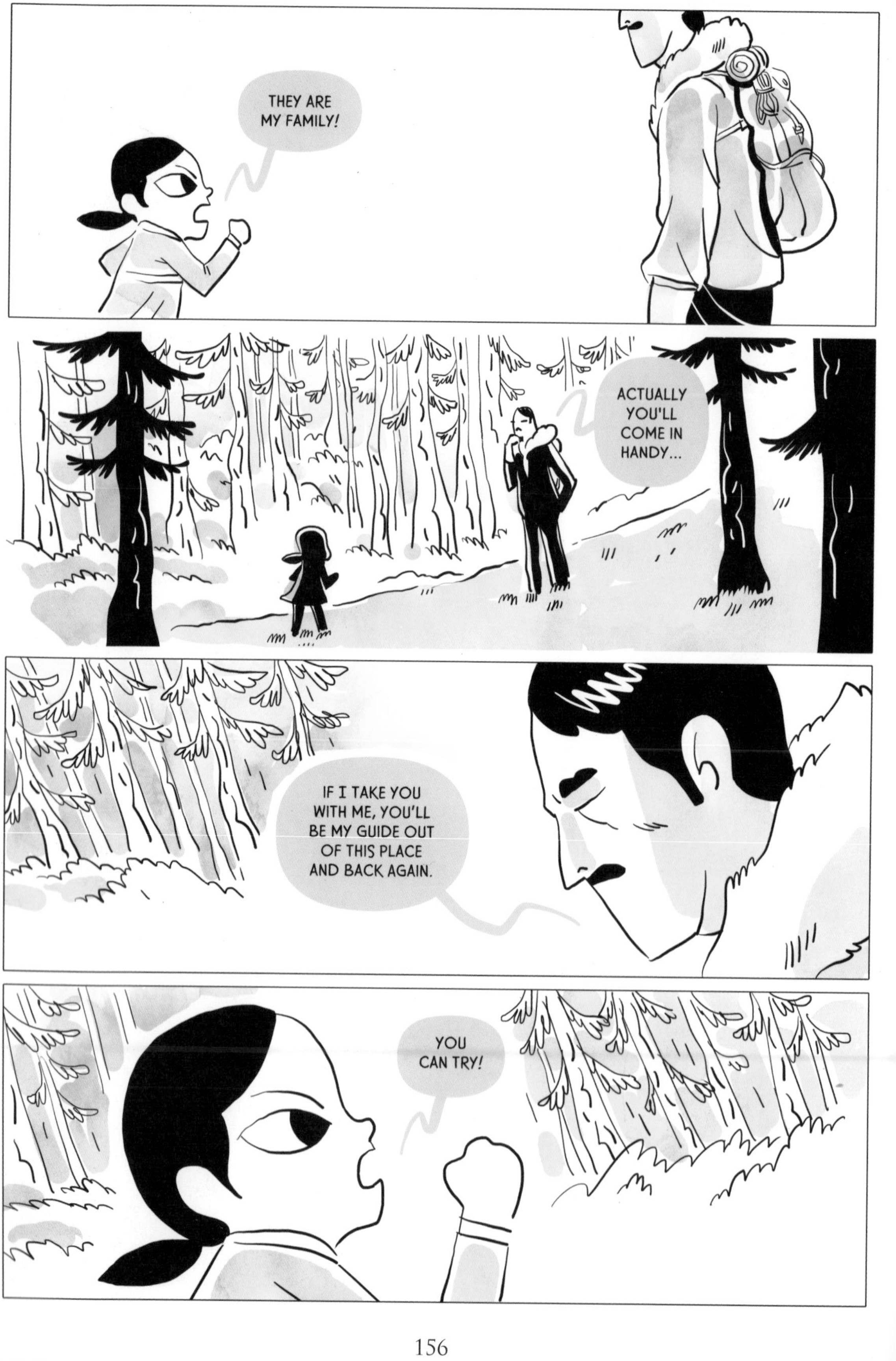
THEY ARE MY FAMILY!
ACTUALLY YOU'LL COME IN HANDY...
IF I TAKE YOU WITH ME, YOU'LL BE MY GUIDE OUT OF THIS PLACE AND BACK AGAIN.
YOU CAN TRY!

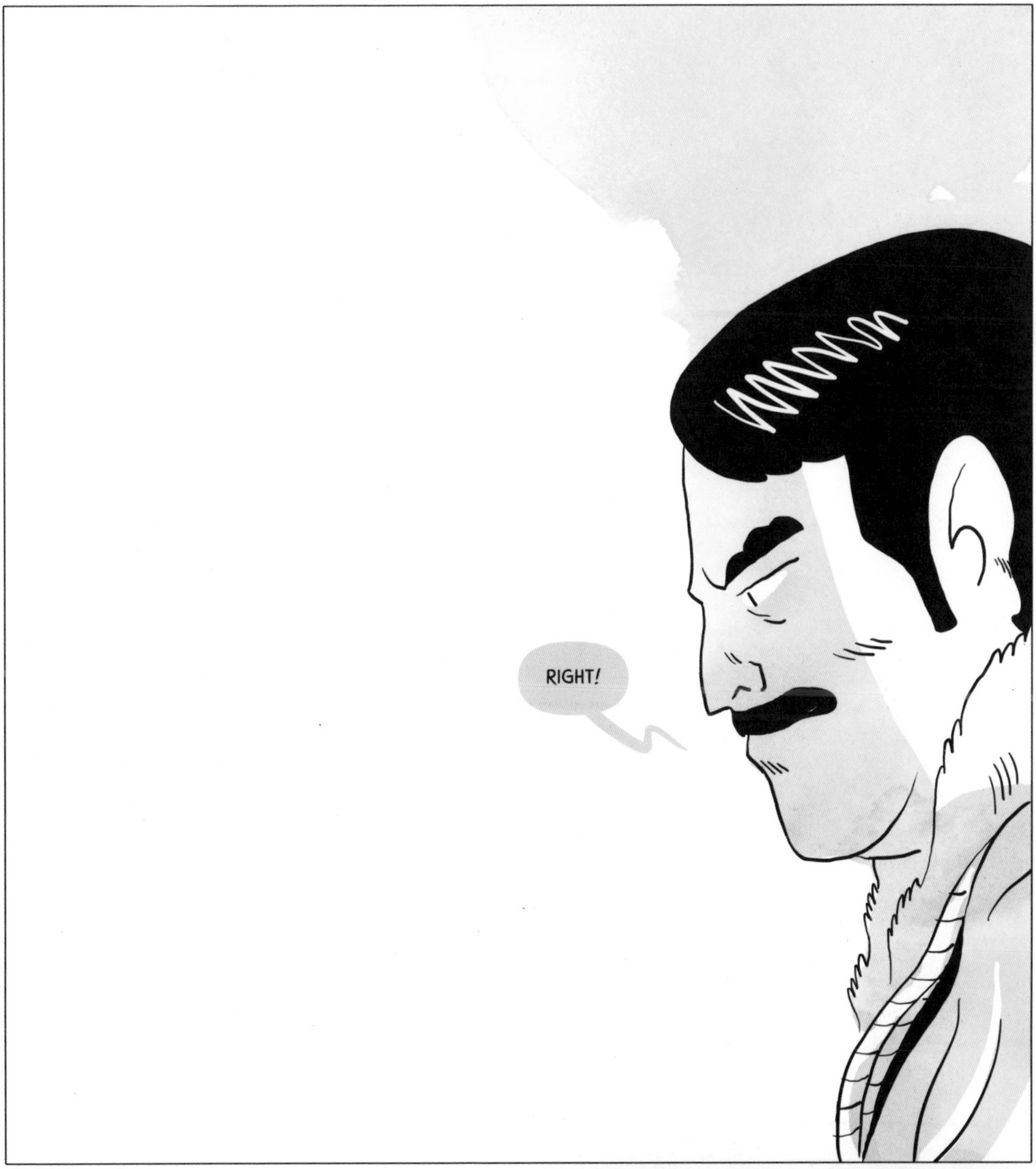
RIGHT!

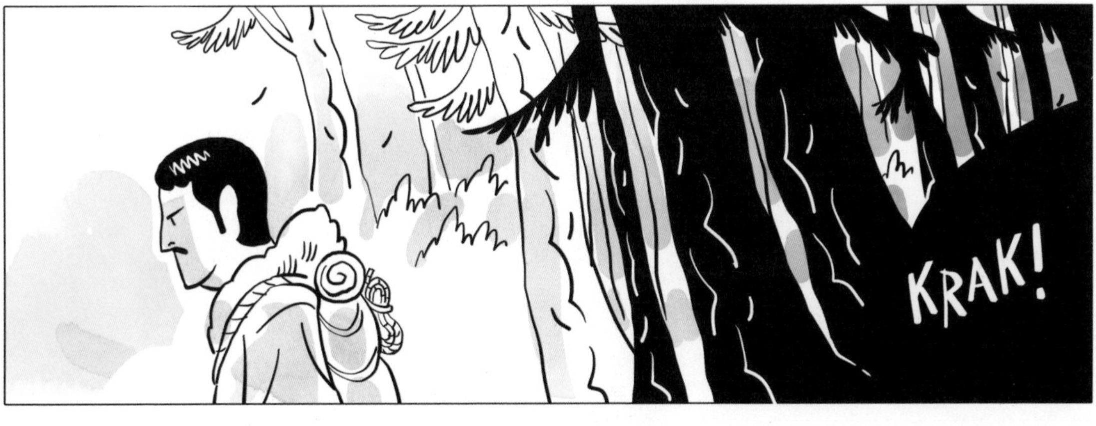
KRAK!

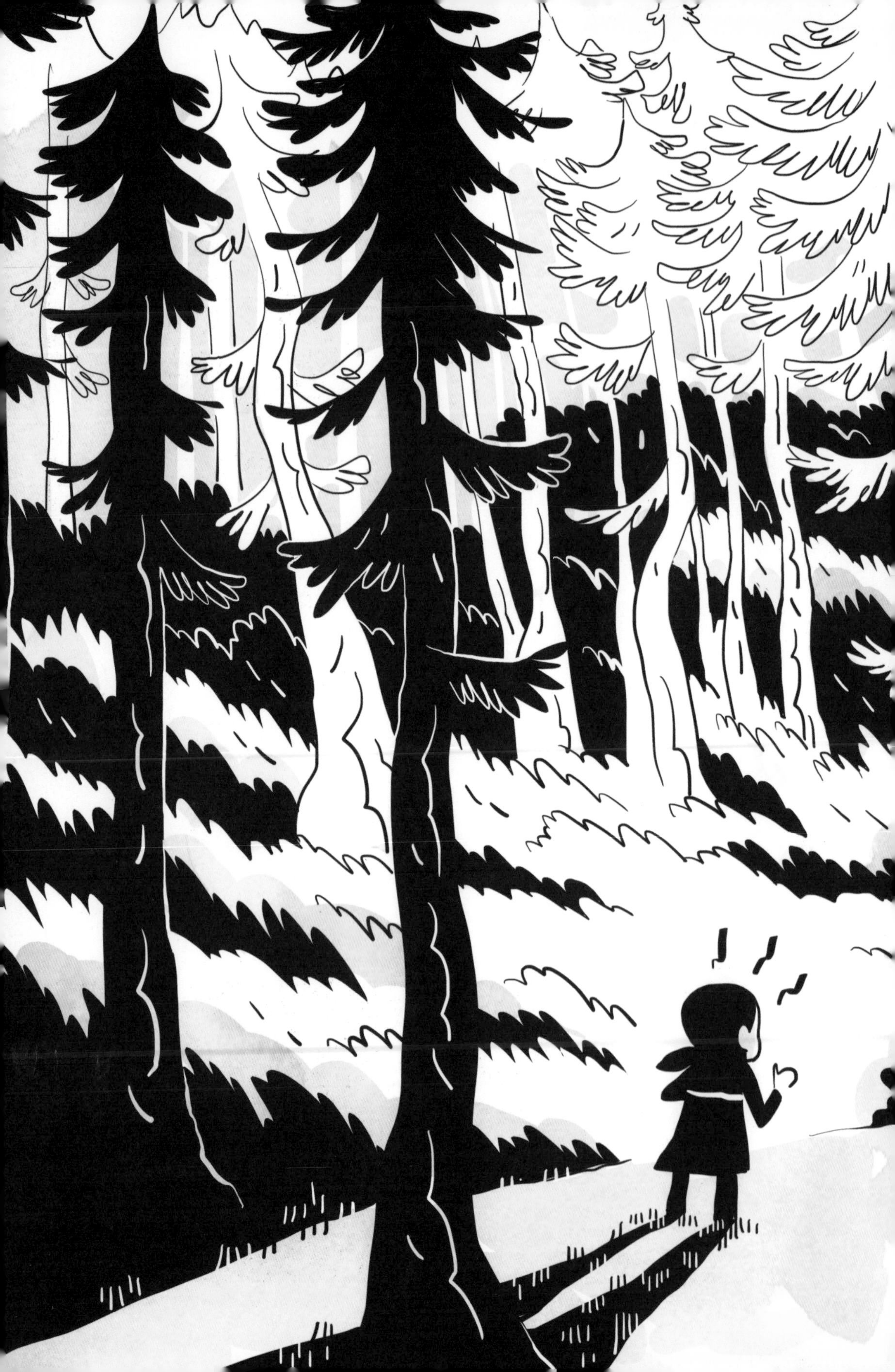

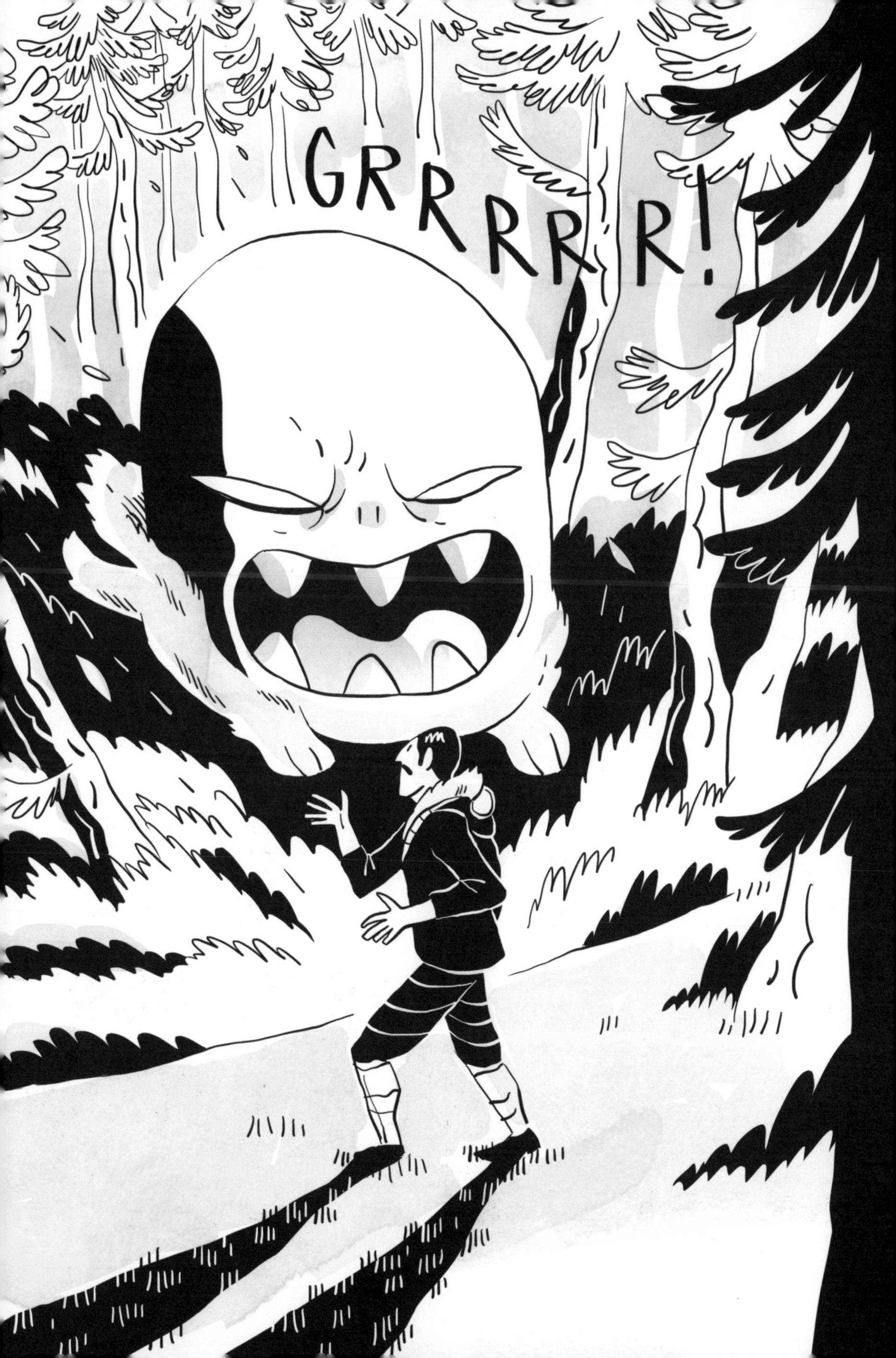
GRRRRRR!

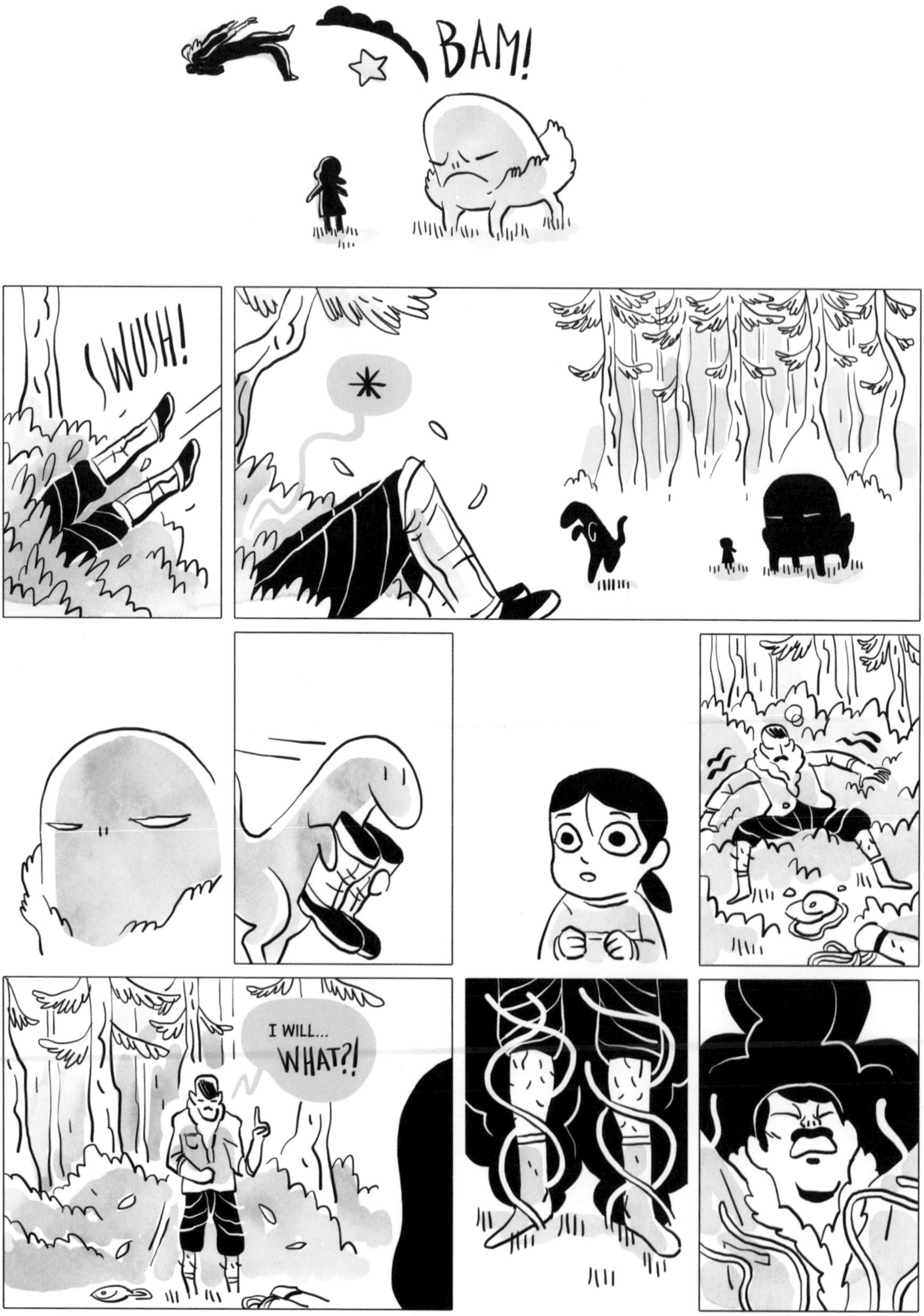
BAM!
SWUSH!
*
I WILL...
WHAT?!

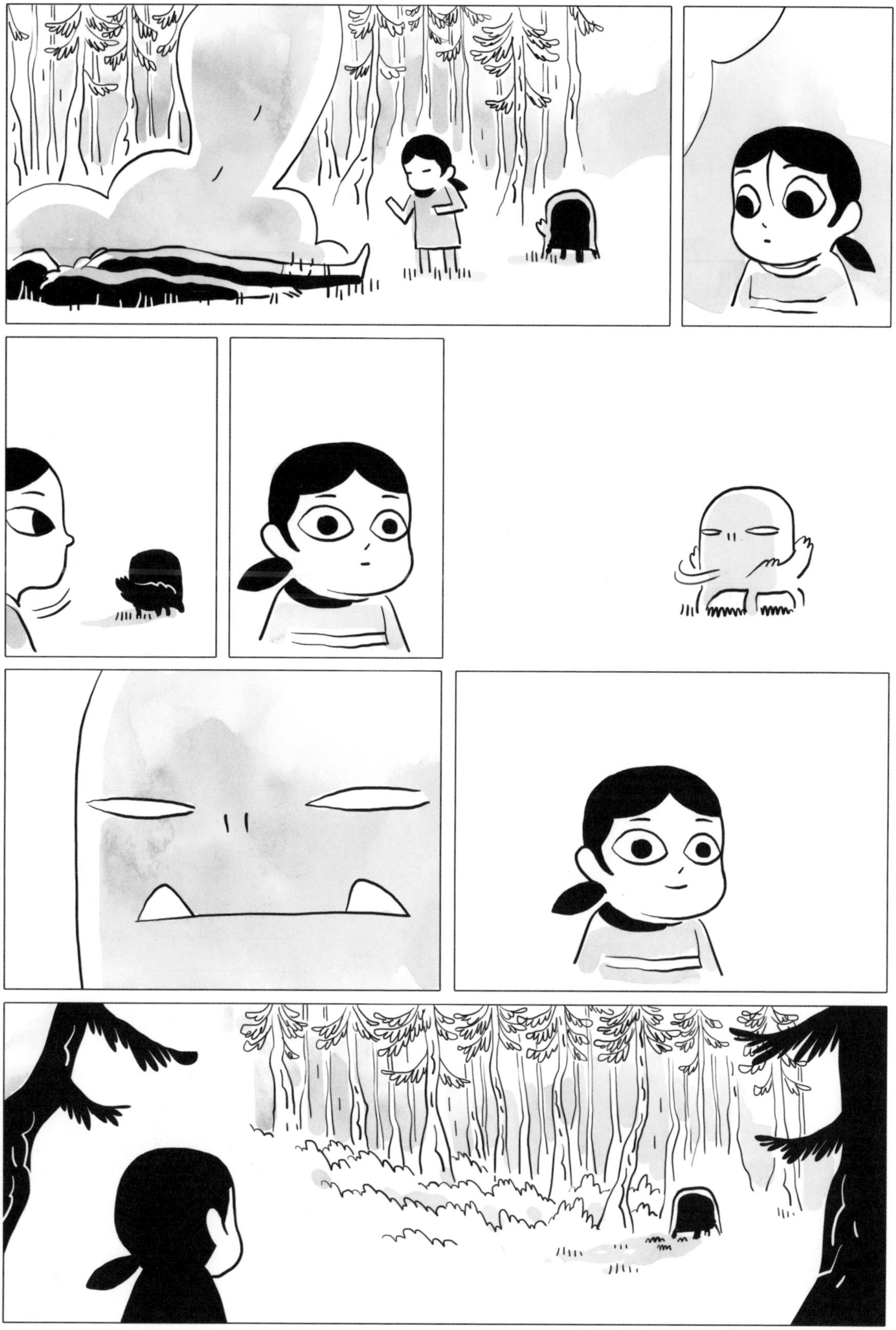

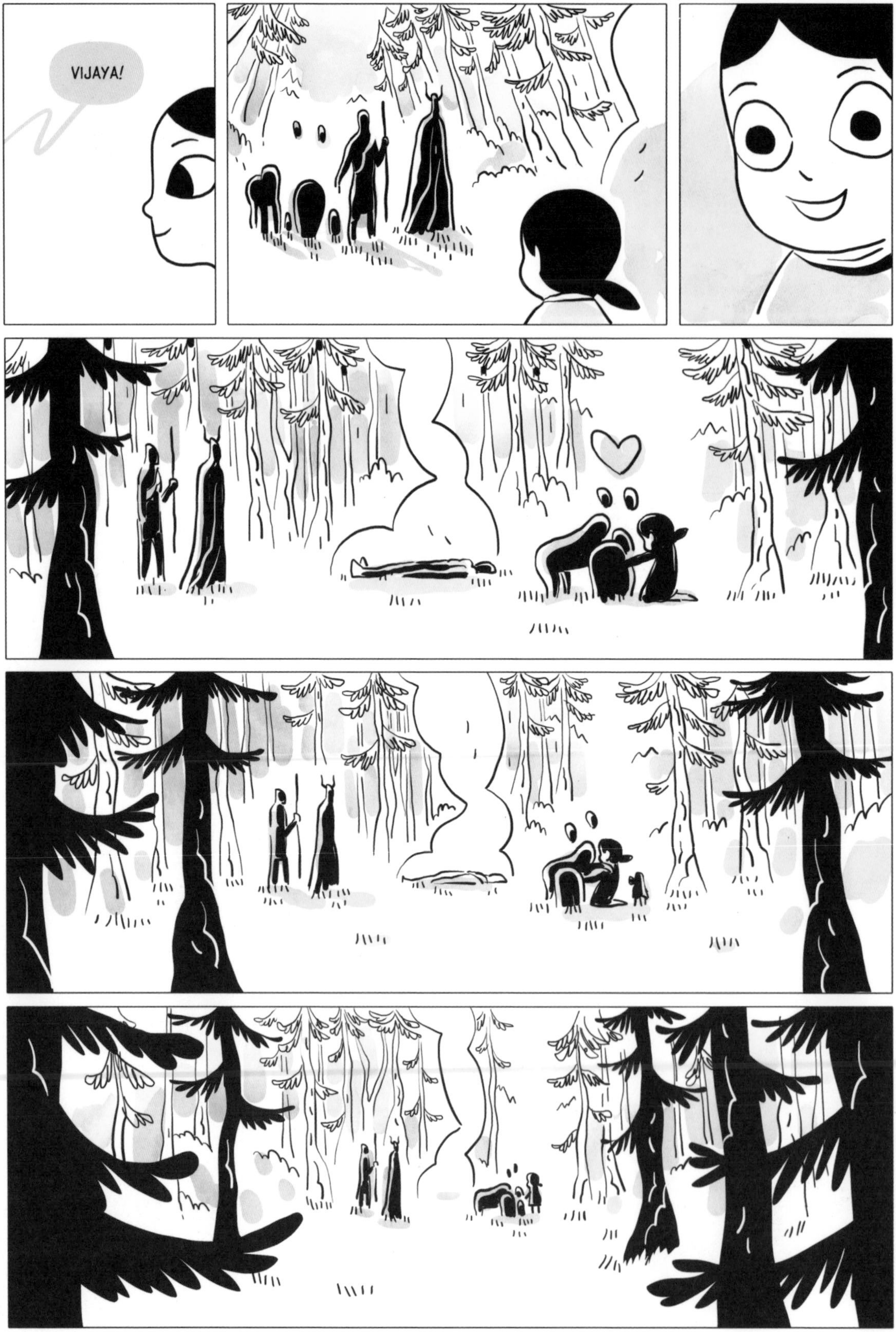
VIJAYA!

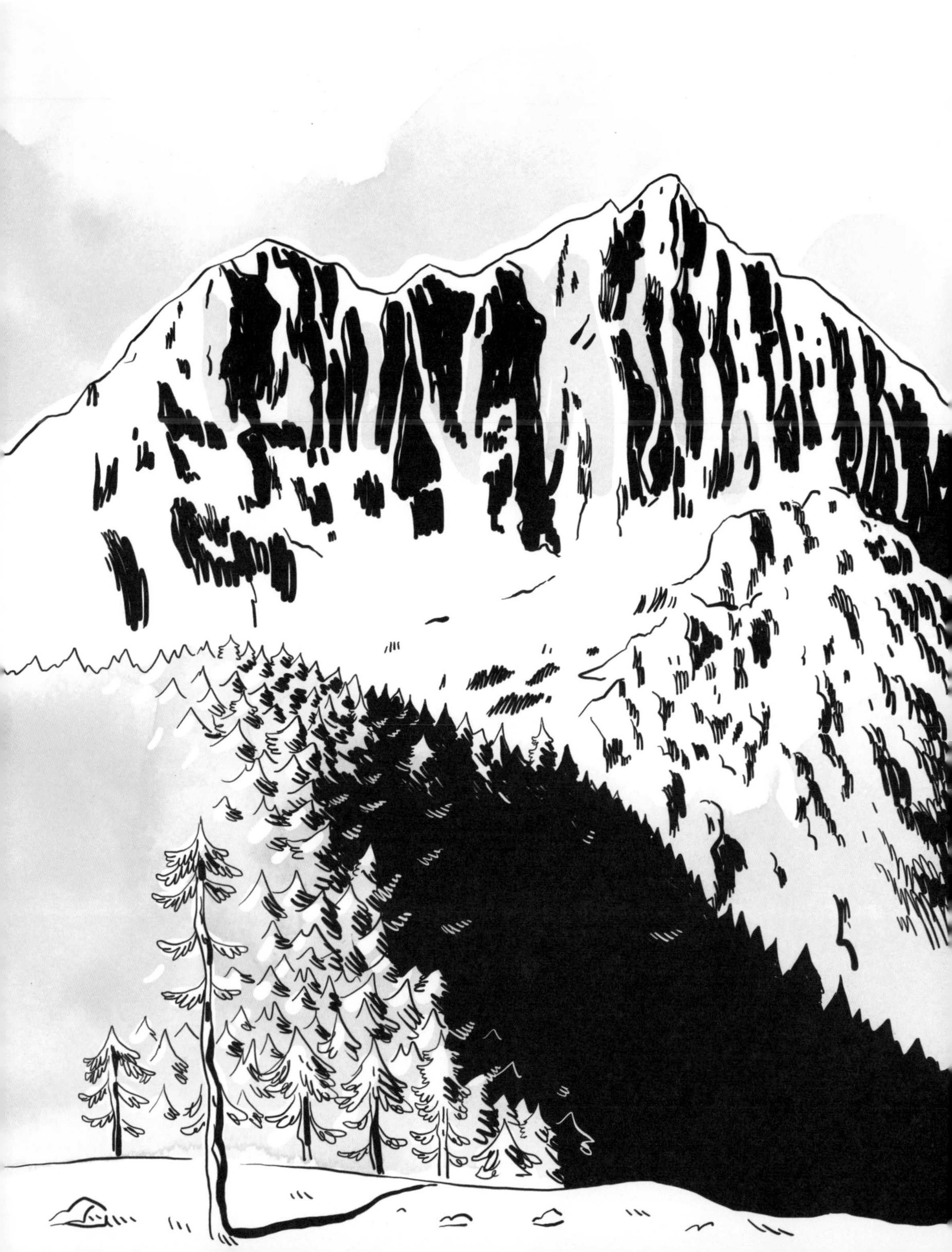

THE HOUSE WILL BE FINISHED IN A COUPLE OF DAYS.

THEY CAUSED SUCH A MESS.

BUT THEY COULD HAVE CAUSED MUCH MORE DAMAGE.

TO USE THE EARTH ELEMENTALS WAS A BRILLIANT IDEA FROM VIJAYA.

THE HUMANS HAVE LEFT THE SANCTUARY NOW.

"ILLUSION WAS REMOVED FROM THEM..."

"AS WELL THEIR MEMORIES OF THIS PLACE."

GUYS, I HAD SUCH A STRANGE DREAM.

"AND THE NATURE AFFECTED..."

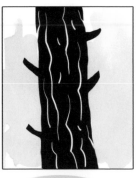

"WILL RECOVER."

YOU MISSED A BRILLIANT OPPORTUNITY...

TO CHANGE THE DESIGN OF YOUR HOUSE, PRASAD.

I HEARD WHAT HAPPENED AND DECIDED TO MAKE A CONTRIBUTION.

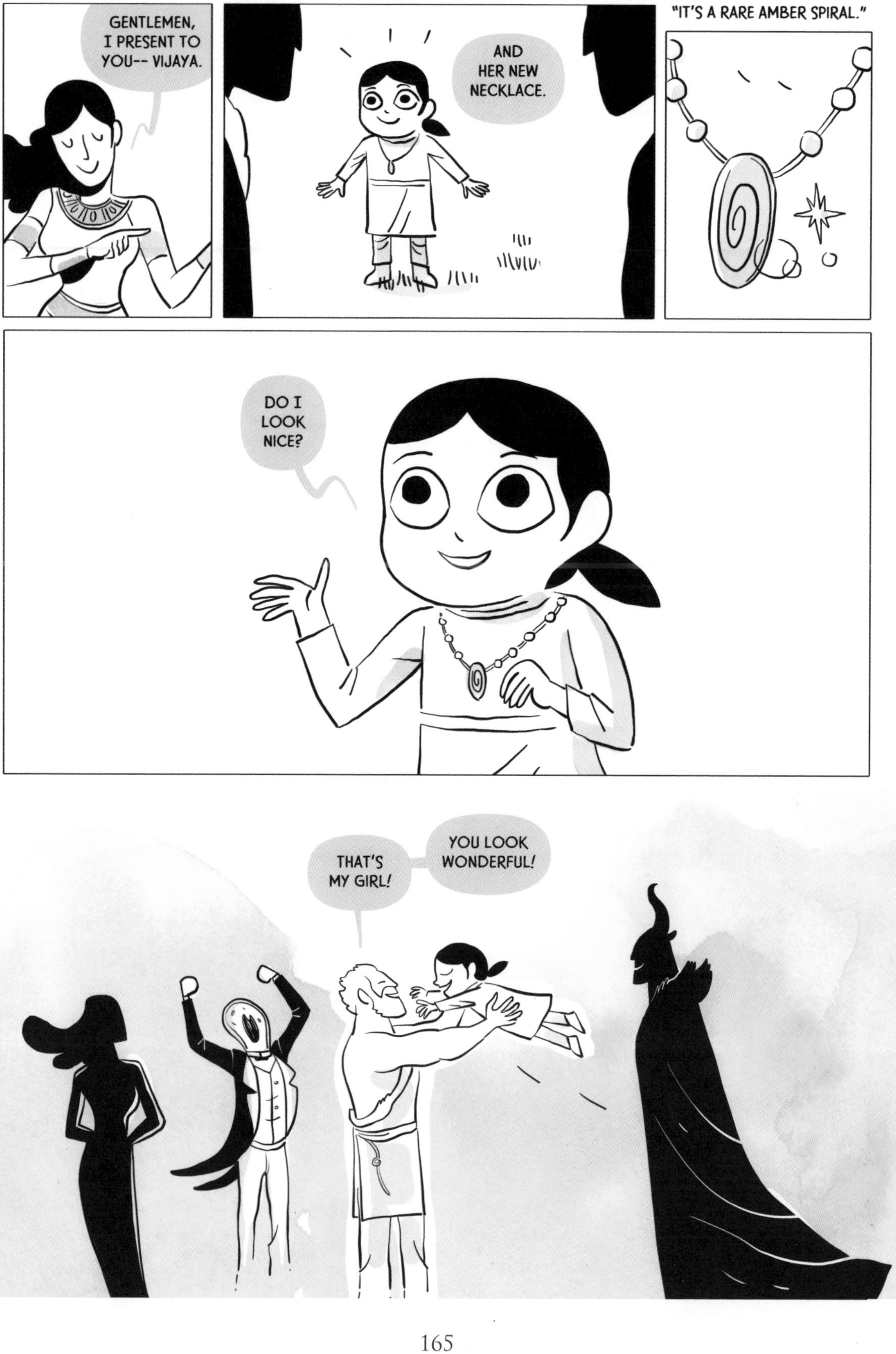
GENTLEMEN, I PRESENT TO YOU-- VIJAYA.
AND HER NEW NECKLACE.
"IT'S A RARE AMBER SPIRAL."
DO I LOOK NICE?
THAT'S MY GIRL!
YOU LOOK WONDERFUL!

MUUAAAP!

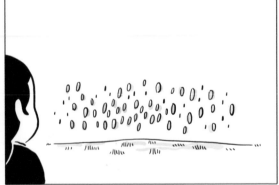

I PRESUME THEY ALL WANT TO SAY -- THANK YOU FOR ALL YOU HAVE DONE.

SHE LOOKS SO MUCH BETTER WITH THAT NECKLACE.

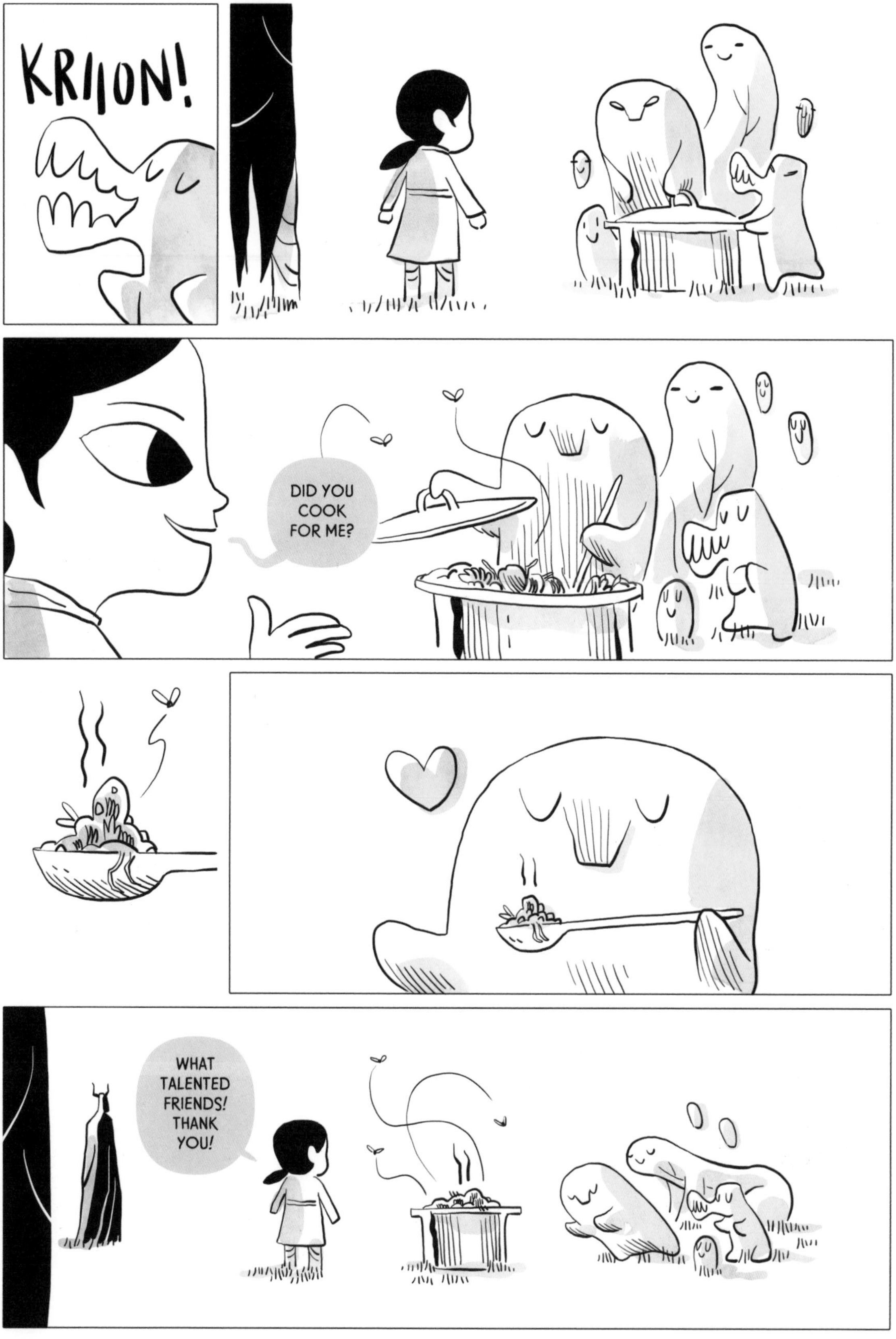
KRIION!
DID YOU COOK FOR ME?
WHAT TALENTED FRIENDS! THANK YOU!

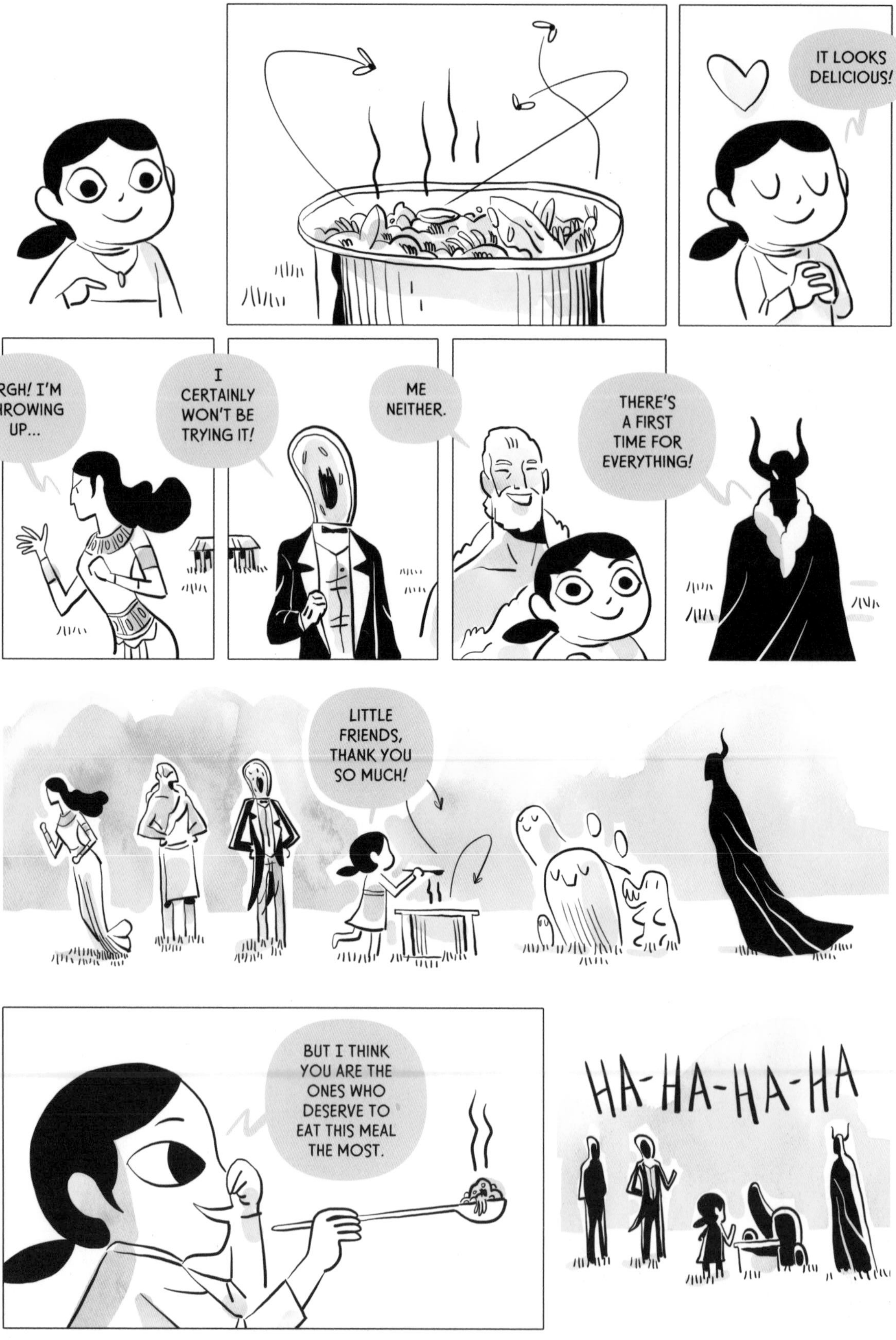
IT LOOKS DELICIOUS!
ARGH! I'M THROWING UP...
I CERTAINLY WON'T BE TRYING IT!
ME NEITHER.
THERE'S A FIRST TIME FOR EVERYTHING!
LITTLE FRIENDS, THANK YOU SO MUCH!
BUT I THINK YOU ARE THE ONES WHO DESERVE TO EAT THIS MEAL THE MOST.
HA-HA-HA-HA

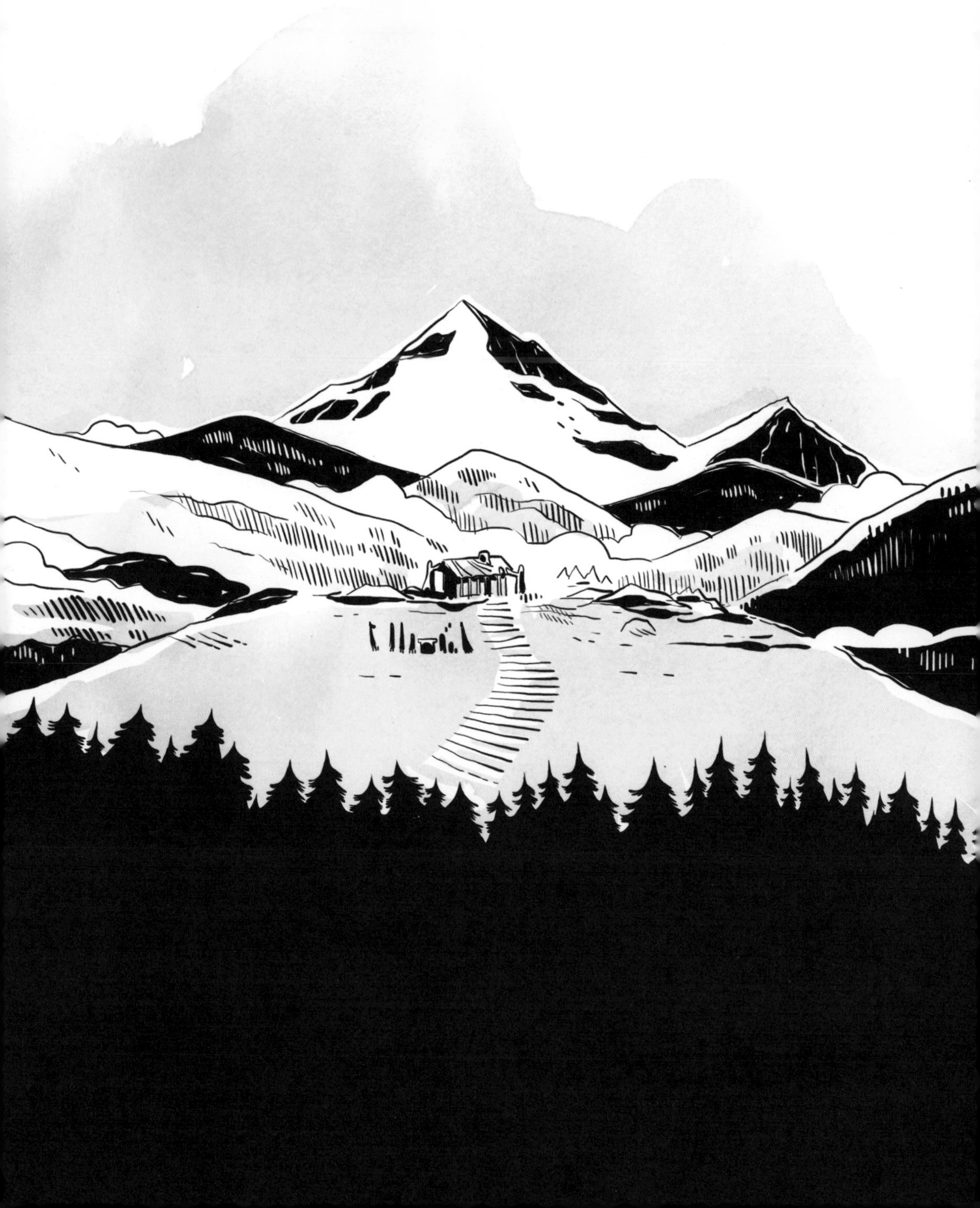

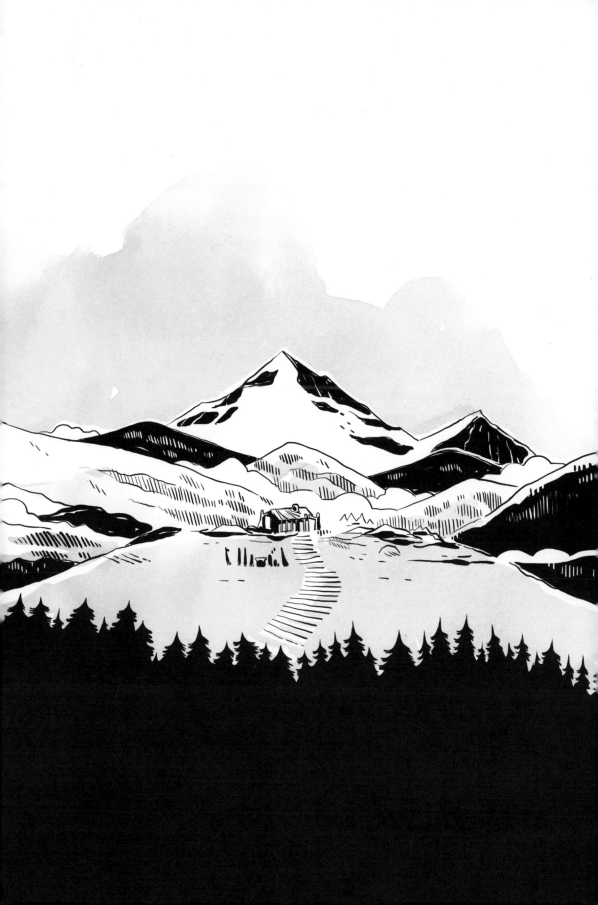

EPILOGUE

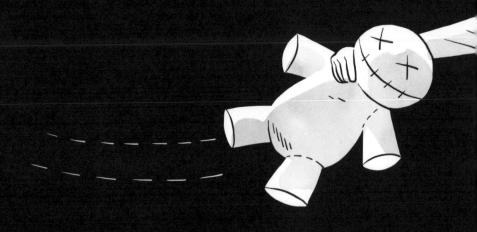

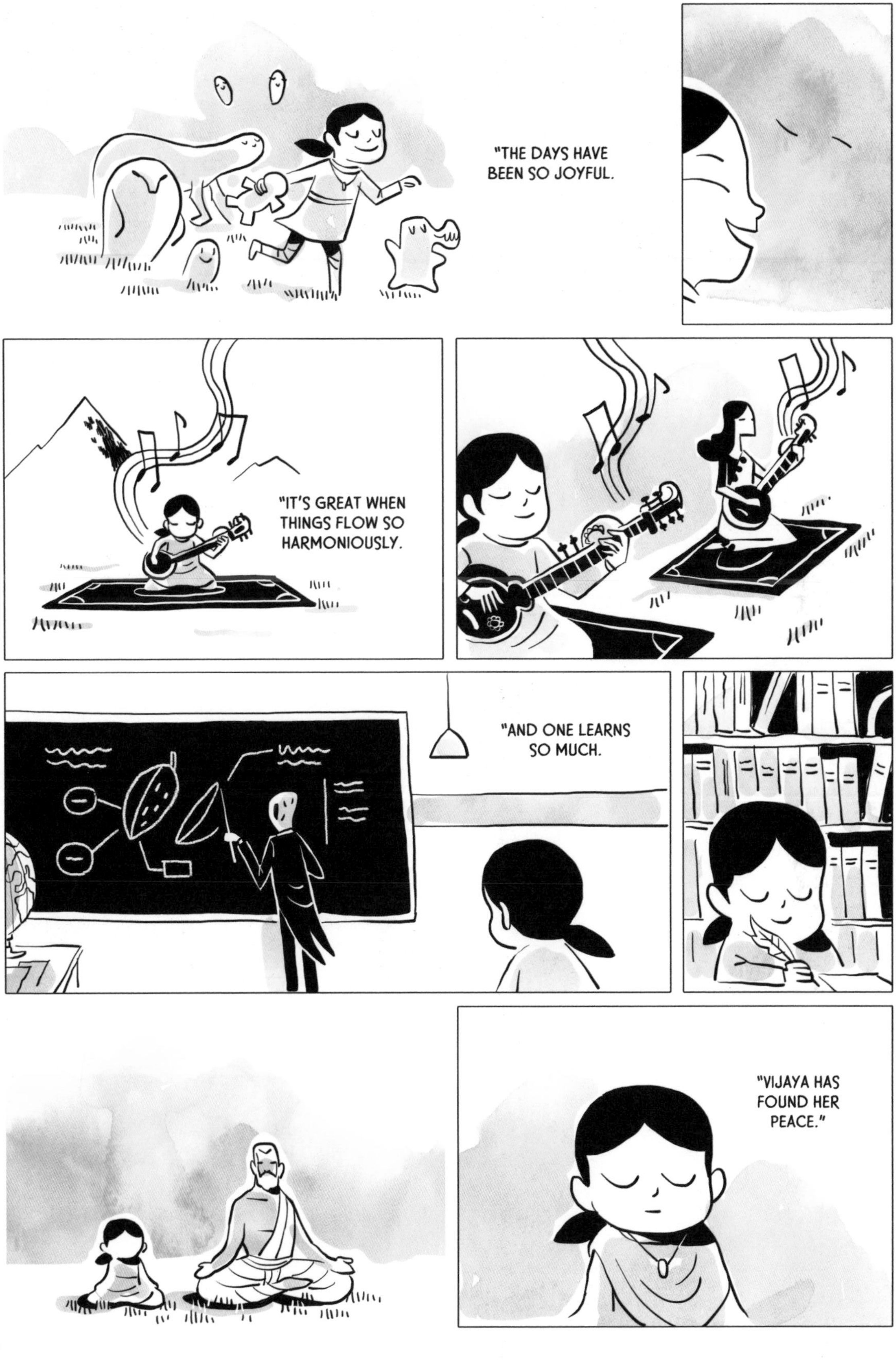
"THE DAYS HAVE BEEN SO JOYFUL.
"IT'S GREAT WHEN THINGS FLOW SO HARMONIOUSLY.
"AND ONE LEARNS SO MUCH.
"VIJAYA HAS FOUND HER PEACE."

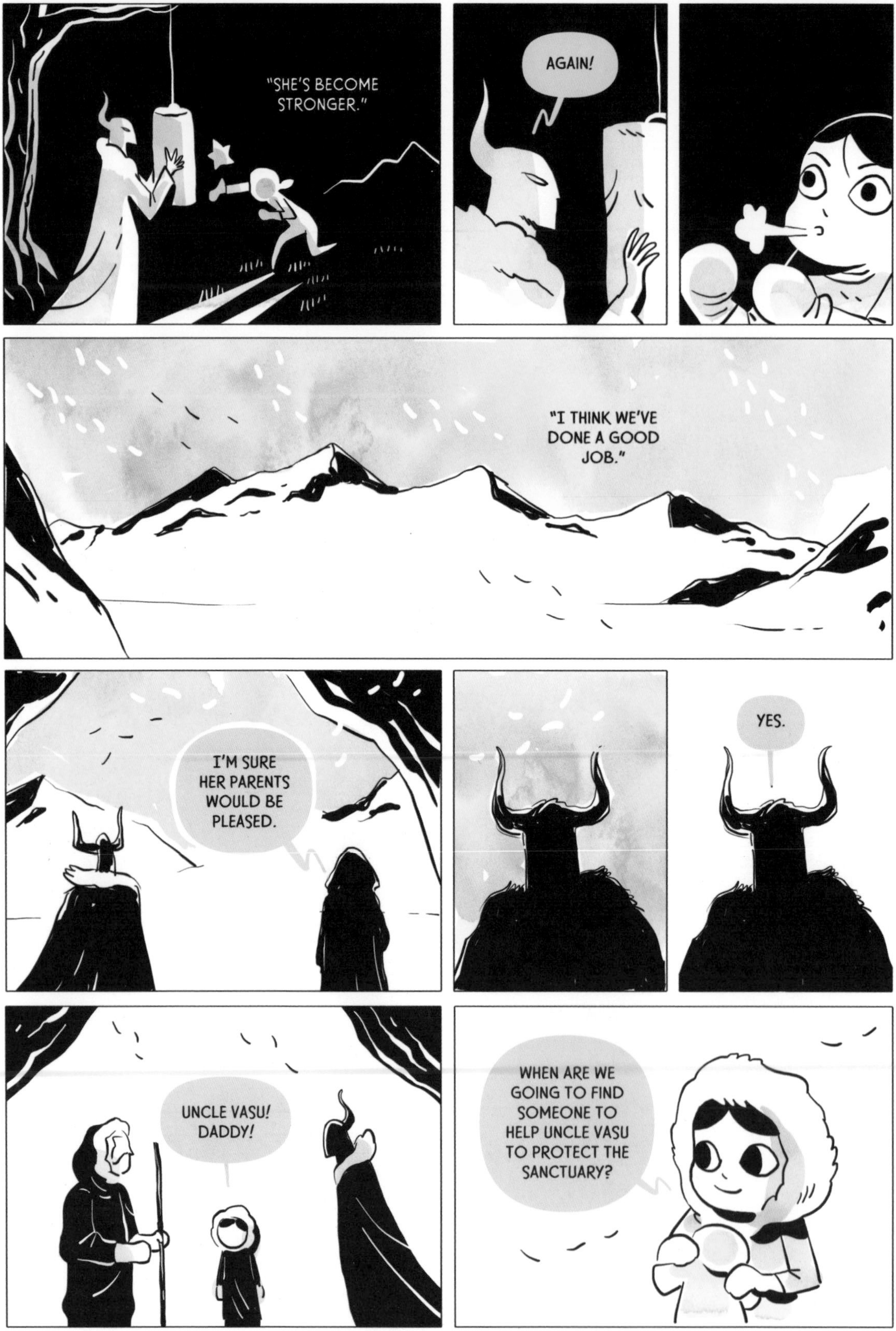
"SHE'S BECOME STRONGER."
AGAIN!
"I THINK WE'VE DONE A GOOD JOB."
I'M SURE HER PARENTS WOULD BE PLEASED.
YES.
UNCLE VASU! DADDY!
WHEN ARE WE GOING TO FIND SOMEONE TO HELP UNCLE VASU TO PROTECT THE SANCTUARY?

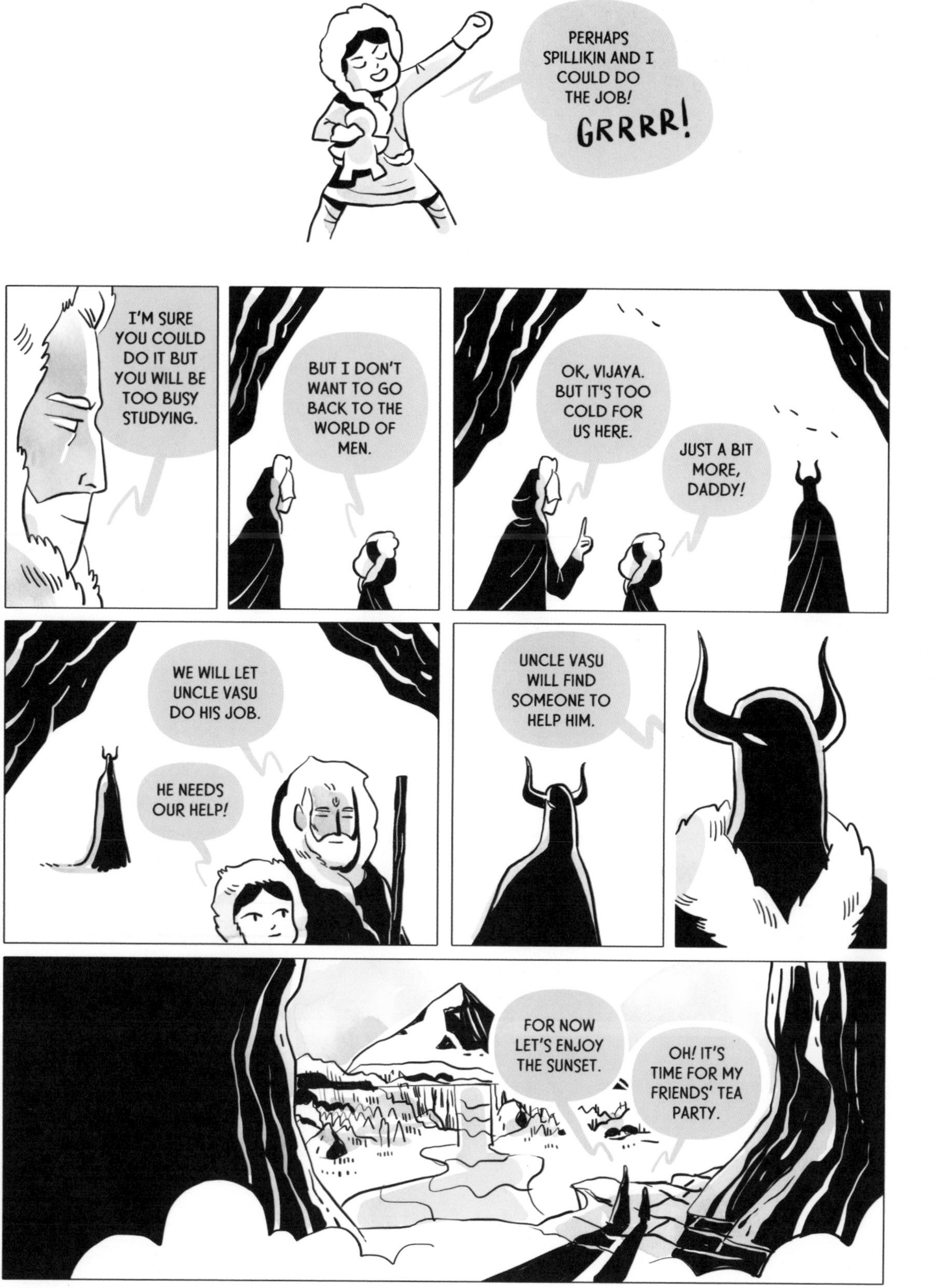
PERHAPS SPILLIKIN AND I COULD DO THE JOB!
GRRRR!
I'M SURE YOU COULD DO IT BUT YOU WILL BE TOO BUSY STUDYING.
BUT I DON'T WANT TO GO BACK TO THE WORLD OF MEN.
OK, VIJAYA. BUT IT'S TOO COLD FOR US HERE.
JUST A BIT MORE, DADDY!
WE WILL LET UNCLE VASU DO HIS JOB.
HE NEEDS OUR HELP!
UNCLE VASU WILL FIND SOMEONE TO HELP HIM.
FOR NOW LET'S ENJOY THE SUNSET.
OH! IT'S TIME FOR MY FRIENDS' TEA PARTY.

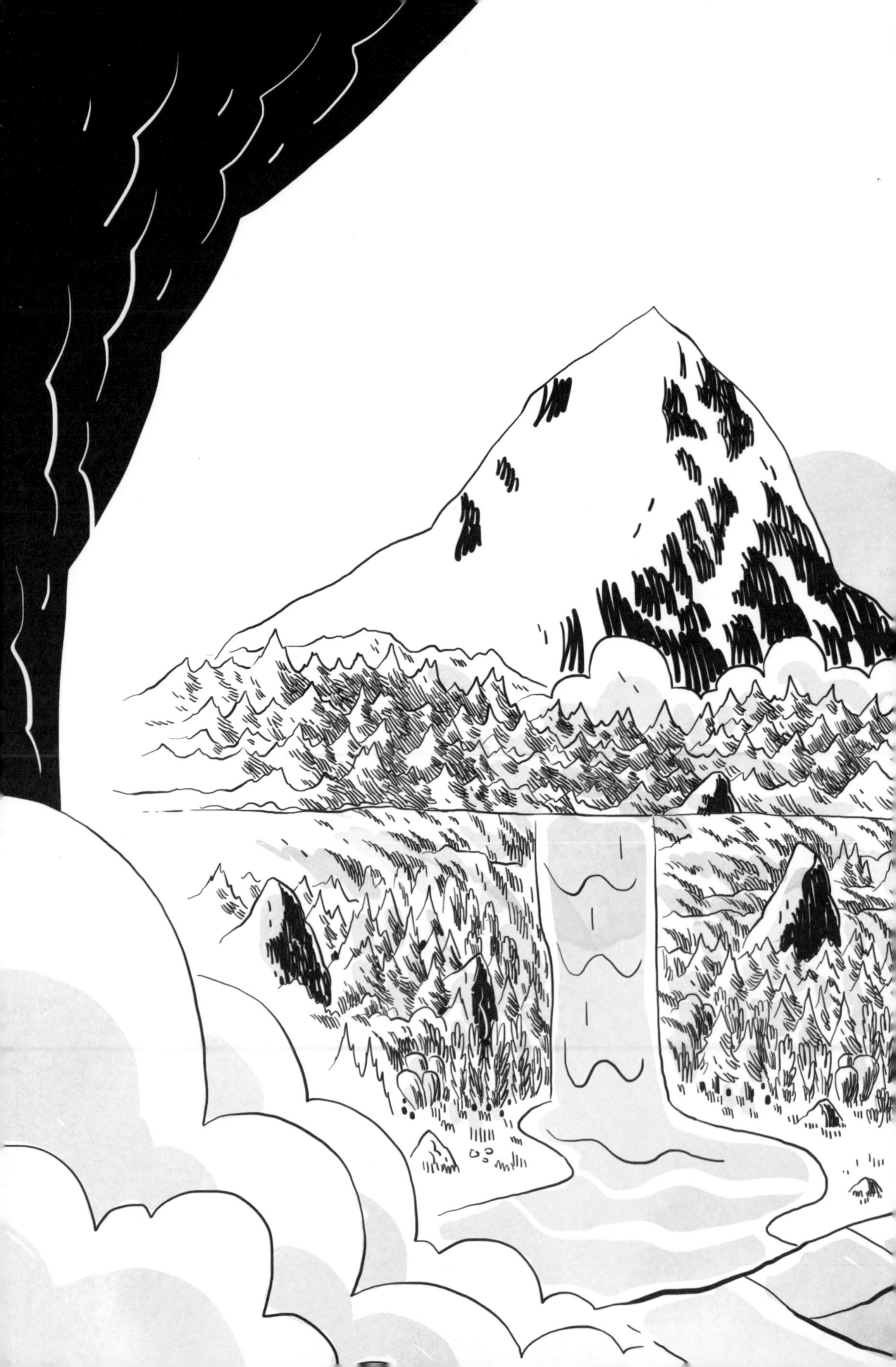

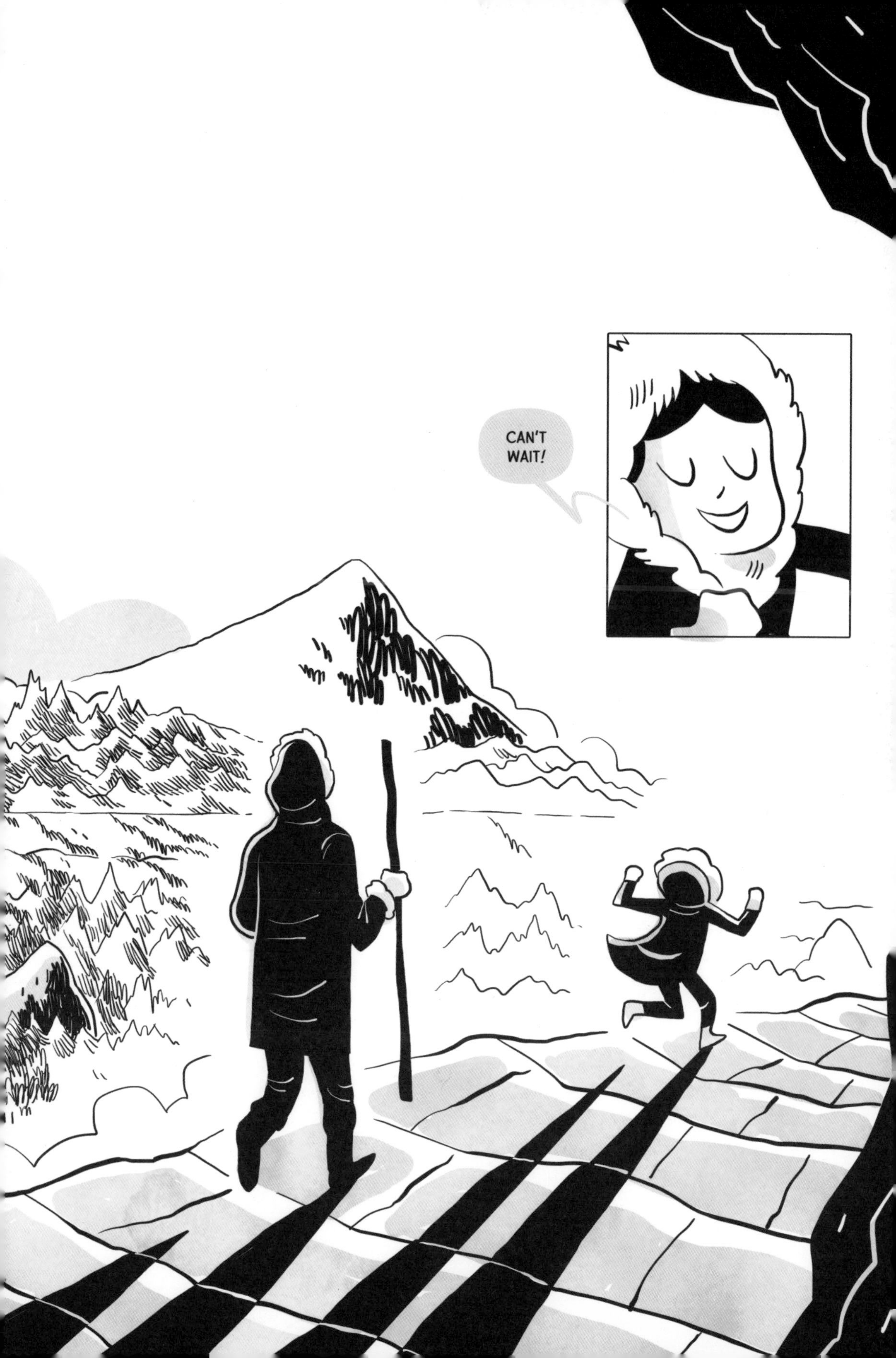
CAN'T WAIT!